A SONG FOR CHARLIE REDBIRD

Earle D. Spencer

SPENCER CREATIVE ENTERPRISES
Depew, New York

Published by Spencer Creative Enterprises, Depew, New York 14043

Cover design by Rickhardt Capidamonte for booknook.biz

Book design by eBooksByBarb for booknook.biz

Author photo by James Roberts

A SONG FOR CHARLIE REDBIRD

Book I

Day Fears and Nightmares

But is there any comfort to be found?
Man is in love and loves what vanishes,
What more is there to say?

Yeats, *Nineteen Hundred and Nineteen*, 1, st. 6

To him who is in fear everything rustles.

Sophocles, *Acrisius*, Fragment 5

CHAPTER 1

LEGS PUMPING, BLONDE hair streaming out behind her, the four-year-old navigated her tricycle down the driveway toward her smiling father.

"Watch me, Daddy, watch me!" she called, proud of her control of the birthday trike.

The ground began trembling and split open, swallowing the little girl and her tricycle.

"D-a-a-a-d-d-d-y!" she cried, her voice echoing off the shaft's raw dirt walls as she fell.

Already kneeling, he dove forward in a desperate attempt to reach his daughter. When he was a foot away from the chasm, the ground shuddered again and sealed itself shut, leaving a pall of foul-smelling dust hanging in the air. He could still hear his daughter screaming, her voice growing fainter as she fell.

"Allison!" he shrieked, tearing at the asphalt until his nails split and his fingers bled.

Mocking bass laughter rose from beneath the ground, filling him until he thought his brain would explode. "Gone, gone, gone!" the laughter mocked.

His windmilling right arm swept the lamp and the alarm clock off the bedside table and onto the floor. Groaning softly, he propped himself up against the headboard. The nightmare slowly eased its grip but the misery remained.

"Shit," he wept, lowering his face onto forearms crossed atop his knees.

Almost seven years gone now. One year less than the duration of he and Jennifer's marriage at the time of their disappearance. Three years longer than his daughter Allison had lived. In five days and a few hours, they will have been missing for seven years.

Jennifer, his wife, never haunted his dreams, although he still loved her and missed her terribly. The gold wedding band had never been off his left ring finger since she had placed it there eight years ago.

Instead, he dreamed of his daughter, Allison Marie, the first of three children he and Jennifer had hoped to have. Now all he had left of her was the terrible nightmare. Not different nightmares, but always the same one, none the less terrifying despite its many repetitions. Always, he stood watching helplessly while she was sucked under the earth by a malevolent but but unseen monster.

During the warmer months the nightmare might visit only once a week. But as summer eased into fall and the anniversary of their disappearance neared, the dream's frequency would increase until it was a nightly occurrence. Sometimes even an afternoon occurrence if he dared to attempt a nap. Often he would stay awake forty-eight hours in a futile effort to escape it. The nightmare haunted him, consumed him.

Finally he rose, stiff from sitting up in bed for over an hour. Stretching as he crossed the bedroom, he saw the two dogs waiting for him just outside the bedroom door.

Both whined and he knelt to give them a reassuring scratch. Susie and Angus, Border Collie-Australian Shepherd crosses, good dogs, the best.

Walking past them, he paused at the top of the stairs and glanced out the window at the lake. The first pale light of dawn was edging westward across the flat water. Continuing down the stairs, he crossed the living room and entered the kitchen. After starting a pot of coffee brewing, he took a seat at the kitchen counter to wait.

Again, he thought of selling the house and moving away. A five bedroom, five bath chalet on fifty acres with seventy-five yards of shoreline on a Northern Minnesota lake would sell quickly for top dollar. Thought of it and again rejected the idea.

Then he thought again of perhaps spending more time at his condominium in Scottsdale. Not that being in Arizona affected the nightmare, it remained the same no matter where he went. Considered maybe leaving after Labor Day and not returning until mid-May. Considered it and again decided against it. He didn't go south to Arizona to escape the rigors of a Northern Minnesota winter, although like many he dreaded the terrible cold and the long dark. Rather, he fled to escape the holiday memories of Jennifer and Allison that would echo through the house.

Ultimately though he rejected any major change in his lifestyle for the same reason that he left the doors unlocked on a three million dollar home when he did leave for Arizona. It was the same reason that he left a message on the answering machine giving his Scottsdale phone number and address and left a note on the kitchen counter containing the same information. Because this might be the year they returned and he wanted their home waiting for them and he wanted them to be able to find him if he was away.

Logically, he knew Jennifer and Allison must be dead. The evidence would not support another conclusion. When divided by the human heart though, logic and hope are often mutually exclusive concepts. So he continued to believe that one day they would return. He had to believe; there was no other choice for him. Because the moment he stopped believing, David Garrison's reason for continuing on would be gone.

CHAPTER 2

THE COMING OF dawn stirred old Charlie Redbird awake. Grasping the ornately carved staff leaning against the wall, he levered himself upright and out of bed on the second try. Leaving the bedroom, he walked down the hall to the living room. Arriving at the cabin's front door, he put his coat on and shoved his bare feet into a pair of battered Wellingtons. Stepping outside, he crossed the small plank porch and descended the three rickety steps to the front yard. Randomly selecting a scrub pine tree, he leaned on the staff and fumbled with the crotch of his long johns.

"A-h-h-h," he sighed happily, making water against the tree.

Finished, Charlie retracted his tackle and spared a moment for the lake's beauty. Argent and crimson flashed westward across the flat grey water as the sun cleared the low hills to the east. Turning away, Charlie looked down the rough corduroy road as it wound into the unnamed hamlet below. Only three lights glowed. At this time last year there had been five, but one family and a young couple had moved away.

"We are a dying people," he thought sadly and not for the first time. "Another generation and even the land will have forgotten us."

Shaking off his pensive mood, Charlie crossed the yard and went back inside the cabin. Opening the firebox in the ancient wood stove, he stirred the coals and threw in a pair of birch logs. Picking up the dented enamel coffee pot, he put in a couple of handfuls of coffee and added water from the kitchen tap. Placing the pot on top of the stove, he pulled a kitchen chair over and took a seat. Rummaging in his coat pocket, he pulled out a pipe and stuffed it full of coarse black tobacco. A dried twig from the can on the shelf by his right hand served as a match after he lit it in the stove. Drawing in a deep lung full of smoke, Charlie waited for the birch logs to fire and warm his bones, his morning brew, and his cabin.

The logs hissed, spat, and finally caught fire, casting flickering shadows over his face. Sixty-nine years old and he felt fine most days. But still. The gift of his fathers had started whispering to him in the deep reaches of the night. This would be his last winter and he would never see another spring.

Death and Charlie Redbird had been nodding acquaintances for over half a century. Now though death no longer bellowed down the arctic winter gales or smashed at his skiff when the autumn winds unexpectedly veered north. None of that now, no more theatrics. Death had entered his home, lurking quietly, patient as a man waiting for a bus.

Charlie was frightened of the pain he knew was coming. He knew better than most how cruel death could be. Still, there were myriad herbs and potions to ease even the most terrible pain, including those sold at Dave's liquor store in Frechette.

Worse than the pain though would be the debilitating effects that could prevent him from acting. Which brought him back yet again to the subject of his sons. At one time Charlie Redbird had two sons, John and Michael. Good boys both. They had died together in a house fire in 1955. Their mother and his wife, Mary, had vanished the same day.

Charlie's grief for his lost family had been terrible, but in time he had healed a little and tried to beget more sons. Tried until his balls felt turned inside out and his guts ached. Tried until his amorous escapades made him a local legend. Tried, but only succeeded in siring eight daughters, all still living. He loved them all, but damn it, he had desperately needed a son.

Without a son, there was no one to pass the mantle of his responsibilities on to. The generational chain stretching back to the dark times would finally be sundered. So at a time when he should have been preparing his spirit for the final journey ahead, he had no choice but to continue on. And he could not fail. Mustn't.

Time was short now. Death was close, very close, and if he was going to act, it had to be soon. David Garrison hadn't left for Arizona yet, the woman and her daughter were drawing near, and the web was almost spun.

Having decided, Charlie slammed the butt of the staff down on the plank floor and sprang erect. The fire roared and flames leaped out of the open firebox toward the ceiling. Dishes, pots, and pans rattled and clattered on their shelves. His shadow grew until it crossed the living room floor and spread up the far wall.

A second later the coffee pot on top of the wood stove boiled over. The dancing flames retreated into the firebox and the room quieted. Charlie Redbird shrank and became just another old man warming himself before a fire on a cold autumn morning.

CHAPTER 3

"MOMMY, ARE WE almost there yet?" the little girl asked.

The child's mother bit back a sharp reply at being asked the same question four times in the last forty-five minutes. They had been driving for three days now since leaving Central Florida and they were both tired.

"No, honey, not yet, it'll be about another three hours," she replied. "Why don't you try and take a nap and let mommy concentrate on her driving."

Concentration was definitely called for. Heavy mist, sometimes changing to rain, was falling on the narrow two-lane road. Tendrils of fog were creeping out of the forests on either side of the road and threatening to shroud the thin ribbon of asphalt. Northern Minnesota in fall, a primeval landscape only lightly touched by the hand of man.

Having spent part of her childhood here she had known what to expect. Even so, claustrophobia was riding her hard. As a child, especially after her friend Jillian disappeared, Gina Tolliver had been terrified of the great woods. The forest's aura of eternity, its lack of light, and the awful noise it made when the wind blew all made her want to shrivel into a fetal ball and whimper. But there had been no other choice and there was no turning back now. Their home in Florida had already been sold and a new job as a middle-school librarian awaited.

Guilt at bringing her daughter here still remained, even though there had been no other alternative. Both she and her husband were only children and both of her parents were deceased. The child's paternal grandparents were long divorced and neither had ever expressed any interest in her. The guilt grew even worse when she found herself wishing that she didn't have a daughter. It would be so much safer and so much easier to be alone, especially when the illness closed in on her.

As if hearing her thoughts, the child sleepily asked, "Mommy, are we going to find daddy when we get there?"

Choking back tears, Gina said, "I don't know, Rachel, we'll have to wait and see what happens."

CHAPTER 4

HE HAD ALWAYS loved it here. The vast forests, the weather, the change of seasons, everything about it delighted him. Today's mist and fog suited him, made him want to sing and dance.

The day had started perfectly. Walking into town, he had spied a young kitten sheltering from the rain on the porch of the Torkelson home. Gathering up the little ball of fur, he had carried it down to the road and thrown it under the wheels of the first passing car. Six-year-old Karen Torkelson's screams when she discovered her pet crushed in the street were the perfect appetizer for today's entree. Speaking of which, he was there.

Climbing up the porch stairs of the Mendelson home, The Wendigo gleefully sang, "Tor-kel-son, Men-del-son, son-of-a-bitch son, but I l-o-o-o-v-e my job!"

Walking into the house, he crossed the living room unseen by Mrs. Mendelson napping on the couch. She immediately fell into a terrible nightmare about a faceless black creature with burning red eyes. Ascending the living room stairs two at a time, The Wendigo entered Oleg Mendelson's bedroom. Crossing the room, the monster stood looking down at the wasted looking old man lying in the bed. Reaching down, the beast hauled the old man upright and slapped him across the face.

"Wakey-wakey, Oleg, you dilapidated old piece of shit!" the monster cheerfully called.

Oleg Mendelson, age seventy-four and a minute away from dying of lymphatic cancer and cirrhosis of the liver, slowly struggled awake. When his eyes finally opened and he saw what was standing there, his jaws gaped wide as he attempted to scream.

"Shut the fuck up, you old rummy!" The Wendigo commanded, placing a huge hand over Oleg's face. "Had 'bout enough out of you for one day."

Noxious blue-black smoke boiled out of Oleg Mendelson's mouth and into the beast's hand. When the monster removed his hand from Mendelson's mouth, the smoke formed into a pressurized jet. Lowering his head, The Wendigo inhaled Mendelson's soul with a look of near sexual ecstasy on his face. Oleg Mendelson's life may have been over but his death was just beginning.

"You're gonna love this, Oleg," the monster said. "No booze, no cigarettes, no porn where you're goin'. You're in for an extended spell of clean living, like say an eternity or two."

Looking down at the corpse, he stopped and listened for a moment.

"What's that you say, Oleg?" The Wendigo asked. "Oh, you're worried about the missus. Don't worry 'bout her, yer old buddy Petey will be over here stickin' it to her before you're even cold, just like he's been doin' for the last thirty years."

Descending the stairs, the monster paused yet again to listen.

"What now?" the monster said. "I, shut the fuck up, you goddamned squarehead!"

Drawing in a deep breath, The Wendigo belched out a great cloud of buzzing horseflies. Using both fists, he pummeled himself on the sides of his head until his eyes rolled back and nothing but the reds showed.

"There now, that's better," he said. "Some people just don't know when to shut up."

Finished descending the stairs, he crossed the living room and headed toward the front door. On the couch, Mrs. Mendelson was still thrashing in the grip of the nightmare.

"Shame on you, Katherine, a woman your age gettin' her undercarriage greased by her hubby's, er, late hubby's best friend," The Wendigo lectured as he exited the house.

Once back on the street, the monster raised his snout and sampled the air. So much here, so much LIFE, just ripe for the taking. Reminding himself of the difference between *gourmet* and *gourmand* didn't help much. The simple truth was there were limits to what he could do, at least for now. But not for much longer.

Redbird was growing old, near death, and nowhere near as smart as he gave himself credit for. That was one visit he was truly looking forward to making. They had old business together, he and Redbird. As far as he was concerned, it couldn't be transacted soon enough. That useless pussy in the big house, Gar-ri-son, was a broken man and had been for years. As for the mad woman and her child, well, they were nothing but a pair of helpless cunts. If mommy thought she was afraid of the big dark woods now, wait until he got hold of her.

Plus it was almost the last week in October, time for his annual dinner party. Road kill like Oleg here was all right, but there was nothing, but nothing, like fresh bloody meat to keep the old picker stuck up.

Cheered by his prospects, The Wendigo whirled with increasing speed until he formed a small tornado in the center of the street. Abruptly stopping, he emerged from the remnants of the funnel cloud dressed in a tux and tails with dancing shoes on his feet. After humming a few bars, he gave voice to *"Singing in the Rain"* and began soft shoeing out of town *a la* Fred Astaire. Unseen and unheard, yet still very much here.

"*Yes,*" the monster thought with great satisfaction, "*everything is going to be just fine.*"

CHAPTER 5

LOOKING AROUND THE rented apartment, Gina tried to tell herself that it was quaint, cute, rustic even. That it had potential. A few curtains here, a rug there, maybe a little paint. Tried, and failed. The place was a dump. Nothing less, nothing more.

They had bought their home in Florida at the end of the boom eighties with a little down and an eternity to pay. Now, in late 1999, she'd sold the house at a fire sale price just to get them here. Cleared enough after the mortgage was paid and the furnishings sold to move and survive until her new job started in January. Maybe, if nothing went wrong. So here they were, water stains, drafts, clanking pipes, and all.

Restless, she got up off the couch and walked into Rachel's bedroom. The little girl was curled up on her left side with the sheets and blankets tangled around her waist. Covering the child up, Gina kissed her on the forehead and gently placed her teddy bear under her arm.

Crossing the living room, she peered out the dirt-smeared window. Nothing out there to see, just the lights in the apartments across the parking lot. Beyond that, halogen lights glowed in the parking lot of Frechette's sole shopping mall. The one and only reason she had rented this place was its location in the center of town away from the surrounding forests. Away also from the house her parents had rented for the five years they had lived here. And away from the house across the street where Jillian had once lived. Better not to think of Jillian now though, not while it was dark outside. Best not to think of her at all, actually.

Ever since they had arrived yesterday, Gina had wanted to collapse into a fetal ball and shriek until the world was empty but for her and the noise. Hugging herself against the fear, she inspected the apartment's doors and windows for the fifth time in three hours. Finding them still locked, she took her pills and climbed into bed. The medications prescribed her brought deep unconsciousness but not true sleep, physical rest without mental peace. The bed began shaking as her body twitched and spasmed in the grip of a nightmare.

Thick ground fog smoked and swirled around the towering pillars of a vast dark forest. A dark figure, barely visible, raced toward her through the murk. Burning red eyes, long yellow fangs, and slashing claws all became clear as the monster closed the last few yards between them. Gina Tolliver desperately tried to wake and scream but couldn't, trapped in the nightmare by her physicians' good intentions.

CHAPTER 6

THE CD CHANGER clicked and the hurdy-gurdy thunder of the Rolling Stones' *"Honky-Tonk Women"* blasted out of the Bose speakers until the windows rattled in their frames. Guns 'n Roses, ZZ Top, Aerosmith, great rock bands, great tunes played loud, REAL LOUD. Hold back the night, the dark. The house was locked down, motion detectors on, security system armed. Everything copasetic. A coffee maker with a full pot sat on the end table next to his right arm. Even though David Garrison hadn't slept for thirty-six hours, he had every intention of remaining awake until at least dawn.

Reaching down, he adjusted the .40 caliber Glock riding in a shoulder holster under his left arm. Two spare magazines for the handgun rode under his armpit on the other side. A Remington riot shotgun loaded with slugs and buckshot was leaning against the left arm of the recliner. Yes sir, he was safe, secure. There was enough firepower within his immediate grasp to kill anything on the North American continent several times over.

If he was so well-armed, so safe, so secure, he wondered, then why was he so frightened? So frightened that he had wedged his shaking body into one corner of the chair. So frightened that he was unable to get up and go down the hall to use the bathroom for fear of what was waiting there for him. What he KNEW was waiting there for him. Too frightened to move, too frightened to sleep, and too frightened to keep on living.

Eventually, despite the thundering rock music and the massive amount of caffeine he'd consumed, David's body betrayed him and he fell deeply asleep. The nightmare of his daughter Allison being swallowed by the earth immediately took him and like Gina Tolliver, he was unable to wake.

Five minutes later, the alarm on the security system began blaring as someone started battering down the front door. Susie and Angus barked anxiously, but David still slept on.

CHAPTER 7

"LOOK, MOMMY, THEY'RE funny looking," Rachel giggled, watching a group of men dressed in day-glow orange crowded around a 4 x 4 pickup truck. "Like Daddy used to wear," she added sadly.

"Yes, honey, that's because it's hunting season and they have to wear orange," Gina said, smiling at her daughter.

It was their first real conversation since she'd found Rachel's window open and her bed empty at 7:30 this morning. Panic growing by the second, Gina had quickly searched the small apartment but couldn't find her. Rachel was gone, vanished just like Jillian all those years ago.

Shoving her bare feet into a pair of white Reeboks, she had run out of the apartment wearing nothing but a pair of panties and a mid-riff tee-shirt. Rachel was sitting on the front steps with the little girl from the apartment next door, admiring her new friend's hamster. Hysterical, Gina had picked her up, crying so hard that it sounded like a long undulating howl. Frightened, Rachel had also started crying as Gina carried her back into the apartment. The neighbor had run out and gathered up her daughter, distressed at the presence of this half-naked harpy near her child.

Once inside, Gina had demanded to know why Rachel had opened the bedroom window and why she had left the apartment without permission. No matter how hard she was pressed, the child had refused to admit that she had opened the window. As for leaving the apartment without permission, Rachel had argued that she hadn't left but had only gone outside to sit on the front steps, and they're part of the apartment too, aren't they? Feeling herself losing control, Gina had marched Rachel into the bedroom after first making sure that the window was closed and locked. Leaving the room, she had closed the door behind her and left Rachel crying on the bed.

Taking a seat on the couch, Gina had tried to calm herself down and succeeded after a fashion. A half-hour later, she had re-entered Rachel's bedroom, walked over to the bed, and hugged her. Mommy had been terribly frightened and worried when she found her gone, Gina had explained, and please don't ever do it again. Nodding agreement, Rachel had wiggled free of her mother's arms and run over to the window. This time, Gina was calm enough to listen to her daughter.

She had seen that Rachel was too short to reach past the lower windowsill. Walking over, Gina had closely examined the window for the first time. Deep gouges ran up the exterior of the frame and the screen was missing. The outer window frame had been pulled halfway out of the wall. Tufts of thick, curly black hair were caught on the jagged splinters of wood.

"I told you, Mommy, but you wouldn't listen," Rachel had said, hurt by her mother's inattention. "The boogie man was at my window last night, but he went away after a little while."

Swallowing hard, Gina had raced her dread to the bathroom. Clutching the toilet's cold porcelain, she had vomited until her stomach hurt and red novas blossomed behind her eyes. Empty at last, she had crawled into the shower and let the stream pound her until the hot water was gone. Emerging from the shower, she had felt a little better. Not good, but better.

Drying and dressing, Gina knew she had to go today before something else happened. By nature, she dreaded the possibility of rejection and had to steel herself for the effort she knew lay ahead. But it had to be today, she couldn't bear to wait any longer. After helping Rachel with her shoes, she had collected her research materials and led the child out to the car.

A horn sounded behind them along with a shouted profanity, startling her. Finally noticing that the light was green, Gina pulled into the intersection, turned left, and headed out of Frechette.

CHAPTER 8

THE DRILL WHINED, almost out of battery power, and slowly drove in the last screw. It had taken him over two hours to repair the front door and frame, and they would still require the attention of a real carpenter. The hour previous to that had been spent scrubbing feces off the hallway floor and out of the locks.

When David had awakened about 6:00 a.m., he was still sitting in the recliner, the holstered pistol biting deep into his side. The lights were still on, the rock music was still thundering, and the alarm on the security system was still blaring away. Struggling out of the chair, he had staggered the few feet to the master alarm panel and shut the system off. According to the digital read-out, an intruder had been detected in the area around the front door at 2:03 a.m. Somehow, he wasn't surprised that neither the security company nor the police had responded to the alarm.

Leaving the den after shutting the music off, he was surprised to see sunlight flooding the normally dim front hallway. The upper right-hand corner of the steel front door and frame had been smashed in about a foot. Through the gap, David could see the tops of the maple trees lining the driveway swaying in the gentle breeze. A dark brown substance that looked and smelt like shit had been forced through the gap and had fallen onto the tiled foyer floor.

Fully awake now, David had become aware that the dogs were missing. Whistling and calling had failed to bring them running, so he had started searching. By the time he had reached the second floor, he was in a near panic, afraid that something else he loved had been taken from him.

At the end of the second floor hallway there was a short flight of steps that led up to the locked attic door. Under these steps there was a crawl space large enough for a small child or two frightened medium sized dogs. It had taken him almost an hour, but he had finally coaxed them out of the cramped space. Slinking out on their bellies, Susie and Angus had laid whimpering at his feet. After a few more minutes of soothing words and some gentle petting, they had reluctantly followed him downstairs.

Sometime during the morning's labors, David had decided that he couldn't go on. It was time, past time, to pack up and relocate. Call a mover to box up the furnishings and then put everything in storage. Just in case Jennifer or Allie should return, he'd leave the house open. As always, he'd leave a note on the kitchen counter and a message on the answering machine. This time though the messages would give his law partner's name, address, and phone number because he planned on traveling for at least the next few months.

The only immediate plans he had made were to pack a couple of bags, load them and the dogs into his SUV, and drive hard until he found salt water and palm trees. Whether the salt water and palm trees were in Southern Florida, Southern California, or Southern Spain didn't much matter, he was going. Once there, wherever there turned out to be, he was going to buy a small villa on the ocean. Sit and drink rum every day and smoke a volume of good dope. Maybe even chase a bikini or six and hopefully catch a couple. See if he could learn to forget, see if he could learn to live without being afraid. Done deal, end of discussion. Even though he felt like a coward and hated himself for running, at least he'd have a life after a fashion.

The car startled David when it drove up. Irritated, he turned to face the intrusion. Never a gregarious man, he didn't welcome company at the best of times. And whatever else these were, they weren't the best of times.

A petite, dark-haired woman got out of the driver's seat with a medium sized box under one arm. The passenger side door swung open but he couldn't see who got out. A little girl about six years old walked around the front of the car and took the woman's hand. Despite his irritation, David couldn't help smiling at the child.

As they approached, David was struck by the woman's drawn face was and the great black circles under her eyes. That, and how thin she was. Gaunt, near emaciated, as if she were dying from some terrible disease. Although certain they'd never met before, her face ignited a flash of recognition in him. Conscious met subconscious and his memory matched her face to one he saw a lot of: his own. The same sunken eyes, the same pale skin stretched drumhead tight over bone. It was discomfiting to look into the face of another, recognize yourself, and see black despair looking back.

"Eh-eh excuse me," Gina stammered, "are, are you Mr. David Garrison?"

"Yes, I am," he replied. "How may I help you?"

"My name is Mrs. Gina Tolliver and I called you late last year after my husband, Eric, disappeared while hunting a few miles north of here," she said, hugging the child to her belly like a shield. "And this is our daughter, Rachel, she's almost six now. We were wondering if we could have an hour of your time. Please?"

"Mrs. Tolliver, I'm very busy," David began, but he was interrupted by Rachel tugging on her mother's hand and whispering urgently in her ear.

Straightening up, Gina asked, "Excuse me, but could we please use your bathroom?"

"Yes, of course," he replied, gesturing toward the house.

Showing them to the downstairs guest bath, David turned and retreated down the hall to the living room. When mother and daughter emerged a few minutes later, he was standing waiting in the center of the room.

"Rachel, do you like Disney movies?" he asked, trying to regain control of the situation.

The little girl smiled and shyly nodded her head.

"Well, let's put *Aladdin* in for you and then your mom and I can have a talk."

Crossing the room, David popped open a cabinet, pulled out a cd, and put it in the player. Leading Rachel over to a pile of cushions on the floor, he turned the television on with the remote control. In seconds the little girl was happily immersed in the animated fairy tale.

"She doesn't need to hear this," David said, leading Gina toward the den in the next room.

Following her through the door, he pulled it closed far enough to muffle their voices, yet left it far enough ajar to see Rachel's head and shoulders. Guiding Gina to an overstuffed arm chair, he took a seat across from her on the couch.

"T-thank you for taking the time," Gina began. "You, you were so nice to me on the phone last year and I was hoping that you could help us."

"Help you how?" David asked, already knowing what she would say and already dreading his response.

"I have a Master's Degree in Library Science and I used to work as an archivist," she continued, sounding steadier now, "So I know how to do historical research. I found your name in a newspaper article because of all the publicity when your wife and daughter disappeared seven years ago. That's when I called you last October because I hoped that you might know something.

"That same newspaper article mentioned there had been a series of disappearances in the Frechette area dating back at least twenty-five years. I already knew a little bit about the disappearances because I lived here for five years when I was a child. My best friend Jillian vanished when we were both seven, that would have been in nineteen seventy-one. And then I let my husband Eric come up here to hunt, he was from just south of the Cities, that was before we moved to Florida, I, I—"

Standing up, David crossed the room and brought her back a box of Kleenex. Knowing that she would probably only get this one chance, Gina brought herself under control with a conscious effort of will.

"I'll, I'll be all right," she apologized, anxious to finish her presentation. "But when I started doing research, I discovered that the disappearances here date back at least three centuries. One of the librarians at the University of Minnesota mentioned that you were involved in the same kind of research, so you know at least some of what I've found out. Several of the newspaper articles mentioned that you were a prominent attorney, so I was hoping that you could help me get an investigation started.

"No-nobody else seems to want to listen to me. I, I want to find out what happened to my husband and whether or not he's still alive. I haven't been well lately, and Rachel needs her father because I don't know how much longer I'll be able to care for her. At least look the materials over. Help us, please?"

Lifting the box off her lap, Gina placed it on the coffee table and pushed it toward David. After a brief battle, she surrendered and sat crying into her hands.

"Let me walk you to the bathroom so you can wash your face," he said, walking around the coffee table and gently taking her arm. "I'll get us something to drink and then we can talk some more."

Dropping Gina off at the bathroom, David crossed the living room on his way to the kitchen. Napping on the pile of cushions, Rachel was oblivious to the adventures of Jasmine and Aladdin. Susie and Angus were sleeping one on each side of her. Smiling down at her and missing his daughter terribly, he moved on to the kitchen. By the time he returned to the den with a pitcher of ice water and a pair of glasses, Gina was already waiting. Pouring them each a glass of water, he sat and gathered his thoughts for a few seconds. Taking a deep breath, he began.

"Mrs. Tolliver, I want you to listen to me very carefully," he said, wanting to keep her pain to a minimum. "I loved my wife and daughter deeply, totally. They've been missing for seven years this month and I still can't get over it and get on with what's left of my life. I don't think I'll ever get over it. Their disappearance shattered my world. And I agree completely with your assertion that something is very wrong here.

"To be blunt, I have a great deal of money. With great wealth comes great power of a sort. When my family disappeared, I called my markers due both here and in Canada. To date there has been three federal and two state investigations of the Frechette disappearances on this side of the border. There have been approximately that many investigations in Canada, which I'm sure you're aware is only thirty miles away.

"I have also hired private contractors to search for my wife and daughter in the month of October. Among them have been the finest guides, hunters, and trackers available for hire in North America.

"For the two years previous to this one, I also hired a six-man team which specializes in rescuing abducted business executives in third-world countries. What they actually are is mercenaries and they are very good at what they do.

"In addition, I also offered a half-million dollar reward to anyone who could tell me what happened to my family or help me find them. Despite everything that has been done, the government investigations, the private contractors, the reward offered, no trace of my wife Jennifer or my daughter Allison has ever been found."

Pausing to sip on the water, he saw that Gina was sitting perfectly still, crying without making a sound. Wanting badly to finish, he pressed on.

"So you see, Mrs. Tolliver, the investigation you want has already taken place many times over. Everyone who has participated in the search has said that there is something badly wrong in and around Frechette, although they can't say what it is. The outdoorsmen, and even the mercenaries, found the woods intimidating and they are not men who are easily frightened.

"If there was anyone or anything to be found out there, it would have been found long ago. Given the quality of the people doing the searching, it's impossible that anyone or anything could escape detection for this long. The only reason they can't find anything is because there's nothing to find. I'm not trying to hurt your feelings, believe me I'm not, but searching for any longer would only be a waste of time."

Taking another sip of ice water, he took a deep breath and continued on, anxious to finish.

"Since Jen and Allie disappeared, I, I have had a recurring nightmare that is slowly destroying my sanity. I believe that you're probably having the same type of dream."

After a few seconds Gina nodded her head, shaking off a fine spray of teardrops that glittered in the light as they flew.

"Then you'll understand," he said, near certain that she wouldn't, "when I tell you that I've decided to give up. I plan to leave Frechette later today and never return. At this point, it's either leave here or die here. And I want to keep on living, or at least I think I do.

"Mrs. Tolliver, Frechette and the area around it has become a very dangerous place these last few years. I suspect it's always been dangerous here. The best advice I can give you is to leave this place, get out, go today before it gets dark. Take that beautiful little girl of yours and run as far and as fast as you can before it's too late.

"In a minute, I'm going to call my bank and ask them to cut you a sight draft. I'll let the amount be a surprise, but it will be more than enough to get you a fresh start somewhere new. Please accept it as a gift, an expression of my hope for a better future for you and Rachel."

"Th-that's it?" Gina asked, collapsing into a weeping ball. "You're, you're giving up?"

"Yes, I am, there's no other choice for me now," he said, getting to his feet and avoiding eye contact with her. "Now if you'll excuse me, I'll make that call."

Walking over to the desk, David made a brief phone call. Crossing the room, he passed behind Gina's chair and gently squeezed her shoulder.

"Think about it, okay? The bank has instructions to hold that draft for you for the next six months," he said as he walked out of the room. "I'll be waiting in the living room with Rachel when you're ready to leave."

CHAPTER 9

"GODDAMN," CHARLIE SILENTLY reflected, *"what a day!"*

And it was nowhere near to being over with yet.

First, his granddaughter Ellen had arrived uninvited from the Twin Cities at 8:30 this morning. Concerned, she had said, for his welfare. Since he acted like he was allergic to the telephone just lately, she had decided to drive up and check on him. Although Charlie knew her concern was genuine, it still aggravated him no end that she was here today of all days.

Second, when Ellen discovered that he was leaving on an errand, she had refused to let him drive because the license plates and inspection sticker on his truck were expired. After a brief argument, Charlie finally surrendered and let her drive. Independent by nature, his forced reliance on her only further annoyed him.

Third, when they stopped for gas in Frechette, they were fifth in line at the check-out counter of the convenience store. Twenty minutes passed while everyone ahead of them either wrote checks, passed credit or debit cards through the store's manual slide imprinter, or asked directions to obscure places.

Fourth, leaving Frechette they had been stopped for speeding by a town cop. They were going 41 mph in a 35 mph zone according to him, but not according to Ellen. Something about the officer felt wrong, so Charlie kept a wary eye on him, the staff resting lightly against his knees. Finally, after about thirty minutes, he handed Ellen the ticket and told them they could go.

Just in time, fifth, to pull out on a winding two-lane road behind a school bus that stopped every fifty yards to drop off elementary school students. After a mile or so, Charlie's jaws were clenched so tightly that he looked like he was storing walnuts inside each cheek for the winter.

None of the delays had felt natural to Charlie, especially getting pulled over by the cop. All day long he'd felt as if he were wading through knee-deep mud. The race was being lost and second place in this contest was no place to be.

Turning her head a fraction, Ellen glanced nervously over at her grandfather. Normally they adored each other. Today though he'd been like a tiger with boils on his ass. Physically he seemed fine, but his disposition sure could use a major overhaul.

"Turn here," Charlie ordered, pointing his finger at a decorative iron gate set in a stone wall.

Tempted to snap at him for his tone, Ellen instead wheeled the car hard right up a long driveway. A large house stood at the end of the drive with a mid-sized silver sedan parked in the circular drive out front. A man and a woman were standing on the porch having some sort of intense conversation or argument from the tense look of their body language. A frightened looking little girl about five or six years old was standing in front of the sedan. Two mixed breed collie dogs were standing at the foot of the porch steps, barking at these latest intruders.

As soon as Charlie saw them he knew he was too late. One had already decided to bolt and the other two would soon go. The mocking bass laughter at the far edge of his consciousness grew a little louder in response.

"Shut the fuck up," Charlie muttered as he climbed out of the car.

Thinking that the remark was aimed at the barking dogs, Ellen shook her head at this latest evidence of her grandfather's foul humor. Puckering up, Charlie loosed a strange, warbling whistle at the dogs and they immediately quieted and lay down. Walking around the front of Ellen's car, he walked toward the little girl, wanting a little time alone with her before the adults on the porch could interfere.

Rachel solemnly watched him approach. A big man, especially from her child's perspective. He had brown skin, long gray braids, and carried a tall black stick. Scary looking. But for some reason she wasn't frightened of him.

"Are you a real Indian?" she asked, wanting to know.

"Yes, little Rachel, I am," he replied, kneeling so they were at eye level and she could see him smile. "Although it's more polite to say First American or Native American."

"Didn't mean to be mean," she quavered, wanting her new friend to like her.

"Oh now, that's all right," he said, afraid that he was losing her. "I brought a present just for you. It'll be our little secret, don't tell mommy or anybody else about it and never take it off. See?"

Reaching into his coat pocket, Charlie pulled out a small beaded bag. Tying the leather thongs around Rachel's neck, he slipped the medicine bag down the front of her tee-shirt.

"Pre-t-t-t-y," she sighed, although strangely enough she didn't want to look at the bag. It felt soft and warm against her skin, just like the kitten mommy had promised her yesterday.

"Remember now, it's our little secret," Charlie prodded, hoping that he could bind her. "You don't tell Mommy or anyone else about it and you don't take it off."

It wasn't much, but it was all he could manage at the moment. When the child nodded her understanding, he stroked her cheek and rose. Walking around the front of the car, he met Gina by the left front fender. Taking a long look, Charlie became more worried than ever.

"Hello, Mrs. Tolliver, I'm—" he began.

"You'll have to excuse me, we-we're leaving," she sobbed, twisting away from him. "I, I—"

"Don't cry now, Gina," Charlie said in a soothing voice, gently holding her left arm. "Just relax; everything is going to be just fine."

Suddenly she felt well, relaxed even, and she had never even met this man before. And although Gina would have been loath to admit it, she had always been frightened of people of other races, especially males.

"See, I have a gift for you," he said, tying the beaded bag around her neck and placing it under the neck of her sweater. "You must never tell anyone about it or take it off, okay?"

"Never tell, never take it off," Gina repeated, a vacant look on her face.

"It was nice meeting you, Gina, but I have to go now," Charlie said, releasing her left elbow.

Gina Tolliver's eyes snapped back into focus and her movements became frenetic again. Dashing around the front of the car, she hurriedly strapped Rachel into the passenger seat. Running back around the car, she leaped behind the wheel and started the engine. Slamming the car into gear, she drove off down the driveway.

As he had held her elbow, Charlie had noticed that Gina's mind smelled and felt like a small electrical fire: all ozone, sparks, and burning wires. And that didn't bode well for what lay ahead.

Turning away, he started walking toward the porch where David Garrison was still standing. Here there might still be a chance of doing some good, of changing the possible outcome. As he approached the porch, Charlie thought about the terrified man he had found deep in the woods almost seven years ago today. David had been nearly hypothermic and out of his mind with fear for his missing family.

"Hello, David, do you remember me?" he asked. "I found you way out in the woods when you got lost searching for Jennifer and Allison. We went back to my cabin and drank coffee and then I drove you back here. Remember?"

David did remember, now that the old man mentioned it. He didn't understand how he could have forgotten such a thing, although he had. Strange.

"David, I can help you if you let me," Charlie said, keeping his voice low. "I—"

"No!" he blurted out. "I'm leaving town shortly. Pl-please leave, right now!"

As he turned his back to enter the house, Charlie grasped his shoulder and commanded, "Stop!"

David froze in place and Charlie walked around in front of him until they were eye-to-eye.

"David," he repeated gently yet again, "I can help—"

"No-no!" he bleated, eyes rolling back until only the whites showed and spittle flew out of his mouth.

Charlie sighed, knowing this particular battle was also lost.

"All right, David," he said. "I have a going away present for you and then you can go. You must never tell anyone about it or take it off. Do you understand?"

"Never tell anyone about it and never take it off," David parroted as Charlie tied the medicine bag around his neck and tucked it under his shirt.

"You can go now, David," Charlie said, releasing his shoulder. "Have a nice trip."

Looking around in confusion, David mumbled, "Bye," and sprinted into the house. Pushing hard, he managed to close the warped front door and lock it. Using his sleeve, Charlie wiped David's spittle off his face. Already weary, he leaned heavily on his staff for a few seconds before descending the porch steps and crossing the yard. When he was almost to Ellen's car, he paused and whistled for the dogs.

Trotting up, Susie and Angus sat happily at his feet. They at least were willing to listen. Kneeling, Charlie petted them both and spoke softly to them for well over a minute. Finished, he rose and eased himself into the passenger seat of Ellen's car.

"You know, Grandpa, some of the things you do really give me the creeps," Ellen said as she started the car and put it in gear.

Ignoring her, Charlie checked the position of the sun in the sky. It was about four o'clock, two hours before dark at this time of year. Not a whole lot of time, but it would have to do.

Turning left onto the county road, she continued in the same vein, "I don't know why—"

"Ellen," Charlie interrupted, "do you ever have a fantasy that you're a distinguished looking black man driving a rich old white lady around in a fancy car?"

"No, I don't," Ellen replied, angered by the interruption, his tone, and the incongruous nature of the question.

"Good," he snapped, "because you ain't drivin' Miss Daisy and I gotta get home! So forget about that damn speeding ticket and put your foot into it!"

Too angry to speak, Ellen accelerated and sped toward Charlie's cabin.

CHAPTER 10

ALL SET. EVERYTHING packed that he was going to need. Setting his bags down by the living room couch, David took a seat and mentally rechecked his preparations.

The suitcases held enough clothes for a couple of weeks, mostly summer-weight stuff. The .40 caliber Glock was strapped under his arm where it would remain until he was well clear of the State of Minnesota. He had loaded the Remington riot shotgun into the SUV earlier. All of his credit cards were in his wallet and his checkbooks were buried deep inside one of the bags.

The house was also ready. All of the doors were unlocked, ready to be opened by Jennifer or Allison. A note to them listing his law partner's name and phone number was sitting on the kitchen counter. A message stating the same information had been left on the answering machine.

The Explorer was gassed up and the road atlas was lying open on the front passenger seat. Getting the oil changed and the tires rotated could wait until he was well south.

The to-do list involved nothing that couldn't be addressed with a few phone calls sometime in the near future. Call the CPAs, personal and corporate. Call the banks, personal and corporate. Call the stockbrokers, personal and corporate. Call the property management company with detailed instructions for maintaining the house and grounds. Call a mover to pack up the furnishings and place them in storage indefinitely.

And that was it, at least for the moment. Nothing else left to do other than to get on with his life. Satisfied with his preparations, David settled back on the couch and indulged in a jaw-cracking yawn. Except for a few short hours of sleep late the previous evening, he had been awake for almost ninety-two hours straight. Snapping his eyes open, David stiffened his body in a conscious effort to fight the overwhelming urge to sleep.

All to no avail. Within forty-five seconds of the yawn, he fell into a deep, dreamless sleep. The time was 5:12 p.m. and the sun was less than ten degrees above the horizon.

CHAPTER 11

WATCHING THE TAIL lights of Ellen's car disappear down the dirt track brought Charlie as low as he had been in years. She was going back to the cities, back to her life there. From the moment of her birth she had been his favorite grandchild and now she was gone, hopefully for good.

Like she had since she was a child, Ellen had wanted to spend the night. Curtly refusing, Charlie had told her to leave. Sensing something was wrong, she had argued with him, demanding to know what was going on. Raging, Charlie had told her to get out and never return. Ellen had left then, crying so hard that she had tripped and fallen in the yard. Watching her struggle to rise had been one of the hardest things Charlie had ever endured, but somehow he had remained inside the cabin.

Having Ellen here, or anywhere near here, was just too dangerous if things went wrong, which they probably would. She'd been hurt badly enough already and he could not, would not, put her at risk again. So Charlie had rained enough fury on her to run her off and ensure that she stayed gone, stayed safe.

He had been given much that was denied to other men, power that was beyond their comprehension. In return, he'd been denied much that other men took for granted. A wife, a comfortable life, and all that went with it. And now the love of a favorite grandchild. It was time, Charlie decided, to call those debts due.

CHAPTER 12

THE REST OF the afternoon and early evening passed in a pleasant pharmaceutical haze. At eight o'clock, Gina finally got Rachel to surrender. By 8:15 the little girl was sleeping soundly, one hand placed near her neck and the other holding her teddy bear.

Walking across the living room, Gina flopped down on the couch. Through the black fog of depression, she bleakly confronted their future. According to David Garrison, the investigation she had wanted so badly had already taken place. In fact, many investigations had taken place. Not that anybody had bothered to tell her. God forbid. Eric was gone for good, and nobody would ever be able to tell her why or how or anything else about what had happened to him.

The move here had been nothing but a fool's errand. So now what? Take the money, she decided, and just go. Accept David Garrison-Of-The-Apparently-Near-Inexhaustible-Fund's gift, as well as his advice, and just go. Leave tomorrow as soon as Rachel was up, fed, and dressed. The desert would do them just fine. Arizona,

Utah, Nevada, somewhere like that, west of the Rockies and east of the Pacific. Somewhere with lots of light and few, preferably no, trees. Somewhere they could start over again, somewhere they could start living again.

Having chosen her course, Gina rose on wobbly legs and staggered into her bedroom. Pausing, she shook out and dry-swallowed a handful of pills from the collection of prescription medications on top of her dresser. As she took off her top, it caught on the beaded medicine bag hanging around her neck. Irritated, she tugged on the obstruction with ever greater effort until the leather thong tore free of the bag. Tugging off the top, she tossed it in a crumbled ball on the room's single chair with the medicine bag tangled up inside it.

Sitting on the side of the bed, Gina struggled out of her jeans and left them lying in a heap on the floor. Swinging her legs up on the bed, she immediately fell into a drugged sleep and began snoring.

CHAPTER 13

THE GODDAMN PHONE wouldn't stop ringing. It kept on ringing until it dragged him up out of the first decent sleep he'd gotten in days. And then of course it stopped. Fully awake now, David was frightened to find himself in total darkness. For five years now he'd slept with a night light on. Fumbling around, he finally found the lamp on the end table and switched it on. There, much better. Looking at the two suitcases next to his feet started a dull stab of panic echoing in his chest. By now he was supposed to be long gone. Why had he fallen asleep?

Just then the phone began ringing again. Calls outside business hours were rare these days and he really didn't want to answer the damn thing, really didn't care who was calling. Finally though he picked the receiver up and said, "Hello?"

"David, this is Jenny, can I talk to you if you have a minute?" a woman's voice asked.

"J-J-Jenny, is that really you?" he stammered, blood pounding in his ears.

"Yes, honey, it's me, I'd like to stop by if—"

"J-Jenny, are you coming home?" he interrupted.

"Yes, we'll be there in a few minutes," Jennifer told him. "Here's Allie, she really misses you."

"Hi, Daddy, I love you," Allison's voice chirped at him.

"David, we have to go now," Jennifer said, laughing now. "We're at a pay phone in Frechette and we're out of change. We'll see you in a little while. Love you, bye now."

The phone clicked in his ear and Jennifer's voice was replaced by the blare of the dial tone. Putting the handset back in the cradle, David stood with tears running down his cheeks and a huge smile on his face. They were coming home. Finally, after all these years, his wife and daughter were coming home to him. They both sounded wonderful, just like the last time he had spoken with them seven years ago.

Overjoyed, David failed to notice that the phone line had burned through at the wall and lay smoldering on the carpet. Nor did he see Susie and Angus streaking off toward their hiding place under the attic stairs.

CHAPTER 14

TURNING IN A slow circle, Charlie carefully surveyed the stone circle located seventy-five yards up the hill next to his cabin. It didn't look like much, just another granite outcropping in the great North Woods. No more than thirty feet wide, if that. Walking over to the fire burning in the center of the circle, he bent down and added another small log. The fire would now burn long enough to get it done. Turning his head, he looked down the hill at the lake just barely visible through the trees. The last red glints of sunset were rapidly vanishing from the calm water.

Charlie was procrastinating and he knew it. If he'd mixed the ingredients wrong or performed the ceremony wrong, he would be dead as a hammer in very short order. There was no other choice though. Age and infirmity were having their way with him and he no longer had the speed or the stamina to keep up with his ancient foe. So it was either perform the dangerous ceremony with all of its risks or cede the battle and the war. An easy enough choice, at least to his way of thinking.

Throughout his long life Charlie had never shirked doing the hard thing. So he began, even though he felt his chances of surviving the night were slim. Kneeling, he pulled an intricately carved pipe and a small beaded pouch from the doeskin bag laying at his feet. He filled the pipe with the mixture in the pouch, a potent combination of ground mushrooms, herbs, nuts, and other plants. Chanting softly, he began walking around the perimeter of the stone circle.

He paused first at the easternmost point of the circle. Raising the pipe above his head with both hands, he offered it to the sun, bringer of life and warmth.

Still chanting, he slowly walked to the southernmost point of the circle. Again he offered up the pipe, this time to the South Wind, bringer of spring rains and fertile crops.

Walking onwards, still chanting, he offered the pipe to the West, keeper of death and darkness, without which there can be no renewal, no dawn.

Finally, Charlie arrived at the last compass point and again raised the pipe with both hands to the North, master of seasons, bringer of winter, guardian of the endless cycle, the yearly wheel of life.

Walking back to the easternmost point to complete the circle, Charlie turned and approached the fire, symbol of man's ascension over the beasts and of the mutability of all things. Reaching into the beaded pouch, he sprinkled some of the herb mix into the fire, making the flames dance and roar.

Taking a seat on the cold stone, Charlie stuck a twig into the fire and waited for it to flame. Applying the burning twig to the pipe's stone bowl, he took a long draw of the bitter mix and offered it up to himself, eldest and wisest of the Poshto children still living on The Great Mother. Struggling not to cough, Charlie smoked until there was nothing remaining in the bowl but a pinch of carbonized cinders. Sitting perfectly still, he waited, fighting impatience, willing something to happen. Ten minutes later he admitted defeat. Bitter frustration and black despair flooded his heart. He'd failed, again. Even having survived the dangerous ceremony seemed little consolation at the moment.

Leaning hard on his staff, Charlie attempted to rise and discovered that he couldn't. Looking down, he saw that his legs had become so long that he could no longer see his feet. When he looked across the stone circle, he didn't recognize it, even though he had been worshiping here for decades.

Ears roaring and head spinning, Charlie lay down on the cold granite outcropping. Grasping the staff with both hands so that it ran in a straight line from his chin to his feet, he lay still and waited. A few seconds later, he started as the stars darkened and the others arrived.

CHAPTER 15

"LOVE YOU, 'BYE now," Jennifer Garrison's voice sweetly said.

Thumb and pinkie extended, The Wendigo dropped an imaginary telephone handset into an equally imaginary cradle formed by his other hand. An audible click sounded as he did so.

"Ah yes," he happily proclaimed, delighted with the ploy, "there's a sucker born every minute and two to take him!"

The simulacrum of W. C. Fields gleefully capered in the moonlight at the foot of David Garrison's driveway. Top hat, waistcoat, cane, lit cigar, and bulbous nose, he was perfect down to the last detail.

Ever since hanging up the phone, David had been pacing around the first floor of the house. Staying still was impossible; his limbs kept wanting to explode into motion. So he paced, at times near jogging.

The knock on the front door startled him. He hadn't heard a car drive up nor had he seen any headlights shine in through the windows. Jennifer and Allison must have wanted to surprise him. Well, they had succeeded. Sprinting across the living room, he accelerated up the hallway toward the front door. Fumbling with the doorknob, he finally got the warped front door opened.

Jennifer and Allison were standing outside on the doorstep. Jennifer, still blonde without a trace of gray, green-eyed and as beautiful as the day he had married her. Still dressed as she was on the day she had disappeared seven years ago.

Allison, with her mother's long blonde hair and green eyes. His baby. Four feet one and a half inches tall wearing a University of Minnesota sweatshirt and children's Reeboks. Still the same after all these years.

Even as he lunged forward to embrace them, David's unconscious tried to shriek a warning. Tried to tell him that Jennifer and Allison's eyes had no pupils, that there was something very wrong about them, but he was past hearing, past caring.

"Hiya, David, you silly fuck!" The Wendigo howled, stepping forward into David's outstretched arms and puckering up. "Here, let me hang a big wet one on ya!"

David's mind, racing so furiously a moment before, shut down in self-defense. All it communicated to its owner were burning red eyes, dagger teeth, and foul carrion breath. Shrieking in terror, David vomited into the monster's face as its stench penetrated deep into his airway. Lashing out his tongue, The Wendigo began licking up the vomit dripping off his face and sucking it back into his cavernous maw.

"*Bon appetit,* motherfucker!" the beast snarled, snapping his jaws forward.

The medicine bag hanging around David's neck detonated, shredding the front of his denim shirt. A blinding flash of blue light smashed into the monster's head, knocking him across the deck and sending him rolling down the steps. The light coalesced into a pulsing caul of sapphire energy fastened over the beast's skull. The air stank of ozone and burning flesh as The Wendigo's skull began cooking inside the hood.

Bellowing in agony, the beast writhed across the ground, trying to free himself from the grip of the tormenting light. Small fires sprang into life wherever the creature's flaming skull brushed up against grass or foliage. Within a few seconds the pulsing cowl of blue light diminished to a soft glow and then vanished. Snarling, the monster staggered to his feet, clawing at its face.

The thick fur on The Wendigo's face had been burned off. The hide underneath was scorched black and leaking thick green lymph. His left eye was a smoking crater. Blackened bone and gristle protruded where his snout had once been. But he was still very much alive. Shaking like a wet dog, the monster loosed a throaty growl. Muscles spasmed and sinews popped as he re-knit himself. Five seconds after getting to his feet, The Wendigo was fully healed.

Leaves, grass, and other debris were sucked up into the gale as he gave voice to his immense fury. The deck railing tore free of its fasteners and sailed off as every window in the front of the house shattered. Caught off balance, David was knocked down and smacked his head hard against the tiled floor.

"You hurt me, prick-asshole-faggot," the monster raged as he charged forward. "I'll—"

"You will do nothing, Trickster," Charlie said, stepping over David and out onto the deck. "Come here and let me teach you pain."

Surprised by Charlie's appearance, The Wendigo skidded to a halt, digging up yards of turf under his clawed feet. Transparent, rimmed by blue fire, Charlie stood leaning on the staff, waiting. Man and demon locked eyes for long seconds. The beast was the first to look away.

"Well, old red nigger," the monster spat out, "Mary sends—"

Leveling the staff, Charlie shot from the hip. The blast of blue fire struck The Wendigo in the chest and sent him flying twenty-five feet through the air. The beast landed in a shrieking ball and Charlie smote him again and then yet again. Howling in pain and fury, the monster vanished in a roar of wind headed toward Frechette.

Turning away, Charlie knelt and put a hand on David's forehead. After a moment, Charlie diagnosed him as suffering from one-third concussion, one-third shock, and one-third physical exhaustion. Although he would have a bad headache when he woke in a few minutes, David would recover fully by morning. Concentrating and singing softly, he gently stroked David's forehead for a few seconds and then got to his feet.

Susie and Angus had arrived from their hiding place upstairs in response to his whistle. Sparing a moment for them, he petted each and told them to ward David until he regained consciousness. Rapping the staff gently on the tiled floor, Charlie vanished in a brilliant flash of blue light.

CHAPTER 16

SON-OF-A-bitches. Cocksuckers. Assholes. Burnt him, hit him with the blue fire. In recognition of his suffering, The Wendigo had awarded himself a Purple Heart which he was now wearing pinned into his bare right chest. A bad start. Fuckers, all of them, especially that goddamn geriatric Indian. Still, the night was young yet. Snare any of the four: Tonto, the yuppie, the loony tune or her whelp, and it was all over but the flowers and the eulogies.

As he had done the night before, the beast crept up to Rachel Tolliver's window. Reaching forward intending to tear the window the rest of the way out of the wall, he yelped in fear and stumbled backwards. Enraged, he snarled and milled around in frantic circles, jaws snapping shut on empty air. The same stench that had surrounded David Garrison was coming from the child's room and the monster wanted no more of old Redbird's magic this night.

Because he was not really alive in the normal sense of the word, The Wendigo could never really die. Because he could never die, the only thing he feared was pain. And the only thing that could cause him pain was the scalding blue fire wielded by the Redbird shamans. The same scalding blue fire that was hanging around the neck of the little girl sleeping on the other side of the window.

"Fucking cunts!" he snarled as he approached Gina's window.

"Ah-ha!" the monster breathed out in malicious delight a moment later.

Peering through the dirty glass, he could see Gina sleeping on her back on top of the covers. Mouth agape, she was drooling and snoring loudly. His sensitive eyes easily detected the faint blue glow emanating from the medicine bag tangled inside the ball of fabric sitting on the chair at the foot of the bed.

"G-i-i-i-n-n-a, wake up sugar, come on darlin', time to p-a-a-r-r-r-t-y." the monster roared at her through the window. "Goddamn it, wake up you drugged out bitch, we've got things to do and places to be!"

It took a while, but Gina's eyes finally fluttered open. She lay still for a moment then drunkenly swung her legs over the side of the bed.

"M-o-o-o-m-m-m-y!" Rachel screamed in terror from the back yard. "Boogie man's gonna get me!"

Staggering to the window, Gina looked outside. Twenty feet away, Rachel was standing in a sea of flowing mist in the midst of a vast forest.

"M-o-o-o-m-m-m-y!" she shrieked again, pointing to the left. "Boogie man's gonna get me! There!"

Fifty feet away, a disturbance rippled the surface of the mist and started speeding toward Rachel. Whimpering, Gina forced the window up, dived through the screen and belly-flopped onto the grass. Bruised and winded, she somehow managed to stagger to her feet. Too late, the monster already had Rachel.

"Oh-h-h G-i-i-n-n-n-a, lookee what I got here!" The Wendigo crowed, picking Rachel up by the neck and shaking her. "Now what are you gonna do, you loony-tune bitch?"

A nauseating *snap!* sounded as the monster broke Rachel's neck. Tossing her body away into the mist, he surged forward toward Gina.

"Turn around, drop your drawers, and bend over 'cuz your daddy's home, slut!" the beast roared as he charged. "But first, a little appetizer for madame before the main course."

Skidding to a halt two feet in front of Gina, The Wendigo grabbed his enormous penis and shook it at her. Smoking black jism flew from the snake-like head and fell on Gina's bare skin, burning her and raising quarter-sized blisters.

"Gina honey," the monster purred, slicing her panties and bra off with a single swipe of a razor-edged claw, "I'm gonna fuck you so hard that you'll die of it and then I'm gonna—"

Swinging hard, Charlie smashed the staff down on The Wendigo's skull. A wave of blue fire engulfed the beast's body. Shreiking in pain he vanished, again taking form as a roaring gale of wind.

The shock wave created by Charlie's blow had shattered windows throughout the apartment complex. Car alarms were going off and lights were coming on in many of the units. People were leaving their apartments to investigate the source of the commotion. Nude, sitting splay-legged on the grass, Gina was screaming mindlessly at the top of her lungs. Events were spinning out of control and Charlie knew that he had to hurry.

Placing one arm around her shoulders and the other under her knees, he picked her up.

"Hush, Gina," he soothed. "Rachel is fine. See, she's right over there waiting for us at the window."

Catching sight of Rachel, Gina's screams quieted to a steady whimpering accompanied by violent shivering. Reaching the window, Charlie eased her through the opening and lowered her to the floor. Standing next to the window, Rachel watched anxiously.

"Hi, Grampa Charlie, I did what you said," the child solemnly told him. "Didn't tell and didn't take it off."

"Yes, Rachel, you did just fine, I'm very proud of you. Can you cover Mommy up with a blanket and take care of her until I get back in a couple of hours?"

Rachel nodded and smiled a little.

"All right then, honey, I'll see you soon," he said, reaching into the room to stroke her hair before vanishing in a flare of blue light.

Walking over to the bed, Rachel tugged off a blanket, covered her whimpering mother with it, and then climbed into her lap. Mother and daughter were still holding each other when the police arrived six minutes later.

CHAPTER 17

A VAST PAIN filled him, making him shriek in agony. Although his body healed almost instantly, the agony inflicted by the blue fire continued echoing down the corridors of his consciousness. Generations of men had turned to dust since the last time he had suffered such pain.

Roaring northwards toward his crèche, he spied a fire burning on a small granite outcropping. A familiar figure lay sleeping next to the fire. Howling his hatred, the beast attacked. The air shimmered and suddenly the granite outcropping was gone. Unable to brake in time, he crashed down headfirst through the trees to the ground below. Rolling to his feet, the monster charged toward the fire burning a few yards away. Seeing who was waiting for him there, he stopped and backed up a couple of steps in a hurry.

At the edge of the granite circle, Charlie stood leaning on his staff. Behind him stood hundreds of generations of Redbird shamans stretching back millennia. All of them somehow standing together on a rock outcropping barely thirty feet wide.

The beast twitched nervously, probing its memories of this very potent magic. The last time he had witnessed it was at this very spot and the ice-sheet was over half a mile thick at the time. Yes, a very long time ago indeed. He had believed such knowledge and power had been lost long ago by the forest dwellers. Time to go, the monster decided, there was great danger here. Before he could escape, Charlie rapped his staff once on the granite and commanded, "Hold!"

Panic filled The Wendigo as the trap was sprung. Body twisting and writhing, he fought desperately to escape. Lowering his staff, Charlie extruded a thick shaft of blue light and circled the demon's chest with it. Cobalt fire raced across the stone outcropping, racing among and up the spectral forms of the gathered Redbird Shamans.

"Come, Dark One," Charlie said, dragging the struggling monster forward a few inches by retracting the noose circling his chest, "step into the circle and free yourself."

Clawed feet digging smoldering grooves in the stony soil, the beast struggled against Charlie's call. Standing rigid, Charlie gripped the staff with white-knuckled hands rimed in blue fire.

Six inches. A foot. Eighteen inches. Two feet. The Wendigo was now a sizzling black sphere of kinetic energy encircled by an equator of blue fire anchored to Charlie's staff. Another foot and the monster would be within reach of the staff and dragged into the circle of waiting shamans. Twelve more inches and the long centuries of terror would be over.

"H-e-e-e-l-l-p m-e-e-e!" the beast gibbered in profound terror.

Sickly yellow-green luminescence attached itself to the noose of blue fire. Sizzling and flaring, it burned through the noose and sent Charlie sprawling backwards onto the stone slab. Expanding, the yellow-green light rapidly enveloped the beast in a protective cocoon. A second later The Wendigo transformed himself into a comet streaking away northwards.

Standing up with his kinfolk's assistance, Charlie watched the monster retreat over the horizon. He was disappointed in the outcome of the battle but not particularly surprised. A realist, he had never expected victory to come so easily. Still, they had been close, never closer.

Threading his way between his spectral kin, Charlie approached the fire still burning at the center of the outcropping. Easing himself down, he re-entered his body and reunited his spiritual and physical selves. Hovering on the edge of sleep, he watched in surprise as the revenants of his ancestors flowed into him. Warmth and a sensation of familial continuity filled him. Seconds later the melding was over. Closing his eyes, Charlie slipped into a deep sleep as the fire burned down and the moon set.

CHAPTER 18

OH-GOD-OH-God-oh-God she was scared! Frightened of the dark since childhood, even now at age thirty-two she still slept with a nightlight on. Despite this, here she was creeping through the dark playing Nancy Drew, girl moron. The full moon had set an hour earlier and now it was darker than Lucifer's bunghole. Born and raised in the Cities, she had spent her entire life under the comforting glow of electric lights. Goddamn rotten son-of-a-bitch, this was all his fault. Telling her to leave, yelling at her at the top of his lungs. Asshole.

Skeletal tree branches scraped and sighed in the stiff breeze and leaves rattled along the ground, testing the limits of her already shaky nerves. Stop, Ellen commanded herself. She stopped. Take a nice deep breath. She breathed. Relax. You must be kidding. All right then, just get on with it.

Stepping forward over a fallen branch, Ellen startled a sleeping ruffled grouse. The bird exploded into noisy flight, sounding like an avian 747 in the night-hushed woods. Chittering indignantly, the grouse button-hooked by her face and flew off to the safety of the deep forest. Letting out a breathy squawk, Ellen stumbled a couple of steps to the right. Heart hammering, blood roaring through her ears, she conquered the urge to scream, barely.

Enough, this was it. *No mas*, out of here. Away from the kamikaze birds, Bambi, Thumper, and whatever the hell else lived here. Once she got home, Ellen promised herself that she would never stray from the bright lights of civilization again. Grandpa was a grown man and then some and if he didn't want her around, that was fine with her. Meanwhile, it was time to beat feet and get the hell out of here.

Firm in her resolve, Ellen reversed course and found that she couldn't recognize anything. Panic began beating its dark wings inside her brain as Ellen realized that she was lost. Not slightly confused or a little uncertain about where she was but Holy-Shit-And-What-The-Fuck-Do-I-Do-Now-Lost. Choke down the panic, the fear, don't cry. Fight the urge to mindlessly run. Breathe. There, better. Be logical, retrace your steps. Pay attention, find your way.

Eyes locked down on the uneven pitch-black ground beneath her feet, Ellen didn't notice the creature until it was on top of her. Moaning softly, it tried to embrace her. Dark holes rested where its eyes should have been and its mouth was frozen open in a leering rictus.

Stumbling sideways, Ellen fell into something soft and yielding. She tried to rise and flee, but her feet couldn't get any purchase on whatever it was she had fallen into. The monster loomed above her, moaning and swinging its arms side-to-side. Self-control fled. Ellen screamed and kept on screaming,

CHAPTER 19

STREAKING NORTH AT treetop level, The Wendigo nursed his hate and pain. Shrieking incoherently, he swore an eternity of revenge against those that had injured him. A ravening need for sustenance consumed him and could not be ignored. Not far from his crèche, he spied a lone hunter and descended to the forest floor. Raising his snout into the air, the beast smelled the hunter's fear and sampled his troubled dreams. He wasn't much more than a boy, lost and separated from his hunting companions. Excellent.

The Wendigo quickly formulated a plan. Making himself comfortable, he waited for dawn to bring everything to fruition. The physical bodies of those he slaughtered were of little concern to him, the merest appetizers. Their terror and their pain was what actually sustained him and allowed him to survive. The victims' terror and pain were maximized when they were fully awake, taken by surprise, and slowly killed. So though he was near starving, he would wait for the lost hunter to wake at sunrise. But that didn't mean that he couldn't enjoy a little snack while he waited.

Placing a forefinger in his mouth, the beast amputated it with one snap of his dagger teeth. Swallowing the morsel whole, he shoved the next digit into his mouth, sheared it off, and swallowed it. Finished with the fifth finger on his left hand, The Wendigo paused only long enough to change hands. By the time the fifth finger on that hand had been devoured, all of the fingers on his left hand had regenerated.

"Always did like finger food," he observed, belching happily.

Finished snacking for the moment, the monster leaned back and contemplated the night's failures. Fury gripped him and he nearly howled, which would have spoiled his meal now slumbering fifty yards away. Biting his lips, the beast slowly calmed himself.

"Minion," he commented aloud, looking over his shoulder toward Frechette, "what a lovely word, what a lovely concept."

CHAPTER 20

"MRS. TOLLIVER, FRECHETTE Police Department, please open the door," a man's booming voice said.

Propped up in a corner of the bedroom, Gina whimpered and rocked mindlessly, the back of her head smacking against the wall with dreadful monotony every couple of seconds. Curled up in the cage of her mother's arms, Rachel was sleeping.

"Mrs. Tolliver, you have until the count of four to open this door or I'll kick it down," the officer said.

"One!" he counted off cheerfully and paused.

"Two!" the voice bellowed in the same gleeful tone.

Rubbing her eyes, Rachel stirred awake, afraid. Worried, she tugged on Gina's hand, but her mother only whimpered and rocked all the harder.

"Three!" the loud voice happily continued before suddenly roaring, "fuck it, I'll huff and I'll puff and I'll blow your house down!"

A splintering crash echoed through the small apartment as the hollow-core front door was battered off its hinges. Patrol Officer Steven Jensen stepped through the opening and walked over the fallen door into the living room. The same Officer Steven Jensen who had raised Charlie's hackles during the traffic-stop the previous afternoon.

Nostrils distended, Jensen sniffed the air seeking his prey. Inhaling deeply, he savored the scent a moment before sprinting down a short hallway. Charging through the door into Gina's bedroom, he skidded to a halt and retreated. Standing outside the door in the hallway, he muttered to himself in a burbling soliloquy.

Frightened, Rachel tried to burrow deeper into her mother's arms. The big man in the uniform on the other side of the door terrified her. Everything about him scared her; the way his head towered up near the ceiling, his sunglasses, and most especially his voice.

Frustrated, Jensen growled, sending spittle flying out of his mouth. The little bitch had one of the Indian's medicine bags tied around her neck and another was lying close to her on a chair. In this current form if either of them detonated, he would be pureed. Literally.

Ah, an idea. Bone cracked and muscles tore as Jensen remade himself. When he took off his sunglasses, he was wearing the face of Eric Tolliver, Rachel's missing father.

"Rachel honey, throw the bag tied around your neck out the window," Jensen said, perfectly mimicking Eric Tolliver's voice. "And the one inside the shirt on the chair too. They're bad things, dirty, dangerous. Hurry up now and do it, that's my girl."

Crying now, Rachel's fingers fumbled at the leather thong around her neck as she attempted to pull it over her head. Her free hand brushed against the beaded bag and she froze. Frowning a little, she remembered Florida. A bright yellow swing set and a matching sand-box in a sunny backyard. The nice smell of hot dogs and hamburgers cooking on the grill. Riding her bike with her friends on their quiet street. Larry, her yellow Labrador dog and Bob her goldfish, both given away when they had to move. Now, Mommy was sick and crying or sleeping all the time. The bike she had gotten for Christmas last year was in storage, wherever that was. And she only had one friend, the little girl next door.

Most of all though, Rachel remembered her father. His easy laughter and how he used to ride her up on his shoulders and how he always had time to read stories to her. Remembered and knew the thing on the other side of the door wasn't her father, not even close. She remembered and got angry the way that only six-year-olds can, a full tilt temper-tantrum that permeated to the core of her being.

"You're a liar!" Rachel shouted, climbing out of her mother's lap. "Not my daddy! You go 'way!"

Unconsciously pulling the medicine bag out from under her shirt, Rachel held it out in front of her as she walked forward. The air in the room shimmered blue and Rachel saw what the creature on the other side of the door really looked like. Instead of frightening her, it only made her all that much angrier.

"Liar-liar-liar!" she screamed, so furious that she could barely speak. "Not my daddy! You get out of here!"

"Gina, honey," the Jensen thing pleaded, "do something with your daughter, she won't lis—"

As her eyes cleared and focused, Gina looked through the curtain of shimmering blue light. Seeing what was standing on the other side of the door, she screamed. Not just any scream, but a great, whooping air-raid siren of a scream. A puddle of urine and feces spread and soaked into the carpet beneath her as fear loosened her sphincters.

"Liar, liar, not my daddy!" Rachel shrieked, walking forward out the bedroom door with the medicine bag clutched protectively in front of her. "You leave my mommy 'lone an go 'way!"

Retreating down the hallway in disbelief, the creature resumed the form of Officer Jensen. Running, retreating, thwarted by a mere child and the power of old Redbird's magic. The instructions had been to deliver the 'toon and her brat alive. But if all else failed, as it was currently doing, the ever reliable center-fire solution would do.

Jensen decided that he would shoot Rachel when he reached the front door and then dive through the opening in the hope that the building would shield him from the expected blast. Preoccupied with keeping his balance while backing down the hall and keeping an eye on the furious and still advancing child, Jensen didn't feel the tug at his right hip until it was too late. Officer Jason Gunther agilely slid by, whirled, and stood facing his partner.

"Honey, go back in the bedroom right now," Gunther told Rachel as he leveled a pair of handguns at Jensen's chest.

Falling silent, Rachel did as she was told and retreated down the hallway to her mother's bedroom. Still screaming, Gina continued rocking and smacking her skull against the wall.

"You're all done, I heard and saw everything," Gunther said, voice quavering, guns shaking in his hands. "Turn around and assume the position against the wall, Steve, or I'll blow your shit away. I swear to God I will."

Gunther was a recent hire, twenty-two years old with the ink on his Criminal Justice degree barely dry. Partnered with Jensen for the last four months, he had initially liked the older man a great deal. Then Jensen had taken a week off at the beginning of October to go on an annual bird hunting trip. When he had returned, Jensen was changed, and not for the better. On three different occasions Gunther had to intervene to prevent him from beating prisoners unconscious, perhaps even to death. Sickened, Gunther had heard Jensen's remarks to female prisoners, watched his hands roam over their bodies. In desperation he had informed his superiors and been met with cold hostility for violating the Eleventh Commandment, "Thou shall not inform on thine partner, never, no matter what happens." When Jensen had sent him to find the manager of the apartment complex, he had known there was going to be trouble.

"You ain't got the nuts for this kind of work, college boy," Jensen snarled, snatching the nightstick out of his utility belt as he charged forward. "Now hold still, this won't take but a second."

Gunther opened fire with both of the Beretta nine-millimeter automatics. Jensen was closing fast, no more than three feet away, point-blank range. Gunther fired five shots, three from his quicker master hand, the right, and two from his slow hand, the left. All five rounds impacted center-of-mass in Jensen's lower chest and upper abdomen.

Screaming as he was shot, Jensen collapsed and landed on his back. Lying motionless, he stared up at the ceiling. Convulsing once, he took a deep, rasping breath and spat an amazing volume of blood up onto the ceiling. Climbing back to his feet as if nothing had happened, he turned and fled out of the apartment into the night.

Still holding the handguns, Gunther stood and watched him go. Five shots, five hits, all center-of-mass. Jensen should have been near dead or nearly dead. Yet he had gotten up and run off as if uninjured. The gore blown out of the exit wounds and splattered all over the living room walls was proof that Jensen hadn't been wearing a bullet-proof vest. This was impossible, it couldn't be—

"Stop this and MOVE!" Gunther ordered himself.

Crossing the living room, he knelt and peered around the splintered door frame at the parking lot. He expected to see Jensen charging back with the twelve-gauge riot shotgun kept in the squad car. In which case, Hollywood action thrillers aside, that would probably be all she wrote.

Instead and to his immense relief, Gunther heard the throaty roar of the squad car's engine starting up and saw the headlights come on. The steel belted radials howled as Jensen accelerated out of the parking lot, sideswiping a pair of cars as he went. The headlights slewed right, raced south down Main Street, and vanished.

Drawing in a shaky breath, Officer Gunther slowly got to his feet. Speaking into the microphone clipped to his left shoulder, he requested backup. Wailing sirens were already clearly audible from the police and fire stations three miles away. Turning, he almost tripped over the little girl standing by his heels.

Hunkering down, he asked, "What's your name?"

"Rachel," she solemnly answered, hugging her teddy bear with both arms. "My Mommy's real sick."

"All right honey, let me go see," he said, standing up. "You stay right here until I get back, okay?"

The child nodded her head and Gunther looked over his shoulder as he walked away to make sure she stayed put. Entering the hallway out of Rachel's sight, he slid one of the pistols into his belt and inserted a fresh clip into the other. Advancing carefully, he checked the bathroom and found it empty. Entering Rachel's bedroom, he looked in the closet and even under the bed and still found nothing.

Easing through the last door in the hallway, he saw a nude woman with a blanket puddled around her hips propped up in the far corner of a bedroom. Large blisters were scattered across her face, breasts, and belly. The stench of urine and feces was thick in the air and there was a dark stain on the carpet beneath her.

Sometime during the insanity of the gunfire, Gina had stopped screaming. Now she was rocking, bouncing off the wall and back again, keening softly to herself. Holstering the pistol, Officer Gunther slowly approached her. Kneeling down, he tried to speak to her. Before he could utter a word, Gina began scrabbling at the floor, trying to escape. Spittle flew out of her mouth as she babbled incoherently and her eyes rolled wildly until only the whites showed.

"Easy now, just relax," Gunther said, standing and hastily backing away.

As soon as he stepped away, Gina began keening again and resumed her monotonous rocking. A dull thud sounded every couple of seconds or so as the back of her head struck the wall. Wincing at the sound, he turned to leave the room and noticed the collection of prescription medications on top of the dresser. Picking up each bottle, he inspected the labels. Glancing back at Gina, Gunther finally recognized what he was seeing. Pity filled him for what lay ahead for her and the beautiful little girl waiting just down the hall.

Leaving the bedroom, he walked through the apartment and found Rachel sitting on the front steps. Plopping down next to her, Gunther felt like he was a thousand years old. Taking off his uniform jacket, he wrapped it around her so that she wouldn't get cold.

"Is my Mommy gonna be all right?" she fearfully asked.

"Yes, honey," Gunther lied, putting an arm around her, "your Mom's gonna be just fine in a little while."

The two sat silently after that, watching the emergency vehicles arrive with lights strobing and sirens blaring. Jensen was right, Gunther decided. He didn't have the stones for law enforcement work and this would be his last shift as a police officer.

CHAPTER 21

THE CHILL ROCK finally prodded Charlie awake. Groaning softly, he rolled over onto his side. A pair of glowing red embers were all that remained of the fire. Moving slowly, he pulled himself erect with the aid of the staff and took a seat on a boulder at the edge of the stone circle. Sighing, he cradled his head in his hands and almost dozed off again. The remnants of the powerful hallucinogen he had smoked were still pounding through his system. Although physically unhurt, he was exhausted. Right at the moment, his sole desire was to sit quietly and wait for the sun to rise. Later, he would see about making a pot of coffee. Or then again, maybe he wouldn't.

The scream echoing up the hill startled him. Another scream closely followed and then another.

"Ellen!" Charlie roared, leaping to his feet. "Ellen honey, where are you?"

Near panic, he started running down the hill. He came not only as Charlie Redbird, but also as the last of the Redbird shamans. Thunder shook the ground as he ran and the early morning stars were blotted out by his shadow. Blue chain-lightning tore the sky above his head. If the Dark One had taken her, Charlie promised himself, this time he would destroy the monster no matter the cost. If he had to unleash the full power of the staff and break the back of the Great Mother he would do so. He would bear no more pain, no more loss.

"Blossom!" Charlie roared, his pet name for her since early childhood. "Blossom honey, where are you?"

Ellen heard, then saw the apparition charging down the hill toward her. Moaning deep in her throat, hands and feet slipping on the mucky ground, she tried to crawl away. And then it was just her grandfather, looking down at her as he leaned on his staff.

"Blossom," he asked after catching a couple of breaths, "why are you laying in my manure pile?"

"I, oh shit, damn it!" she exclaimed in disgust, realizing now what she had fallen into. "Gross!"

Still intoxicated, Charlie began laughing helplessly.

"W-w-well," he commented, laughing so hard that he could barely speak, "it, it happens!"

Convulsed with laughter he fell to his knees, paralyzed by his own sally.

"That goddamned scarecrow of yours scared me," Ellen yelled, trying and failing to get her feet under her, "and when I tried to get away, I fell into this pile of shit!"

For decades, Charlie had been an accomplished tinkerer. The scarecrow had been mounted on a wooden crucifix attached to an old car spring set into a five gallon plastic bucket filled with concrete. Tin cans with holes knocked into the sides had been tied to his arms. When the wind blew, which was usually in these parts, the scarecrow swayed on the car spring and the tin cans moaned. Its face was loosely modeled on one that had haunted Charlie's nightmares for decades. As Ellen could testify, it was a highly effective straw man.

On the third try, Ellen finally extricated herself from the manure pile. Genuine organic cow shit covered her from head to toe.

"I'm glad you think this is so goddamned funny!" she shouted, crying hard now. "I come up here to see if you're all right and you're hateful to me. I get scared to death by your scarecrow and fall into a stinking pile of cow shit and you think it's funny! I'll get some clean clothes out of my car and take a shower and leave. That is if you don't mind me being in your house. You're a mean, spiteful old man! You just leave me alone!"

Tirade finished, Ellen turned on her heel and stomped off toward her car. Her departure sobered Charlie instantly. Things between them couldn't be allowed to end like this; he just couldn't bear it again.

"Ellen Blossom, please come back," he pleaded. "I am a rude old man sometimes. There is great danger here now and I was afraid something else would happen to you. So I was cruel to you because I knew that would be the only thing that would make you go away and stay away."

Stopping, Ellen turned and faced her grandfather.

"Blossom, if you are still angry with me I will understand. Much as I love you and much as I wish you could stay here, it's better if you go back to the Cities and stay there. It's just too dangerous for you to be here right now."

"Don't you think that at age thirty-two I'm entitled to make my own decisions?" she asked, anger percolating just under the surface of her voice. "Besides which, living in the Cities hasn't kept me safe yet, so why should it now?"

Smart enough to know when he was on the losing end of an argument, Charlie just smiled, nodded, and kept quiet.

"Good then, I'd like to stay if it's all right with you," Ellen said, smiling a little. "Provided you tell me what's going on here. You've been hiding something for years and if it's dangerous, I deserve to know."

"Yes, Blossom, of course you can stay as long as you realize that it's very dangerous," Charlie replied, already worrying about her safety. "And you're only going to get the Reader's Digest version of what's been going on because it's a long, complicated story. Now let's get you inside and cleaned up, we have a lot to do today and we need to get going."

Thirty minutes later, Ellen preceded Charlie out the front door and waited for him to lock it. Climbing down the rickety porch steps to the front yard, Charlie led her over to his ancient Chevy pick-up truck. Somehow, and she couldn't imagine how he'd done it given the time-frame, he'd managed to get the plates renewed and gotten a new inspection sticker.

"It's best if we take my truck this time," he told her. "In case something happens, it would be better if your car wasn't seen. Would you mind driving please, I had a rough night and I'm pretty tired."

Deciding she was better off not knowing what the unnamed "something" might entail, Ellen took the keys out of his outstretched hand and climbed behind the wheel. Twisting the key in the ignition, she swallowed hard to keep from laughing at the amazing clatter her grandfather's beloved old pick-up made as it started.

"So you mean it's all true?" Ellen asked as they waited for the truck to warm up. "All those old stories we got told at bedtime when we were kids about the Redbird shamans and the Trickster were true?"

"Not all true, Blossom, no. Most of what you heard were old granny tales, but there are some grains of truth in them."

"Well I—" she began, biting off her sentence when Charlie suddenly stiffened on the seat next to her. "Grandpa, what's wrong, tell me—"

"I'm all right," Charlie told her as his body relaxed. "The woman and little girl from yesterday, Gina and Rachel Tolliver, have been taken by the Frechette Police Department. They are in great danger and we must hurry!"

Nodding, Ellen swung the pick-up truck out onto the dirt track and accelerated toward Frechette.

CHAPTER 22

HOLDING HIS BREATH, Dwayne Hutchinson placed another piece of green wood on the fire and prayed that it would burn. He was lost and had been since mid-afternoon yesterday. Dwayne was a big boy. Fat, to put it in uncharitable terms. Seventeen years old, he stood five feet, eight inches tall and weighed 294 pounds. Adding to his charms was a virulent case of acne that could pass for leprosy in dim light.

Originally left out, Dwayne had agitated to be included on this hunting trip. His stepfather, a former NFL wide receiver and now a successful business man, had been opposed. So had his older stepbrother, currently a starting middle linebacker on the University of Minnesota football team with NFL aspirations of his own. But Dwayne's mother had intervened and he had been included, albeit not willingly.

Or, as his stepfather Creighton had not so tactfully put it, "Dwayne, you mother Lenora has threatened to shut off what little pussy I still get from her unless I take you deer hunting. So you can go, but as we tell rookies in the NFL, shut up, do what you're told, and don't fuck up."

And now Dwayne had fucked up, BIG TIME. Yesterday afternoon he had climbed down from his tree stand to relieve himself. Glad of the opportunity to escape the confined stand, he had decided to take a walk. After following a stream for a little while he had seen some squirrels and gotten distracted. Gotten lost, to be perfectly honest about it.

The survival pack containing his compass, map, emergency rations, and water bottle was right where he had left it. Sitting on the ground propped up against the bole of the tree his stand was in. Wherever in the hell that might be. Currently, Dwayne's on-hand survival inventory consisted of three waterproof matches, a five-inch drop-point skinning knife, and a bolt action Remington 30-06 rifle with a loaded four-shot magazine. Not much to survive with in one of the most remote wilderness areas in the lower forty-eight states. It was late October in Northern Minnesota and it could snow anytime.

Closing his eyes, Dwayne could already hear Creighton Richards', late of the NFL, cutting, sarcastic remarks. Which were sure to be echoed by his step brother Montgomery Richards, soon to be of the NFL. Worse yet, he could hear his mother Lenora's murmured excuses and see her downcast eyes, her disappointment in him. Huddled by the smoky fire, dressed head-to-toe in hunter orange, rifle at his side, Dwayne Hutchinson re-sembled a well-armed weather balloon that had suffered a crash landing and subsequent clinical depression.

Time to choose, he decided, the lady or the tiger. If he fired three shots in rapid succession, the hunter's distress signal, someone might find him. If no one heard the shots though, he would be left with only one round and from here to China to walk. Or, he could use one of the bullets on himself and be spared the expected NFL roast. No, he decided, that was a little premature just yet. Besides which, he didn't want to give the bastards the satisfaction. Or, he could just sit here and wait to be rescued. Or more likely, freeze like an orange Popsicle in a day or two.

So, Dwayne decided, from here to China it would be. Put the rising sun to his left and start walking south toward the lake and possible rescue. Although he wasn't certain of the distance, he didn't believe it was further than thirty miles or so. Thirty miles through one of the harshest woodland environments on the continent. Beyond question, one thing could be said about Dwayne Hutchinson. He might have been grossly obese, uglier than a mud fence and none too bright, but he damn sure was an optimist.

And then Dwayne saw the deer and with it his possible salvation. The animal was a white-tailed buck, a beauty with at least seven points on each of his antler's main beams. The deer's configuration was perfect, its colors a symphony of earth-tone hues. The buck was a lifetime trophy, one for the record books by anyone's standards.

If he could kill the buck, Dwayne knew that his fat would be out of the fire. He could claim that he cut the animal's track yesterday afternoon and followed it until dark. Resuming at first light, he had tracked the buck down and killed it. His step-sadists would have to believe him. The buck's body and rack would be undeniable concrete evidence. He would have beaten them at their own game. Most importantly, he, Dwayne Hutchinson, would be one of the boys. For once he would belong.

Moving slowly and quietly, Dwayne knelt and raised the rifle to his shoulder. A twig lying next to the fire snapped under his left knee and he froze in terror. The buck merely looked at him and obligingly turned broadsides. Fifty yards away, no more. The buck's image danced around inside the telescopic scope as Dwayne struggled to settle the cross hairs just behind the deer's shoulder. A case of buck fever that was rapidly approaching Ebola-like proportions swept through him. In desperation he finally jerked on the trigger and fired.

When the rifle fell out of recoil, Dwayne saw the buck leap once, crash down on his knees, and collapse. Dead, apparently. A fresh gash in a large birch tree five yards to the left and ten yards beyond the fallen deer escaped his notice.

Leaping to his feet, Dwayne hooted. He hollered. He whistled. He stomped his feet. He Twisted. He Frugged. He Chickened. He set American dance back at least fifty years. Launching into a wobbling trot, Dwayne propelled his ponderous bulk over to the fallen buck. The light was gone out of the deer's eyes and a large exit wound gaped just behind its right shoulder.

Fighting down an urge to simultaneously cry and vomit, Dwayne prepared himself for what came next. The buck had to be bled out and field dressed. Euphemisms aside, it meant that the deer's blood had to be drained out by cutting its throat and then removing its viscera from its body cavity.

Grabbing the left antler, he turned the buck's head, exposing its throat. Taking a deep breath, Dwayne shoved the skinning knife into the buck's throat up to the hilt and the animal exploded back to life. Within a second The Wendigo had resumed his true form and was up on his feet, raging. Only the antlers remained unchanged, protruding from the top of the monster's skull. Pulling the knife out of his throat, he flung it away. Gobbling in terror, Dwayne tried to back away.

"Well hiya there, Dwayne, you fat fuck!" the beast roared, seizing him by the throat. "Think I'll return the favor and see how long it takes me to field dress your fat ass, but in reverse order."

Wallowing in the pain and terror he inflicted, The Wendigo took seven long, slow minutes to field-dress Dwayne Hutchinson. For six of those minutes, Dwayne was conscious or semi-conscious. His agonized screams could be heard from over a mile away.

Finished with the last morsel, the monster daintily licked his fingers. Waste not, want not. A quick twirl and he was Elvis at forty, sequined jump suit and cape sparkling in the early dawn light.

"O-h-h-h, I'm all shook up," he sang, protruding belly rumbling. "Yo, you in there, Dwayne, you gotta lay off the saturated fats, you're killin' me here. Startin' now, Pork, you're goin' on a diet that would give Jenny Craig a wet spot."

Two hundred yards away, Creighton and Montgomery Richards were calling Dwayne's name. Another quick twirl and the monster transformed from Elvis into Snagglepuss, the insouciant 1960's cartoon character.

"Exit, stage left!" he proclaimed, accelerating northwards and vanishing from sight in seconds.

Breathing hard, Creighton and Montgomery Richards arrived in the clearing two minutes later. Although they closely examined the ground, they saw nothing. There was no sign that Dwayne Hutchinson had died here or ever even been here. There were no tracks, no blood, no fire or traces of it, nothing. Even Dwayne's rifle and skinning knife were gone. After a couple of minutes the two men continued on, seeking the source of the terrible screams they had heard a few minutes earlier.

CHAPTER 23

SLAMMING ERECT, CHARLIE squeezed his eyes shut and clutched the staff with both hands.

The Wendigo's dining habits were never a joy to behold.

"Grandpa," Ellen asked, giving him a worried look, "What's—"

"I'm fine, Ellen," he said, body slowly relaxing. "That's the building just up ahead on the right. Go ahead and pull into the side lot and park near the back."

Stepping on the brake pedal with both feet, Ellen slowed the pick-up and turned into the parking lot. Uneasy, Charlie carefully surveyed the area, senses tingling. Danger, but not particularly close. Twisting in the seat, he faced Ellen and held her with his bottomless black eyes.

"Listen to me carefully, Blossom," he said, urgency permeating his tone. "In a minute, I am going into that building and get Rachel, the little girl. When I'm gone, if you feel afraid or something seems wrong, you are to run, on foot or in the truck, whatever seems best at the time. Don't stop or wait or look for me, I'll be fine and catch up with you later at David Garrison's, that's the big house we visited late yesterday afternoon. Mind me now, this is very important. Do you understand what I just said?"

Ellen nodded uncertainly, already worried. Smiling, Charlie reached over and squeezed her hand. Climbing out of the truck, he headed off across the parking lot toward the front door. Stepping up on the sidewalk, he paused and examined the building in front of him. The gusting wind disturbed his long grey braids and scattered leaves around his feet.

"Minnesota Department of Human Services" was written across the front of the three story red brick building in large black letters. The grim structure was over half a century old and had been used for the same purpose since the Second World War.

The wailing sobs of long forgotten children drifted down the wind and eddied around Charlie. Knuckles whitening on the staff, he frowned, carving deep lines into his face. Sighing, he wished yet again that he was the instrument, not the reed. Wished again that he rightfully possessed the power instead of being its reluctant guardian. Wished, because there were so many things that he would change if he could.

Taking a sip of coffee, the building's security guard watched an elderly gentleman approach the building's front doors on one of the two video monitors mounted on his desks. Natty looking old dude, he genially thought. Blue jeans, sweater, hiking boots, and a stylish jacket zipped shut against the day's chill. He looked like somebody's well-tanned, white-haired southern grandfather up for a visit with one of the little darlin's. Which damn sure wasn't about to happen.

Remaining seated, the guard watched him struggle through the double set of doors. A cynical smile spread across his face as he watched the old man hobble across the lobby leaning heavily on his sick. Arriving at the security desk, the elderly gentleman politely cleared his throat and stood there waiting. The security guard ignored him for long seconds and then officiously snapped, "Help you?"

"Yes, well, I hope so," the old man hesitantly said. "My great-granddaughter Rachel Tolliver is here and I've come to take her home with me."

"Sorry, sir," the guard brusquely replied, enjoying himself immensely, "children are not released from this facility without a valid court order and prior authorization from the Minnesota Department of Human Services."

"Well, could I please see her, if only for a minute?" the elderly man pleaded, managing to look both hopeful and crestfallen at the same time.

"Sorry, sir," the security officer replied in the same clipped tone. "Visiting hours are eight to ten and three to five, Monday through Saturday. Today is Sunday and there are no visiting hours. We have rules in this facility, you know."

Finished speaking, the guard leaned and crossed his arms across his chest. Smug, secure in his authority, invulnerable behind the bastion of the security desk and its flanking video monitors.

"Oh, no," the old man sighed, pulling a small piece of paper out of his jacket pocket. "Then could you please tell me how to find this address in Frechette? It's where my granddaughter lives."

Eager to show off his knowledge, the security guard rocked forward and reached across the desk for the slip of paper. The old man's hand flashed out and the guard was snared.

"Take me to Rachel Tolliver," Charlie commanded, keeping a firm grip on the guard's arm as he led him out from behind the security desk. "Now, damn it!"

Placing the staff in the small of the guard's back, Charlie allowed the man to lead him across the lobby. Arriving at a security door, the guard pulled a magnetic swipe card out of his right breast pocket and passed it through a scanner. A buzzer briefly sounded and the heavy steel door slid open. The two passed through the security portal and it clanked shut behind them.

These new surroundings didn't suit Rachel at all. She didn't like the cramped little room with the dirty linoleum floor. Wire mesh covered the outside of the only window and it wouldn't open. She didn't like the little bed with the single itchy blanket on it. Only one hard little chair to sit on. No storybooks and no TV to watch cartoons on, either. She didn't like any of it, period.

Worried about and missing her mother, Rachel had spent most of the morning crying. A mean looking old lady with thick glasses named Mrs. Riley had told her that after lunch she would be going to live with a foster family. Rachel didn't understand, she didn't know anybody named Foster and she wanted to live with her mom.

The door buzzed and opened and the policeman from downstairs walked into the room. Certain now that she was being taken away from her mother, Rachel pressed up against the wall and started crying. Face in her hands, she wailed inconsolably.

"Now, sweetie, don't you cry," Charlie told her from behind the guard. "We're getting out of here right now and going to get your mom"

Lowering her hands, Rachel launched herself off the wall and hugged his knees. Caught off balance, Charlie struggled to keep his feet, hug her, and control the guard all at the same time. Somehow, he managed.

"Grampa Charlie, Grampa Charlie!" Rachel said. "I thought you forgot about me!"

"No, Rachel, of course I didn't forget about you," Charlie replied, gently stroking her hair and compelling her at the same time. "Now why don't you go stand over by the door while I take care of Officer Friday here."

Releasing his knees, Rachel stepped away and stood near the door.

"'kay Grampa Charlie," she dreamily told him, "I'll wait right over there."

Satisfied that Rachel wouldn't wander, Charlie turned his attention to the slack-jawed guard. Hurting the man was out of the question but a lesson needed to be taught. Frog marching him over to the bed, Charlie directed him to lie down. The guard was so tall that his head hung over the head of the child-sized bed and his butt and elled-legs hung over the foot.

"Sleep long," Charlie commanded, tapping him lightly on the chest with the staff.

In response, the guard's eyes closed and his breathing slowed to the regular rhythm of sleep. When he awoke in a few hours' time, he would have a migraine headache from being compelled by the staff and his back would feel like it had been run over by a freight train. But no lasting physical harm would have been done. Walking over to Rachel, Charlie took her hand and released the compulsion.

"You ready to get out of here, Rachel?" he asked, smiling down at her.

"Yes, Grampa Charlie, I am. I don't like it here," she replied, tugging him toward the door in her eagerness to leave.

At the room's threshold, Charlie reined Rachel in for a moment and looked back at the sleeping security guard.

"Remember now," he mockingly told the sleeping guard, "we have rules in this facility, you know."

Climbing out of the truck, Ellen had one foot down on the asphalt when Charlie and Rachel walked out of the institution's side door. Getting back behind the wheel, she started the truck and intercepted them halfway across the parking lot. Helping Rachel up into the truck, Charlie climbed in after her. Opening his mouth, he started to admonish Ellen for disobeying his instructions. Seeing her nostrils flare and her chin left, he thought better of it and deftly changed the subject.

"We're fine, Blossom," Charlie said, answering her unasked question. "We're going to the hospital next, please."

On the short ride across Frechette, he introduced Rachel and Ellen to each other.

Getting out of the truck in the hospital's back parking lot, Charlie told Rachel, "You wait right here with Ellen and I'll be back with your mom in a few minutes."

Walking around the truck, he walked up to Ellen's window and softly said, "Not that you'll listen, but if anything goes wrong, take Rachel and go to David Garrison's house and I'll be along as soon as I can."

Patting her on the shoulder to and smiling to take the sting out of his words, Charlie headed off across the parking lot, staff clicking on the pavement as he went. Rachel watched him go, thinking.

"I wish Grampa Charlie really was my grampa," she told Ellen, twisting in the seat to look up at her. "My real

Grampa Henry, he's my daddy's daddy, he doesn't like little kids so I really don't have a grampa."

"Why of course he's your grandpa," Ellen said, hugging her. "Among our people adopted grandparents are very common and are the same as regular grandparents. He's my real grandpa but we can share."

Delighted with Ellen's answer, Rachel smiled up at her, greatly liking this beautiful woman with the long black hair and brown skin. Yawning, she lay down on Ellen's lap and was asleep in seconds. Sitting quietly, fighting to stay awake, Ellen nervously stroked the child's hair and worried about her grandfather.

Charlie had feared that the hospital would surpass his abilities. The glamour was limited to short range and he could only bedazzle a few people at a time with it. As it turned out, his fears were groundless.

Consulting the lobby directory and map, he learned the location of the psychiatric holding rooms. Walking down a side hallway, he found himself in front of a windowless steel security door. A magnetic card lock similar to the one in the children's home was mounted on the wall a few inches to the right of the door frame. The desk to the left of the door frame was deserted. Since entering the hospital Charlie had seen only four people and none since entering the side hallway.

Placing the end of the staff against the center of the metal door, Charlie twitched his will and a blue spark erupted. The bolt retracted with a *click!* and he pushed the door open and walked through it chuckling out loud. Technology and hi-tech gadgets always tickled him. A small *cul-de-sac* containing two doorways lay just beyond the security portal. The one on the left was empty. The one on the right held Gina Tolliver. Pushing a button on the right-hand wall opened the door and he walked into the room.

Wrapped in a strait-jacket, eyes vacant, Gina sat perfectly still with her back propped into a corner of the padded room. She didn't move, didn't flinch, didn't even blink as he approached. Catatonic, her eyes blankly stared out from some unfathomable inner space. Only the slow rise and fall of her chest proved that she was still alive.

Kneeling down, Charlie reached out for her and then hesitated. What came next was as delicate as brain surgery with no margin for error. Reaching out again, he grasped Gina's temples between his palms and leaned the staff against her body. Repulsed by the roiling black smoke and dancing shadows cascading through her mind, Charlie flinched and jerked his hands away. Gina was extremely ill and had been for a very long time, probably since childhood. Taking a deep breath, he placed his hands back on her temples and concentrated. Soft blue light danced and flickered around Gina's skull for over a minute. Finished, Charlie released her and picked up the staff.

"Gina," he said, gently shaking her shoulder, "wake up, it's time to go."

Moaning softly, Gina slowly opened her eyes. Opening her mouth to scream, she abruptly stopped and started smiling.

"I feel so good!" she exulted, eyes shining now. "Thank you!"

Well pleased but still very concerned, Charlie smiled back at her. Though Gina seemed happy and healthy, radiant even, the slightest tap could easily shatter her again. And when it happened, this time the damage would be irreparable. That time was coming soon, he was certain of it.

"Ray-ray-Rachel," she stammered, grief making her voice shake, "las-last night—"

"Rachel's waiting right outside in the parking lot," Charlie soothed, struggling with the Velcro fasteners on the strait jacket. "Soon as I figure out how to get this damn thing off you, we'll go find her."

A few seconds later he got the last fastener unbuckled and Gina wiggled out of the canvas restraint. Grasping both of her hands, Charlie helped her stand. He led her to the door and found that it had closed. Placing the butt of the staff against the door, he boosted a small charge into it, mindful not to set the room's padding on fire. The portal clicked open and he led Gina out into the deserted *cul-de-sac.*

Repeating the process with the security door, Charlie stuck his head out into the hallway and saw that it was still empty. There was another metal door a few feet away with a large red sign on its panic bar proclaiming, "Not an exit, alarm will sound if door is opened." Walking up to it, Charlie rapped the sign with the staff. Blue fire danced along the panic bar and the door flew open without the alarm sounding. Grinning at being five-for-five on the day, he led Gina out into the hospital's rear parking lot.

Ellen was growing more uneasy by the second. Resisting the urge to fidget for fear of waking Rachel, she watched an elderly man and a much younger woman start crossing the parking lot hand-in-hand. Looking down, Ellen smiled at the sleeping child and smoothed down an errant lock of hair. Such a beautiful little girl, she wished yet again that it was possible for her— The elderly man was somehow opening the truck's passenger side door though she had locked it and double checked to make sure that it was secure.

"Run!" Ellen's mind screamed at her. *"Go, hurry, something's wrong!"*

Fingers fumbling on the keys, Ellen started the engine with a roar and reached for the shifter. Her abrupt movements awakened Rachel, who sensed her panic and started crying.

"Blossom, easy, it's me," Charlie said.

"Jesus, Grandpa, you scared me!" Ellen gasped, heart still hammering. "How did—"

"Never mind that now," he interrupted. "It won't be long before someone notices Rachel and Gina are gone so we have to hurry. Right now, we need to go the park on Walden Street and park at the end in the trees where the picnic area is. I'm going to drop all of you off there and then go to Gina's apartment to pick her medicines up and get them both some clothes. Then I'm going to come back and pick you up and we're all going to David Garrison's house."

"Mommy-Mommy-Mommy!" Rachel cried, leaping into her mother's arms and making further conversation impossible for the moment.

Climbing in, Charlie closed the door and they headed toward the park.

CHAPTER 24

IRRITATED, AL DAGLOWSKI yanked hard on the leash, jerking the Pomeranian dog on the other end forward a good foot. Tootsie for Christ's sake, his wife Laurie's dog, a goddamn yap monster if ever there was one. What self-respecting male wanted to promenade down the street towing a yapping, pissing, shitting ball of red fur named Tootsie? J-e-e-e-sus!

Four times a day, rain or shine or snow or dark of night, he had to drag Tootsie down here to the park to do her business. That or listen to Laurie run her beaters at him all goddamn day. Married almost fifty wonderful years now and she could still rag just as well as she could the day that he made the terrible mistake of walking up the aisle with her. Better, in fact. A half-century of using him as a human whetstone had honed her tongue to surgical sharpness. Bitch. J-e-e-e-sus!

Walking up to the edge of the park, he saw a battered police cruiser parked directly across the street in a strip mall parking lot. The sheet metal along the vehicle's entire right side was stove in as was the right headlight.

The windshield and right passenger-side windows were spider-webbed with cracks. The car's light bar was askew, its plastic housing shattered on the right side.

Black spots exploded in Al Daglowski's vision as his blood pressure soared. He'd worked hard his entire life and always paid his taxes on time. And he hadn't paid them so some idiot with a badge and a uniform could use town property in a demolition derby. As soon as he got a break in the traffic, he and this useless damn dog were going to cross the street and ask the goddamn fool behind the wheel what had happened to his tax dollars. J-e-e-e-sus!

Officer Steven Jensen was sitting behind the wheel of the damaged cruiser drinking coffee from a thermos. He failed to notice that the coffee was leaking out of a pair of bullet holes in his upper abdomen. Or that three other bullet holes were dripping blood and body fluids down his torso, steadily contributing to the pool of gore he was sitting in.

A red Nissan pulled into the parking space diagonally ahead and to the left of the cruiser. Four young women, coeds from the local community college, got out and headed toward the coffee shop at the end of the strip mall. The last co-ed in line, a petite brunette, felt a gale of wind blast her skirt up around her waist and unseen hands jerk her panties down around her ankles. A second later the same invisible hands pulled her skirt down around her feet.

"Sm-o-o-o-k-k-in-n-n'!" Jensen roared in delight, pounding the dashboard so hard that the cruiser rocked on its suspension.

Taking one look at what was inside the police car, the petite co-ed fled screaming across the parking lot, skirt and panties forgotten. With her startled friends in close pursuit, she ran shrieking into the coffee shop.

The same gale that blew the co-ed's skirt up deposited her panties inside the police cruiser. Snatching them out of midair, Jensen sniffed appreciatively at the faint blood scent. Opening wide, he shoved the panties into his mouth, swallowed them, and belched mightily.

"A bit fruity on the tongue and not nearly red enough for my taste," he critiqued in a wine critic's plummy tones as a look of mock dismay spread across his face. "Goddamn lady, when was the last time you washed that thing?"

"You there, I want to speak to you!" Al Daglowski shouted, impatiently waiting for one last vehicle to pass so that he could finish crossing the street.

Snarling, Jensen turned his head searching for the source of the annoying voice. An ancient pick-up truck passed in front of a furious looking old man as Jensen watched Ellen, Charlie, and the Tollivers drive by.

"Hot damn and I owe it all to the power of clean livin'!" he crowed, snatching the radio microphone out of its dash bracket. "Unit Eight in pursuit of a Chevy pick-up truck, tag Minnesota 88579. Vehicle's occupants are Charlie Redbird, Ellen Talltrees, Gina and Rachel Tolliver. Copy that, you fucking pinheads?"

"Copy, Eight," the dispatcher said, "return to—"

"Shut the fuck up, moron!" Jensen replied, ripping the microphone free of the radio and tossing it out the window.

"Ellen, forget the park, we are in danger!" Charlie said, twisting in the seat and looking back at the police car. "Head to David Garrison's house. Hurry, go!"

"Lights, camera, action," Jensen roared as he started the cruiser and switched on the siren and emergency lights. "Head 'em up, move 'em ou-t-t-t!"

Slamming the transmission into Drive, he floored the accelerator and sent the cruiser charging toward the sidewalk. As the front wheels jumped the curb, he cut the steering wheel hard left and slid into the road with tires screaming. Less than ten feet away from the on-coming cruiser, Al Daglowski stood frozen in the center of the street with a look of stark terror on his face.

"Bye-bye, Al, you tightwad fuck!" Jensen howled as the cruiser struck the old man and sent him flying.

Fifteen feet later Al Daglowski's flight was terminally interrupted by a telephone pole. Uninjured when the jagged sheet metal on the cruiser's right front end sliced through her leash, Tootsie the Pomeranian wandered over and sniffed at the bloody body laying at the base of the telephone pole. Squatting delicately, she spritzed Al Daglowski's face. J-e-e-e-sus!

Inside the cab of the pick-up truck panic was spreading as the police cruiser rapidly closed on them.

"Be calm now, I need you all to be quiet," Charlie ordered, compelling them with the staff while he tried to think of something.

"Grandpa, that's the cop from yesterday," Ellen said, remembering the way the man's eyes had roamed over her breasts, so frightened that even the staff's compulsion couldn't soothe her. "I, I'm really scared!"

"Don't worry, Blossom, I won't let him hurt you," he told her, expressing a great deal more confidence than he felt at the moment.

Charlie was exhausted. With the exception of a very short nap, he'd been awake in one form or another for over twenty-four very strenuous hours. Last February he had turned sixty-nine years old and right now he felt every minute of it and more.

"Grandpa, here he comes!" Ellen wailed, clutching the steering wheel with both hands. "He's gonna ram us!"

Raising the staff, Charlie slammed it down on the floorboards and the ancient pick-up truck instantly accelerated thirty miles an hour. Smoke began billowing out of the truck's engine compartment and blue fire shot out of the tailpipe. Strain etched Charlie's features and a thin stream of blood began trickling from his right nostril and down the front of his jacket.

"He's caught up to us!" Ellen said, fighting to hold the truck on the road. "He's gonna try and ram us again!"

A blue wall, a buffer, appeared between the accelerating police cruiser and the laboring pick-up truck. The police car smashed into the barrier, knocking itself back and the pick-up truck forward. Black flowers blossomed in Charlie's vision as his other nostril started leaking blood.

"Please, I need a break here," he silently prayed. *"I ain't got much left. I, the girls, help us, please."*

Sometimes prayers are answered and Charlie got his break, many tons of it, in the person of Andre Deering. Twenty-two years old, wearing aviator sunglasses, a western shirt, cowboy hat, and Tony Lama boots. Garth Brooks blasting away on the CD player. Country cool. Driving a long-nosed Kenworth tractor pulling an empty log trailer at eighty miles an hour. Amped up on enough meth-amphetamine to drive nonstop from here to Bejing and back provided he could find a road. Two hundred yards away in the opposite lane and closing fast.

Concentrating, Charlie gathered himself up for the effort, knowing this was his last, best chance. Grasping the staff with both hands, he wrenched it violently to the left, grunting with the effort.

The cruiser's steering wheel spun hard left, twisting Jensen's hands off and breaking his wrists. The police car crossed the center line and struck the Kenworth tractor head-on at a combined closing velocity of over 160 miles per hour. Deering didn't even have time to think about stepping on the brakes before the impact. Although injured, he managed to stop his rig two hundred and twenty-five yards after the collision.

The Crown Victoria police cruiser was a cube of burning metal welded to the front of the Kenworth tractor. Although he was never certain later whether it was the concussion, the monster load of meth-amphetamine he'd done, or maybe both, but Andre Deering thought he saw something reptilian writhing and screaming as it burned to death inside the crushed cruiser.

"Grampa Charlie?" Rachel asked, frightened by the sight of the blood soaking his jacket and shirt front.

Blood was pouring freely out of Charlie's nostrils and his head lolled bonelessly on his neck. His black eyes were rimmed by networks of exploded capillaries and his breathing was uneven. Her grandfather was having a stroke, Ellen was sure of it. Crying and cursing at the worn brakes, she finally brought the truck to a halt on the dirt shoulder. Jumping out, she ran around the truck and jerked Charlie's door open.

"I am fine now, Blossom, just a little nose bleed, that's all," he told her. "Now would you please drive us to David Garrison's house?"

"No," Ellen replied, running practiced hands over him. "Now you hush and let me do what I have to do."

Pulse eighty-five beats per minute and rock solid. Without a blood pressure cuff it was hard to tell, but the great arteries near the surface of his neck didn't look distended. His respiration, at least without a stethoscope, sounded strong and clear. Eyes fine, pupil dilation normal, blink and impact reflexes normal.

"I'm all right, Blossom, don't worry," he reassured her, smiling a little. "But we have to go; it is still very dangerous for us here."

A flicker of blue fire dancing across his hands caught Ellen's attention as she closed the door. Drawing in a long breath, Ellen continued around the truck. Climbing behind the wheel, she started the engine and pulled back out on the road.

CHAPTER 25

FAR AND NOT so far away, a wild thunderstorm raged along the summits of a low range of hills. Lightning flashed and thunder rolled from black anvil-head thunderclouds towering miles overhead. Rain, sleet, and hail pounded down. Winds in excess of 100 miles per hour snapped off trees and scoured the vegetation. A funnel cloud snaked down even though tornadoes were rare here, especially in this season. The meteorological phenomena raging above the hills mirrored the fury of the being living below them.

They had escaped, all of them, time after time. Aided each time by old Redbird who seemed able to cheat death no matter how it was dealt. And now they were together: red man, white man, mad woman and child. But still, their gathering was of no real importance. There would still be many opportunities yet to finish them. Even so, The Wendigo didn't like having his grand scheme set askew in the smallest degree.

Without understanding why, the monster raged on. Millennia had passed since he had last worried and he no longer comprehended that emotion. So instead he raged.

CHAPTER 26

CHARLIE AND THE others barely caught David in time. As they drove up he was walking down the path toward the dock. A backpack and a scoped assault rifle were on his back. Turning in response to Ellen's honk, he saw Charlie climbing out of the truck. At first David thought he had been seriously injured because of the blood soaking his jacket and shirt.

"I'm fine, David," Charlie said before he could ask. "Where are you going?"

"I, that thing, the monster from last night," David replied, swallowing hard, "it has Jennifer and Allie. I know it now, and I'm going to kill it and bring them home or die trying."

"David, you can't kill it alone, it's impossible. Can you please help us, we're in a lot of trouble and we need to talk about everything that has happened and about the monster. After that, if you still want to go after him alone, it will be your decision."

Mulling over Charlie's request for a full thirty seconds, David finally said, "Yeah, all right, tell me what's happened."

Charlie, occasionally interrupted by the others, told David about the morning's events.

When Charlie finally finished speaking, David whistled and commented, "When you folks set out to break a few laws, you don't half mess around."

Thinking quickly, he told Charlie to pull the pickup inside the garage. Following the truck in, David took off the backpack and rifle and leaned them against the wall. After asking everyone to go inside the house, he took a padlock off a hook and trotted down the driveway. Arriving at the gate, he swung it shut and padlocked it. Hearing sirens approaching, he concealed himself behind a stand of pine trees and watched the road through the locked gate. A pair of state police cars raced by heading toward Frechette, light bars flashing and sirens howling.

Leaving the cover of the trees, David trotted back up the driveway. Entering the garage, he closed the door and locked it. Picking up a shovel, a rake, and a hoe, he threw them into the bed of the pick-up. A bag of fertilizer and an empty gas can were added for good measure. Closing the tailgate, he circled the truck, pressing his hands and especially his fingers against the sheet metal. Climbing into the cab, he repeated the process.

Entering the house, David went straight to his office and hand wrote a bill of sale to avoid leaving any traces on his computer. Taking a checkbook out of the office safe, he wrote a pre-dated check to Charlie. Joining the others in the kitchen, David handed the check to Charlie and told him to keep it in his wallet. Both men signed the bill of sale and Ellen witnessed it. David was now the owner of Charlie's twenty-two-year-old pick-up truck and had been for the past three days. The ruse wasn't anywhere near air-tight, but it wasn't half bad and it was all he could think of at the moment. Returning to the office, he made a copy of the bill of sale and placed it on a corner of his desk. Joining the others in the kitchen, he gave Charlie the handwritten original.

Looking hard at him, David said, "All right, Charlie, you've made me an accessory after the fact to everything from kidnapping a minor child to the felony murder of a police officer. I'd like some answers about everything that's been going on around here. So tell me about it. Everything. Now."

CHAPTER 27

"MY NAME IS Charles Lantot Redbird," he began, introducing himself in the ancient tradition of storytellers everywhere, "last of the Redbird shamans and eldest of the Poshto children still living on the Great Mother. This is the story of The Wendigo, which translated into English means Wind Walker, and of your places in that story. So I don't confuse you, he, The Wendigo, is also known as the Trickster or the Dark One by our people.

"A very long time ago, about twenty-five thousand years, give or take a couple, the Poshto people migrated over the land bridge from Asia into North America. After another thousand to fifteen-hundred years we ended up in Central Canada not too far north of here.

"When we, the Poshto, arrived in October time all those thousands of years ago, we discovered a tribe of white people living in the area. They were Celts who had fled religious persecution in their native Britain and settled here. Peaceful and prosperous, they welcomed the Poshto to their village, actually a small town.

"Not that it's any excuse, there can be no excuse for such a thing, but the Poshto were ravaged by their travels and they wanted what the Celts had. The second night after their arrival, the Poshto attacked just before dawn and killed all but three of the Celts.

"The Celtic chief, Lodan, who was also their shaman, escaped. With him were a woman named Elhira who had been driven mad by the murder of her husband and three oldest children. Elhira's youngest child, a daughter named Cortha, also escaped with the adults. All three were wounded and near death. Somehow though they managed to climb a hill just outside the town and reach a ledge on top.

"The three Celts were spotted by the Poshto when they were halfway up the hill. A war-party immediately started pursuing them. That party was led by Nantot, one of my lineal forefathers. Seeing the Poshto warriors approach, the Celts stopped trying to escape, sat down, and waited to die.

"When the war-party was about twenty-five yards away, Lodan tapped Elhira and Cortha with his staff, killing them instantly with its power. Enraged at what had been done to his people, Lodan struck the stone with his staff and called forth The Wendigo from the great darkness beyond. Just before the monster killed him, Lodan threw his staff at the Poshto war party.

"The lead warrior, my forefather Nantot Redbird, snatched the staff out of midair. By doing so he bound himself and countless generations of his male descendants to its service. In some of the old legends the staff is called the Redbird Bane because of the terrible price we have paid for our ancestors' crimes. It is the same staff as the one I am now holding in my hand.

"Using the staff, Nantot was able to drive The Wendigo away, but not before the monster killed the other five members of the war-party. As Nantot wielded the staff in those first few moments, it spoke to him, prophesying what was to come. For as long as he existed in this world, The Wendigo could roam free for the first three weeks, well actually it's twenty days, of October. During these twenty days he can claim the souls of the dying. He can also enslave the living and turn them into his familiars. The policemen that chased us earlier today, Jensen, was one such creature. For the last ten days of the month, the Dark One can roam free, slaughtering all whom he finds and keeping their souls for his own. The only thing that would limit The Wendigo's evil would be a Redbird shaman wielding the staff against him during the month of October.

"For millennia it has been so. The last part of the prophecy says there shall be one last Redbird shaman, one without a son to assume the mantle of his responsibilities. That shaman is me. My sons John and Michael were killed in a house-fire set by the Trickster's creatures and burned to death. That was the same day my wife Mary was abducted and delivered to the monster. Her screams as he torments her have haunted my every moment ever since and I, I— Anyway. So, as I told you, I am the last of the Redbird shamans and at last our long servitude is nearly at an end.

"In the time of the last Redbird shaman, the descendants of the three Celts murdered on the hilltop shall draw together. Together with the last shaman, that's me remember, they shall battle The Wendigo and cast him from our world forever. At the end of the battle, the staff shall pass back to the lineal descendant of the Celtic shaman Lodan. A time of great peace and beauty may come to pass, although the prophecy is a little unclear at the very end.

"If the descendants of the murdered Celts don't band together with the last Redbird shaman, the Dark One will hunt them down one-by-one and kill them within a week of each other. The final one to fall will be the last Redbird shaman, yours truly. And when I fall, the staff will come into The Wendigo's possession. The only thing the Dark One fears, the only thing that can truly hurt him or limit him will be his. Freed, The Wendigo will slaughter his way across the planet until there is nothing left alive. No people, no animals, no fish, no insects, no plants, nothing. This is not an overstatement on my part but rather what the staff has foretold.

"You, David Garrison, in case you haven't guessed, are the lineal descendant of the Celtic shaman, Lodan. In time, and this is my great hope, you will be the next staff bearer and usher in the great time of peace and beauty briefly mentioned at the end of the prophecy.

"You, Gina and Rachel Tolliver, are the descendants of the Celtic woman Elhira and her daughter Cortha. For all of us there are only two choices: stand together or die separately. You have all seen at least some of what The Wendigo can do. Know this: he will never give up until he succeeds. I need to take a break now and give everybody a little time to consider what I've just said. When I get back, I'd like to say a few more words and then we'll see what everybody thinks. Like the rest of my anatomy, my bladder is old. David, I'd appreciate it if you could point me toward a bathroom."

Smiling, David rose and pointed Charlie toward one bathroom and Rachel, Gina, and Ellen toward another. Walking into the kitchen, he put a large frozen pizza in the microwave and started piling meat, cheese, and bread for sandwiches on a platter. As his hands worked, David's mind digested what Charlie had told them. During the several trips required to pile everything onto the dining-room table, he kept on thinking. Finished, he took a seat and impatiently waited for the others to get back. Just about the time he was getting ready to go look for them, they all trooped in together. Sitting down, they cast appreciative glances at the food and then looked expectantly at Charlie.

"I will be brief," he said, smiling, "even us long-winded old farts get hungry sometimes. You don't have to wait on me to finish, please go ahead and eat.

"I'm not trying to upset you, especially at mealtime, but I would like to apologize to Rachel, Gina, and David for the loss of your loved ones. It is the duty of the Redbird shamans to keep the world safe from The Wendigo and I failed. The death of my sons has forced me to carry the staff decades longer than any of my forefathers. The Dark One is ageless and I am aged and these last few years he has surpassed me. Although I am terribly sorry for your loss, please believe me when I tell you that I've done everything I can and it is still not enough."

"That's all right, Charlie," David said. "I got a good look at that thing last night for the first time and it's not your fault."

Gina remained silent but nodded her head in agreement and after a moment so did Rachel. Relieved, Charlie gathered his thoughts for a moment before continuing.

"One of the things the staff does is tell its wielder when his death is near. Late last year I was bitten by The Trickster and absorbed a huge amount of venom. This last couple of weeks the staff has begun whispering to me in the night. This will be my last winter; I will not live to see another spring. I—"

"Grandpa," Ellen burst out, crying, "There are specialists in the Cities and—"

"Not this time, Blossom," Charlie sadly told her. "If this were curable, I'd do it myself with the staff. But it isn't, not by me, not by anyone. I've had a hard life but a good one, and I am not afraid to die."

"And if you believe that one," Charlie thought as he reached out and gave her hand a squeeze, *"I've got a bridge in Brooklyn that I'd like to sell."*

"My entire adult life," he continued after taking a sip of soda, "has been spent battling this terrible evil. I will not sit back and wait for the rotting sickness to take me or for The Wendigo to hunt me down at his leisure. When I finish this nice meal David has prepared, I am going to war on it one last time. Alone if I have to, but hopefully with Rachel, Gina, and David."

"I'm going with you, Charlie," David immediately said. "I don't know whether or not I can bring Jen and Allie back, but I mean to destroy that thing or die trying. I'm in until the end, wherever that takes us."

"M-m-me, too," Gina stammered, fighting hard to keep her composure. "I, I was diagnosed with schizophrenia three years ago, but that thing is going to keep after us until it get us, me and Rachel. G-god, I am so scared, but we're going to go."

"Good," Charlie said, taking her hand and calming her before any damage could be done. "We're all scared, Gina, every last one of us."

"I'm goin' too!" Rachel declared, making the adults smile. "I'm not afraid of no boogie man!"

"Grandpa," Ellen began in the tone and with the look that Charlie had been dreading ever since he had begun speaking, "Why can't I—?"

"Be still, all of you!" Charlie ordered, raising a hand to silence them.

Leveling his staff at a pair of French doors twenty feet away, Charlie loosed a bolt of sapphire energy. The doors flew open and the blue beam of light lassoed the creature outside on the deck. Hooting and screeching, the great horned owl was pulled through the doorway levitated halfway between the floor and the ceiling.

"Well now, skulker, I thought I heard you out there a while ago," Charlie cheerfully told the bird. "You know, I once ate an owl back in the winter of 1958. I stuffed it with apples, raisins, and breadcrumbs. It was pretty good, but kind of tough. Maybe I'll do the same thing to you, but I'll marinate you first."

"Fuck you, Indian," the owl spat at him, green sparks shooting from its eyes. "I'll kill—"

"Be quiet, fool," Charlie ordered, tightening the sap phire band around the bird's middle until it screeched in pain. "Tell your idiot master I'm coming and the battle has begun. You will forget everything else you have seen or heard and remember only that. Understand?"

When the owl didn't respond, he torqued the lariat down another notch.

"Yes, yes, don't hurt, don't hurt!" the bird begged.

"Good," Charlie said. "You aren't as dumb as you look but it's really close. Now you're going to make like Tom Cruise in *Top Gun*."

"What, what?" The owl squawked in terror as Charlie winched it toward him a couple of feet. "Don't hurt, don't—"

Blue fire erupted out of the staff's head as Charlie slammed its butt down on the kitchen floor. The Great Horned Owl was catapulted through the French doors like a navy fighter plane being launched off a carrier's deck. Blue fire erupted out of the bird's tail feathers as it hurtled northwards over the lake. The owl's outraged screeching carried back to Charlie and the other until it vanished into the dusk.

"Don't you know that got his attention," David said, impressed and starting to laugh, finding nothing incongruous about a talking owl after everything else that had happened.

Suddenly they were all laughing, roaring until their sides hurt and it happened. Five individuals who moments before had been little more than strangers were now transformed into a group. Not a well-defined or a cohesive group but a group nevertheless. Their laughter slowly died away but their smiles remained.

"Well," Charlie said, reaching for the plate of sliced meats, "everybody eat up. We need to leave tonight and there's still a lot to do."

CHAPTER 28

THE GREAT HORNED owl lay crushed against the cave wall in a pile of bloody feathers. Souls captured by The Wendigo left phosphorescent trails in the darkness as they streaked about, terrified by his wrath. Howling in rage, the Dark One caromed around the vast cavern, moving so rapidly that his form was a kinetic blur of pulsing yellow-green light. Boulders the size of small cars were gouged out of the schist in showers of incandescent sparks as he collided with the cave's floor, ceiling, and walls. Faster and faster he careened until the crèche was filled with a whirling cyclone of ricocheting stone and crackling yellow-green energy.

Stupid fucking bird, idiotic damn creature. All it had to do was be silent, listen, and report back what it had heard. Instead, the moron had gotten too close and had been captured by Redbird. The owl had paid for its stupidity and would continue to pay.

Without accurate intelligence, the Trickster could not calculate the forces arrayed against him in the coming battle. All he knew for certain was that Redbird was coming, and soon. No surprise there, old news. The presence of the other three or the lack thereof was an open question, a cipher on which the entire battle could turn.

Though he had many forces and stratagems available to him, he was still worried. Worry had given way to fear, causing him to rage mindlessly. For the first time in the long ages since he had been summoned here, The Wendigo was terrified, fearful that he wouldn't survive the coming confrontation. Charlie Redbird had won the opening skirmish of the final battle.

CHAPTER 29

"I AM SORRY, Blossom, but no," Charlie told her.

"But, Grandpa," she argued, crying now. "I—"

"No, Ellen, not this time," he interrupted, lying wholeheartedly. "There is no mention in the prophecy of an unrelated fifth party being involved. If you go, you may alter the prophecy and cause us to fail. So you must stay here and manage this end of things."

In fact, Charlie neither knew nor believed any such thing. The final battle had been foretold long eons ago when the creator first sprinkled light across the heavens. Even if it was broadcast on prime time network television, it would make no difference; the battle would go forward to its ultimate conclusion. Just because the prophecy was silent about the presence of non-descendants did not mean they were forbidden to be present. Charlie knew that the battle would be terribly dangerous and some of those who went probably wouldn't be coming home again. So no matter what she had to say, Ellen wasn't going.

"Ah, ah, all right," she said, still crying. "If you say so."

Heaving a huge internal sigh of relief, Charlie put an arm around her and gently squeezed. His granddaughter was an intelligent young woman and very hard to fool. This moment had worried him since she'd first become involved with his plans.

"Let's go look at the lake," Charlie said, steering her toward the end of the dock.

Voices on the shore finally disturbed them and broke the moment. Rachel, Gina, and David were walking down the dock carrying backpacks. David had lent Rachel and Gina gear that had once belonged to Jennifer and Allison. Everything was a size too large or a size too small, but it would have to do.

"Is that thing legal?" Ellen asked, pointing at the scoped assault rifle slung over David's shoulder.

The trial lawyer always lurking in David's subconscious surfaced and he replied, "Depends on who you ask."

Annoyed, Ellen turned her back so that he couldn't read her expression. Why, she wondered, did this undeniably handsome and undeniably nice and undeniably wealthy man annoy her so much? Although she didn't know it, he was asking himself the same thing about her, only in far stronger terms.

David stepped off the dock and down onto the deck of his inflatable launch. Reaching up, he began transferring the gear piled on the dock to the launch's rear deck. Finished, he walked forward and entered the pilothouse. Inserting the keys into the ignition, he pushed the twin starter buttons. First the starboard, then the port, outboard engine coughed and started.

Leaving the pilothouse, David walked back to the stern of the launch and climbed back onto the dock. Opening a white fiberglass storage box, he began handing out life preservers. After making sure everyone knew how to put them on correctly, he put one on himself and stepped back across onto the launch. He whistled and Susie and Angus jumped down onto the launch and lay down in the stern. First Rachel, then Gina, and finally Ellen took his hands and stepped across onto the boat while Charlie stood protectively behind them. Putting one foot up on the starboard pontoon, he reached out to link hands with Charlie.

"David, I have to do something before we leave," he said. "It'll only take a few minutes and then we can be on our way."

Turning away, Charlie walked down the dock toward the shoreline, staff tapping on the weathered boards. Reaching the shore, he turned left and made his way over to a rocky point about fifty yards away. Minding his footing on the uneven rocks, he walked out to the end and stood looking at the dark water and the surrounding forest. Despite all the tragedy and pain, he had always loved living here. This land was embedded in the deepest memories of he and his people. More than anything, he wanted to finish his life and die in peace here, but he knew it wasn't to be.

Suddenly, he smashed the staff down on the rock beneath his feet and cleaved it. Water gushed into the fissure and boiled, cloaking his lower body in clouds of steam. Energy surged up the staff, shooting high into the night sky and exploding into a massive burst of blue chain-lightning. Thunder rolled as a gale howled out of the trees and out onto the lake. Standing ramrod straight, Charlie grew until he towered over the surrounding white pines. Throwing his head back, he loosed a long, undulating shriek, the ancient battle-cry of Clan Redbird.

"I am Charles Lantot Redbird," he roared, "last of the Redbird shamans and I am coming for you, you murdering prick! Prepare yourself because I mean to finish you!"

As quickly as it had begun, it was over. The lightning vanished, the thunder quieted, and the gale dropped. Walking off the rocky promontory, Charlie headed back toward the dock. He might be old and soon to die, but he refused to skulk along like some creeping night thing. The last of the Redbird shamans, he would go into battle cloaked in pride and power as befitted the last of his line. As Charlie walked up the dock toward the launch, there was a spring in his step and a broad smile on his face.

Book II

A Strange and Distant Land

Do not set your eyes on things far off.

Pindar, *Pythian Odes*, III, I, 39

CHAPTER 30

WALKING DOWN THE starboard side of the launch, David untied and pulled the dock lines in. Taking a seat behind the wheel in the pilothouse, he put the engines in gear. After one last look at his home, he advanced the throttles and started across the lake. After speaking with Ellen for a moment, Charlie joined him.

"David, thank you for calling your law partner for Ellen," he said. "I'm still worried about what could happen to her while we're gone, but there's nothing else I can think of to do."

"She'll be fine; Terry's a fine man and a great lawyer. If you don't mind, there's a question I'd like to ask."

"Go ahead, let 'er rip."

"How come we have to take the boat across the lake and walk in? I could've chartered us a helicopter and we could've been there by noon tomorrow."

For nearly a minute Charlie sat thinking about his answer.

"Well, for one thing, David, a helicopter can't take us where we need to go," he finally replied. "And for another, there is more involved than just getting there. A process is involved, a rationale. What we are undertaking is as much about the journey as it is about the destination. Maybe a better way to put it is that without a journey, there cannot be a destination. Do you understand what I'm trying to say?"

"I think so," David replied, trying to wrap his mind around the conundrum. "What is the sound of one hand clapping?"

"Now you're getting it!" Charlie said and they both started laughing.

The staff, propped up between Charlie's knees, began emitting a faint blue glow. In response, a blue line began fluorescing in the water just off the launch's starboard bow.

"What's that?" David asked, steering away from the possible hazard.

"That's a part of the Redbird Navigation System," Charlie told him with a grin. "Just follow it like a lane on a highway and it will take us where we need to go."

Altering course a few degrees, David centered the bow on the narrow band of glowing blue light. An hour and a quarter later the narrow ribbon of blue light terminated at a narrow patch of rocky shingle where David beached the boat. Climbing over the bow, he whistled for Susie and Angus and lifted them down to dry ground. Telling the dogs to stay close, he began stacking their gear on the shore as the others handed it to him.

Kissing Rachel on the forehead, Ellen told her, "You take good care of mommy on your trip, okay?"

"I will, Auntie Ellen, I promise," Rachel said.

With Gina and Ellen holding her arms, Rachel stood balanced on the bow. Reaching up, David wrapped his arms around her and carried her over to the pile of gear.

Setting Rachel down on a backpack, he whistled for the dogs and they trotted over and lay down at her feet.

Hugging Gina, Ellen said, "When you get back, you and Rachel come see me. I'll worry about you when you're gone."

Fighting hard not to cry, Gina nodded and took a seat on the bow. Swinging her legs over, she dropped down into David's arms. Looking over his shoulder at Ellen and Charlie, he decided to walk her over to Rachel and take a break on one of the packs.

Struggling to remain calm, Ellen etched this moment on her memory; certain these were their last few moments together.

"Grandpa, you're not coming back, are you?" she asked, crying.

"No, Blossom, probably not," Charlie replied, barely able to speak. "One way or another, my time here is almost done. But death, mine or anybody else's, isn't what you think. I'll always love you and always be with you no matter what. All you have to do is think of me and I'll be there for you. So there really is nothing to be sad or cry about. Let's make our last time together a happy one and just stand here and look at the stars. See how pretty they are?"

Minutes passed while the two stood with their arms wrapped around each other.

"Blossom, you need to get going," Charlie finally said. "You've got a long ways to go and it's getting late."

Hugging her grandfather hard on last time, Ellen kissed him on the cheek and stood watching as David helped him down from the bow. A second later, David scrambled back aboard and together they walked back into the pilothouse.

"Do you have any questions about taking the boat back across the lake?" he asked. "The autopilot and the plot tracker are all set, just like we talked about. If you have any questions, now's the time to ask."

"I'll be fine, don't worry," she told him, expressing a confidence she was nowhere near to feeling.

"Do you remember what to do if you're questioned by the police?"

"Yes, I tell them that I have nothing to say and that I want to call my lawyer, your friend Terry Thomas," Ellen replied, concentrating on remembering what he had told her earlier.

"Sounds to me like you've got it down," he said, hoping that she didn't hear the doubt in his voice.

Formerly a prosecutor, David could sense a crystalline fragility in Ellen Talltrees and he knew that a hard word could break her. If she was arrested, which he considered very likely, those doing the questioning would be experts with hard words.

"There is one thing, though," Ellen said, looking away, trying to hide the tears. "My grandpa, would you please look after him? He's old and sick and I, I—".

"I'll do my best, I promise," David told her, although he had no idea what, if anything, he could do.

An awkward moment passed and he finally said, "Well, I guess you're all set. As soon as we get back, I'll call you the first chance I get. Take care and we'll see you soon."

Ellen nodded her head and David started walking forward. Rachel, Gina, and Charlie were standing together on the shingle. As David lowered himself off the bow to the ground, they walked over and joined him. The worst moment, the hardest, was here. The time when those that go and those that stay part company was at hand. Besides death, there are few divisions in human affairs as painful.

Waving a final goodbye, Ellen entered the pilothouse and took a seat behind the wheel. Walking forward a couple of steps, David and Charlie put their shoulders on the bow and shoved the launch off the shore. First the starboard, then the port, outboard slammed into reverse. Weaving erratically, Ellen began backing out into the lake. Crying silently, Charlie Redbird stood watching her go, heartbroken. A black surge of hatred filled him for the fate and the monster that had brought him to this pass.

"Some of the people, some of the time, old man," he thought bitterly, remembering his recent soothing words to his granddaughter.

Reaching out, David squeezed Charlie's shoulder and stepped to one side a few feet. Grateful for his friend's discretion, Charlie collected himself and joined him a minute later. The two men stood watching as Ellen backed the boat in a ragged half circle and then took the engines out of gear. White water boiled at the launch's stern as the engines were slammed into forward. The boat veered first to starboard, then to port, then to starboard again. The launch began drifting to port again and then its course steadied to a few points west of south as Ellen engaged the autopilot.

"She'll be fine, Charlie, don't worry," David said, wincing despite himself.

"You know, she was the same way when she was learning to drive a car," Charlie told him. "I hope you've got insurance on that boat, you might need it."

The two stood on the shore watching the launch until its running lights were swallowed by the night. Turning away from the lake, they walked a few yards up the shingle and joined Rachel, Gina, and the dogs.

"We need to go a little ways tonight," Charlie announced, "but not too far, just a couple of hundred yards or so."

A moment of comic relief ensued while David showed Rachel and Gina how to put on a backpack and adjust the straps. Shouldering his pack, David watched as Charlie slipped his arms through the shoulder straps of an intricately woven pack-basket.

Turning to face them, Charlie set the order of march, saying, "I will go first, Gina and Rachel next, then David and the dogs. It will be dark in the woods, but don't worry, there's nothing to be afraid of."

Stepping off smartly for a man approaching his seventh decade of life, Charlie led them into the forest, a faint blue light glowing at the tip of his staff. Following closely on his heels, Gina clutched Rachel's hand, frightened of the night-shrouded woods. Flanked by his dogs, David brought up the rear, mindful not to lose sight of the faint blue beacon just ahead of him.

Two minutes later, Charlie stopped and said, "All right, we're there, everybody can relax for a minute."

Rachel, Gina, and David instinctively crowded together in the dark. Stepping forward, Charlie mumbled something under his breath and rapped the staff on the ground. A wooden door materialized which appeared perfectly solid and not the least bit ethereal. It was constructed of smooth planks fastened together by horizontal wrought iron straps. A wrought iron thumb-latch served as a doorknob. "ENTER" was written in glowing blue capitals in the center of the door. Bathed in its faint blue luminescence, Rachel, Gina, and David stood gaping in wonder at the portal.

"Feel free to look at it," Charlie said, "it won't hurt you but it will stay locked until I open it."

Giggling, Rachel stepped forward and knocked twice on the door. The raps created by her small fist echoed around the small clearing and faded into the surrounding forest. Stepping up behind her daughter, Gina placed her right palm flat against the glowing wood.

"It's warm," she said, withdrawing her hand, "and it sort of tickles."

Stepping to one side, David examined the door's edge, or tried to. When he walked around behind the door, he saw nothing and had an unobstructed view of the others. Yet when he waved, it was plain from their expressions they couldn't see him. Returning to where the door's edge should have been, David placed one hand flat on the wooden front surface while shoving his other arm through the door's non-existent back up to the elbow. Gina had been right; it did tickle, sort of. Actually though the sensation was more akin to a deep, tingling itch in the center of his forearms and hands.

Jerking his arms back, he muttered, "Jesus, that feels weird!"

"Everyone done looking at the door?" Charlie asked. "I know you have a lot of questions, but I'd like to ask you to hold them until tomorrow. Right now, it's getting late and I want to go through the door and camp for the night."

Everyone mumbled their assent and Charlie continued.

"This door is one of many that opens on First Land, but it's the only one that is convenient for our purposes. These doors are always located on the borders of First Land on the roads which lead to its center, which is where we're trying to go.

"First Land is just that, the first land of the planet Earth, which the Poshto people call the Great Mother, which is also our name for the creator. First Land is the skeleton, the bones that give shape and form to the world we normally live in. I know this is hard to grasp, but are you with me so far?

The others nodded their understanding and Charlie pressed on, anxious to pass through the doorway and camp.

"All who seek entrance to First Land must do so of their own free will or else they cannot enter. Do you understand?"

Again, everyone indicated their understanding.

"Good, we shall begin," Charlie said, kneeling in front of Rachel. "Rachel Tolliver, little flower from Florida, land of flowers, do you want to go through the door and enter First Land?"

Gina started to help her daughter answer, but Rachel cut her off saying, "Yes, Grampa Charlie, I wanna go through the magic door and see what's on the other side."

"Good," Charlie told her with a smile as he got to his feet.

Standing now in front of Gina, he asked, "Gina Tolliver, mother of Rachel, late of Orlando, Florida and now living in Frechette, Minnesota, do you desire to pass through the portal and enter First Land?"

"Y-y-yes, I do," she replied, not sounding at all convinced.

"Good enough," Charlie told her, taking a step sideways and standing now in front of David.

"And you, David Garrison, of the State of Minnesota, Town of Frechette, do you desire to pass through the portal and enter First Land?"

"Yes, I do," he answered, excitement evident in his voice. "I just gotta see what's on the other side of that door!"

"Good," Charlie said again, kneeling and whistling for the dogs. "Susie and Angus, faithful companions of David Garrison, do you desire to pass through the door and enter First Land?"

The dogs barked once and felt silent. None of the others found it odd that Charlie had questioned the dogs. Somehow, it seemed proper.

"Excellent, all of you!" Charlie said, well-pleased.

Rising, he turned, faced the door, and said, "I, Charles Lantot Redbird, last of the Redbird shamans, from just outside Frechette, Minnesota in the American state of Minnesota, desire to pass through this portal with my friends and enter First Land."

Rapping sharply on the door with the staff, Charlie commanded, "Open!"

An audible click sounded as the portal unlocked itself. Grasping the thumb latch, Charlie popped it up and swung the door open. Ushering the others through the doorway, he then passed through himself and allowed the door to swing shut behind him. "EXIT" was written in glowing block capitals on this side of the door.

Rachel, Gina, and David were standing in the center of a grassy track, wide-eyed with wonder. The air was intoxicating, smelling of flowers, grasses, and trees, as free of pollution as it was at the dawn of creation eons before. Overhead, bright stars twinkled in alien constellations.

Watching his friends, Charlie smiled, enjoying their sense of awe. Over fifty years ago he had entered First Land for the first time at this very spot and had been unable to move for over an hour, frozen in wonder at its overwhelming beauty. Fatigue began gnawing at his knees and back and he reluctantly broke the spell.

"Okay, everybody, as you can see we ain't in Kansas anymore, or anywhere close to it. They'll be plenty of time to look around tomorrow as we walk plus you can see more in daylight anyway. It's getting late and we need to make camp for the night. Let's go into this building over here and settle in."

The others followed Charlie over to a large stone building set back a few yards off the grassy track. Staff glowing, he led them into a large common room with ledges on three sides for sleeping. A large fireplace took up most of the fourth wall. An arched doorway in the center of the rear wall led to a combination bath and outhouse with a hand-operated water pump thrusting up from a polished stone bowl in the middle of the floor.

"This building is called a way-station," Charlie explained, using the staff to light a wall sconce. "It's left over from when First World was inhabited, which it hasn't been since a little after modern humans first appeared in our world. This one, and the other way-stations, are relics from that time. Since structures don't deteriorate here like they do in our world, many of them are still standing, but most aren't in as good condition as this one. As you saw from the plaque on the front door when we came in, this is Station Number Thirty-Two. The way-stations are for any traveler's use, including ours, so make yourselves at home, we're here for the night."

Rachel, Gina, and David all tried to ask questions at once, wanting more information about this wondrous place.

"Whoa, now!" Charlie said, raising his hands and smiling. "It's late and I'm very tired. Right now, I'm going outside and smoke my pipe and have a last look around. After that, and I mean directly after that, I'm going to bed. We'll have plenty of time to talk in the morning."

Rachel, Gina, and David reluctantly bit off their questions and began unrolling their sleeping bags. Pulling his pipe out of his pocket, Charlie stepped out the door and pulled it closed behind him. Sitting down on a stone bench to the right of the door, he loaded and lit his pipe. Taking a deep draw of the aromatic smoke, he murmured a long "ah-h-h" in appreciation.

Since giving up the bottle, that great poisoner of aboriginal peoples everywhere, the pipe had been his only true vice. Its worn black bowl had been a source of vast comfort to him through some very dark days. Never mind that it was helping speed the venom that was even now gnawing away at him, Charlie considered it a more than even trade. Senior citizens in his line of work usually didn't come to a pleasant end, so he wasn't about to surrender one of his few remaining pleasures now that the Great Mystery was at hand.

Looking around, Charlie soaked in the beauty surrounding him, enraptured by it. He thought of the wisdom of his distant cousins, the Navaho, and their prayers to beauty. It didn't seem possible, but it had been almost ten years since he had last visited First Land. Sadly, the old saw was true: when the bones get old, the feet get slow. It was even harder to believe that this would be his last visit here. Harder yet to believe was just how terribly dangerous this place was despite its spectacular beauty.

The pipe began gurgling its tar song and Charlie knocked the cake out against the sole of his boot. Rising to his feet, joints protesting, he took one last appreciative look around and turned to enter the way-station. A blur of motion flashed across the corner of his left eye and he whirled, tracking it with the staff. A nightingale leveled out at treetop level and sped away to the north. Charlie started to bring the bird down, but changed his mind at the last second and quelled the staff's fire.

"Nightingale, night thief," his father's voice chanted down the long corridors of his memory. "Cries out in joy at death, one of Trickster's oldest friends, one of his chief spies, but not too bright."

For at least the first twenty-four to thirty-six hours, Charlie had hoped their presence in First Land would remain undetected. After that, he knew concealment would be nearly impossible. The enemy was too strong here, too fey, for them to remain hidden long. Letting the nightingale go might have been a mistake, but he didn't think so. Often knowing what the enemy knew, or what he thought he knew, was a huge advantage.

Entering the way-station, Charlie barred the front door behind him and made sure the rear entrance was also barred. Rachel and Gina were curled up together in a mummy bag on a ledge at the rear of the room. A few feet away and at right angles to them, David was also wrapped in a sleeping bag on a ledge with the dogs lying on the floor next to him. Humans and dogs alike were moaning softly and twitching as nightmares began creeping in on them.

Singing softly in Poshto, Charlie stroked each of their foreheads, including the dogs. Each quieted immediately and fell into a deep, dreamless sleep. The brief incantations would hold their nightmares at bay for the few hours remaining until dawn. Tomorrow night he would prepare a herbal brew that would help them sleep, but it was too complicated to prepare for just a few hours rest.

Getting into his sleeping bag, Charlie confronted a bleak truth yet again. When The Wendigo sent the nightmares, he almost always revealed more than he intended. So Charlie had no choice but to let the monster torment him in the hope of learning something useful. Still though, it wouldn't make for a restful night's sleep. Lying on his back, Charlie braced himself for the coming nightmare and prayed for at least a couple of hours sleep before dawn arrived.

CHAPTER 31

SQUIRMING IN THE helmsman's seat, Ellen tried to ease the kinks out of her back. Fear was making her muscles knot up and ache. When she was seven, a group of older children had thrown her into the deep end of a swimming pool. If a nearby lifeguard hadn't snatched her off the bottom of the pool, she would have drowned. For years after she had nightmares about looking up from the pool's bottom, green light filtering down from the surface as chlorinated water gushed into her lungs. During her first year of college she had taken swimming lessons and turned herself into a weak swimmer. Even so, she would always be afraid of the water. That, and the dark. And now here she was, stuck in the middle of both.

The ETA function on the launch's Sat-Nav autopilot indicated twenty-two minutes left to run. Twenty-two minutes until the auto-pilot delivered her fifty yards from the end of David Garrison's dock. Five minutes after that, Ellen hoped to be safely ashore.

"Dear God," she prayed softly aloud, "just let me get my dogs on dry land and I'll never drive another boat. Ever. Amen."

When the ETA function ticked down to fourteen minutes, Ellen began to believe, really believe, that she would make it. A brilliant white light flared into life just off the port bow, blinding and frightening her. Eyes tearing, she raised he arms in a vain attempt to protect her vision from the high-intensity searchlight.

"This is the Minnesota Lake Patrol," an amplified voice boomed out across the water, "Stop your vessel immediately, then go stand in the stern and don't move!"

Blinded, Ellen fumbled around the control console and finally found the combination transmission/throttle levers and pulled them back into neutral. The computerized autopilot began flashing and beeping, warning that the boat was now drifting off course. Still blinded by the searchlight, Ellen groped her way out of the pilothouse and made her way to the stern. Shivering in the cold air, she stood waiting, uncertain about what came next. She heard the Lake Patrol vessel approach and felt it bump up against the launch's port side. The deck rocked under her feet as someone climbed aboard from the other vessel.

When Ellen was handcuffed and placed in the stern of the Lake Patrol skiff, the ETA function on the launch's autopilot indicated twelve minutes and forty-two seconds left to run.

CHAPTER 32

THE NIGHTINGALE THAT Charlie had spared was perched on a clawed digit fully a yard long. Chirping and warbling, the bird reported what she had seen. The beast held her at eye level, head cocked, listening intently. When the bird finished her report, the monster emitted a loud, grumbling sound. He was laughing, delighted. The nightingale, certain that death was near, trilled shrilly, fluffed her feathers, and shit on her perch.

"No, no, little spy," The Wendigo soothed in gravelly tones. "You have done well and I am very pleased with you. Go now and I will call you when I need you."

The nightingale took wing and the monster absently licked its now vacant finger. Things were looking up, starting to break his way. The Indian bitch was taken and securely under wraps. There wasn't anything he could do to her now because he was fresh out of instruments. Her goddamned grandfather has seen to that. But no matter, he already had a new recruit in mind and would have her snared a little after dawn.

Shortly after that, Redbird's granddaughter would be his.

As for the four, he now knew their location and the direction they would approach from. They would be disposed of long before they came close enough to pose a threat. Once they were taken and the staff was his, why, why—

"Soon!" The Wendigo shrieked in delight, pounding his clawed feet on the stone floor until sparks flew. "Real fucking soon!"

CHAPTER 33

CHARLIE ROSE EARLY while it was still dark. The way-station had grown cold during the night so he built a fire. Rummaging in his pack basket, he pulled out a battered blue-enamel coffee pot. Filling the pot with water and coffee, he set it on a grate in the fireplace. Lighting his pipe, he sat patiently waiting for the coffee to brew.

As usual, and especially at this time of year, he'd spent a restless night. The Dark One had tormented Charlie with special fervor as if trying to avenge himself for the recent small defeats he had suffered. But there were compensations.

Like many shamans, Charlie Redbird could commune with the dead. During the night, he had spoken briefly with his Mary, his wife when the monster's attention was elsewhere. The news she had brought him wasn't good.

Ellen had been arrested by the authorities almost within sight of David's dock and was now being held in the county jail. Alarmed, Charlie had climbed out of the sleeping bag intending to start back for Frechette immediately. After a moment though, he sighed and climbed back into the bag. Much still depended on him and he had no choice but to keep going forward. Always a realist, he hadn't bothered to tell himself not to worry. After a while, Mary had come back, kissed him goodbye, and said that she would see him soon. All in all, it hadn't made for a restful night.

A few minutes later the others began stirring and shifting in their sleeping bags. By the time everyone had finished their ablutions in the combination bath/outhouse, Charlie had breakfast ready. Prepared from dehydrated rations the meal wasn't going to win any culinary medals, but it would serve its purpose.

When everyone was finished eating, Charlie announced with a smile, "As I promised last night, I will now entertain questions from our studio audience."

Walking over to Charlie, Rachel looked up at him and asked, "Grampa Charlie, how long are we going camping for? I wanna go to school and I miss cartoons."

Smiling down at her, he replied, "Honey, I really don't know how long we'll be camping for, time is different here. But don't you worry, you'll get to go to school and watch cartoons as soon as we get back."

Satisfied, Rachel walked back to Gina and crawled into her lap. Smiling, David raised his hand.

"The moderator recognizes Mr. Garrison," Charlie intoned.

"Charlie," David asked, serious now, "I know you tried to explain it to us last night, but where are we again and why are we hunting the monster here?"

"That's two questions, David," Charlie replied, laughing. "But that's all right. We are in First Land, oldest of the realities connected to Earth, the Great

Mother. Think of this place as a hub like an airport or train station with branches or routes going all over to other realities. The shape, the nature of these realities, is determined by their proximity to First Land. There are four reasons why we are here, all good.

"First, the authorities are looking for us by now. Obviously, it is much easier for us to hide from them here than in Sellater, which by the way is the proper name for our reality, what we call Earth. First Land, you might say, is out of their jurisdiction. Way out.

"Second, here in First Land, magic is still very powerful. While magic has been dwindling away for many centuries in our world, here it is still vital, strong. Magic is the essence, the core of this place. I, we, are much stronger here than we would be at home and we are going to need all the help we can get.

"Third, the monster lives here and it is easier to get at him here and send him back where he belongs. If we tried to fight him at home, he'd almost certainly run here and hide. Then we'd still have to make the trip here to find him. So it was easier just to come here and have done with it.

"Fourth, although the prophecy is silent about where the final battle will take place, I am ninety-nine percent certain that it will take place here in First Land. So again, it was just easier to come here and get it done and over with.

"I hope you understood all I just said. I know it's confusing, but the more you think about it, the more sense it makes."

Gina and David nodded at Charlie while Rachel yawned and fell asleep in her mother's lap. After a few seconds, Gina hesitantly held up her hand.

"Ms. Tolliver, you have the floor," Charlie told her.

"N-now that we're here, wh-what do we have to do to get rid of the monster and how long is it going to take?"

Hearing the fragility in her voice, Charlie started worrying and replied, "First, we have to find him. That will take anywhere between a few days and a couple of weeks and we'll be in the center of First Land when it happens. The magic is strongest there, so that's where we want to be because we will be at our strongest there. He, our enemy, knows this and will try and stop us before we get there.

"As to how it will happen, how the battle itself will go, I don't know. The prophecy is silent and states only that the staff will tell us when the proper time comes. That's really all I can tell you for the moment. Now, does anybody have any other questions?"

Charlie looked at the others for a long moment, hoping that they were fresh out of questions. Unsettled by all they had just heard, they just silently looked back at him.

"Everything will be fine, don't worry," Charlie told them, trying to sound confident. "There are a few more things I'd like to talk about before we leave. As you may have noticed, I have not called our enemy by his name. Doing so makes him aware of you, conscious of you, so be careful what you say.

"I can't remember whether or not I told you, but we will be walking for our entire time here. At one time there were horses here, but not now. As we walk, it is very important that we stay together and look out for each other.

"As you saw last night, First Land is beautiful beyond the power of words to describe. Unfortunately, it's as dangerous as it is beautiful. There are perils here beyond your comprehension. Because these dangers are beyond your understanding, it is critical, vital, that you do what I tell you when I tell you. If anyone has a problem with that, I will take you home now and we can all wait for death to find us there."

Thinking of Ellen, Charlie prayed that either Gina or David would disagree and give him the excuse to turn back he so desperately wanted. They both just nodded and waited for him to continue speaking.

"Good," Charlie said, masking his disappointment, "I'm glad we agree. Now that I've frightened you, let me say that although dangerous, this is an enchanted place, full of wonders. If we are careful and lucky, our trip together will be a wonderful experience, one that you will always remember."

Finished speaking, Charlie rose and started loading his pack basket. The others followed his example and soon they were ready to leave. After extinguishing the fire, he led them outside. They all paused just outside the way-station's door, enraptured by the verdant beauty of First Land. Dew glistened on grass and leaves, refracting the sunlight into myriad crystalline shards of light. No pollutants had ever soiled the air and only a lingering hint of wood smoke from their recent fire mixed with nature's scents. Pulling the hood of his sweatshirt up against the chill October air, Charlie stepped out onto the grassy track.

A grey stone monolith protruded from the ground a few feet to their left. On one face of the monument a plaque read "Sellater" in a host of languages with an arrow pointing at the door twenty-five yards away. On the stele's opposite face, also in a multitude of languages, another plaque simply said "North" with an arrow pointing up the grassy track.

Leaning on the staff, Charlie started walking north up the trace. Holding Rachel's hand, Gina fell in a couple of steps behind him. David brought up the rear, assault rifle slung over his right shoulder. Happily patrolling their flock, Susie and Angus trotted up and down the file.

Although Rachel, Gina, and David were unaware of it, a critical moment had just passed. From this point forward, there was no turning back. For better or worse, they were on their way.

CHAPTER 34

SITTING ON A steel-framed bunk, back resting against a grey cinder block wall, arms and face resting on her upraised knees, Ellen Talltrees was a study in abject misery. "Coulter County Jail" was stenciled in black block capital letters across the back of the oversized orange jump suit she was wearing. Like many people, she had a fear of confined spaces and it was currently eating away at her courage. Hearing distant footsteps ringing on the concrete floor, she raised her head to listen. Lowering her head onto her knees again, Ellen considered the litany of crimes she was accused of.

Kidnaping of a minor child from state custody.

Kidnaping of an incompetent adult from state custody.

Felony murder in the death of the elderly pedestrian.

Felony murder in the death of the pursuing police officer.

And that, the prosecutor had informed her, was just for starters. Squeezing her tired eyes shut, Ellen choked back nausea and near hysterical panic. The footsteps in the corridor halted outside her cell and she raised her head to look. A female sheriff's deputy was standing on the other side of the bars.

"Well, lookee here," the deputy spat, an evil leer spreading across her face, "fresh meat. I'll be the one transportin' you down to Stanleyville, that's the state prison for women, sugar. And you and me, darlin', we're gonna become real good friends. In-ti-mate friends, you could say."

Repulsed, Ellen scrabbled back on the bunk. Grasping the bars, the deputy pressed her face forward until her nose and mouth were crushed between the bars. Smoldering red fire flooded her eyes, swallowing the green irises that had been there a moment before. When she opened her mouth to speak, a forked tongue flicked out between dagger teeth.

"Heya bitch, let's hula!" the deputy-thing roared, forked tongue wetly slapping down on the concrete floor inside the cell. "Whadayasay! Whadayasay! Whadayasay!"

Just after dawn, Deputy Sheriff Elizabeth Railes had pulled off the road at an isolated rest area just outside Frechette intending to relieve herself and smoke a joint. Or, as she thought of it, pump the old bilge and polish the little grey cells before reporting in for another shift at the human zoo. She had just left the Ladies' Room, lit joint in hand, when something dark and terrible came raging out of the forest and seized her. The Wendigo had a new pawn and Deputy Sheriff Elizabeth Railes had just committed her last act of self-indulgence.

Throwing her head back and covering her eyes, Ellen shrieked. A scream so powerful that she felt it course up and out of her like a living thing. Almost out of air, she stopped screaming long enough to take a huge gulp of air. Sensing something different, she peered out from between her fingers, but the deputy was gone. Feeling another scream rising, she locked her jaws together and willed it back. If she screamed again, Ellen knew she might never stop. So she thrust her knuckles into her mouth and bit down hard, relishing the distraction the pain offered.

When a guard passed three minutes later, Ellen was sitting on the bunk, muttering and crying. Despair and madness were both common here. The pretty Native American prisoner in Cell 217 was in the belly of the beast named Justice now and her humanity was forfeit. Unconcerned, the guard continued on her rounds, wondering what kind of slop the employee cafeteria was serving for lunch today.

CHAPTER 35

AT MID-MORNING, THEY stopped and rested on soft turf next to a rushing stream. Gina and David were both a little downcast. It was starting to sink in for them just how alien First Land was and how very far from home they were. Opening the top of his backpack, David pulled out a water purifier and started assembling it.

"David, you won't need that," Charlie said. "The water here is pure as is everything else. Taste it and see."

Gathering up their water bottles, David scrambled down to the water's edge. Cupping a hand, he dipped it into the fast moving water, shocked at how cold it was. Raising his hand to his mouth, he took a sip. The water delighted his palette with its freshness and made his teeth tingle. Smiling at the sensation, he filled the water bottles and handed them up to Gina. Climbing up the brook's bank, he rejoined the others and took a seat on the soft grass. Tearing open the wrapper on a nut bar, he had just taken the first bite when Rachel pointed at something.

"Mommy, what's that?" she asked, sounding a little frightened.

A glowing cloud of light resembling a massive swarm of fireflies was rapidly closing on them from the left. Choking down the dry mouthful of nut snack, David jumped to his feet, swinging the assault rifle up to his shoulder as he stood. Crouched on their bellies, Susie and Angus growled, fangs showing. The luminous swarm slowed and then stopped about five feet away from him.

"No, no, it's all right," Charlie said, hastily rising and standing between David and the swarm. "I'm sorry, I should have told you earlier, but I wanted it to be a surprise."

"Yeah, well, you succeeded," David told him. "What are they?"

"In the Poshto tongue they are called Oplathen. Translated, it means ones who bring joy."

Taking a step forward, Charlie opened his arms wide. The cloud of light immediately surged forward and enveloped him from head-to-toe. Delighted, he began laughing softly. The swarm continued advancing and wrapped the others in its radiant light.

"Look, Mommy, fairies!" Rachel giggled, examining one of the creatures perched on the end of her right index finger.

Gina and David were also both filled with joy at the presence of these tiny beings. Susie and Angus were also covered by the creatures. Susie lay on her belly, eyes closed, moaning happily. Angus was lying silently on his back, right rear leg twitching the way it will when something tickles that special spot on a dog.

Gina held out the back of her right hand at eye level and several of the Oplathen obliged her and landed. The creatures were tiny, something more than a quarter but less than half an inch tall. Their skin was a golden honey color. Shaggy brown or black hair framed pointed, elfin faces with deep-set blue eyes. Gossamer dragon-fly wings were arranged in two rows of three each down the center of their backs. One of the Oplathen took flight, kissed Gina on the end of her nose, and perched upside down on her left eyebrow. Looking down into her eye, it crooned a song of pure delight. Entranced, Gina couldn't stop laughing.

After a few minute, Charlie raised his arms and said, "Enough, little ones. I am glad to see you again and my friends are very glad to meet you. But we have much to do and far to go, so please ease up just a little."

The light emanating from the swarm of Oplathen immediately dimmed in response to Charlie's request. The pervasive sensation of intoxicating joy they were all feeling diminished to a deep-seated feeling of well-being.

"Thank you, my friends," Charlie said. "Your affection for us surpasses our ability to perceive you."

Turning to the others, he explained, "The Oplathen's great gift is the bringing of joy. They have no other purpose, not that they need one. Were they allowed to do so, they would hold us enraptured indefinitely. But since they are not evil creatures, they stop as soon as they are asked. The Oplathen are the canaries in the mineshaft of First Land. Whenever you see them, all is well. But if they suddenly leave or fail to appear by mid-morning, then danger is very near. They are among the oldest of all who live in First Land and they hate our enemy with a passion.

"And now, we really should get a move on. Time is different here and we've been stopped a lot longer than you think. I'd like to cover another few miles before sunset and then we can camp."

Heeding Charlie's words, Rachel, Gina, and David put their packs on. Cloaked in the radiant cloud of Oplathen and flanked by the dogs, they stepped out onto the grassy track and started walking north again.

CHAPTER 36

GODDAMN. ATTORNEY TERRY Thomas was seething, jaws clenched so tightly that they ached. The day had been one delay and nuisance after another. Rain. Road construction. Detours. Traffic. And now he was late by nearly an hour. Neither the car phone nor his damn cell phone could get any reception, just white noise. Up here in the Great-Northern-Heavily-Forested-Ass-End-Of-Nowhere, there apparently weren't any pay phones. There weren't even any buildings a pay phone could be located in.

He had never understood why David Garrison, his best friend and law partner, had insisted on living up here. Their office in the Cities had been more than busy enough to support both of them. Then Jennifer and little Allison had disappeared all those years ago. And still David refused to leave, hoping and praying that someday they would return. At this time of year, near the anniversary of their disappearance, Terry suffered terrible nightmares about a monster with burning red eyes who— Enough, he told himself, he wouldn't think about that right now, especially not here.

And now, to top it all off, there was a cop riding on his back bumper. Here he was driving a Mercedes sedan that could outrun the Starship Enterprise and he was plodding along like your Aunt Hermione in her asthmatic 1982 Plymouth Reliant. The fact that Frechette, Minnesota was surrounded by a thirty-five miles per hour speed zone that apparently started in Northern Iowa and extended up to the Arctic Circle wasn't helping anything either.

After getting lost and driving around in circles for fifteen minutes, a difficult feat in a town as small as Frechette, Terry finally found the courthouse. Every parking spot for blocks were taken up by various media outlets and courtroom gawkers all turned out to watch the preliminary hearing for Frechette's one woman crime wave.

Finally finding a vacant parking spot on a side street three blocks away, Terry parked the Benz and got out. Taking a bead on the courthouse's cupola which loomed above the intervening buildings, he started jogging. Three steps later, he thrust his left foot, currently encased in a hand sewn Italian loafer made from the tanned skin of a gen-u-ine alligator, ankle deep into a mud puddle. Freezing water soaked through the shoe and started soaking his gen-u-ine Argyll sock. Gritting his teeth, Terry jogged on.

Arriving in front of the courthouse, he paused a moment to catch his breath and survey the sidewalk circus. Talking heads from the various media outlets along with their remudas of cameramen and support staff were present. A First American activist group in traditional native dress was standing on one side of the courthouse, waving placards and chanting. On the other side of the building, a victim's rights group was also waving signs and chanting. It was an election year and a local candidate for governor was standing at the base of the courthouse steps being interviewed by one of the TV news reporters. Officers from the Frechette Police Department were blocking the main entrance into the courthouse, looking like they wished they were somewhere saner, like say Afghanistan.

All the elements of high drama or low farce that surrounds high profile criminal trials in the American justice system were cocked and ready. Taking a deep breath to steady himself, Terry walked up the courthouse steps and introduced himself to the senior officer. The clamor of voices at the base of the steps immediately trebled in volume.

One of the officers hustled Terry inside the courthouse and ushered him through the metal detector. Pushing through the crowd in the hallway, he led Terry to a large courtroom at the rear of the building. Entering the room, Terry was self-conscious about the squelching noise his soaked left shoe was making on the carpeted floor and the wet tracks it was leaving. Looking toward the front of the room, he felt his gut tighten and his pulse start hammering. Judge Thornton Osgood sat rigidly behind the bench, brown pop-eyes glaring. The same Judge Thornton Osgood that he and David Garrison had gotten reversed by the Minnesota State Supreme Court almost a decade earlier.

"Counsel," Judge Osborne called out in his booming voice, gesturing Terry forward with a crooked finger, "approach!"

Obeying the command, Terry walked past the bar to the bench and bravely sallied, "Good afternoon, Your Honor, nice to see you again."

"We'll see about that," Osgood replied, pop-eyes never wavering, never blinking.

Judge Osgood then launched into a blistering ten-minute diatribe about the merits of attorneys being on time in court. In those few minutes, Terry Thomas ate enough crow to last until Christmas with leftovers and soups lasting well into the new year. Near the end, he found himself doing what David Garrison had named the Osgood Shuffle. Rocking sideways, Terry shifted from one foot to the other in response to the ass-chewing the judge was meting out.

Finally winding down, Judge Osgood leaned forward and snapped, "Tell me, Mr. Thomas, are you prepared to adequately represent your client today? That is your job, you know."

Swallowing hard, feeling the sweat dripping down his forehead and armpits, Terry politely answered, "If I may have half an hour with my client, we'll be ready to proceed, Your Honor."

"You have your half-hour, counselor, and not a second longer! Court is recessed until then!" the judge roared, smashing his gavel down and storming off the bench.

Startled, Terry flinched and watched the judge stalk off, looking like a great flapping black bird in his loose robes.

"Ill-natured, cantankerous old bastard," he muttered to himself, vastly relieved at being off the hook at least for the moment.

Sitting shackled in a small holding area, Ellen watched him approach.

"Hi, Ms. Talltrees, I'm Terry Thomas, your attorney," he said, ignoring the shackles and reaching out to shake her hand. "I apologize for being late; it's been a hell of a day so far. I don't want you to worry; everything is going to be just fine. We just need to have a quick talk before the judge gets back on the bench."

"Hello, th, that's okay, thank you for coming," Ellen replied, surprised to find that she really *did* believe that things would turn out all right.

Suddenly, she caught sight of The Trickster's pawn just across the courtroom. Looking around to make sure no one was watching, the creature lasciviously wiggled its tongue at her. Ellen decided to tell Terry everything, or as much of it as she could manage in the time allotted. When the bailiff brought them forward to the defense table prior to court being called back into session, Terry Thomas was deep in thought.

"All rise!" the bailiff barked and they all rose.

Black robes flapping, Judge Osgood ascended the bench.

"Court is now in session," he announced, smacking down the gavel. "You may be seated. Are counsel ready to proceed?"

"Yes, Your Honor," both lawyers answered in unison.

"Mr. Ridley, you may proceed," Judge Osborne instructed.

Terry Thomas sat down while the prosecutor launched into a droning litany of the crimes Ellen was accused of. Looking over, she was surprised to see that Terry was sitting with his eyes closed. For a moment she was afraid that he was falling asleep and then she realized that he was listening intently to what Ridley was saying.

When the prosecutor was finally finished speaking, the judge asked, "How does the accused plea?"

Helping Ellen to her feet, Terry gently elbowed her and she said, “Not guilty, your honor.”

“The accused’s plea is duly noted,” Judge Osgood stated. “Does the state have a bail recommendation?”

“Yes, Your Honor,” Ridley began. “In light of the serious nature of these crimes and their impact on the comm—”

“A bail recommendation if you please, counsel, not a closing argument,” the judge snapped.

“Ye, yes, Your Honor,” the prosecutor stammered, face flushing red. “The people request that bail be denied in this case.”

“How says the defense,” Osgood inquired. “Please keep in mind my previous admonition to Mr. Ridley.”

“Your Honor,” Terry Thomas began, “the accused, Ms. Talltrees, has no prior criminal record whatsoever. She has deep family roots both here in Frechette and in the Twin Cities. The State has produced no evidence whatsoever to support the enumerated charges. In light of these facts, the defense requests that Ms. Talltrees be released on her own recognizance.”

Smiling for the first time, Judge Osgood said, “Sorry, Mr. Thomas, but not today. In view of the nature of these crimes, bail is set at $750,000.00. Cash.”

Ellen’ vision swam and for one terrible moment she thought that she was going to faint. A sound intruded on her consciousness and she realized that Terry Thomas was speaking again.

“Your Honor, Ms. Talltrees will satisfy that bail immediately with a sight draft. She has expressed extreme concern about her personal safety while in custody. With your permission, I would like to accompany her while she is processed out.”

Judge Thornton Osgood was livid. His color had faded to pasty grey and veins throbbed in his forehead and neck. An excited clamor just short of shouting broke out in the courtroom. There were moments, and this was one of them, when Terry Thomas truly loved his job.

"I will have order in the court or I will order it cleared!" the judge roared. "Bailiff, please accompany Ms. Talltrees and Mr. Thomas while she is processed for release on bail. Usual restrictions to apply."

With a final weak tap of the gavel, Judge Osgood announced, "Court is dismissed," and fled from the bench.

CHAPTER 37

CHARLIE AND THE others had been walking for the better part of an hour after leaving the stream when the raven first appeared. The bird overflew the walkers and their accompanying cloud of Oplathen at a height of fifty feet, croaking out the strange rusty cry of its kind. Landing in the center of the grassy track a hundred yards ahead, the raven waited until they had closed to within fifty feet before taking flight. It overflew Charlie and the others again, uttering its strange rasping cry and again settled in the center of the grassy track a hundred yards ahead. Susie and Angus, dedicated pursuers of all things avian, stayed close to David and contented themselves with growling at the bird. As the afternoon wore away and the shadows grew long, the raven continued repeating its strange behavior.

Gina finally spoke up, saying, "Charlie, I don't like that bird, it's scaring me."

"Don't like that ugly black bird," Rachel echoed.

"Nor should you," Charlie told them. "The raven is one of his creatures, one of his favorites."

"I can feel it looking inside of me," David called up from the rear of the line, sounding uneasy. "If you want, I can pop him with the rifle next time he lands."

"Yes, David, I know," Charlie replied, raising his voice a little so that it would carry. "Perceptions are heightened here; it's the magic that does it. Please don't shoot him; I have a use for him."

"How many of these whatever they are, these creatures, does he have?" Gina asked.

"All carrion eaters, all that live by night, all reptiles, and all humans that he can lay his hand on in the month of October," Charlie recited from long memory.

Repulsed, Gina and David shuddered. Frightened by the adults' reactions, Rachel clutched her mother's hand and looked like she wanted to cry.

"Don't get all upset, now," Charlie said. "We're a long ways from being helpless. David, it is very important that you keep the dogs on their leash for the rest of the day and not lose control of them."

Whistling Susie and Angus in, David clipped a short leash with a pair of snap-hooks on one end to their collars. Without breaking stride, Charlie bespoke the Oplathen. In response, the Oplathen's light increased in intensity until Charlie and the others were squinting from the fiery brightness of it.

The sudden flare of the Oplathen's light frightened the raven into flight. Circling high overhead now, the bird squawked down its disapproval at the walkers below. Cloaked by the radiant cloud, Charlie and the others continued walking northwards with the raven squawking high above all the while. After a mile or so, Charlie led them into a way-station, smaller and far more dilapidated than the one they had used the previous night.

Silent now, the bird glided down and lit on a nearby treetop. Head cocked, it watched and listened. The raven saw the way-station door swing shut and heard the bar slide into place. A few minutes later, a thin finger of wood smoke started rising out of the crumbling chimney. Satisfied, the raven took wing eastwards at maximum speed. Two miles later, the bird circled once around a wooded hilltop and landed.

CHAPTER 38

THE RAVEN LIT on a massive shoulder and started reporting what it has seen. When the shoulder's owner tilted his to listen, a swinging gold hoop earring almost knocked the bird off its perch. Finished reciting, the bird anxiously awaited the listener's reaction.

Gently stroking the raven's feathers, Mancun said, "You have done well, little friend. Go find a tree and rest; we will have work to do later."

Croaking his relief, the raven lifted off and flew over to a nearby birch tree. Looking across the fire at the intertwined balls of rutting flesh, Mancun was amazed yet again. Two women and three men, using every position and every orifice for countless years, and yet they still couldn't get enough of each other. If lust wasn't blind, it damn sure was persistent.

"Brother and sisters," he called out in his ringing voice, "we have work and it is time. Come gather and hear me."

The balls of flesh quickly separated themselves into discrete individuals. Dressing hurriedly, they sat down by the fire. All of them were emitting a faint, sickly green light. The whites, irises, and pupils of their eyes were blood red. They were the Lapushtan, the Dark One's storm troopers, his pet reivers and slayers.

Mancun, their leader, had been a Poshto warrior specializing in murder, rape, torture, and cannibalism. He had been taken in 1403 at age twenty-seven and treasured ever since.

Pierre LaCroix, second in command, was French by birth. In life, he had been both a slaver and a whiskey seller. In 1695 he had been transporting a coffle of young native girls south when the Dark One took him at age thirty-two.

John Lowery, an Englishman, had been a successful fur trader and a serial killer of anything human. His personal score was at 132 victims when he was killed by The Wendigo in 1779 at age thirty-one.

Jasper Finley, an American, had been a scalp hunter. Forty-two First American scalps were drying on a pole at the center of his camp when he was slaughtered by the Dark One in 1802 at age twenty-nine.

Anne Fullerton, a beautiful white woman with long red hair, had been a part-time prostitute and full-time serial widow. She had murdered her husbands, eight in all, as fast as she could marry them. Husband Number Nine had been taking her towards present-day Minneapolis when The Wendigo seized her in 1832 at age twenty-four.

Mary LeFevre, a French Canadian, had been a nurse who serially murdered twenty-two of her patients, many of them children. She had been arrested and was being transported towards Ottawa in 1903 when the Trickster decided to spare the State the expense of a trial and harvested her at age thirty.

Individually and collectively, the Lapushtan were the darkest gems in their master's vast collection. In recognition of their unique abilities, he had reanimated them and allowed them to run on a loose leash. They were his dark pets, reserved for those special occasions when he chose to send only the very best.

"As the Master promised," Mancun began, "the old shaman and his party are in the old way-station on the North Road. We will—"

As Mancun watched in utter fury, Jasper Finley popped Mary LeFevre's left breast out of her blouse and pinched the nipple. Smiling happily, she leaned over and stuck her tongue in his ear. Leaping to his feet, Mancun windmilled a large flint tomahawk up from the small of his back, over his shoulder, and down. The razor sharp stone blade cleanly amputated Finley's hand at the wrist and sliced LeFevre's exposed breast in half at the nipple. Kicking both of his screaming subordinates in the face, Mancun sent them crashing down the hillside. Striding down the hill slope, he snatched Finley and LeFevre up by the hair of their heads. Spreading his arms wide, he smashed their skulls together. Keeping a firm grip on their hair, he knelt until he was at eye level with them.

Ignoring the gore fountaining into his face from their wounds, Mancun shook them both and hissed, "Hear me well, brother and sister. I have neither the time nor the patience to discipline you further. If I have any further problems with you, I will turn you over to the Master and he can deal with you. Understood?"

LeFevre and Finley made wet, grunting noises of assent.

"Good, I'm glad we understand each other," he said, smashing their heads together again and flinging them to the ground.

Ascending the slope, Mancun reached the top and seated himself by the fire. LeFevre and Finley rejoined the circle a few seconds later, their flesh making gassy, gurgling sounds as it rejuvenated in pulsing flashes of green light.

"As I was saying," Mancun began, glaring at the two offenders, "we will leave in a minute. By the time we get to the way-station on the North Road, it will be fully dark and Redbird and the others will not be able to see us coming. The raven will fly over first and make sure all is well. If everything is fine, and I'm sure it will be, we attack then."

Pointing at Lowery, Finley, Fullerton, and LeFevre, he directed, "You four will man the front of the ram we made earlier and smash down the station's door with it. LaCroix and I will go in first, the rest of you follow as quickly as you can."

Pausing for emphasis, Mancun pounded the earth with his fist to hammer home the most critical part of his orders.

"The old shaman, Redbird, must be killed immediately. He is the only dangerous one in their party. No one is to touch or pick up his staff but me. The others, a man, woman, and a child, are to be taken alive and brought to the Master. If this is not done right, if there are any mistakes, it will go hard on you, on us, the Master will see to that. Got it? All right then, let's go."

The others rose and followed Mancun over to an eclectic pile of weaponry that included a cavalry saber, a spear, a bow and a quiver of arrows, an M-16 assault rifle with eight spare clips, and four hand grenades. Finished selecting and strapping on weapons, they all walked over to a ten-foot long white pine log.

One end of the log had been chopped into a rough point and charred in the fire to harden it. Three stout branches protruding from opposite sides of the trunk served as handholds. Lining up by threes on each side, the Lapushtan easily lifted the massive log on Mancun's command. He whistled sharply, and the raven took flight and started circling overhead. Stepping off at a slow walk, they started down the slope and soon accelerated to a jogging pace, carrying the huge log as if it were a twig.

Reaching the forest floor, the Lapushtan headed west on a well-worn trail. Frenzied crashing and flapping on either side of the trace preceded them as they advanced. All of the forest creatures that could flee, did. Those that couldn't cowered and hid in their burrows. Death was afoot in the wood tonight and all that lived here knew it.

Twenty minutes later, the Lapushtan halted under a stand of maple trees at the edge of a clearing. The way-station where Charlie and his party had camped for the night was twenty-five yards away. The pungent scent of wood smoke hung in the still night air. The smoke plume rising out of the station's chimney was a lighter shadow in the deeper dark and plainly visible to their enhanced vision.

Stepping away from the log, Mancun whistled for the raven. Gliding down, the bird perched on his shoulder, croaked once, and flew off. Turning slowly through 360 degrees, Mancun searched for any sign of danger or ambush. Sensing no danger, Mancun waved LaCroix toward the rear of the log and joined him there. He rapped once on the log with his tomahawk and the four bearers dropped the ram from shoulder to hip level. Taking one last look around, he rapped the log twice more with the tomahawk and the Lapushtan began charging toward the way-station.

Gathering momentum, they accelerated across the small clearing. Fifteen feet from the way-station's door, the four bearers swung the battering ram back as far as they could and reached maximum speed. Lowery, positioned at the right front handhold, grunted an order. He and the other bearers flung the massive ram at the station's door and rolled out of the way.

The ancient wooden door exploded inwards. Shrieking, upraised tomahawk in one hand, Mancun sprinted down the fallen ram and leaped through the doorway. LaCroix, waving a huge Bowie knife, was close on his heels. The four bearers scrambled to their feet and were inside the building within ten seconds of the ram striking the door. Cawing, the raven entered last, just behind Finley.

Crouched in a fighting stance, stone tomahawk held high above his right shoulder, Mancun scanned the small, smoke-filled room. He could sense, even smell, the presence of his prey, but he could not see them. Redbird especially worried him. They had old business together and he knew far better than to underestimate the old man.

"Spread out!" Mancun ordered. "Check the back room. They're here, I can smell them. Remember, I want them all alive except for old Redbird. Don't touch his staff, that is for me alone."

The other Lapushtan were turning to follow his orders when Charlie's voice rang out.

"Looking for me, trash?" he asked from over on the hearth, a wisp of smoke rising from his pipe.

Sucking in his breath, Mancun rose to his full height of 6'8". Roaring until his scalp lock shook, he attacked.

"You die tonight, old fuck!" he raged, tomahawk already beginning its fatal down stroke as he charged forward.

"I will die, but not tonight, fool," Charlie replied just before he vanished.

Left in the space Charlie had occupied was a beaded medicine bag pulsing with sapphire light. Propelled forward by inertia, unable to arrest the tomahawk's downward swing, Mancun smashed his shins into the stone hearth and crashed headfirst into the fire. LaCroix, following a step behind, watched in disbelief as the stone tomahawk's downswing buried it up to the haft in his right knee cap.

The other four Lapushtan were milling about in confusion. Flapping around their heads, the raven croaked in panic. Sitting on the floor with his back to the wall, LaCroix was bellowing in agony and trying unsuccessfully to pull the tomahawk out of his knee.

Rolling out of the fire, buckskins burning and smoking, Mancun roared, "Run, you fucking idiots, we—"

Enhanced by the eldritch environment of First Land, the medicine bag detonated. The way-station didn't so much explode as lift-off and take flight. Stones weighing hundreds of pounds were flung over half a mile away. A glowing blue crater filled with roiling steam was all that remained of the building. A single black feather, bent and charred, drifted down and landed in the center of the depression.

In common with their maker, the Lapushtan were supernatural creatures who could not die because they weren't alive in the normal sense of the word. But also like him, they were capable of feeling pain. And they were feeling pain now, an infinity of it. Pain so terrible that they would have all chosen the mercy of death had it been possible. Disembodied now as six flashes of pale green light; they fled shrieking northwards to the uncertain protection and doubtful mercy of their master.

CHAPTER 39

TAKING A DEEP draw off his pipe, Charlie sat waiting for the expected explosion. A second later the ground trembled and a distant roar echoed out over the forest. A flash of blue light coursed across the night sky, blotting out the stars.

Well pleased, Charlie laughed and said, "Ouch, I just know that had to hurt!"

Of all the Dark One's many familiars, he bore an especially black hatred for the Lapushtan and in particular for Mancun. Although there was still an account owing on their part, he considered tonight's ambush as going a fair way toward evening the score.

Rising to his feet, Charlie walked across the small meadow and joined the others. Taking a seat at the small fire, he took a small aluminum saucepan of boiling water off the coals. Adding a generous handful of dried herbs to the water, he set the pan aside and left the mixture to steep.

"Big bang, Grampa Charlie," Rachel observed.

Still tickled with the success of his ambush, Charlie smiled and said, "Yes, honey, it was a beaut for sure."

As soon as Charlie had realized what the raven was doing and for whom, he had formulated a plan. Keeping everyone moving to maintain the illusion of normalcy, Charlie had rummaged through his pack basket and found a medicine bag. Holding it out at arm's length in the palm of his hand, he had whistled softly. Forty or fifty of the Oplathen had detached themselves from the main swarm and landed on the medicine bag. Their light had flickered, then steadied as they lifted the bag off Charlie's palm like so many tiny helicopters and flew off with it.

Charlie had immediately halted and cast a glamour around the members of his party, cloaking them from view. Aided by the enhanced atmosphere of First Land, he simultaneously cast an illusion that he and the others were still walking down the grassy track amidst the glowing cloud of Oplathen. The raven continued circling the glowing swarm, croaking away, and Charlie knew for a certainty that the spy had been fooled.

Enveloped in the glamour, they had stood motionless in the center of the track until the Oplathen and the raven were out of sight. Turning left off the track, Charlie had led them along a small stream to a meadow. After asking Gina and David to start dinner, he had left them and moved further across the meadow.

Sitting cross-legged in the soft grass, Charlie had put the finishing touches on his ambush, including barring the way-station door and starting a fire. By the time the raven had flown away to report, the hard part was done and there was nothing to do but wait. Lingering long enough to watch Mancun bury his tomahawk deep into LaCroix's kneecap, Charlie had then retreated back to his physical form a few seconds ahead of the massive explosion.

The cans of beef stew sitting on the bed of glowing coals started bubbling, reminding everyone that they were hungry. Lining up their cups, Charlie portioned out the herbal potion steeping in the saucepan, straining it with a spoon as he poured.

"This will keep the dreams away tonight and help you sleep," he explained. "But be warned, it sure doesn't taste very good. That's why we're drinking it before we eat in case it makes you sick. I hope it won't, but it might."

David went first, barely managing to choke the foul brew down.

"Man, that's rank!" he exclaimed, swallowing hard to keep the potion where it belonged.

Looking doubtful, Gina went next, swallowing the potion in one long gulp.

"That's awful!" she gasped, hand covering her mouth as her stomach churned.

"Fifty years of brewing this stuff and it still tastes as bad as the first time I made it," Charlie said, chugging the noxious liquid in one long pull and shuddering at the taste.

Forewarned by her elders' reactions, Rachel hesitantly took a sip and started coughing.

"That's enough for a little thing like you," Charlie said, taking the cup from her. "You should sleep just fine now."

"That was gross, Grampa Charlie!" Rachel sputtered. "Not nice to be mean to little kids!"

"I'm sorry, honey, but you need that so you can sleep tonight," he explained. "Now why don't you come over here and eat with me."

Rachel crawled into Charlie's lap while Gina and David pulled the cans of stew off the coals. Pinning the cans between a pair of forked sticks, David poured the stew into their mess kits while Gina handed them out. Hungry, they sat eating without talking, enjoying the bland stew.

After they were finished eating, Charlie lit his pipe and said, "For the next couple of days we're going to leave the road and travel through the forest. We stung him and his pretty good today, which will infuriate him. His creatures will be out in force in a matter of hours searching for us by dawn at the latest. I want to be deep in the forest by first light just to be on the safe side."

Looking at the night shrouded trees at the edge of the meadow, Gina shivered, remembering her nightmare. David looked thoughtful and a little worried.

"Don't worry, we'll be fine," Charlie assured them, trying to convince himself as he spoke.

By the time the trash was buried and the mess kits scrubbed clean, Charlie's potion had started taking effect. Yawning, Rachel, Gina, and David crawled into their sleeping bags and soon fell into a deep, dreamless sleep. Decades of use had raised Charlie's tolerance to the elixir, so he wasn't sleepy just yet. Walking the few feet over to the rushing stream, he lit his pipe and stood thinking.

If the others could have known his thoughts, they wouldn't have slept well nearly as well. Charlie Redbird, eldest and wisest member of a people that had dwelled in the great northern forests for millennia, was terrified by this wood. He didn't want to lead his friends into it, but there was no other alternative. The Dark One had suffered a major defeat today and his minions would be out in force soon looking to even the score. If they tried to remain on the road, they would be spotted no later than mid-morning, attacked shortly after, and dead by noontime at the latest. So they had to risk the forest, there was no other choice. Hawking, Charlie spit toward the wood, expressing his contempt for it and for his own fears.

Tasting tar, he knocked the dottle out of his pipe and walked back to the campfire. Throwing on a few sticks of kindling on the fire, Charlie unrolled his sleeping bag and took one last look at the surrounding forest. Feeling drowsy as the potion finally kicked in, he crawled into the bag, hoping that tomorrow would be a better day than he feared.

CHAPTER 40

THINGS WEREN'T GOING well anywhere. Against all odds he had suffered major defeats on all fronts.

The Indian girl had escaped with the help of that damn smooth-tongued lawyer and Garrison's wealth. Well, he wasn't through with her yet, he still had a card or two left to play.

Old Redbird had not only eluded the Lapushtan, he had ambushed them and temporarily destroyed their corporeal forms. The Lapushtan, his pet terrors, defeated by a dying old shaman. It just wasn't beyond belief, it was fucking incomprehensible, a disaster.

Storming across the crèche, The Wendigo charged toward the six Lapushtan who were suspended from the ceiling by their ankles. He had reanimated their physical forms and turned the other prisoners loose on them. Barbarity is never worse than when the tormented gain dominion over their tormentors. Tongue ripped out, Mancun saw his master approaching and began gurgling in terror.

Swinging his right leg back, the Dark One kicked Mancun in the belly with all of his might. Mancun's body cavity exploded, spraying out viscera as his body flew up and smashed against the rough stone ceiling. As he fell, the Dark One connected with another kick and launched him back up to the ceiling. Enraged, the monster continued until there was nothing left of his chief lieutenant but a pair of bloody feet dangling from the leg irons. Fury growing progressively worse, The Wendigo proceeded down the line of chained Lapushtan, kicking each until there was nothing left in the shackles but bloody shreds. Idiots, all of them, fucking useless, nothing but a bunch of goddamned morons.

Feeling better now, The Wendigo stalked across the cavern and took a seat on his throne. Picking up a three foot wide obsidian circle, he gently exhaled on the polished surface, clouding it. Concentrating, he patiently waited for the clouded surface to clear, anxious to see what the scrying stone would reveal. The stone mirror cleared and the Dark One cast a net of consciousness out seeking Charlie Redbird. The ebony surface of the mirror shimmered and a ground level view of a dense forest appeared. The patch of forest was vaguely familiar, but he couldn't understand what, if anything, the mirror was trying to tell him.

Next, The Wendigo sought Ellen Talltrees. The surface of the obsidian mirror roiled for a few seconds before clearing and showing an aerial view of Frechette from about ten thousand feet. Exasperated, the Dark One gently laid the mirror down, being careful not to shatter the delicate stone. As it often did, the scrying stone had shown him riddles, concealing as much as it revealed.

Redbird was somewhere in the southern forests of First Land, no surprise there. The Indian bitch, his granddaughter, was still in the Frechette area, which did surprise him. After her recent experiences there, he had thought she would flee as far and as fast as she possibly could. Not that it would have done her any good; he could find her now no matter where she went.

Still, even though he couldn't determine his enemies exact locations, there were steps he could take. Cheered by his prospects, The Wendigo rose from the stone throne. Breaking into a run, he charged toward the chained row of Lapushtan. Screaming, they writhed in terror on the end of their chains as the Dark One cocked his right leg back and began tormenting them anew.

CHAPTER 41

IT WAS COLD in the pre-dawn darkness. Glittering hoar-frost clung on grass and branch, reflecting the firelight. Everyone was quiet, already tired before the day had properly begun. Packing up after a hasty breakfast, Charlie paused for a moment to set the order of march.

"Rachel and Gina, I want you directly behind me on my heels. Gina, you are to hold on to my coat with one hand and hang on to Rachel with the other. Okay?"

Looking fearful, Gina nodded her understanding.

"David, I want you directly behind Rachel and Gina. Leash your dogs; it will be very dangerous for them to run free today. We'll stop in about half an hour; there are some things I will need to tell you then. We need to be under the cover of the trees before sunup, so let's go."

Shouldering their packs, everyone silently fell into line and followed Charlie toward the darkened wood. Finding a faint trace, he led them into the forest, a dim blue light glowing at the tip of his staff. The dense trees formed an interlocking canopy of branches overhead, blocking the faint moonlight. Bringing up the rear with Susie and

Angus, David struggled along in the dark, stumbling over exposed tree roots and hoping that he wouldn't lose sight of the blue beacon a couple of yards ahead. Ten minutes after they entered the forest, the raucous cries of a flock of crows sounded to the north.

Extinguishing the staff, Charlie led them beneath the ground hugging branches of a towering fir tree and hissed, "Be still now and no talking."

Thirty seconds later a murder of crows flew by at tree-top level and bore away to the southeast. Relieved, Charlie watched them vanish from sight, but knew they were only a small part of the forces scouring First Land for them.

"All right," Charlie said, "we can go on now."

Daylight was now filtering down through the dense umbrella of branches overhead, allowing them to walk with greater speed and confidence. A few minutes later, they saw brighter light ahead as the trees began thinning out. Continuing on, they came to the edge of the forest and saw a hundred yard wide strip of bramble bushes stretching east to west as far as the eye could see. On the other side of the thorn barrier, another forest began, looming dark and ominous in the early morning light.

The Oplathen swarmed them as Charlie took a seat under a silver birch tree and signaled the others to join him. Knowing there would be few, if any, opportunities to smoke in the hours ahead, he lit his pipe and took a deep draw. The Oplathen flitted about his head, delighting in the aromatic cloud of smoke he was producing.

"They like tobacco smoke, always have," Charlie said, smiling a little then turning serious. "We're now going to have that talk I mentioned earlier. Across the thorn barrier over there lays the Tintaen Forest, which we are going to try and cross today. The Tintaen is not like other forests, it is very dangerous.

"Many centuries ago, even before the Poshto left Asia, the Tintaen were an evil people. For their crimes, they were spelled into trees and made immortal by a shaman whose name has long since been forgotten.

"The Tintaen hate all that walks, slithers, or flies free. They kill anything they catch in their domain without exception. When I was young and new to the staff, I accidentally wandered into the Tintaen Forest and got lost. For three days and nights we battled and I barely escaped with my life. This will be my first time back inside the Tintaen Forest in almost fifty years.

"Were there any other route, any other choice, I would take it, but there isn't any. His creatures are sweeping First Land and he will have us by noontime if we stay out in the open.

"We must hide and yet move forward and the only way to do that is by passing through the Tintaen Forest. I'm sorry, but this is the only way."

Sensing her mother's fear, Rachel curled up in Gina's lap and hid her face.

"Charlie, can't you use the thingy, the glamour, and we can sneak by?" Gina asked, starting to rock.

"No, I'm afraid not," he replied, reaching out and stopping her mid-rock. "The Tintaen are among the oldest creatures living in First Land, far older than even the magic in the staff. The glamour won't fool them, not for a second. They would see through it immediately."

Biting her lower lip, Gina turned her head away and buried her face in Rachel's hair.

"I've got the rifle," David said, unconsciously fondling the weapon's stock, "and you have the staff. Couldn't we go back on the road and fight our way north and get there in a day or two, maybe less?"

"No, it wouldn't work that way," Charlie told him. "Once we were spotted, and it wouldn't take long, his creatures would keep coming until they overwhelmed us by sheer weight of numbers. Distance, like time, is different here. We might get there in a couple of days, but it might take us as long as a couple of weeks, there's no way to tell."

"Well, how long do you think it will take for us to get through the Tintaen Forest?"

"Hopefully just today, but maybe as long as two or three days, depending on how it goes once we get in there."

"Yeah, all right," David said, reaching down to scratch Susie and Angus. "Let's get started then, sitting here thinking about it isn't improving my outlook any."

"Good, the sooner we start, the sooner were through the forest," Charlie said as he rose, trying to muster a smile but failing. "With your permission, I would like to keep the dogs with me so you can look after Rachel. Gina will walk with me and the dogs. Stay on my heels no matter what happens. Don't be afraid to use the rifle if they get too close. It won't kill them, but it will hurt and frighten them. All right then, let's go."

With Gina holding his left arm and the dogs ranging ahead on their leash, Charlie stepped out of the edge of the forest. David followed close behind, Rachel clutching his left hand. Approaching the chest high bramble thicket, Charlie leveled the staff and commanded, "Burn!"

Coruscating blue fire scythed through the thorn bushes, burning open a narrow path. A grating, high pitched keening filled the air as the brambles flamed and died. Grimacing, Charlie led them forward, using the staff twice more to clear their way.

Three minutes later, they emerged on the other side of the bramble thicket and stood facing the Tintaen Forest. A mildewed wet odor of things long dead drifted out of the forest on the faint morning breeze. Thick tendrils of white mist curled around the trees' boles, obscuring their lower branches.

As Charlie started toward the forest, the Oplathen's glowing radiance blinked out as they dematerialized. A pair of crows flew out of the forest behind them and flew away north, their annoying cries echoing out over the trees.

"Shit!" Charlie swore, angry at being spotted by the Dark One's spies.

"Will they follow us into the woods or call for reinforcements or something?" David asked.

"No, they won't follow us because they know they would die in the forest" Charlie replied. "Still, they now know exactly where we are and that is bad enough."

CHAPTER 42

"CAREFUL NOW," SHE silently cautioned herself. *"This is no time to get careless."*

Keeping one hand on the cabin's log wall to steady herself, she eased along, concentrating on being as soundless as possible. She knew she'd heard and seen something in the woods a few yards ahead, she was certain of it.

Pulse hammering, she took another silent step forward. Her left foot was in mid-air, creeping toward a landing, when a shadow flashed across her peripheral vision. As she turned her head to look, a three-foot length of birch firewood smashed into the right side of her skull.

There were no exploding stars, no pain, just sudden darkness. Limp, she slid down the log wall and lay in a jumbled heap of limbs on the ground.

CHAPTER 43

SETTING A QUICK pace, Charlie led them into the edge of the Tintaen Forest. The tendrils of mist thickened, reducing the surrounding trees to blurred grey columns, making it difficult to see anything. Susie and Angus, walking ahead of Charlie on their leash, suddenly backed into his legs and nearly knocked him over. Crouched on their bellies, hackles raised, they growled with fangs bared.

"We will stop now for a moment," Charlie said, turning to make sure Rachel and David were behind him. "I need to have a word with these creatures. David, be ready with that rifle. If anything happens, go ahead and shoot."

Raising the staff, Charlie smashed it down hard on the ground. A blue flash shot across across the ground, dissipating the mist and revealing the true nature of the forest. The Tintaen were covered in a scaly, grey bark that was reptilian in appearance. Protuberant knots and growths were present on all of their boles. A gentle breeze began rising, making their branches rattle and sigh. The knots and growths on their boles writhed and took on definition. The upper deformities became noses and fanged mouths. The Tintaen's eyes were round, lidless, and filled with a terrible fury. The lower knots transformed themselves into misshapen breasts and genitals.

Gina whimpered as her nightmare came to life. Keeping a firm hold on her arm, Charlie tried to keep her mind from unraveling. Burying her face in David's belly, Rachel began crying and reached for Gina. Gripping the stock of the assault rifle with one hand, David held Rachel steady with the other.

"Stand and be strong," Charlie commanded, "or else we are lost!"

Somehow, Rachel, Gina, and David collected themselves and regained a semblance of composure. Sitting on Charlie's feet, pressed up against his shins, Susie and Angus snarled at the Tintaen.

The breeze continued rising and soughed, "You will die today, Redbird. All of you will die today."

Handing Gina back to David, Charlie knelt and looped the dogs' leash around his ankle. Standing, he shot upwards, becoming a towering figure rimmed in blue flames taller than the surrounding Tintaen.

"Hear me well, old ones!" he roared. "I am Charles Lantot Redbird, last of the Redbird shamans, and I am no longer the helpless boy you attacked so many years ago. We will pass through your domain unmolested today or else you will feel the scourge of my fire and burn in its flames like the rotten old wood that you are!"

Ghostly, mocking laughter filled the air. The Tintaen on either side of Charlie whipped branches out toward his feet. A supple creeper lashed out and snaked around Rachel and Gina, trying to pull them into the depths of the forest. A hard blow to his pack knocked David flat on his face.

"Now, David, shoot!" Charlie roared as his staff erupted with blue fire.

Rolling into a prone position, David sighted on the Tintaen trying to snatch Rachel and Gina and fired. A fist-sized hole exploded in the monster's cheek and smoking green sap started dripping out of the wound. Shrieking in pain, the creature whipped its creeper back, flinging Rachel and Gina to the ground. Sighting and firing, David continued shooting until the rifle's twelve shot clip was empty.

Wielding the staff in a horizontal arc, Charlie scythed through the Tintaen, decapitating them. Smoking stumps were all that remained of seven of them when he finally stopped.

Returning to normal size, Charlie leaned heavily on his staff, eyes closed, gasping for breath. Wielding the staff took a physical toll and it had been years since he had loosed such a concentrated barrage. Opening his eyes and looking down, his worse fears were confirmed.

"I think we're all right," David called, climbing to his feet and slamming a fresh clip into the assault rifle.

Still sprawled out on the ground, Rachel and Gina were clinging to each other, crying. Walking over, David helped them to their feet and tried to calm them down.

"It's all right, we're fine," he said, hugging them both.

"David, I'm sorry, but you're wrong," Charlie sadly told him. "They got Angus. A branch was wrapping around my ankle and he bit it. Before I could do anything, it snapped back, cut the leash, and dragged him off. I, I'm sorry, I know how much he meant to you."

David's arms dropped away from Rachel and Gina. There was a rustle of motion a few yards back in the forest and suddenly something was flying through the air. Angus' broken body crashed down at David's feet. The Tintaen's mocking laughter sighed down the wind and increased in volume. His back to the others, David knelt and cradled the eviscerated body of his old friend. Whining anxiously, Susie crawled over on her belly, unable to understand what was wrong.

Depressed and desperately lonely after Allison and Jennifer's disappearance, he had decided to get himself a dog. Looking in the classified section of the local paper under pets, he saw an ad proclaiming "1/2 Bor. Coll., 1/2 Aus. Shep., $175.00 Firm" and listing a local phone number. Calling for directions, he had driven over on a rainy day to look at the puppies.

Following the convoluted directions, he had eventually arrived at an isolated farmhouse. Standing with rain dripping down the back of his collar, he had knocked on the peeling front door and waited. And waited. A gaunt woman in her fifties with flinty eyes finally opened the door and ushered him in. Leading him through the threadbare house, she guided him out the backdoor to a ramshackle shed attached to the house's rear wall. Opening the door, she tugged on a pull chain and turned on a bare hundred watt bulb hanging from the stained plywood ceiling. Gesturing him inside, she turned away and silently left.

Stooping down to pass through the low doorway, David entered the dimly lit shed and saw a reclining bitch and six squirming black and white puppies. Hunkering down, he had whistled softly until the bitch came over and sniffed his fingers, puppies in tow. After a second's hesitation, the puppies mobbed his legs in a warm, furry pile.

Although David was never certain why later, he had lifted a female puppy out of the center of the pile. Liking her immediately, he knew that he would keep her. Having become something of an authority on loneliness, he had impulsively decided that the female would need another puppy for company. A male puppy was licking his free hand, frantically vying for attention. Surprising himself by laughing, David scooped the male puppy up and stood.

The puppies were only eight weeks old, so they fit easily in the cargo pockets of his parka. Backing out of the shed, he had deliberately left the light on and regretfully closed the door on the puppies. David had knocked twice on the back door, but after five minutes the woman still hadn't appeared. Wading through the wet, overgrown grass to the front door, he had knocked again and got the same response. Growing cold and a little annoyed, he had started the truck, put the puppies on the front passenger side floorboard, and turned the heat on. Digging a pen and a paper out of the clutter in the glove compartment, he wrote a short note listing his name and phone number. Folding $350.00 inside the sheet of paper, he shoved the note into a battered mailbox at the end of the drive as he backed out onto the county road. Already attached to the puppies, he had hoped the grim woman wouldn't call and she never did.

On the way home, David had named the puppies Susie and Angus after the characters in a dimly remembered novel. From the moment they arrived, they claimed his home and made it their own. The two charging balls of black and white fur banished the house's gloomy silence to the dark graveyard hours after midnight and before dawn. Nothing was safe from their depredations. Kitchen trash, shoes, socks, rugs, and furniture were all thoroughly teethed and investigated. Most importantly though, they kept him company and gave him something to smile about even on the darkest days.

He had brought his two friends to this awful place and now Angus was dead, killed by a nightmare given life. His fault and no one else's.

Walking up, Charlie put a hand on his friend's shoulder and said, "David, I know you're upset, but we need to get going, the day is getting past us."

"I, I thought you said these things couldn't move."

"They can't, it would take them all day to move five feet. But the Tintaen have long, supple arms with razor edges and they're very quick. As you saw, it's more than enough."

David nodded and said, "I won't leave him here for these things. I'm going to carry him out and bury him somewhere safe."

"Good," Charlie told him, squeezing his shoulder. "We'll take turns carrying him. It shouldn't be too much further, no more than four or five hours."

Rising, David carried Angus' body over to his pack. Releasing the drawstring on top of the main cargo compartment intending to pull out a plastic groundsheet, he had an idea. Pulling out the plastic groundsheet, he laid it flat and wrapped Angus in its folds. Reaching back into the pack's main cargo compartment, he snapped open the fluorescent orange box lying on top. Removing the object inside the box, David quickly put it in the right side pocket of his parka. Standing, he walked over to Charlie.

"There's something I need to do before we move on," he said, a grim smile on his face.

Turning away and taking a couple of steps, David stood facing the nearest Tintaen thirty feet away.

"Think it's funny that you killed my dog?" he shouted, startling his friends. "Enjoyed that, did you?"

The haunting, cynical laughter trebled in volume. The Tintaen rustled their myriad branches, expressing their amusement, their contempt. Reaching into his parka pocket, David drew the compact flare gun and fired in one fluid motion. Sizzling in the cold air as it flew, the magnesium flare shot into the open maw of the closest Tintaen and down its gullet. The creature began shrieking as smoke poured from its mouth. White flames suddenly appeared at the Tintaen's roots and flashed upwards to its crown. Screaming helplessly, the creature writhed in agony as the flames engulfed it. The mocking laughter abruptly ceased and the sound of rustling branches died away to nothing.

"Now that's entertainment!" David screamed. "That was for my dog, Angus, and it's just a beginning! 'Cause I'm gonna come back here and burn every last one of you motherfuckers just like your friend here! I'll leave none of you alive! None of you!"

Wrapping his arms around David, Charlie tried to calm him. After struggling for a few seconds, David quieted and stood with his chest heaving and his hands on his knees. The two men silently watched the Tintaen burn until nothing was left but a pile of grey, smoking ashes.

"Are you going to be all right, David?" Charlie asked.

"Yeah, I'll be all right. But I meant what I told them. I am going to come back here and burn them down, every last one of them. No matter how long it takes, I am going to torch them, I swear it."

Charlie knew a thing or six about what black hatred could do, how it could warp a person. But he also knew this wasn't the time or the place to raise the subject with his friend. Taking David's arm, Charlie steered him toward their jumbled pile of gear. Rachel and Gina were waiting there, eyes huge. Releasing David, Charlie folded them into his arms.

Hugging them, Charlie was relieved to find Rachel unscarred. Terrified of the Tintaen, and deeply upset over the death of Angus, but still fundamentally sound. Childhood resilience would leave her with nothing worse than an occasional nightmare that would soon fade away as she grew older.

Gina though was a different story. Probing, Charlie found roiling black smoke creeping through some of the recently repaired cracks in her psyche. A chorus of voices, birthed in some dark place where mind meets soul, babbled and giggled just under the surface of her consciousness. Concentrating, he drove the churning black smoke back through the cracks in her mind, mending them as he went. He silenced the babbling voices and sent them back to their black places of abode. Mostly. Try as he might, thin tendrils of black smoke still crept in here and there. The voices no longer spoke, but rather whispered in a hollow echo as if from the bottom of an unfathomable chasm. Gina's mind was injured and close to unraveling completely. If she was to have any chance of further recovery, she had to get away from the Tintaen as soon as possible.

Turning, he saw that David already had his pack on with Angus' body strapped to the top. Rachel also had her pack on and was standing next to David holding his hand. After helping Gina into her pack, he put on his pack basket on with David's help. Striking out northward, Charlie set a brisk pace, leading them away from the charnel clearing with it decapitated and smoldering Tintaen. They marched as before, Charlie with Gina on his arm with David bringing up the rear holding Rachel's hand. The only difference was Susie, now leashed to David's belt and happy to be there.

Wary now, the Tintaen rustled their branches and uttered strange, high-pitched whistles as they passed but otherwise left them alone. On the few occasions when their rustling and whistling became louder, seeming to herald further violence, David would raise the flare pistol dangling in his right fist and Charlie would cause the staff to flare blue fire. The Tintaen would immediately become still, only to start rustling and whistling a few minutes later. The creatures' volume would gradually increase until David and Charlie were forced to brandish their weapons again and the cycle would start anew.

As Charlie and the others marched northwards, the day became increasingly colder. Within an hour, they were wearing their hats and gloves, parkas zipped up to their chins. The wind kept rising, driving cold out of the north, tearing their eyes and making it difficult to walk a true course.

Two hours after leaving the charnel clearing, they took a short break in a jumble of boulders. Sitting with their backs to the biting wind, they snacked on nut bars and passed around a bottle of fruit drink re-hydrated from powdered mix.

"We have done well," Charlie announced, pausing to take a sip of the fruit drink. "We should be away from the Tintaen in an hour and a half or so. Which is good, because it is going to snow hard tonight and I want to be well away from them before we make camp."

Looking up at the clear blue sky, David swallowed the last of the dry, crumbly nut bar and wondered why some people claimed to enjoy the damn things.

"You sure about that snow, Charlie?" he asked. "It sure doesn't look like it's going to snow."

"Yes, David, I'm sure, positive."

"How's that? The staff tell you or something?"

"No," Charlie said, laughing, "My left big toe told me. I broke it years ago and now it aches like hell whenever it's going to rain or snow."

Looking at him for a moment, David laughed and said, "Okay, Charlie, you da man. If you tell me it's gonna snow out of a clear blue sky because you're left big toe told you so, then by God, it's gonna snow!"

"Good, David, I'm glad you believe me," Charlie told him, smiling as he took Gina's arm and turned back into the frigid wind. "I'll tell you what, if it's not snowing by the time we make camp tonight, I'll gather all the firewood and cook dinner. Deal?"

"Deal!" David replied, laughing as he took Rachel by the hand and fell in behind Gina and Charlie.

Charlie was glad for the laughter's release, it eased him and made a grim situation a little more bearable. They were all bone-tired in a very dangerous place with a bad winter storm brewing. Humor helped, a lot.

The wind kept rising, moaning and crying around the tangled limbs of the Tintaen, mixing its voice in with their alien rustles and whistles, creating a discordant, nerve-grating symphony. An hour later, they were forced to stop again and lower their ski-masks against the wind's cutting chill.

Cold and tired, Rachel was stumbling and having trouble keeping up. Picking her up with his left arm, David staggered along under her off-center weight combined with that of Angus's body strapped to the top of his pack. The wind increased yet again even as the rustling and whistling faded away to nothing. Suddenly, they were standing in open space and free of the claustrophobic Tintaen Forest.

Another bramble thorn thicket in a long corridor of broken, stony ground lay directly ahead. A forest of mixed birch, maple, and fir trees lay on the far side of the thorn barrier. Free of the Tintaen's interlocking canopy of branches, they could see churning, slate-grey clouds towering thousands of feet into the air a few miles to the north. Pausing, David looked at the oncoming storm and grinned.

Stepping forward, Charlie started burning through the brambles with the staff. Something smashed into David's left shoulder and bicep, knocking him and Rachel to the ground. Crying hysterically, Rachel was holding the back of her head with both hands. When David reached out for her, his left arm refused to move. A five-foot long branch lay on the ground between them, a parting missile from the Tintaen.

Charlie trotted over with Gina following a couple of steps behind him. Pulling down her hood and removing her hat, he examined the back of Rachel's skull with gentle fingers. To his great relief, he found nothing worse than a fist-sized bump. Even so, the blow had hurt and frightened her. Leaving her to Gina's care, he turned and saw David sitting on the ground, cradling his left arm.

"I, I can't feel my arm," David said, raw panic lurking just under the surface of his voice. "I, I think it's broken."

"Let me have a look," Charlie said. "Even if it's broken, I can set it easily enough."

After helping remove his parka, sweater, and shirts, Charlie was finally able to examine David's arm. His entire upper arm from elbow to shoulder was swelling and turning a bruised purple color. Probing, Charlie gently squeezed the bruise with practiced fingers while softly singing.

"You're a lucky man, David," he said as he withdrew his hand. "Your arm's not broken, but it is badly bruised and it's gonna hurt like hell for a few hours. The branch smashed the big nerve that runs from your shoulder to your fingers, deadening it, which is why you couldn't move your arm. You'll start getting the feeling back in a minute, although from the looks of that bruise, you may wish it stayed numb."

While David dressed, Charlie pulled a tee-shirt out of his pack and fashioned it into a sling. Draping it around David's neck and placing his arm inside, Charlie pronounced him fit to travel.

"You're right," David said, wincing. "The feeling is coming back into my arm and it really aches, especially now that I've got this pack on."

"I only want to go about a mile into these next woods and then we're done for the day," Charlie told him.

Concerned about David's arm and wanting to make camp before the storm hit, Charlie hurried back to the bramble tangle and started burning his way through. A popping noise sounded and he whirled, expecting another attack from the Tintaen. Standing with his legs braced apart, David stood watching a magnesium flare scud low over the Tintaen Forest on the driving gale wind. The flare struck the crown of a Tintaen, causing it to burst into flame and start shrieking.

"David, that wasn't a very smart thing to do!" Charlie snapped. "The whole point of risking the Tintaen Forest was so we could hide and now you're shooting off flares while we're out in the open! He already knows where we went in, and unless we're very lucky, now he'll know where we came out! Short of hiring a sky writer, I can't think of a better way to announce where we are!"

Seething, Charlie turned away and started burning through the bramble thicket with the staff's fire. Frightened by his anger, Rachel and Gina followed silently behind him. Realizing the stupidity of his act, David mumbled, "Sorry," and took his place at the end of the file. Taking deep breaths to get a grip on his anger, Charlie wearily led them out of the far side of the bramble thicket, already regretting losing his temper. Still, it galled him that David could be so careless in such a dangerous situation.

So far they had been incredibly lucky. They had escaped and successfully ambushed the Dark One's pet terrors, the Lapushtan. The battle with the Tintaen could have easily gone against them or with far worse casualties than just poor Angus. The impact from the branch which had struck Rachel and David could have easily killed them both if the Tintaen's aim had been just a little truer.

To waste all their good fortune on a pointless act of revenge had been more than Charlie could bear and his temper had snapped. The flare might have gone unnoticed, it hadn't risen far above the trees, and visibility was poor and getting worse by the minute. The Tintaen's screams as it burned to death might have gone unheard. Somehow though Charlie doubted it and knew they'd been seen. Luck in his experience was unforgiving of human stupidity. Worried, he led them forward with long strides toward the cover of the forest just ahead. Neither he nor the others spotted the timber wolf lying on her belly three hundred yards downwind.

Attracted by the flare's light and the Tintaen's screams, she had gone to ground as soon as she had scented the humans and their dog. Ears pointing forward, she watched with keen yellow eyes as they entered the wood and disappeared. Ten minutes later, sure she was safe, the wolf rose and started northward with the long, ground-covering lope of her kind. He would be pleased and her reward would be great.

CHAPTER 44

STRUGGLING INTO CONSCIOUSNESS, she groaned at the white-hot agony pulsing down the right side of her skull. Her right eye refused to open and it felt like the entire right side of her head had been crushed in. Coughing weakly, she spat out a thick wad of phlegm and blood. A searing thunderbolt of pain coursed across her face as the jagged ends of her right cheekbone grated together.

Fully awake now, she realized that she was sitting upright in a chair. Or more accurately, confined sitting upright in a chair in a darkened room. Escape, she had to get out of here, get away from this awful place. Groaning at the pain it caused her, she tested the limits of her bonds. As the realization that she was tightly bound at the neck, elbows, wrists, waist, knees, and ankles sank in, she almost started screaming. Growing desperate, she tried to rock the chair over on its side and discovered that it was solidly attached to the floor. Taking a shallow breath, she leaned her head back and smacked her head against a wall. Fresh waves of pain surged through her skull and she almost lost consciousness again.

The sound of a key being inserted into a lock sounded off to her left. A door creaked open and her tormentor stepped through, turning on a light switch with an audible *click!*. Harsh fluorescent light lanced out, causing her good eye to tear and close. When she reopened her eye, a blurred figure was standing a few feet away, watching her. As she blinked the tears away, the menacing figure gradually came into focus. Ellen Talltrees was leaning against the rough dirt wall of her grandfather's root cellar, his double-barreled ten-gauge shotgun pointed at her captive.

"Hi there, you don't look like you're feeling too well," Ellen said. "Remember me? We met while I was in jail and you threatened to rape me."

"I'm a deputy sheriff," the thing bound to the chair said, "and you'd be well advised to release me immediately. You're in enough trouble as it is."

"No, I don't think so. You're one of that thing's creatures. And you're right; I am in enough trouble as it is. Enough so that I'd have to be out of my mind to turn you lose."

"I need a doctor," the thing whined. "You hurt me real bad. If I die, you're a murderer."

"No," Ellen snapped, getting angry now, "you don't need a doctor. You died as soon as that thing got hold of you and you can't murder something that's already dead."

"F-u-u-u-c-c-king bitch!" the creature roared, forked tongue lashing out as she struggled to free herself. "Kill you, kill you, kill you!"

With a cautious eye toward an uncertain future, Charlie had built the chair well. It was constructed of spruce 2 x 4's and 3/4 inch marine grade plywood fastened together with stainless steel hardware. The chair's four legs were each mounted in five gallon plastic buckets filled with cement and buried flush into the dirt floor. Stainless steel bolts, also mounted in buckets of cement, secured the chair's solid back to the wall. Yards, rolls, of duct tape secured the creature to the chair.

Despite the chair's sturdy construction and the yards of tape binding it, the creature's manic thrashing still caused the wood to groan alarmingly. Frightened, Ellen slid along the dirt wall. When she reached the door, her prisoner was still struggling and raving.

"Shut up and listen!" she yelled with no result other than the creature doubling its already considerable volume.

Hanging on for dear life, Ellen gently squeezed the shotgun's front trigger. The gun's recoil slammed her back into the wooden door as its thunder crashed through the small cellar. A basketball-sized chunk of dirt wall exploded a yard to the left of the creature, showering its head and shoulders with clods of dirt.

Ears ringing and shoulder aching, Ellen screamed, "Shut up or the next one goes through your head and that should be enough to kill even you, asshole!"

The creature immediately fell silent and watched her with wary, predatory eyes.

"I want to know what's happening to my grandfather and I want to know now," Ellen said, placing her finger on the shotgun's rear trigger.

The creature started ranting again, saw Ellen's finger tightening on the gun's rear trigger, and knew that it was a squeeze away from ending this existence.

"Don't hurt, don't hurt, I'll tell," it pleaded. "Don't think Master has found him yet, but don't know for sure. But he'll be found, can't escape this time."

Knowing this was as much truth as she was likely to get from the creature, Ellen relaxed her finger and pointed the shotgun at the ceiling. The thing immediately began ranting and struggling again. Exasperated, Ellen lowered the shotgun to hip level and her prisoner quieted again. Holding the heavy gun with one hand, she reached into the right hip pocket of her jeans and pulled out one of Charlie's medicine bags.

"Know what this is?" she asked, taking a step forward and thrusting the medicine bag toward the creature.

Her prisoner recoiled back in the chair, clearly frightened of the talisman.

"Good, I thought so," Ellen said. "But just in case you've forgotten some of the finer points, I'll refresh your memory. What I have in my hand is one of my grandfather's medicine bags. According to him, if you come near it, it will explode and kill you. Your boss and some of his stronger creatures can survive the explosion of one of these things at close range, but you can't. Short of sitting on a nuclear weapon and pulling the trigger, you couldn't get much deader. Got it?"

Snarling, the creature nodded its head, sending fine drops of spittle flying off its chin.

"Good, 'cause here's the deal. I'm leaving in a minute and I'm going to hang this medicine bag on the doorknob on this side. Even if you somehow manage to get loose, if you try to go through the door or get anywhere near it, the medicine bag will blow you clear to Hong Kong. If you continue making noise, I'm going to get on the other side of this seriously heavy door, throw the bag at you like a hand grenade, slam the door, and duck. Understand?"

The creature again nodded its understanding.

"Good, let's keep it that way," Ellen snapped. "I'll be around, so don't get any stupid ideas."

Leaving the light on, she hung the medicine bag on the doorknob, walked through the door, and slammed it closed behind her. Ignoring the creature's whining, she slid a pair of heavy steel bars across the door and snapped shut a padlock in the hasp at the end of each bar.

Turning away from the door, Ellen walked the two steps over to the ladder and climbed back up to the living room. Setting the shotgun down, she swung the trap door shut and locked it. Taking hold of a large braided rug, she dragged it across the wooden floor and covered the trap door. Grunting from the effort, she wrestled a five-foot long plank table over and centered it on the rug. Done, finally.

Walking across the room, Ellen collapsed on the couch, exhausted. As usual, her grandfather's prescience had been unerring, unnerving even. Although he had erred by twenty-four hours on when, he had predicted her arrest and subsequent bond. He had also foretold that the Dark One would send one of his pawns after her, probably while she was incarcerated and helpless. He had also predicted that once the pawn had her scent it would continue seeking her, so she had to kill it.

When Ellen saw the thing drive up to the cabin, she had fled, making sure that the creature saw her. Circling the cabin, she had hidden behind the woodpile with a hefty length of birch firewood in her hand. When the creature turned the corner and started easing along the cabin's rear wall, Ellen had charged, certain that it would sense her.

At the last second the creature had turned its head, but it was too late. Swinging with all of her might, Ellen had smashed the length of firewood down on the right side of the thing's skull. The creature had collapsed in a limp pile and she had hammered its skull three more times to make sure it was dead. The Trickster's human pawns died as soon as they were taken, her grandfather had explained, and it was merciful to kill their reanimated physical forms and allow the human spirit trapped within to pass on. Still, it made her stomach churn to physically abuse anything. After smashing the creature's skull for a fourth time, she had leaned over, hands on knees, and puked until her guts ached and her eyes watered.

The problem was the damn thing wouldn't die, it kept reviving. The first time it had happened, Ellen had shrieked mid-hurl, snatched up the birch log, and whopped it a couple of more times. The creature lay still for a minute, then started stirring and Ellen had beat it some more. After a little while it had started moving again, and she had beat it some more.

Teetering on the black edge of hysteria, Ellen had giggled helplessly. Here it was, mid-afternoon, and she was standing behind her grandfather's cabin pounding the ever-living shit out of a monster that refused to die. The cabin was isolated, but Charlie was a popular man and someone could stop by at any time. And her arm was getting tired and it was cold outside.

Deciding to risk the noise and finish it, Ellen had struck the creature a couple of more times and started toward the cabin's front door intending to get Charlie's shotgun. Three steps later a premonition had stopped her dead in her tracks.

"NO!" a voice inside Ellen's head had roared, frightening her. "YOU NEED IT ALIVE!"

Taking a deep breath, Ellen had fought to hold on to what few marbles she had left. There are, she told herself, no such goddamn things as premonitions, they're just old wives' tales, that's all.

"Yes," the voice inside her head had told her, "Just like there's no such thing as magic or monsters or—"

"Oh, all right, damn it, I'll keep it alive!" Ellen had wailed aloud. "Just give me a minute to think about what to do."

Jogging around the corner of the cabin, Ellen had slid to a stop in the front yard. Thin fingers of mist were creeping out of the trees lining the dirt track. The cabin's one door faced the track. If anybody drove by or walked out of the woods while she was dragging the creature inside, she would be caught for sure. Or —

"Quit diddlin' and get it done," she had told herself.

Trotting back around the cabin's corner, she had seen that the creature was up on its hands and knees. Shaking its injured head back and forth, the thing was attempting to rise. Amazed, Ellen stopped so quickly her knees hurt. It couldn't be, it was impossible, yet here the damn thing was trying to get up. Furious, Ellen had picked up her trusty length of birch firewood off the ground and attacked.

If she had beaten the creature earlier, by comparison this time Ellen inflicted a genuine-by-God-mojo on it. Grasping the length of firewood with both hands, she had hammered the thing's skull until her breath came in great whooping sobs and black spots danced in her vision. One final swing and the length of firewood had snapped off just above her hands.

Casting the butt of her club away, Ellen had swallowed her revulsion and grabbed the creature's arms. Digging in with both heels, she had pulled hard and almost went over flat on her ass. The creature had weighed next to nothing, no more than seventy-five pounds, if that. It was as if the evil inside it was devouring the creature from the inside out. Catching her balance, Ellen had easily dragged the thing to the corner of the cabin and laid it down against the rear wall.

Running out to the dirt track, Ellen had looked both ways but had seen and heard nothing. Jogging back to the cabin, she had climbed the porch steps and flung the front door open. Trotting back around the cabin, she had kneeled and grabbed the creature's arms again. Now for the hard part, the dicey part. After one last listen, Ellen had sprinted toward the cabin door, towing the unconscious creature behind her. The thing was so light that its body had left the ground as Ellen ran up the porch steps and pulled it through the doorway into the cabin. Slamming the door shut, Ellen had had locked it and leaned against it, breathing hard. A vehicle had approached from Frechette, stereo blasting out a country tune. The vehicle had slowed and then driven away, music fading away into silence. Squeezing her eyes shut, Ellen exhaled a long wheezing breath.

Hurrying now, afraid that the next vehicle would stop, Ellen had moved the heavy table, dragged back the rug, and opened the trapdoor. Turning, she had seen that the creature was stirring again. Picking the thing up by the heels, she had dropped it headfirst through the trap door to the dirt floor seven feet below. Landing with a wet crunching sound, the creature had ended up on its stomach with its head looking over its right shoulder.

Charlie always kept several rolls of duct tape, his In-Case-Everything-Else-Fails-Fixit, on a shelf near the wood stove. Sliding two rolls over each arm like bracelets, Ellen had climbed down the rickety ladder and dragged the creature into the cellar.

Originally, Charlie had excavated the space under the cabin as a still-room to distill his moonshine in. Later, after he quit drinking and his war with the Dark One intensified, he converted the space into a crude holding cell. Propping the creature up, Ellen began securing it to the reinforced chair with the duct tape. Fifteen minutes and many yards of tape later, she was finished.

Encased in grey shiny wrappings, the creature had resembled a pharaoh mummified by a demented hardware store clerk. Clicks and grating noises had emanated from inside the creature as its head suddenly spun around off its shoulder and faced front. Ellen had stood watching as a deep gash in its forehead closed and sealed, leaving no trace of a scar. The thing was healing and regenerating itself. The creature wasn't conscious yet, but it probably wouldn't be long before it was. Leaving the cellar, Ellen had secured the heavy door behind her and had hung the medicine bag on the doorknob as a precaution. Climbing back up the ladder, she had closed the trapdoor and concealed it with the rug and table.

And this had been the easy part.

Grabbing a change of clothes from her bag in the bedroom, Ellen had headed for the shower to wash off the creature's blood. Emerging clean a few minutes later, she had dressed in jeans, hiking boots, a heavy sweater, and a parka. Getting a nurse's scrub cap and two pairs of latex gloves from her bag, she had stuffed them into her coat pocket. Throwing her blood-stained clothes in a black plastic bag, she had picked up Charlie's flashlight from the shelf by the front door and walked outside.

Locking the front door behind her, she had walked around the cabin to the incinerator barrel out back.

Pausing, Ellen had slowly rotated through 360 degrees, watching, listening. Seeing and hearing nothing, she had placed the bag of soiled clothing in the bottom of the burn barrel. She then placed the two pieces of the club she had used earlier on top of the clothes. Opening the door to Charlie's rickety garden shed, she had paused a moment to glare at his scarecrow and the manure pile next to it. Through the shed's single window she had seen that her car was still parked out of sight along the back wall. Picking up a red jerry can, she had walked back to the incinerator.

Unscrewing the can's filler cap, she had poured about a quart of kerosene into the burn barrel. Digging in her hip pocket, she had pulled out a kitchen match, struck it on the barrel's metal rim, and flicked it inside. The puddled kerosene had whooshed into flame, leaping up into the night until Ellen dropped the perforated lid on the barrel. Returning the jerry can to the shed, she then headed off across the yard and suddenly stopped.

Swearing under her breath, Ellen ran back into the cabin, hoping that she could find what she needed. Opening a kitchen cupboard, she found the primary ingredient for her grandfather's infamous five-alarm chili sitting on the shelf. Making sure the lid was screwed on tight; she put the large plastic bottle of cayenne pepper in her coat pocket and walked back outside.

Approaching her prisoner's car, an elderly Taurus, Ellen had stopped while she was still ten feet away and considered her next moves. This next bit was tricky and there was no room at all for error, none. She could leave no traces of her presence if she hoped to escape detection. Making sure her hair was still tied back, she had pulled the surgical cap out of her pocket and put it on. Pulling on the latex gloves, she had walked up to the car, opened the driver's door and climbed behind the wheel. The keys were dangling from the ignition, which had made her sigh with relief. Placing her grandfather's flashlight on the passenger seat, she had seen her prisoner's purse sitting on the passenger-side floor-mat. Good, she would need it later.

Certain it was here somewhere, Ellen had begun groping around the driver's seat. While she had been whaling on the creature with the club, she was certain that she had smelled, ah, there it was. Her hand closed on a glass bottle wedged under the driver's seat and she pulled it out. Opening the door just enough to turn the dome light on, she had held the bottle up to the light and seen that it was a half-full fifth of cheap vodka.

Following a strong flash of intuition, Ellen had opened the glove box. Fishing through the clutter, she had retrieved a white metal Band-Aid box and opened it. Inside there was an amber vial filled with what looked to be about a gram of Colombia's finest, four rolled joints, and about half a dozen round white pills with an embossed triangle logo. Apparently her captive had a concrete monkey on its back the size of King Kong. All the better, it would help when the time came. Placing her finds next to the flashlight on the passenger's seat, Ellen had leaned back, taken a deep breath, and focused on what came next.

"Just a couple more things, darlin', and we're home and dry," she said aloud, encouraging herself, trying to make herself believe.

Turning the ignition key, she had waited for a long second before the engine finally chugged into reluctant life. Turning on the headlights, she had put the car in gear and headed toward Frechette. Although she had only two and a half miles to drive, it took Ellen the better part of a half hour to get there. Her route took her down various dirt and paved roads and through any number of dark intersections and unmarked turnings. Finally, twenty-four minutes after she had pulled out of Charlie's driveway, she arrived. Snowflakes started drifting down as she pulled into the gravel parking lot. A flashing neon sign mounted on a trailer proudly proclaimed:

Mother's Bar and Grill
All Nude Revue
Live Music Every Nite
If we ain't got it,
It would probably kill you anyway.

Mother's was reputedly the worst dive north of the Cities and south of Canada. Outside the city limits of Frechette proper, it was a popular watering hole with local construction and timber workers. Supposedly owned by a motorcycle gang, Mother's supported the local law enforcement community with never ending arrests for prostitution, drugs, violence, and assorted alcohol violations. Editorials were written, state and local politicians blustered, but nothing much ever seemed to change. Mother's rolled on down the years, dispensing alcohol and mayhem in equal measures. It was perfect for Ellen's purposes.

The tires started kicking up rattling volleys of gravel against the car's undercarriage and she had felt her stomach start churning. If anything was going to go wrong, if she was going to be seen and later identified, it would be in the next few minutes. Swallowing hard, tasting bile, Ellen had slowly driven past the low cinder block building housing the bar. A group of four men clustered around the front door shouted lewd remarks as she drove past but made no move to follow her.

Accelerating slightly, Ellen had driven around the side of the building and found what she was looking for. A dualie pickup truck was parked at the end of the lot near the woods. She had parked the Taurus on the truck's far side, concealing it from all but the very rear of the lot and the surrounding forest. Getting out of the car, she had peered into the truck and found it empty.

Climbing back into the car, she had picked up her prisoner's purse and upended it over the front seats, front floorboards, and the center console. Picking up the wallet, she had removed the thirty-five dollars inside and thrown the credit cards down on the passenger side floorboard. Throwing the now empty wallet down at her feet, she had picked up the amber vial and sprinkled the cocaine inside over the center console and floor-mounted transmission lever. The rolled joints had been thrown around the front seats and on top of the dashboard. The white pills with the triangle logo and the amber vial had been tossed in a backhanded spray across the rear seat.

Now for the finishing touch, the clincher. Picking up the bottle of vodka, Ellen had shaken it out in short spurts in a 180 degree arc from the windshield to the right side of the rear seat. Holding Charlie's flashlight out at arms' length over the center console, she had swung the empty bottle against it as hard as she could, shattering the glass. Reaching into her pocket, Ellen had pulled out a plastic baggie containing a clump of the creature's bloodstained hair. Pulling the hair out of the bag, she had pressed several strands of it onto the glass shards from the broken liquor bottle. Pulling a larger baggie out of her coat, she had put the smaller bag that had contained the bloody hair inside and then put the larger bag back in her pocket. There, finished. The perfect crime and the perfect crime scene, or so she hoped. Taking on last look around the car's interior, she had decided that it would do, it would have to.

Leaving the keys in the ignition, Ellen had gotten out of the car and sprinted for the cover of the woods carrying Charlie's flashlight. Twenty steps later, she had been swallowed by the dark woods. Footprints in the fresh falling snow marked her passage. Once safely inside the forest, she had halted and took several deep breaths, trying to stay calm.

Charlie's cabin was about two and a half miles to the east, about a forty-five minute walk through the woods. They'd come this way often when she was a teenager, out on long afternoon walks searching for wildflowers and mushrooms. The trail was pretty much flat and Ellen had been certain that she still remembered the way back to the cabin. Well, pretty certain anyway.

Slipping off the scrub cap and the surgical gloves, she had stuffed them into the plastic baggie in her parka pocket. Pulling on a knit watch cap and snowmobile gloves, she had pulled out the large bottle of cayenne pepper from her other pocket. Popping open the top, Ellen had spread a thick line of the fiery pepper across her footprints. Years ago Charlie had told her about the pepper trap, laughing and saying that it was an old Indian trick.

"Blossom," he had told her one day as they were out walking, "if you spread red pepper across your trail, a dog that's following your scent will run nose first into it and that's it for him. After that, he couldn't smell ammonia if you pumped it up his nose with a fire hose."

At the time, Ellen had thought it was a bizarre thing to say, cruel even. Now she wondered how he would know such a thing, what circumstances had caused him to learn it. One thing she did know for certain now was that her grandfather had never told her anything needlessly. Whatever the lesson he intended, she needed to remember it because it was important. Was he all right now, she had wondered, safe. He was old and sick and it was cold outside and—

"Stop this right now!" she had ordered herself, fighting back the tears. "This is no time to get mush-brained, so get a move on!"

Following her own command, Ellen had started jogging up the narrow trail. Ever since cobbling her plan of action together a couple of hours earlier, she had dreaded what came next. Although she had wandered these woods for years with her grandfather, she had never felt safe. Instead, surprisingly, her fear fell away and was replaced by a sense of wonder. The falling snow caught and reflected the flashlight's beam, illuminating the surrounding forest with an ethereal fairy light. The falling snow masked and softened the trees' forbidding outlines, transforming them into objects of surpassing natural beauty.

Slowing to a walk, Ellen gazed about, enraptured. For the first time she truly understood her grandfather's love for this place. Why despite the bigotry, the lack of opportunity, and the terrible winters he remained so firmly rooted to this land, the two intertwined in each other.

After a minute or two Ellen had shaken off her reverie and picked up her pace, but the feeling of delight had lingered. Every couple of hundred yards she would stop and pour another line of pepper across her tracks.

Fifteen minutes later she had come to a paved county road as expected. Pleased with her navigation so far, she had stepped behind a fir tree and looked up and down the road, looking and listening. Seeing and hearing nothing, she had taken a deep breath and sprinted across the road, her tracks standing out in bold relief against the fresh fallen snow. Reaching the cover of the woods on the far side of the road, Ellen turned and looked back at the telltale footprints. The snow was coming down harder now, slashing down the wind. With any luck her tracks should be drifted over within a half-hour or so.

Turning her back on the county road, Ellen had started back into the woods at a fast walk. Snow geysered as a brown monstrosity exploded into snorting life a yard in front of her toes and exploded upwards. Screaming in panic, Ellen stumbled backwards and fell flat on her back. The yearling whitetail buck leaped across her shins and bounded off across the road.

"Oh man," she sighed aloud, climbing to her feet. "What is it with me and this place anyway?"

Setting off up the path, Ellen had headed toward the cabin. Ten minutes later she stepped out into the clearing behind Charlie's storage shed. Surveying the ground for tracks and seeing none but her own, she had walked up to the incinerator and pulled the plastic baggie out of her pocket. Dropping the incriminating evidence into the burn barrel, she had splashed on some kerosene and threw in a lit match. Putting the lid back on the barrel, she had crossed the clearing and crept along the cabin's side wall, stopping at the front corner.

Taking a quick look around the corner, Ellen had seen that both the road and the front yard were empty. Running for the front door, she had stepped inside and had pulled it closed behind her. Locking it, she had leaned up against the worn wood, closed her eyes, and drawn in a long, ragged breath. Made it. Home, safe, and dry, at least so far. One last hard thing to do and then she could rest.

Pushing off the door, Ellen had crossed the room and taken the shotgun down off the wall pegs. Cracking the breech open, she had loaded the gun and had stuffed some spare shells into her pockets. Pulling the table and rug away from the trap door, she had climbed down and confronted her prisoner.

Now, a half-hour later, Ellen was lying on the couch, wrapped in a patchwork quilt made by Mary Redbird almost fifty years earlier. The shotgun was down on the floor within easy reach. From down below in the root cellar, she could faintly hear the creature babbling and cursing. Huddling under the quilt, she curled into a ball and tried hard not to cry. Failed. She couldn't help it, she was just so goddamned scared all the time. Her grandfather was gone and, and—. A few minutes later, Ellen calmed herself and lay with a forearm across her eyes. Soon after, she fell into an uneasy sleep peopled by dark phantoms in a white monochromatic landscape.

Outside, the low howling down off the Arctic Circle stalled just north of Frechette, spinning and gathering energy. For nearly half an hour, the wind veered counterclockwise around the compass. Steadying out of the north, the wind then rapidly increased to fifty miles an hour with higher gusts. It was going to, as they say in these parts, snow a bitch.

CHAPTER 45

LOOKING DOWN THE granite slope, he saw a grey shape battling its way upwards against the driving gale, struggling to maintain her footing on the slick, snow-covered stone.

"Protect!" The Wendigo ordered, snapping his massive fingers.

A bubble of green light formed around the she-wolf, sheltering her from the storm.

Sweeping his arm to one side, he commanded, "Clear!"

The snow lying on the slope ahead of the wolf vanished and the firmer footing let her increase her speed a little. Entering the crèche, she collapsed at the Dark One's feet. Blood flecked foam dripped from her muzzle and her breath came in great wheezing gasps.

"Tell me what you have seen, little sister," he said, gently stroking her cheeks and ears with a clawed finger.

The wolf opened her jaws to report but instead her head collapsed and thumped against the stone floor. Sensing her death was at hand and desperately needing her information, The Wendigo reached down and snapped her neck with a short flick of his finger.

"Know that in me you shall have eternal life," he said as the she-wolf sprang erect. "Now, little pretty, tell me what you have seen this day."

The wolf yapped and barked while the beast crouched next to her, listening intently. Finished reporting, she dropped to her belly and licked his foot. Reaching down, he scratched the top of her head with a curved talon.

"You have done well, I am pleased," he crooned, lovingly scratching her cheek and ears. "Go now and rest, we will speak later."

The Wendigo stood and watched as the wolf walked over to a distant corner of the crèche and lay down. As he had suspected, Redbird and his friends were somewhere just north of the Tintaen Forest. Earlier, the scrying stone had revealed a faint, sputtering light somewhere to the south, cloaked in the developing storm. Striding over to the creche's entrance, he stood looking out at the storm, thinking.

"Now here's a golden oldie from our rock n' roll vault," the Dark One said, mimicking a Top 40 DJ, "hasn't been heard in at least a millennia or two."

Inhaling, he loosed a low-frequency, whistling cry out into the depths of the winter storm. Repeating the strange cry twice more, he then turned his head, listened intently, and then began smiling.

"Hot damn!" he crowed. "Had me worried there for a second, thought I'd gone tone deaf."

Storming across the cavern, feet striking up sparks, he charged up to the Lapushtan still hanging in a row from the ceiling. Cocking his right leg back, he advanced down the row, kicking each of them in the head and sending them crashing up against the ceiling.

"Think you brainless assholes can do something right for a change if I give you another chance?" he roared.

Unable to speak without their tongues, the Lapushtan made various wet noises of assent. Snapping his fingers, the Dark One caused green fire to melt through their ankle shackles. Their necks and skulls fractured as they landed headfirst on the stone floor many feet below.

"Good, I'll see you in my office as soon as you get your shit together," he ordered, walking off and muttering. "Now there's an oxymoron if ever there was one!"

Approaching the dais, The Wendigo climbed up and took a seat on the carved stone throne. Picking up the scrying stone, he gently exhaled on the polished black surface. When the breath mist cleared, Charlie Redbird appeared in the mirror, leaning on his staff atop a wooded knoll. Wind driven snow whipped around his face and clung to his braids.

Aware of the Dark One's scrutiny, Charlie glared, lips curled in disdain. The scrying mirror began pulsing with blue light. Caught by surprise, The Wendigo juggled the smoking stone mirror from hand-to-hand, a magical hot potato. As his fingers began charring and blistering, he was forced to drop the fragile mirror, shattering it into myriad fragment against the hard stone floor. Enraged, he stomped down on the obsidian shards, grinding them to dust under his pounding feet. The mirror was irreplaceable, unique, and had been the only one of its kind left in existence. The magic that had created it had been lost long eons before he had even been summoned here.

Still, all was not lost. He recognized the hill where Old Redbird had been standing and knew the area well. Soon, after tonight, he wouldn't need the mirror anyway. His enemies would be dead and he would be loose in the world. His own native abilities would more than make up for the loss of the bauble.

"Red man, when I catch you tonight," The Wendigo roared, rage reigniting, "you will wish you burned with your whelps all those years ago!"

CHAPTER 46

LEANING HEAVILY ON his staff, Charlie stood atop the wooded knoll, snow blowing in his face, tired and annoyed. The destruction of the obsidian scrying mirror exasperated him no end. For decades he had known of the mirror's existence and coveted it for himself. Now it was gone, a priceless treasure destroyed forever.

A spasm seized Charlie's chest, causing him to bend at the waist, coughing hard. Expectorating a large wad of phlegm, he spit it on a nearby blackberry bush. Hunkering down, he distastefully examined the ropy green mass and noted the flecks of bright lung blood speckled throughout it. Whatever entered First Land tended to accelerate and his disease was no exception. They needed to hurry; his time was very short now.

Reaching into his pocket, Charlie pulled out a small doeskin bag and took out a healthy pinch of the medicinal herbs inside. Placing the mixture in his mouth, he slowly chewed, enjoying the astringent mint taste. A moment later the deep throbbing ache in his chest eased and he tongued the wet mass over between his cheek and gum.

As the pain eased, some of Charlie's fatigue lifted and his mental balance returned. Leaning on the staff, he threw back his head and laughed, delighting in the sound. Here he was with one foot in the grave and the other on a banana peel, and he was fussing about the destruction of a magical artifact that wasn't his to begin with. The Dark One had seen him and probably now knew their location. It was snowing to beat hell and getting worse by the minute. The human condition was, he reflected, often imbecilic to the point of total idiocy.

Looking down one side of the knoll, Charlie could see Rachel playing unsupervised in the snow twenty yards from their campsite. Down the slope on the other side, David was struggling to bury Angus, hampered by his bruised arm. Charlie wanted to simultaneously herd Rachel back to her mother and help David bury Angus before it got any later.

"Too many Indians and not enough chief," he thought, unable to decide which task had priority.

Spotting Rachel, Gina settled the issue by running over and fetching her. Protesting, Rachel was dragged back to the campsite by the hand, Gina lecturing her every step of the way. Smiling, Charlie turned away and carefully picked his way down the slope. Trenching tool in hand, David paused and silently watched him approach. Sliding the last three feet down the slope, Charlie braked to a halt with the aid of the staff.

"David, I have come to apologize," he said, wanting an end to the tension between them. "You did a very foolish, even dangerous thing, but I had no business speaking to you like that. Sometimes I am a cantankerous old man and I am truly sorry for what I said to you. I hope we can still be friends."

Ready to lash out, David suddenly felt the anger drain out of him.

"No, Charlie, you were right, it was a stupid damn thing to do," he replied. "I knew, know, better than to do something idiotic like that. I don't understand what got into me, Angus dying, this place, I just don't know. Of course we're still friends, at least I hope we are."

"It's First Land, David, it does strange things to people," Charlie told him, smiling a little. "Now why don't you let me help you dig this hole. It's not getting any warmer out here and we need to get back to camp because I don't like leaving Gina and Rachel alone."

Taking turns with the trenching tool, the two men soon had a hole four feet deep hacked out of the frozen soil. With Charlie helping, David lowered Angus' body down into the grave. Working quickly, they scraped the loose dirt back into the grave and covered it with fist sized rocks from the nearby stream bank.

"I'll wait over there for you, out of the wind," Charlie said, pointing at a small grove of silver birch trees. "We can walk around the hill to camp; I'm too damn old to be climbing up and down snow covered slopes in the dark."

As Charlie walked away, David dropped to his knees in the snow. Taking off his right glove, he reached down and placed his palm on the cold stones covering the grave. Standing under the shelter of the birch trees, Charlie sadly watched his friend's bowed back, the grief evident in his posture. Rising, David put on his glove and walked over to Charlie, feet kicking up clouds of snow.

Ten minutes later they walked into camp and found Rachel happily putting the finishing touches on a family of five snowmen. Three larger ones, one with braids made out of fallen spruce boughs, one child sized, and one that bore a slight resemblance to a dog. Reminded of his daughter Allison, David found himself smiling. Susie trotted up, happy to see him, and he reached down to scratch her ears.

Pleased by the upswing in his friend's move, Charlie said, "Good thing Gina started the fire and got dinner or else you'd be humping wood and cooking on top of everything else."

"Oh, yeah!" David laughed, remembering their wager. "Remind me never to bet against a wise old shaman when it comes to the weather."

"Especially one that hates lugging wood, although I really don't mind cooking," Charlie said.

After rounding up Rachel and Susie, they walked over to the fire and found that dinner was ready. Everyone ate the re-hydrated rations, but with no particular enthusiasm. Pulling his battered coffeepot out of his pack basket, Charlie filled it with water and regretfully added the last of the ground coffee from the small can. Putting the pot on the fire, he sat back and waited for it to brew.

Reaching for the small pan of steeping herbs near his right knee, Charlie portioned out three cups of his sleeping potion. After some good natured arm twisting, he persuaded them all to drink the foul brew but drank none himself. Shortly after, Rachel and Gina retreated into their tent, doubled up their sleeping bags, climbed inside, and fell asleep. Remaining outside, David talked to Charlie for a few minutes before the potion took effect. Barley able to keep his eyes open, he crawled inside their tent and went to sleep.

Pulling the coffee pot off the fire, Charlie poured a cup and wrapped the pot in a flannel shirt to keep it warm.

Carrying it over to their tent, he cleared the snow off a flat rock near the door and set the pot down. Dragging his sleeping bag to the door, Charlie arranged himself so that he was sitting cross-legged inside it with the bag draped up over his shoulders. Filling and lighting his pipe, he took a deep draw and chased it with a sip of coffee.

Surveying the terrain, Charlie considered what he had heard earlier. Or might have heard, it was impossible to tell with the wind whistling and howling through the trees. It was probably nothing to worry about, he concluded, just a good case of nerves. Still, getting careless wouldn't do, so he had skipped his dose of sleeping potion in order to stay alert and keep watch.

As the night wore on the blizzard worsened, wind-driven curtains of snow dropping visibility below fifty feet. Seemingly impervious to the wind, snow, and cold, Charlie sat wrapped in the sleeping bag, smoking and drinking now cold coffee. Occasionally he would drift off for a few minutes, walking the sleep paths of the elderly between yesterday and today. Mostly though he stayed awake, snow accumulating on the sleeping bag and the sliver of face he exposed. A totem, timeless, eternal.

CHAPTER 47

TURNING TO THE other Lapushtan standing in a line before him, Mancun started threading his way between them, lightly caressing each of their throats with the stone tomahawk as he passed.

"Hear me well, brothers and sisters," he hissed, voice barely audible in the raging storm. "No fuck-ups this time, none. I will not suffer the Master's torments on your behalf again. One mistake, one fuck-up from any of you, or all of you, it doesn't matter to me, and I will take your head and burn it. That will kill even you and send you on to the darkness beyond. Understand?"

Glaring, Mancun waited until each of his subordinates muttered assent and lowered their eyes.

"Good," he said, facial muscles bulging in rage. "We'll go over it one more time to make sure you get it right. Leave none of them alive; kill them on sight, if they're not already dead by the time you get there. No matter if they're alive or dead, take their heads to show the Master. That will prove to him that they're dead and that we have succeeded. The old shaman's staff is for me alone; call me as soon as you find it. If you touch the staff, you will answer both to me and the Master and the questions we will ask would make a stone scream for mercy. Got it?"

Catching each of their gazes, Mancun held it until each Lapushtan indicated his or her understanding. Satisfied, he turned and led them to the edge of a rock shelf a few yards away. A host of yellow-green eyes were looking up in silence at them. Bears, moose, lynx, deer, bobcats, foxes, even mink, were all waiting. Some of the animals were alive, others recently dead and reanimated for the occasion. Several packs of grey wolves, the Dark One's prize coursers, paced restlessly through the mob of animals.

All had answered The Wendigo's call, the Spell of Ralatan. The incantation bound all wild things that walked on four legs to his will. The spell was effective only during the dark hours of a single day a year. But this was the night of that day, Mancun reflected as he leaped into space, and it was more than sufficient for the task at hand. Landing thirty-five feet below, he tucked into a shoulder roll and somersaulted to his feet. Looking around, he saw the other Lapushtan climbing to their feet after leaping from the ledge above. Signaling the others forward with his tomahawk, he started southwards at a slow trot.

Flanking Mancun, the other Lapushtan advanced at the same pace, driving the herd of wildlife ahead of them. Gradually increasing their speed, they drove the animals downhill to the forest below. The herd remained silent as it advanced but still shook the earth and knocked down trees with the weight of its passage. The warmth of the animals' breath created a roiling fog bank which combined with the blowing snow decreased visibility to zero. Vision wasn't important now though, the Dark One and his Lapushtan pawns would provide all the guidance the herd needed.

Two hours later, Mancun raised his face to the howling storm and inhaled deeply, detecting the faint scent of wood smoke even amidst the zoo musk of the herd. They were close now, very close. Gesturing at the flanking Lapushtan to pick up the pace, he sprinted forward into the mob of wildlife. Reaching the front of the herd, he seized the left beam of a bull moose's antlers and vaulted onto the massive animal's back. The scent of wood smoke was stronger now, filling his senses, maddening him. Reaching forward, he seized the moose's ears and smashed its ribs with his powerful legs, urging the beast into a shambling gallop. Staring forward between the animal's antlers, Mancun spied his prey standing immobile at the base of a small hill.

Turning, Charlie shouted something to his companions, but they remained frozen, too frightened to flee. Blood lust surging, Mancun shrieked with joy as he slashed the moose's shoulder to the bone with the tomahawk, causing it to bellow in agony as it frantically reached top speed. The other Lapushtan were also mutilating the animals around them, causing the wounded beasts to stampede the rest of the herd in their panic and pain.

Charlie and the others watched in horror as the maddened herd of wildlife stampeded down-slope toward them. The new snow, now nearly eighteen inches deep, formed a powdery bow-wave six-feet tall at the front of the stampede, making it appear as if a mammalian avalanche was thundering down the hill.

Raising his tomahawk, Mancun charged down on Charlie Redbird. Howling in triumph, he swept down onto the flat, swinging the tomahawk sidearm with all of his might. Screaming, Charlie tried to leap aside but the flint blade bit deeply into the side of his neck, beheading him at the adam's apple.

The wave of stampeding animals broke over Rachel, Gina, and David, trampling them under tons of charging wildlife. The tiny clearing was obscured by a boiling cloud of powdery snow fifty feet tall, churned up by the maddened animals as they circled, making sure of their kills. When the beasts finally quieted and the snow settled back to the ground, nothing human was left alive in the clearing.

CHAPTER 48

EXPRESSION GRIM, CHARLIE stood concealed in the dark shadows of a towering blue spruce, observing the chaos in the clearing 150 yards away. Fifteen minutes earlier, he had been dozing wrapped in the sleeping bag when the staff fetched him a sharp crack over the right eye. Startled awake, forehead stinging and eye watering, he had grabbed the staff intending to smash it against a nearby rock.

"What in the hell do you think you're doing?" he had roared and then the staff had told him.

Rising as quickly as his old bones allowed, Charlie had tried to urge strength and speed into his sleep-numbed legs. Waking the others, he had gotten them moving toward the tree line at the edge of the small clearing. Bringing up the rear, he had managed to cast a glamour over Rachel's snowmen and reach the shelter of the trees just before Mancun crested the lip of the hill and started down the slope.

"Charlie, what are we going to do now?" David asked, fear evident in his voice.

Starting to reply, Charlie hesitated, thinking. They had escaped with little more than the clothes on their backs. He had his staff, pipe, and tobacco. David had his sidearm, a 40 caliber Glock. Rachel and Gina had dressed and fled, taking nothing with them. Everything else, all their gear, had been destroyed under by the stampeding wildlife. Even so, he refused to surrender. In a very real sense he was their chief and he would lead them forward for as long as he was able.

Turning to face his friends, Charlie said, "We have a little time yet, so let's sit down and talk for a minute."

Walking back further into the shelter of the trees, Charlie eased himself down onto the snowy ground. David and Susie sat facing him at his right knee, Gina at his left knee with Rachel in her lap. Filling his pipe, he coaxed it into life and took a satisfying mouthful of smoke.

Passing the pipe to David, he said, "I want you to take a little and hold it in your mouth. Don't try and inhale it like cigarette smoke or it will turn you inside out."

Taking a hesitant draw, David was surprised by the pleasant taste of the tobacco. Smiling a little, he handed the pipe back to Charlie. Gina was handed the pipe next, and she too was surprised by the smoke's smooth flavor.

"You too, Sugar," Charlie said to Rachel. "You are very much a part of our circle. Just a little bit though."

Gina nodded her reluctant approval and Rachel put the stem into her mouth and took a draw.

After a second, she said, "Good! Can I have some more?"

"No, honey," Charlie laughed, taking the pipe from her. "You've had enough."

Taking a long draw, Charlie held the smoke in his mouth for a moment and then exhaled a long, arcing plume of smoke over his friends' heads.

"So, our circle is joined in smoke, as is proper in times like these," he began. "What you just saw was an ancient spell called the Ralatan. For the dark hours of a single day a year, it causes all wild things that walk on four legs to seek the death of any human they can find. Right now, because they missed us a few minutes ago and there's nobody else available, the animal are kicking the hell out of the Lapushtan, the apparitions you saw herding them. When dawn comes in about three hours, the spell will end and the animals will revert back to their true natures.

"After sunrise, the Lapushtan will be free of the attacking animals and they will immediately start hunting for us, probably helped by packs of wolves. Our chances of escaping them are nearly non-existent. Even if we do, without our equipment we will probably die of exposure within forty-eight hours. Despite all this, it is my intention to continue on and try to finish what we started. If the rest of you don't want to go forward, I will understand and we will make our stand here."

"Not me, Charlie," David said. "I say we keep going. I didn't come this far just to give up when it gets hard and sit under a tree waiting to be butchered like a prize hog."

"I, I agree," Gina stammered. "I, I'm really scared and if we don't do something, those things will get us for sure. M-m-maybe something will happen and we can get away again."

"Me too, Grampa Charlie," Rachel chimed in. "I don't like it here, I'm scared of the monsters with the animals."

"Good, I'm very proud of all of you," Charlie said, pleased that they were all bearing up better than he had expected, especially Gina. "We are going to march as far and as fast as we can. All right then, let's go!"

Rising, Charlie led them north up a slight slope, chewing on the medicinal herbs to ease the ache in his chest as he walked. The fresh snow, drifted thigh-deep in spots, immediately started hindering their progress. Reaching the top of the knoll, he noticed that the storm was decreasing in severity and shuddered. The heart of the Arctic low that had spawned the blizzard was about to arrive and it was going to get brutally cold.

CHAPTER 49

WITH A PERFECTION honed by centuries of constant practice, Mancun had swung his tomahawk with the speed and power necessary to behead a human being. When the tomahawk's blade bit into the soft neck of Rachel's snowman, the unexpected lack of resistance cartwheeled him over the moose's head and under its hooves. The stampeding herd of wildlife thundered over him a second later, trampling him into green phosphorescent pulp.

The moose, its senses heightened and maddened by the Spell of Ralatan, returned seconds later to attack the hated two-legged thing again. For the next three hours, the massive animal, along with its brethren in the herd, stomped, clawed, and bit Mancun and the other Lapushtan every time their crushed bodies showed the slightest sign of reanimation.

At dawn's first light, a strange, warbling whistle rose from beneath the earth and a reddish cinnamon-colored mist formed over the small clearing. The Spell of Ralatan was over, releasing the creatures held in its thrall. The animals capable of doing so fled to the shelter of the surrounding forest. Some dropped dead of exhaustion while others stood immobile, too weary to move. A few, mainly predators, continued attacking the fallen Lapushtan.

Free of the crushing weight of multiple assailants, Mancun's flesh reknit itself within seconds in a series of liquid-sounding pops. Rolling to his feet, he seized a mink chewing on his lower lip and crushed it. He uttered a short, hooting cry and the flint tomahawk launched itself from snow bank thirty feet away and flew into his right hand. Gliding across the snow covered ground, he charged the bull moose that had tormented him so for the last few hours. The moose was near death from exhaustion, long ropes of bloody saliva hanging from his jaws as he struggled to breathe. Standing splay-legged with his head lowered, the animal made no effort to escape as Mancun closed.

Seizing the moose's right antler with his left hand, Mancun levered the animal's head up and swung his tomahawk overhand with his right. The stone blade smashed down and cleaved the moose's skull cleanly to the end of its muzzle. Dropping the tomahawk as its blade emerged dead center out of the animal's nose, he grabbed the two pieces of skull, one in each hand, and tore the moose's head from its neck.

Flinging the two pieces of skull aside, Mancun raised his clenched fists and howled his rage to the leaden sky. It was inconceivable, impossible, that he had failed again. Even before his sack dropped and his voice changed, he had always won, always dominated.

When he was thirteen, he had chased a whitetail buck down after a five-mile pursuit and killed it with his bare hands. At eighteen, now wielding the fearsome stone tomahawk, Mancun had stalked a grizzly bear for over a week. Waiting until the animal slept, he had crept up and struck off its head, his first beheading. For months he was in a black rage because it had taken him two strokes to decapitate the great bear. Its claws still hung on a leather thong around his neck, a constant reminder of the price of weakness. Between the ages of nineteen and twenty-seven, he had roamed the length and width of North and Central America, killing, raping, and plundering.

In late April of his twenty-seventh year, he had been camped in a small Aztec village in Northern Mexico. Having just finished slaughtering the inhabitants, he was waiting for a spit full of human livers to finish cooking and thinking about despoiling the four Aztec women tied together in the corner when the vision had struck.

In the flickering flames, Mancun had beheld himself seated on a throne of skulls, the ground around him soaked in blood. The sun was high in the sky, ringed in red, and a vast army stood silently awaiting his command. Frightened female captives stood to one side, certain of their fate. Off to the left in the mid-distance a small village stood, the one where he was born. His, all his, the vision promised, if he could arrive home by the time of golden leaves. Jolting awake, Mancun had been amazed to see the sun rising even though the livers were barely cooked. From the beginning, he had always known that he was special, meant for greatness on a grand scale. Now it was time to put idle pleasures behind him and assume the mantle of his life's work. But only if could reach the land of his birth before the leaves fell.

Springing to his feet, Mancun had drawn his tomahawk and leaped over the fire. Approaching the captive women, he had jerked each of their heads up by the hair and slit their throats. Working quickly, he had removed their livers, wrapped them in leaves, and put them in a tanned doeskin bag. After all, a man had to eat. Time was short, the road ahead was long, and every hour wasted hunting threatened to deny him his rightful destiny.

For months, seven days a week, eighteen hours out of every twenty-four, Mancun had traveled north-northeast at a ground-covering lope. Finally, on a drizzly afternoon in the third week of October 1403, he had crossed a small river into the country of his birth. Emaciated, he had jogged on, frantic at the lateness of the season.

Three miles from his home village, The Wendigo had struck. Leaping out from behind a birch tree, the monster had glared at him and then collapsed to the ground, convulsed with laughter. Mancun had frozen in place, cautious but not the least bit afraid.

"Mancun the Great, Mancun the Terrible, Mancun the scourge of all that lives," The Dark One mocked, thrashing about in helpless mirth. "You're nothin' but another scrawny, moth-eaten Indian and a goddamn slow Indian at that. I 'bout starved to death waiting for you to get here. Good thing I like ribs, 'cause that's all you got, you useless, skinny piece of shit."

Understanding had flooded Mancun and he now realized the magnitude of the deception played upon him. The endless days without food, the vast distances traveled, his vision of dominion, all for naught because of this babbling liar thrashing about on the ground in front of him. Shrieking, he had attacked and the battle was joined.

Despite his jeering tone, the Dark One had been impressed, near certain that he had chosen well. For over twenty minutes the two had fought, neither able to mortally wound the other. Finally, at minute twenty-four, The Wendigo had disemboweled Mancun with a slashing backhand blow and it was over.

No foe, before or since, had ever lasted near that long in combat with him. Positive that he had his man, the Dark One reanimated Mancun and repeated his earlier job offer. Delighted to discover that he had not been deceived, Mancun accepted immediately after emphasizing that but for his diminished physical state, the master-servant relationship would have been reversed. Vanity and all, The Wendigo had the lieutenant he needed. The darkest of the dark days had just begun.

Over time, Mancun had found his position with The Wendigo to be as advertised, even better in most regards. Pride yet intact, he still insisted that he had not been defeated but rather recruited, selected for a higher calling. Out of the vast legion over which his master held sway, including his fellow Lapushtan, he alone was fulfilled. He alone would not have returned to his former life if given an opportunity to do so, would resist such a change down to the core of his being.

The only fly in Mancun's ointment was his master's erratic temperament, which was variable to outright terrible even at the best of times. Given the current situation, he sourly reflected, His Nibs was going to have a hair up his ass the size of a redwood tree. And the Dark one would hold him, his chief lieutenant, responsible for the snug fit.

The consequences of another failure had been made clear before they had left the crèche the previous evening. If Redbird and the others escaped, he and the rest of the Lapushtan would be permanently disembodied and left to the not-so-tender-mercies of their many victims. Worse yet, as his master was well aware, he would have to spend eternity contemplating his own ineptitude.

So Mancun couldn't fail. Mustn't. And yet he was perilously close to doing just that. Again. He was six hundred and twenty three years old and he had never been beaten, not once. Elevated to a higher status once, but never defeated, not ever. And now, within forty-eight hours he had been defeated once and was dangerously close to having it happen again. It was simply beyond belief. Beaten by a dying old town Indian only fit for standing in front of a cigar store. Defeated by humanity's sheep, white people, two of them female, and one a child. Beaten. It was fucking inconceivable.

Screaming in frustration, Mancun leaped over the moose's sprawled body, accelerated, and caught a fleeing timber wolf by the tail. Flipping the wolf up into the air, he caught the animal by the throat on its way down and stared into its yellow eyes.

"Hear me, little grey brother," he hissed. "You and yours and me and mine are going hunting today. I want the old Indian and the three whites dead by afternoon. Fail me and I will find you and yours, tie you down, cook you tail first, and eat you while you're still alive. Understand?"

The wolf whined assent and Mancun flung it away from him. Scrambling upright, the wolf yapped to its kin, and they immediately began casting about in ever larger circles, searching for scent. A pack of wolves had once stolen a venison haunch from Mancun back in his human days. The punishment he had inflicted on the thieving animals was the same as the one he had just described. Over the course of eight successive days, he ran the offenders down, then cooked and devoured them while they were still alive. As a result, his current threat was perfectly credible, driving the wolves to hunt in a near panic.

Looking up, Mancun saw that it had almost stopped snowing and the sky was turning the flat gunmetal color that presages arctic cold. The weather would not seriously affect him or his allies, but it would hinder, maybe even kill, their prey. Whistling sharply, he signaled the other Lapushtan to line up in front of him. As before, he walked down the line stroking each of their throats with the stone tomahawk as he passed.

"Listen well," he said. "We are not going back until we take Redbird and the whites. Pay attention, don't lag, and stay close to the wolves. Remember, I want their heads and the shaman's staff is for me alone. For your own sakes, don't forget our earlier conversation about what will happen if you screw up."

Frightened of their leader, the other Lapushtan nodded their understanding. Turning away from them, Mancun watched the timber wolves scour the surrounding hills and forest. A long, undulating howl sounded a half-mile away to the northeast. Their prey's scent had been detected, their tracks cut. Motioning his subordinates to follow, Mancun started running toward the rising chorus of wolf voices. The hunt was on.

CHAPTER 50

HALFWAY UP A gentle hillside, they sat huddled around a small fire in the center of a small grove of birch saplings. The air temperature was thirty degrees below zero Fahrenheit slashing down a thirty-knot breeze straight out of the north, killing the fire's warmth. Legs numb, they had collapsed amongst the boulders, unable to continue on, starting to die of exposure.

Gina sat holding Rachel in her lap, weakly rocking her, trying to make her wake up. Arms locked across his chest, David sat shivering uncontrollably. Under his drawn up knees, Susie lay on her belly, still, near death. Staff resting across his thighs, Charlie sat smoking his pipe, watching the blue smoke billow down the wind before vanishing. It was now early afternoon and he had succeeded in keeping them moving for nearly eight hours and twenty miles. But even the staff's power had limits and now they were all starting to freeze to death. As the staff bearer Charlie was shielded to a greater degree, but now he could feel the icy daggers of the terrible cold starting to carve deep into his flesh. .

At first, Charlie had enjoyed some limited success at deceiving their pursuers. Using every deception learned in a long and dangerous life, he had confused and delayed their enemies for a few hours. But it was for naught. Three hours ago, the wild howls of a huge pack of wolves had erupted a few miles to the southeast. Desperate, he had pushed on until his friends had collapsed. The wolves' cries had been growing steadily louder as they sensed the nearness of their prey. Another few minutes, he guessed, no more than half an hour, and the wolves and their Lapushtan handlers would burst out of the woods and it would be over.

A long, screeching howl of pure agony forty-five minutes earlier had been Charlie's sole satisfaction for the day. The lead wolf, probably an alpha male by the sound, had charged muzzle first into the cayenne pepper trap he had laid down. The wolf's screams of agony had scaled up for well over a minute before being suddenly cut off by one of the Lapushtan. Despite their desperate situation, Charlie had stopped and laughed, savoring the moment. Frightened into obedience by tales of the grey scourge when he was a child, pursued by them on more than one occasion as an adult, he had hated wolves for his entire life. Still, it was only a small victory, one wolf out of at least a hundred. Far more intelligent than dogs with sharper senses and superior communications skills, the other wolves would be wary now and nearly impossible to fool or injure.

Taking a long draw on his pipe, Charlie heard it bubble, tasted tar, and knocked the cake out of the bowl. Wrapping the pipe up in its deerskin pouch, he stuffed it in his pocket and bleakly contemplated what came next. When the Lapushtan and the wolves began their final assault up the hill, he was going to kill his friends with the staff's power and start them on their long journey home.

And then, his last obligation fulfilled and the burden of leadership lifted, Charlie planned to stand and confront his enemies. Let them learn why the legend of the Redbird shamans echoed down the centuries; let them witness the full power of the staff unleashed. He would smite them, slaughter them until the very bones of the earth shook. When his enemies came near to taking him, as he knew they eventually would, Charlie planned to end his life, sending himself and hopefully the staff onwards. It would be his last battle and he was looking forward to it with a savage exultance.

A deep pain racked Charlie's chest and he spat out a large wad of bloody phlegm onto the snow. If his companions noticed, they gave no sign. Fingers cold and numb, he fished around in his pocket and withdrew the deerskin pouch containing the medicinal herbs. Popping some of the mixture into his mouth, he chewed rapidly, grateful for the near instant relief the herbs brought.

When Charlie looked up after replacing the pouch in his pocket, a wolf was standing at the forest's edge. Savoring the phlegm's blood scent, the animal stared at him for a long moment before loosing a short, yapping cry. Within a minute over a hundred other wolves had joined it. The Lapushtan strode out of the trees and stood waiting at the rear of the pack. The wolves in the center parted and slunk away to either side as a shadowy form sprinted out of the forest and took his place in front of them. Mancun.

"Old man,!" he roared out across the yards, voice filled with hate. "We have business together, you and I! I am going to kill and you are going to die!"

It was time. Leaning on his staff, Charlie rose, unable to feel his frozen legs. Glaring at Mancun, hating him, he summoned the power in the staff. Blue fire leaped and danced along its carved length as Charlie prepared himself for what lay ahead. Mancun shrieked and the wolf pack surged forward with the other Lapushtan bringing up the rear.

Weeping, tears freezing on his face, Charlie brought the blazing staff down to hip level. All he could see of his friends were the hats on the tops of their heads as they sat motionless with their faces down, already near death from the terrible cold. Feeling deeply ashamed at his gratitude for not having to look into their eyes as they died, Charlie amped up the staff and started to strike. A shadow flitted across the corner of his left eye and he felt a feather of displaced air sigh by his ear.

"*Too slow!*" Charlie told himself as he turned to face the threat. "*You've waited too long and now we all must pay.*"

CHAPTER 51

EXHAUSTED, ELLEN HAD slept until mid-morning. Hungry after such a long sleep, she had started cooking breakfast. While waiting for the cast-iron skillet to heat, she picked up the remote control lying on the kitchen counter and clicked the TV on. After channel surfing for a few seconds she found a local newscast and turned up the volume.

A head and shoulders shot of President Bill Clinton was replaced by a wide-angle shot of Mother's parking lot. The camera panned left and right, then zoomed in on a group of parked police vehicles near the lot's rear corner. Yellow crime scene tape was strung in a thirty-yard square centered on her prisoner's Ford Taurus. Several police officers were performing official looking tasks in and around the car.

The camera cut away and focused on an immaculately dressed female reporter holding a microphone. Why was it, Ellen wondered with irritable irreverence, that female tele-journalists were almost always beautiful white women who almost always sounded like they were about to reach orgasm as they reported the latest catastrophe of the day? It was almost as if there was a crew member kneeling just below the bottom frame of the picture with a microphone poking it —. Well, never mind.

"State and local law enforcement officials are investigating the mysterious disappearance of Coulter County Deputy Sherrif Elizabeth Railes," the reporter breathlessly gushed, eyes sparkling, cheeks rosy, perfect teeth glinting in the weak autumn sunlight. "Deputy Railes was last seen around eight o'clock last night driving into the parking lot of Mother's Bar just outside Frechette, which you can see directly behind me. Mother's is notorious throughout Northern Minnesota for many incidents and arrests involving drugs, prostitution, and violence. The bar is rumored to be owned by an out-of-state motorcycle gang with close ties to organized crime. Officers on the scene have said little beyond the fact that they fear foul play is involved."

Smiling vacuously, the reporter paused a second to breathe. Where, Ellen wondered, did the idiot store all the air necessary to rattle on so?

"Lieutenant David Kendricks, Public Information Officer for the Minnesota Bureau of Investigation would like to make the following statement to our viewer audience," the reporter said, now making stern eye contact with the camera.

The shot widened to show the reporter and the officer standing side-by-side, then pulled in tight on the lieutenant's face. Behind and to his right, a K-9 officer was slowly walking out of the woods leading a german shepherd dog on a leash. The animal was sneezing, coughing, and trying to bury its muzzle in the snow.

"Coulter County Sheriff's Deputy Elizabeth Railes left her workplace, The Coulter County Jail, yesterday morning at about eleven-thirty saying that she was sick with the flu," Officer Kendricks said. "When Deputy Railes failed to return home by ten in the evening, her roommate became concerned and called the Coulter County Jail to find out if she was working overtime. When informed that Ms. Railes had gone home sick at eleven-thirty in the morning, her roommate notified law enforcement.

"State and local law enforcement agencies began searching for Deputy Railes immediately. At approximately seven o'clock this morning her vehicle was discovered in the parking lot of Mother's Bar directly behind me. Although the Minnesota Bureau of Investigation will not discuss specific details of this case, we will go on the record and state that we fear violence was involved in Deputy Railes disappearance. Anyone who saw Deputy Railes after she left her workplace at eleven-thirty yesterday morning, has current knowledge of her whereabouts, or knows what may have happened to her is strongly encouraged to contact their nearest law enforcement agency immediately. Thank you."

A picture of Deputy Railes appeared on the screen above a pair of telephone numbers, one an 800 number.

"Elizabeth Railes is thirty-two years old, five feet, six inches tall, and weighs one hundred and thirty pounds," the reporter intoned from off screen. "She has green eyes and shoulder-length brown hair.

The picture of Deputy Railes was replaced by that of the reporter standing in front of Mother's parking lot.

"Ms. Railes is a nine-year veteran of the Coulter County Sheriff's Department," the reporter continued, sounding near tears. "She is well-liked in her home community of Thetford and is active in her church and in local charities. Her family, friends, and co-workers miss her. If you have any information concerning Elizabeth Railes' disappearance or current whereabouts, please contact the Minnesota Bureau of Investigation or one of your local law enforcement agencies. Back to you, Jim."

The camera switched back to the studio and Ellen turned off the television. Near laughter at the reporter's closing statement, she suddenly paused, thinking. Saddened, she realized that the reporter was probably right. Elizabeth Railes probably had been a nice person, albeit one with some very serious substance abuse problems. Now she wasn't even a person, just an empty husk animated by the evil that had stolen her life.

A strange pinging noise sounded behind Ellen and she became aware of the smell of overheated metal. Startled, she turned and saw the cast-iron skillet glowing cherry red and dancing with kinetic energy on the stove-eye. Crossing the kitchen, she shut the burner off. Putting on an oven mitt, she wrapped a heavy dish towel around the pan's handle and carried it outside. The skillet steamed and hissed when she thrust it into a snow bank by the front steps. While she was waiting for the pan to cool, she heard a car coming up the road and turned to look.

A Minnesota State Police cruiser drove by the cabin at a walking pace. The single officer inside stared out at her, head swiveling to keep her in view as the car advanced down the road. About the time Ellen was positive that he was going to pull over and stop, he accelerated hard toward Frechette, tires kicking up a spray of slushy dirt.

Watching him drive off, Ellen stood with her knees shaking and her arms locked across her chest. For the next half-hour, she remained outside waiting to see if the officer returned. Her feet were numb and her teeth chattering from the cold, but she couldn't retreat to the warmth inside. If the officer came back and stopped, she had to meet him outside in the yard. She couldn't risk letting him in or near the cabin because he might discover what was in the cellar.

Finally, Ellen decided that it was time to go inside or freeze where she stood. Picking up the skillet, she walked inside, grateful for the wave of heat that greeted her when she opened the door. Locking the door, she made sure that all of the curtains and blinds in the cabin were drawn and down.

The thing imprisoned in the cellar suddenly began howling, "H-e-e-e-l-l-l-p-p-p-!", its volume reaching an incredible level within seconds. Glassware was jumping on the kitchen shelves and the windows were rattling in their frames. Any passerby, even one in a car with the windows up and the radio on, would be able to hear the creature shrieking.

Frantic, Ellen pulled the rug and the table aside, grabbed the shotgun, and climbed down into the cellar. Fumbling with the padlocks, she finally got the door opened and entered the cellar. Something brushed her left foot and she lowered her head to look. Jarred loose from the doorknob by the creature's vocal shockwaves, her grandfather's medicine bag was lying on the dirt floor with its contents spilled out. Frightened by the loss of the bag but unwilling to retreat, Ellen raised the shotgun to her shoulder and took a step forward. Seeing her raise the gun, the creature immediately quieted, cutting off a howl on a protracted L. Dust hung thick in the cellar, sucked off the bare dirt walls and floor by the force of the thing's cries. The creature began muttering as the dusty air at the end of the cellar started shimmering with a putrescent green glow.

Not knowing what to expect, Ellen retreated a step as an image of her grandfather appeared in the green glimmer. Looking near frozen, he was standing on a snow covered hillside facing a pack of wolves. His posture bespoke weariness and defeat.

An apparition, a nightmare given form, strode to the front of the pack. Nearly seven feet tall and heavily muscled, he was a First American with a greased scalp-lock and blood-red eyes. Alternating streaks of red, yellow, and blue war paint highlighted the cruel lines and planes of his face. Despite the cold, he was wearing only a loincloth with fringed buckskin leggings. He was the personification of every fear, every night-terror, that had ever haunted the dark corners of the human psyche.

The warrior chopped a wicked looking stone tomahawk down and sent the pack of wolves charging forward. Other dimly seen apparitions herded the pack from the rear. Turning away from the attacking pack, her grandfather called blue fire out of his staff. Rachel, Gina, and David slowly came into view, huddled motionless in their parkas. Weeping, Charlie lowered the staff to hip level and Ellen knew that he had surrendered and that his death was near. The glimmer flickered and suddenly the image of her grandfather vanished.

"Wait, come back!" Ellen begged, crying, feet sliding on the loose dirt as she charged forward. "Don't hurt him, please don't!"

The glimmer sizzled and popped as The Wendigo materialized. Recognizing what she was seeing, Ellen started scrambling backwards. An arctic gale, foul with carrion stench, howled out of the glimmer and smashed her back against the heavy wooden door. The heavy shotgun slipped out of her hands and smashed down stock first on top of her right foot.

"Come back? Why, sugar, I've never been gone, just haven't been getting out much lately," the beast roared, leaning forward out of the glimmer. "But that's all gonna change real soon. Know what I mean, toots? As for your dear, sweet, old granddaddy, hurt is too weak a word for what I'm gonna to do to that prick."

Ellen slid down the rough wooden door and collapsed on the dirt floor. The beast continued extending itself out of the glimmer until it was leaning over her with talons raised.

"B-i-i-i-t-t-t-ch!" he shrieked, soaking her in a flood of fecal matter that spewed from his maw. "Some night soon, real soon, there's gonna be a knock on your door. And let me tell you, you red cunt, it ain't gonna be Big Ed and the Prize Patrol. It's gonna be me and my prize patrol and you're gonna be the prize, all hot, wet, and juicy. Know what I mean there, squaw?"

Finished speaking, the monster's voice degenerated into a howling bellow as his raised talons swept down. Shrieking, Ellen threw up her forearms to shield her face and rolled onto her right side, eyes squeezed shut. A slight breeze tickled her face, heralding the death blow. A few seconds passed before she muster the courage to open her eyes. Peering out from behind her crossed forearms, she discovered that the Dark One was gone, vanished. The only evidence of his presence was thick, swirling clouds of dust and the filth which caked her from head to toe.

A little while later, composure regained, Ellen lowered her hands and blew out a ragged breath. Well, that was it then. Her grandfather was dead, she was almost certain of it. Cry for him later, now it was time to tidy up the loose ends. Soonest begun, soonest done. Wearily climbing to her feet, Ellen picked up the shotgun and took aim at her prisoner's head.

"DON'T KILL IT!" a voice bellowed deep inside her mind, its volume making her cry out in pain. "YOU NEED IT ALIVE! I ALREADY TOLD YOU THIS ONCE! PAY ATTENTION WHEN I TELL YOU SOMETHING!"

After all she had been through over the last couple of days, Ellen wasn't about to quibble over a mere voice in her head.

"Okay, if you say so," she sighed, lowering the shotgun. "Although I don't know why, that thing is really dangerous and it wants to kill me. And you don't have to be so rude about it or talk so loud; you're giving me a migraine."

"Now, dearie, don't fuss so, it's unbecoming in such a pretty and accomplished young lady. You'll just have to trust your mother in this matter. After all, that's what mothers are for," a woman's dulcet voice whispered deep in her consciousness before vanishing in a soft *pop!* of white noise.

"Roger, over and out," Ellen muttered, backing out of the cellar door and locking it behind her.

Climbing up through the trapdoor, she set the shotgun down and concealed the opening with the rug and the table. Keeping the shotgun with her, she shuffled into the bathroom and stripped out of her filth-encrusted clothing. Stepping inside the shower stall, Ellen wedged herself into a corner and stood thinking while the hot water sluiced over her.

If her grandfather was dead, she didn't believe she would have been instructed by dear old Mom, whoever or whatever she was, to keep her prisoner alive. The question that begged an answer though was if he did somehow manage to get home, would she still be alive to see it?

CHAPTER 52

EVEN THOUGH HE knew the battle was already lost, Charlie whirled, staff blazing, determined to fight to the end. A red brick wall dropped to earth six inches from his nose and nearly crushed his toes. Ablaze with blue fire, the staff bounced harmlessly off the brickwork and knocked him sprawling. Laughing, Charlie scrambled back to his feet, knowing that he had to hurry. The sudden hundred degree rise in temperature had caused a thick fog to form, masking but not concealing the figures milling around the yard's perimeter.

Charlie reached the others in one long stride. Motionless, they were sitting huddled together, tendrils of fog rising off their frost-rimed bodies. Blue fire erupted as he tapped each of them gently on the head with the staff, causing them to seizure-thrash their way back to consciousness. Wincing, mentally apologizing for his rough treatment of them, Charlie jerked them to their feet.

"Listen to me now," he told them, "we don't have much time. We are going to the front door of this house and I am going to knock. When the door opens, I will do all the talking. You are to remain silent no matter what happens or else all is lost. Okay?"

Rachel, Gina, and David all slowly nodded their heads, still half-snared in the cold death sleep.

Taking Rachel from Gina's arms, he said, "Good, we must hurry before things change."

Leading them across the small front yard, Charlie noticed the fog roiling about ten yards to his right. Without missing a stride or pausing, he lowered the staff and sent an arc of blue fire scything down the length of the fog bank. The mist-shrouded figures shrieked in agony and the churning fog became still. Walking up the cracked sidewalk, Charlie felt the ground beneath his feet start trembling.

A basso sound of immense and rapidly accelerating power began emanating from the brick duplex house. Holding Rachel tight with his left arm, Charlie broke into shambling run. Climbing the three steps to the concrete stoop, he knocked on the front door in a peculiar rhythm. *Rap!* pause, *rap!, rap!,* and after an even longer pause, *rap!*.

As the sound of the last *rap!* faded, the thundering roar was suddenly cut off and the ground stopped shaking. Leaning on his staff, Charlie stood patiently waiting. Crowded close behind him on the narrow stoop, David stood with his arm protectively around Gina with Susie whimpering at his feet.

The front door flew open and a small pugnacious looking man stepped out of the house, crowding Charlie and the others back toward the edge of the stoop. Wearing polyester work pants and a plain white shirt, he was dressed like an average American blue-collar worker from an earlier era.

The man's face though was extraordinary. Veins pulsed and throbbed on both sides of his neck, which supported an out-thrust, rounded chin. Choleric spots flushed across both cheeks, accented by his white hair. His bright blue eyes bulged until it was a wonder they remained in his head. Death from terminal apoplexy appeared imminent, near certain.

"Yews, Redboid!" the man roared in a thick New York accent, thrusting a cold cigar clamped in his right hand at Charlie's chest for emphasis. "What are yews doin' heah? I told yews to stay away. Jeez, are yews thick or somethink?"

"Holy shit, it's, it's," David mumbled, unable to remember who the man was but certain that he had seen or met him before.

"What's dem woids comin' out of yews mouth, sonny?" the man bellowed, stepping forward. "Yews watch yews language, dares women and kids heah!"

Startled, David backed up a step, heels extending out into space. Arms windmilling, he started falling off the stoop. Just in time, Gina caught him around the waist and dragged him away from the edge.

"Now I've had about enough outta yews!" the man shouted, so angry that even his ears were flushed red. "Yews get outta hea—"

Anticipating the outburst, Charlie had already dropped to one knee, smacking David on the left instep with the staff as a not-so-subtle signal to be silent.

"Eldest," he interrupted, "we humbly apologize for intruding upon your privacy and beseech you for sanctuary, our need is dire."

"Sanctuary is granted, you and yours are welcome in my home," The Eldest replied in a clipped voice without a trace of accent. "May peace find you and remain with you always."

"And with you, Eldest," Charlie replied as he rose, relief evident in his voice.

"Well, come on in, don't just stand there all day," The Eldest said, turning and gesturing them toward the door. "Hurry up and, now jeez, wouldya lookit that."

Glancing where his finger pointed, they saw a pair of feet clothed in dirty red and white stockings protruding from beneath the wall next to the stoop. Turning to look, Gina caught a glimpse of The Eldest out of the corner of her right eye. Only it wasn't a man, but rather a huge creature covered in thick grey fur with large, oval black eyes.

"Somethin' botherin' yews there, Missus?" The Eldest asked, cheeks flushing, eyes starting to bulge.

Fearing another outburst, Gina violently shook her head in mute denial.

"Good, I wouldn't want nuthin' to be botherin' yews, now would I?" The Eldest said, the flush slowly leaving his cheeks. "Yews know, I got the worst luck wit this house. Dem feet stickin' outta there, do they belong to an ugly broad by any chance?"

"Yes, Eldest, her name was Mary LeFevre," Charlie answered. "And she was ugly from the inside out."

"See, last time, it was an ugly broad too," The Eldest told them. "There was a little girl and a tornado, well, never mind that anyway. I guess my homeowner's will cover it. Come on in now, I ain't got all day, ya know."

Opening the door, The Eldest gestured for them to enter. Still holding Rachel in the crook of his left arm, Charlie went in first with Gina following close behind. As David stepped forward, The Eldest shot an arm out, blocking him. Bumping into the out-thrust arm, David grunted in pain, his short-ribs feeling as if they'd just collided with a steel I-beam.

"What's dat now?" The Eldest asked, pointing down at Susie. "I'll have yews know I ain't runnin' no kennel heah."

"Eldest," David said, hoping that he was using the correct form of address, "that's my dog, Susie. I'm afraid that if I leave her out here, those things in the fog will kill her."

"Nah, won't happen, not in this neighborhood," The Eldest assured him, pointing his cigar around the yard. "So just go ahead and leave her out here. Now let's quit yappin' like a pair of old women hangin' over a backyard fence and go inside."

"S, sir, Eldest, if we can't come inside, would it be all right if we stayed here on your stoop for the night? That way I know she'll be safe and we won't be in your way."

Winding up for a major eruption, The Eldest suddenly deflated and said, "Okay there, Sonny, if you're that worried about the mutt, you can bring her inside. I won't have anybody bein' afraid around heah. But if she does her business in the house, you're cleaning it up. Unnerstand?"

Too relieved to speak, David just nodded and The Eldest waved him and Susie forward toward the door.

As David passed, he heard The Eldest mumble to himself, "Yews know, I just don't get it. Dem things, they don't talk, they can't sing or dance, they leave hair all ovah the place, they gotta be fed and watered, their messes gotta be picked up, and they die almost as soon as they're born. So why do they bother with the damn things?"

Entering the house, David saw the others standing in a small living room crowded with overstuffed furniture.

Slamming the door, The Eldest walked into the room, crowding it even further.

"Well, heah we all are," he announced cheerfully. "Make yewselves at home, we don't stand on formalities 'round heah. I gotta say though, yews people look a little rough and yews don't smell none too good either. Kinda rank, if yews know what I mean. If yews'd like to freshen up, and I really wish yews would, the bathrooms are at the top of the stairs ovah dare. Ladies to the right, gents to the right, dogs at the end of the hall.

Feeling embarrassed and self-conscious, Charlie and the others filed up the narrow stairway. As promised, a pair of doors marked "Ladies" and "Gents" stood at the top of the stairs. Barking happily, Susie vanished through a two-foot by two-foot swinging door at the end of the hall with a picture of a dog on it. Eying the narrow wooden door, David silently motioned for Charlie to enter.

"C'mon, David, there's more than enough room for both of us," Charlie said, taking him by the arm and steering him through the door.

Releasing David's arm, Charlie closed the door behind them. Turning, he found his friend staring in shock at the vast room stretching out in front of them. The white marble floor stretched away into the distance until it merged with the ceiling several miles away. Glazed ceramic tiles adorned soaring walls that rose to join a vaulted ceiling pierced with stained glass skylights many stories above their heads. Bath fixtures of every shape and description were scattered indiscriminately throughout the vast space.

"Can't be, not possible, the house isn't big enough, no house or structure is," David whispered, squeezing his eyes shut, hands balled into shaking fists by his side.

"Holy shit, things just keep getting weirder and weirder. I don't understand and I can't keep—"

"Easy, David, easy," Charlie said, putting an arm around his shoulders. "Everything's fine, you're perfectly safe, just hang in there. After we leave tomorrow, I'll explain everything. Just don't speak to The Eldest unless he speaks to you first and take no offense at anything he says or does or else he will deny us sanctuary and turn us out."

Drawing in a long breath, David held it for a long five count before slowly exhaling. Dredging up a wan smile, he nodded at Charlie and said, "Sorry, guess I was letting things get to me there for a second."

Squeezing his shoulder, Charlie smiled and headed off into the depths of the bathhouse. Needing to use the facilities, David approached a strange looking toilet, one of many standing on the open floor.

Heeding an intuitive flash, he asked, "A little privacy here, please?"

A blur of motion close to his face caused him to retreat a step and blink in reflex. When his vision steadied, David found himself standing enclosed in a luxurious private toilet stall paneled with oiled teak wood. Rails for the handicapped, four in all, were bolted to the door and formed a hollow square. A small first-aid kit and an emergency oxygen bottle were fastened to the door inside the square. The toilet paper holder, located in the traditional spot just to the right of the Great White Porcelain God, was decorated in a patriotic red, white, and blue motif. The first sheet of bath tissue showed a picture of the State of Alabama and where its capital, Montgomery, was located. Presumably the tissue would spool onto Wyoming and Cheyenne forty-nine sheets later before returning to Alabama and starting over.

The toilet was unique, alien even. Instead of the usual arrangement, the tank on this fixture sat in the center of the floor with the seat attached behind. A shiny brass plaque on the tank read, “In loving memory of Joseph Bramagh, inventor of the flush toilet, Pimlico, Great Britain, 1778."

Feeling uneasy but confronted with a undeniable need, David unbuckled and cautiously took a seat on the contraption. To his surprise, the seat was comfortable, cushy even. The tank rumbled and a slot opened in its top and extruded the sports section of the New York Times, headlines trumpeting Yankees pitcher Don Larson’s perfect outing in the fifth game of the 1956 World Series. A pair of speakers popped out of the sides of the tank and began delivering the Emergency Broadcasting System spiel in tinny tones. At the test’s conclusion, there was a brief moment of silence before Beethoven’s “Ode to Joy” soared out of the speakers, sounding as if a full symphony orchestra and choral section were present with David having the best seat in the house.

Near to bolting, David paused and slowly dropped back down on the seat. Crossing and resting his forearms on the tank’s top, he surprised himself by laughing. Enjoying the sound, realizing how much he had missed it, he kept on until he was roaring, tears rolling down his face. Events, at least in his estimation, had gotten so strange that there was nothing else to do but laugh. Besides which, he really liked Beethoven and he really had to go.

After reacquainting himself with a major chunk of American geography, David stood, finished. As he flushed the toilet and started walking away, Ludwig V.

was suddenly replaced by The Eldest's voice as the sports page and speakers retracted back into the toilet's tank.

"Now yews remembah to wash yews hands. And for cry-sakes, use some of that air freshener on the counter first, it smells like yews been eatin' enchiladas or some damn thing."

"Yes, Eldest, right away," David replied, determined to obey Charlie's instructions to the letter, but unable to keep himself from laughing.

Walking over to the vanity counter, he picked up a floral can of air freshener, pointed it, and squeezed the trigger. Thick billowing smoke, reeking of gardenias, spurted out of the can. Startled, David released the trigger, but the aerosol can continued spewing the noxious smoke. Coughing, eyes watering, he put the can back on the vanity counter and retreated out the door before he suffocated.

"Yews make sure yews wash dem mitts," The Eldest's chided from behind his back. "Yews ain't visitin' in France or Eye-tie Land or one of dem places where there ain't no in-doah plumbin', heah?"

Turning to face the voice, David beheld the toilet stall he had recently occupied being slowly levitated toward the ceiling, contrails of gardenia-scented smoke trailing in its wake.

"Well, whatta 'bout dem hands, Sonny!" The Eldest roared, startling David out of his reverie.

"Right away, Eldest," he replied, hustling over to the nearest sink. "Right now!"

As he twisted the ornate swan-shaped taps, the flowing water gurgled, "Sheesh, some people's kids, ya know, they just don't lissen, gotta tell 'em everything two, three times. Now when I was a kid," until fading away to the normal sound of running water. Taken aback but fearing another lecture, David grabbed a bar of soap off the counter, plunged his hands into the warm water and worked up a thick lather. Rinsing off, he dried his hands on a plush hand towel. Hanging the damp towel on a convenient rack, he turned away to search for a shower stall amid the myriad plumbing fixtures.

Ten feet away, another cubicle had materialized, door standing ajar. Stepping inside, he found a spa complete with all of the amenities. On the left, trapped behind a foggy glass door, cloud of steam rolled in a cedar-lined sauna. In the center of the cubicle there was a tiled, multi-nozzle shower with a padded bench to sit on. To the right, a large Jacuzzi tub was bubbling away. Stripping off his clothes as he went, David headed toward the shower.

A basso-profundo voice asked, “Master, would you like a massage before you bathe?”

Covering his groin with his shirt, David turned and found himself nose-to-chest with a giant of a man. Hastily backing up a couple of steps, he stopped and gaped in amazement at the spectacle. The loin-cloth clad giant wasn’t as broad as he was tall, but it was close.

“Excuse me for startling you, Master,” the giant boomed, flexing fingers the size of bratwursts. “I am Achmed, your masseuse. If you’ll step over here to the table, I will massage away the aches and pains in your back.

“Ungh, no thank you,” David replied, not wanting this monster near his back or any other part of his anatomy. “I really don’t like massages; it’s kind of like a phobia. But thank you for the offer; it’s very kind of you to ask.”

“Pardon me for disturbing you, Master David,” the masseuse said, sweeping down into a surprisingly graceful bow for such a huge man before turning away. "Perhaps another time."

Loosing a soft whistle of relief and shaking his head, David turned to enter the shower and collided with a petite Japanese woman. Yelping in alarm, he leaped back and became aware of three things.

First, having put down his shirt in anticipation of entering the shower, he was now naked. Second, the Asian woman in front of him was similarly attired. Third, she was beautiful, lovely, lush, exquisite, pick your superlative adjective, they were all applicable.

Opening his mouth to speak, David slammed his jaw shut when he realized that he didn't have a damn thing to say.

"Hello, David," she said, reaching out to take his hands. "My name is Nagamura Sachiko and I am your bath girl. Please step into the shower and I will bathe you."

"I, I, I, whoa there, hold up a minute," he stammered, freeing himself after a short struggle. "In my culture, we bathe alone. And besides which, I'm married."

"David, don't you like me? I can tell that you do, and it doesn't matter that you're married," she pouted, staring pointedly at his rapidly growing erection. "I can arrange for another bath girl if you like, perhaps a Greek or a Roman? Or maybe you would prefer a bath boy, I can—"

"No, no," he interrupted, covering his groin with his hands. "I like you just fine, you're lovely. And I don't want another girl and I'm not at all interested in boys. It's just that I'm married and I prefer to bathe alone."

"If you say so, David," she sighed, teardrops glistening at the corners of her almond-shaped eyes. "Goodbye for now, but I may look in on you later."

Casting one last longing look at his crotch, she swayed off toward the door. Mesmerized by the swing off her perfect buttocks, David stood watching her walk away. When she was finally gone from sight, David blew out a long breath, trying to clear her scent from her mind.

"Son, if they start giving out medals for moral fortitude, you damn sure ought to be first in line," he muttered as he adjusted the flow and temperature of the six shower nozzles.

Across the hall, Rachel and Gina were sitting together in a sunken marble tub awash in bubble bath with an armada of twelve multi-colored fluorescent ducklings swimming circles around them. Seventy-five feet away from David, Charlie was submerged up to his neck in a bubbling Jacuzzi, lit pipe hanging from the right corner of his mouth. In contrast to David's, theirs had been a self-service bathing experience.

Awaking from a short nap, David rose from the comfortable padded bench and shut off the water. Sticking his head out of the steamy shower stall, he made sure there weren't any other bath attendants lurking in the spa. Finding the room empty, he stepped out and toweled off, half-disappointed that the Japanese bath girl hadn't returned. Well, more than half, he grinned to himself. And what the hell, it sure didn't hurt to look, and what a look it had been.

His clothes were neatly folded and stacked on the changing bench, boots sitting on the floor below. Picking up his tee-shirt, he noticed that it had been laundered and wondered how long he had slept in the shower. As he started to put the shirt on, he noticed that it was inside out. Straightening out the shirt, he slipped it on and noticed that the pocket was on the wrong side. On a hunch he checked the rest of his clothes and discovered that while they too were freshly washed, everything was inside out with the buttons, snaps, and pockets all on the wrong sides.

Appreciative of the thoughtfulness of the act but a little aggravated, he took a seat on the bench and muttered, "Beware the frustrated Japanese bath girl's revenge."

Finally finished dressing, he reached down for his boots and stopped, groaning aloud. The boots had been cleaned, but they were laced in reverse, from the tops down toward the toes. An intricate chain-knot dangled at the end of each lace. It took him ten minutes, but David finally got the knots undone and re-laced the boots. Finished, he stood and walked out of the cubicle, hoping Charlie was somewhere nearby. As he left the spa, David heard a soft whistle. Charlie was standing about fifty feet away, waiting near the door.

As he walked up, Charlie asked, "Are you enjoying yourself, David?"

"Yeah, I am," he replied after a moment's thought. "At least so far."

"Good, I thought you would. We should go, I think I just heard Gina and Rachel in the hall."

Entering the narrow hallway, they found Rachel and Gina waiting for them. Susie was also there, wearing a new pink collar with a red bow.

"But Mommy," Rachel pleaded, near tears. "I like the baby duckies, why can't I play with them some more?"

"Because, honey, they're not yours, and they have to stay in the bathroom," Gina patiently told her. "Maybe the nice man will let you play with them later if you ask him nicely."

"'Kay," Rachel sniffed, signifying by her tone that she intended to do just that.

"We should go downstairs," Charlie told them. "We've been up here quite a while and it's not polite to keep our host waiting."

Filing down the stairs, they followed Charlie into the living room. Rising from his chair, The Eldest watched them enter the room. Smiling, he said, "There now, that's better, ain't it? Yews people was rank enough to offend the E, P, and A."

"Yes, Eldest, we feel much better, thank you," Charlie replied, unperturbed. "Please allow me to introduce my friends, it was rude of me not to do so earlier. May I present Mrs. Gina—"

"That's all right, Redboid, I don't really expect manners from yews anyhow, seein' as how yews an aborigine and all," The Eldest interrupted, waving his cigar in dismissal. "Besides which I already read all about yews in the pay-puh. See?"

Reaching down, The Eldest picked up a newspaper off the end table next to his chair. Unfolding it, he held the paper across his chest so they could see it. The paper's masthead identified it as "The Newly Yolked Times". Directly below, banner headlines proclaimed in marching block capitals, "REDBOID EXPEDITION FEARED LOST". Beneath the headline there was a color photo of Ellen Talltrees looking forlornly across the lake.

"I gotta say, Redboid, that if what the pay-puh here says is true, not that I believe anything I read in the pay-puh mind yews, this is a real bunch of losers yews is travelin' with. I been watchin' NCN and they say the same thing, not that I believe anything dem liberals on TV say. And now on top of everything else yews is lost, or at least seriously confused. Sheesh, I just don't know about yews people."

Pausing, The Eldest stepped forward and kneeled in front of Rachel.

"Say, I like yews though," he told her, smiling. "I useta have me a little girl, then she went and got married. Well, never mind that now. I'll bet yews hungry, ain'tcha sweetie?"

Not knowing what to make of this strange man, Rachel turned and hugged Gina's leg. Extending a forefinger, The Eldest reached out and gently touched the top of her head.

"I know, I know," he said, face wrinkled and scowling in concentration. "Yews like dem, dem cheerful foods that come in a box with the clown on it. Come on now, honey, yews gotta help me out heah, I can't figure it out all by myself."

"Happy Meal," Rachel said, eyes big, yearning plain in her voice.

"Well, yews wait just a minute, Missy, and I'll get yews one of dese Happy Meals," The Eldest said, rising to his feet. "Now if yews will just follow me, yews can take a seat in the dining room while I sees to dinnuh."

Stepping through a doorway off the living room, he gestured them forward with a grand sweep of his arms.

"Heah we are," he announced. "It's kinda homey, but we've enjoyed many a fine meal heah."

Spode china, Waterford crystal goblets, and Oneida sterling silver flatware glittered beneath a Tiffany chandelier on a linen-draped table set for French service. Classical music played softly from hidden speakers.

"Well, sit down, sit down," he said as he walked toward a door at the rear of the room. "Shouldn't be but a minute, supposed to be fast food, ain't it?"

As The Eldest opened the door, a wave of humid air fragrant with the scent of exotic foods filled the dining room. A clattering metallic din and multi-lingual shouting signaled the presence of an international *brigade de cuisine* working at full tilt. As the door swung shut behind him, the olfactory and auditory assault was suddenly cut off and the room became quiet again.

Struggling against the thick Persian carpet, David pulled out a pair of chairs away from the table and seated Rachel and Gina. Seating himself, he opened his mouth to speak but Charlie silenced both he and Gina with the cautionary wave of a hand.

"Tomorrow after we leave, I will explain as best I can, but not before," Charlie told them.

"How'd you know I was going to ask a question?" David asked, puzzled.

"Because you had that blank, inquiring look I've come to know and love so well," Charlie replied, grinning.

Embarrassed, David hung his head and laughed, but otherwise kept silent. The Eldest's minute turned into a half-hour, making them all fidgety and a little irritable. As hungry children are apt to do, Rachel was getting fussy, near tears. A noise near her feet caught her attention, causing her to look down. A half-dozen multi-colored ducklings were gathered around the front legs of her chair. Laughing in delight, hunger forgotten, she eeled down out of her chair.

Looking up, Rachel noticed something strange. There was no tablecloth or dishes above her head, only a clear table with a bunch of funny lines and shapes on it with the adults sitting around the edges. Peeking out from under the table into the dining room, she saw a console with chairs, computers, and flashing lights, just like on *Star Trek*. Cool! Rachel thought about telling her mother about her discoveries but decided she'd rather play with the ducklings.

"Here we are, dinnuh is soived," The Eldest announced, staggering through the swinging door, face and chest hidden behind a serving tray stacked high with plates and silver room-service covers. "Yew know, dem damn chefs, they can't cook anything American, at least not in a hurry. And then if it ain't the cookin' sherry, it's the scotch, or dem hoibs they grow in the garden, or da waitresses, or who knows what all. Anyways, I apologize for dinnuh bein' late, ain't good mannuhs, if yews know what I mean."

Seeing The Eldest bringing the overloaded service tray in for an emergency landing, Charlie and David hastily cleared a spot in the middle of the table. Narrowly avoiding Gina's head, he half-dropped, half-slid the tray onto the table.

"Dare we are, all ready to eat," he said. "But there's one thing we gotta do foist."

Removing the top room-service cover with a flourish, he revealed a cut-crystal finger bowl filled with warm, soapy water with red rose petals floating on top. The bowl was sitting on top of a hand-towel embroidered with the gothic initials "RT".

"Dis heah is foah the young missy," he explained, carrying the plate, towel, and finger-bowl around the table. "She's gotta wash dem mitts aftuh playin' with dem barnyard animals or else she won't be fit to eat with civilized people."

Holding Rachel's wrists, Gina gently dipped her hands into the warm, sudsy water while The Eldest held the plate and bowl for her. Finished, Rachel took her hands out of the water and Gina carefully dried them. Pacing the damp towel back on the plate, Gina smiled up at him, mindful of Charlie's injunction not to speak unless spoken to.

"Dare now, dat's bettuh," he proclaimed, walking back around the table. "Now wees ready to eat like civilized folks."

Rounding the table, The Eldest covered the plate and bowl with the room-service cover. Flicking his wrist, he sent the covered plate flying toward the far wall like a Frisbee. A small service window slid open and the covered plate sailed through with a couple of inches to spare on each side. As David and the others winced and sat waiting for the inevitable crash, the service window closed and the room remained silent.

"My bounty be yours in time of famine," The Eldest said, using the accent-less, clipped tone he reserved for formal occasions, "and water in time of drought."

"And you also, Eldest, now and always," Charlie replied, bowing his head.

"Let's eat, I'm starvin', yews must be too," The Eldest said, uncovering and passing out plates.

Cardboard boxes and paper wrappers in bright primary colors were neatly stacked on each plate. Pouring carefully, The Eldest emptied Styrofoam drink containers into his guests' Waterford goblets. The last dish he uncovered was for Susie, a deep bowl with orange and blue tissue paper stretched across the top. Their host had just taken his seat when a great crash sounded from the front of the house.

"Surrender your guests, old fuck, and we will let you live!" a voice roared.

"Mancun!" Charlie said in disbelief.

Rachel crawled into Gina's lap and started crying. Leaping to his feet, David sent his chair crashing over onto its back. Ears back and belly on the ground, Susie crouched snarling between his feet.

"None need fear who are granted sanctuary in my home," The Eldest said as he rose. "So say I, The Eldest, who was the first of all things in the beginning and who shall be the last of all things in the end."

Repeated tremors shook the house as the front door was battered down. The voices of Lapushtan and wolf joined together in a soaring chorus of malevolent glee.

"I think not!" The Eldest said, his entire head and neck flushing bright red. "Dese people just doan know when theys well off!"

The Eldest's strides looked slow, almost a caricature of a bulldog roll. Yet a blink later he was dressed in plaid CPO jacket with a porkpie hat crammed down on his head, unlit cigar hanging down from the corner of his mouth. And then he vanished.

"Charlie, we have to help him!" David yelled, starting to run toward the front of the house. "They'll kill—"

"Steady now!" Charlie said, rapping his staff on the carpet for emphasis and hooking David by the arm to stop him. "A close-quarter battle with the Lapushtan is out of our league. If The Eldest falls, we can make our stand here as well as anywhere, so let's just wait and see what happens."

The triumphant howls of malicious glee were suddenly cut off and all was silent for a few seconds. The initial shrieks of agony were all from the Lapushtan, but soon wailing wolf voices joined in. Underlying the screams was a throbbing basso roar of pure fury. Soon the cries faded away into the distance until only occasional muted shrieks were heard. A few minutes later The Eldest startled them by materializing in the doorway and then stalking across the room.

"Excuse my bad manners in leavin' so abrupt like," he said, halting by the table. "But dem damn La Putzes make me forget myself. I tole them a million times to stay away from heah, but dey doan lissen. Yew shouldn't worry 'bout dem anymore, I'm gettin' old, but I can still run dem off on da worst day I ever had.

"By the way dare, Redboid, I'd appreciate it if yews'd lean yews shillelagh against da wall ovah dare. Aladdin and his dimwit siblin's woiked themselves cross-eyed sewin' the zillion knot in dis heah cah-put, so I'd appreciate it if you quit thumpin' on it wit dat hoo-doo stick of yours. Now, if yews'll excuse me again, I gotta go wash my hands so dat I'll be fit to associate wit civilized people."

Rising, Charlie crossed the room and leaned his staff against the far wall. At the same moment, The Eldest strode down the length of the dining room and entered the kitchen. As soon as the door swung shut behind him, he re-emerged and headed back toward the dining room table. The two arrived at the table together, Charlie standing and politely waiting for his host to sit down.

"Sit down, sit down," The Eldest said. "Yews go ahead and eat now, don't wait on me, we doan stand on ceremony 'round heah."

Despite the delay the food was still hot. Upon opening the bright cardboard boxes, they noticed that while the food smelled delicious, its preparation and presentation were bizarre. The breading for the chicken nuggets and the cheese for the burgers were stuffed inside of those items. The french fries stood in neat blocks, bristling like scrub brushes. The soda had inverted with the ice, creating pools of clear liquid at the top of their goblets.

Picking up a burger, David thought he felt it move in his hand. Glancing down, he caught a glimpse of tubular red-brown shapes writhing in his hand. Repulsed, he started to drop the slimy mess, but he blinked and the burger returned. Hungry, he decided he was going to eat no matter what was on the menu. Raising the burger to his mouth, he took an exploratory bite and found that it was delicious.

"Everything all right dare, Counselor?" The Eldest inquired. "Reason I ask is dat yews never can tell what dem foreign chefs of mine will put in somethin'. I mean yews wouldn't believe some of da things dem people eat."

"Yes, Eldest, the food is wonderful" David replied.

The cuisine was excellent and apparently never ending. When something was consumed by one of the diners it was somehow immediately replaced, creating a never ending supply of food and drink. So they ate, and ate, and then ate some more. It took a while but finally they could eat no more.

"Well, I gotta say that was a fine meal if I do say so myself, and I do," The Eldest said. "Well, yews must be tired, so I think we'll call it a night. Bedrooms for all is upstairs, you'll find 'em easy enough.

"Davy, yews make sure yews waters dat mutt of yours unless yews wanna be scrubbin' all night. Yews'll see where once yews is upstairs.

"Redboid, and I guess the rest of yews too, we'll have us a serious discussion about current events tomorrow after breakfast. Good night, sleep well, and I'll sees yews in da mornin'.

With no pyrotechnics or other theatrics, The Eldest vanished. One second he was there and the next he was gone.

"I think we should follow our host's example," Charlie said, choking back a huge yawn. "I don't know about anybody else, but I can't stay awake much longer."

While Charlie crossed the room to collect his staff, David picked up Rachel, fast asleep in her mother's lap. After climbing the stairs, they easily found the bedrooms. An engraved brass plate in the center of a door on the lefthand side of the hallway read, "Mrs. Gina Tolliver, BA, MA, and Miss Rachel Tolliver". Directly across the hall, a similar plaque in the center of another door proclaimed, "Charles Lantot Redbird, Shaman, Healer, and Artist". The plaque on the door next to it read, "Mr. David Adam Garrison, Esq., BA, MBA, JD, and Susie, female canine companion of indeterminate education". A bright neon sign in the center of a door at the far end of the hall announced, "Dogs Watered Here."

Handing Rachel to her mother, David said good night and led Susie down the hall. Following her through the neon-lit doorway, he found himself in a small park. Lush green grass sloped downhill to a small oval-shaped pond. Various varieties of trees, shrubs, and flowers were planted in decorative groupings throughout the park. Different sizes of stones and rocks were also scattered about, everything from small pebbles to large granite boulders. Mailboxes and fire hydrants from many nations stood lined up in orderly rows. Susie hesitated, then introduced herself to a bed of red tulips planted around the base of a French mailbox.

"Good choice, dats a smart dog," The Eldest said from behind David's shoulder, startling him. "Never met a Frenchy yet that I like, arrogant bastids they are. And sheesh, da things dem people eat."

Sticking a cigar into his mouth, The Eldest pulled a match from his pocket and lit it on a thumbnail. Inhaling, he rotated the cigar between his fingers, toasting it until it was drawing evenly.

"I want yews to know, counselor, that if it were possible for me to lift the burden of what lays ahead from yews, I would," he continued, face solemn and wreathed in smoke. "But I can't, nobody can. Yews is a good boy, Davy, so I think yews'll be fine. But ya know, yews really should go easier on yewself. Yews can't be responsible for everything that goes wrong in the woild. Nobody can, not yews, not even me for dat mattuh."

"I, I, thank you, Eldest," David said, suddenly feeling near tears.

"Yews a good boy, Davey, a fine boy," The Eldest repeated, reaching out and squeezing his shoulder.

And then he was gone, the only evidence of his presence a lingering cloud of pungent cigar smoke. Bone weary, David whistled for Susie and headed toward the door. Letting Susie out into the hallway, he closed the door and watched it transmute itself into just another section of paneled wall. Shaking his head, he led Susie down the hall to their bedroom. Upon entering the room, he found a luxurious suite complete with sitting room, bedroom, and bath.

An old-fashioned nightshirt and tasseled nightcap were laid out on the bed. Getting undressed, David pulled the nightshirt over his head. Dubious about the cap, he examined it for a few seconds and then decided he would try it on. Placing the cap on his head, he looked at his reflection in the mirror. He decided that it looked jaunty, sporty even.

Yawning until his jaws popped, David swung his legs up on the bed and climbed under the covers. Propping himself up on an elbow, he reached out and turned off the lamp on the bedside table. Smiling in anticipation, he propelled his head toward the pillow with the attitude of man intent on some serious slumber.

Colored novae whirled in his vision, his eyes teared, and his ears rang from the pain of smacking his skull against the softball-sized lump of chocolate laying on the pillow. Groaning, he grabbed the piece of chocolate and placed it on the bedside table. Rubbing the back of his head, David lay down, rolled over on his side, and fell deeply asleep within seconds.

CHAPTER 53

THE CREATURE THAT had been Deputy Sheriff Elizabeth Railes hummed happily. Slipping an arm under the duct tape, it reached up and scratched its nose, dislodging large flakes of dead skin. Finished scratching, it reinserted its arm back between the chair's arm and the loops of duct tape. Its flesh was too far decomposed now for the tape to grip it. It sat in the chair now by choice, not by coercion. Be still, it had been told, and wait. Don't reveal your new freedom, pretend you're still bound. Be patient, it had been told, and the woman upstairs will be yours.

Nostrils distended, forked tongue flickering, it savored the scent of the woman sleeping a few feet above on the other side of the plank ceiling. It could taste the light taint of Ellen's sweat and the slight cinnamon aroma of her skin. Underlying it all was the musk of Ellen's sex, a mélange of wet rich odors akin to fresh plowed earth in the spring.

Rocking slightly, the creature sat wallowing in the scents drifting down from the ceiling. The woman would be its soon and the pleasures then would far transcend the olfactory. Soon, it had been told, very soon indeed.

CHAPTER 54

TAKING A SEAT on the polished throne, the Dark One looked down at the bloody figure lying on the floor. The Lapushtan, his prize terrors, were gone, destroyed. All save Mancun laying a few feet below and he was so badly wounded that he probably wouldn't survive.

Boarding The Eldest's ship had been a bold but foolish stratagem. The Lapushtan had broken through the forward cargo hatch hoping to kill Redbird and the whites, seize the staff, and somehow escape in the ensuing confusion. But as soon as the hatch was breached The Eldest had attacked, unveiled in his true form.

Anne Fullerton and John Lowery died first on the access ladder directly below the breached cargo hatch. Jasper Finley had gotten another ten feet before he too was destroyed. Mancun and Pierre LaCroix, the fleetest of their brethren and sisters, were fifty-feet away from the bottom of the access ladder when The Eldest caught up with them. Hearing his footsteps closing on them, knowing that death was near, Mancun had slowed a little. Red eyes bulging in terror, LaCroix had started to pass him when Mancun lashed out with his right arm and sent his longtime lieutenant crashing to the ground. Legs pounding, Mancun had accelerated and hit full speed, running for his life.

Six strides later he was back in the shelter of the forest. For long centuries nothing that ran on two legs or four had been swifter, and none knew these forests better than he. A blur of motion a yard ahead caught his attention but it was too late.

Bones and tissue pulped with a wet cracking sound as Mancun's face smashed into The Eldest's iron right fist. As Mancun's momentum continued driving him forward, The Eldest caught him around the waist, flipped him over, and pile-drove him skull first into the ground. Removing the flint tomahawk from Mancun's belt, The Eldest then used the blunt end to systematically break every bone in the warrior's body. Deaf to the cries of centuries of victims, Mancun now shrieked his torment to the uncaring sky and begged for release from pain.

Flipping the tomahawk end-for-end, The Eldest caught it by the handle, blade now facing forward. Kneeling, he jerked Mancun's loincloth down and slashed open a six-inch incision in his lower belly. Reaching down with his free hand, The Eldest fished around in the bloody incision and withdrew a slimy loop of intestine. Raising the loop of gut a few inches, he swung the tomahawk down in a smooth arc and cleanly severed it. Allowing the bowel end to fall, he then pulled out fifteen feet of intestines out of the incision and coiled the ropy mass on Mancun's chest. Finished, he stood and dropped the stone tomahawk on top of the pile of viscera.

"Sheesh, yews know, I just don't know how these people tolerate havin' all that filth inside 'em," he muttered, wiping the gore off his hands by dragging them through the snow. “Doan seem very sanitary, if yews ask me.”

Swinging his right leg back, he planted a solid kick to the side of Mancun’s skull.

“Look at me, Sonny, I know for a fact yews ain’t dead, yews ain’t made that way,” The Eldest said. “I’d be more than happy to see yews get there, but She says the balance must be maintained and dat’s dat. But that doan mean I can’t get yews attention.”

Turned his head, Mancun focused his vision on the vast grey figure towering over him.

“Mancun Tehostel, you are a cad, a scoundrel, and an im-be-cile of the first order,” The Eldest intoned in Oxford-accented English, sounding like an Old Bailey jurist. “You are hereby arrested, charged, tried, and convicted of multiple counts of murder, rape, torture, cannibalism, and of being a general law-breaking pain-in-the-ass. Your sentence having already been served, you are hereby ordered released into the custody of your employer, perfidious scum that he is.”

Pounding his right foot against the ground, Mancun gurgled once and lost consciousness.

“Oh jeez, I forgot,” The Eldest declared, snapping his fingers. “Yews’ll be needin’ a ride home seein’ as how, if yews’ll excuse the observation, yews ain’t exactly ambulatory at the moment.

Cupping his hands around his mouth, The Eldest uttered a pair of low, hooting cries. In response, a similar call drifted down the wind followed by a distant crashing in the underbrush. He repeated the strange call again and again received an immediate response. The crashing in the underbrush intensified and then quieted as a large bull moose trotted into the clearing.

"Well, I gotta say, Bullwinkle," The Eldest said, reaching out and gently scratching the animal's muzzle, "yews ain't the handsomest or smartest creature on the Great Mother, but yews is one of the strongest. In a minute heah I'm gonna load that meatbag ovuh dare on da ground onto yews back. Den I want yews to deliver him down the street to the low-rent neighborhood, yews knows the one I mean. Pitch him right through da door and den take off."

The moose stomped his hooves and snorted, eyes rolling in fear.

"Yews just relax dare, yews woikin' for me now so yews ain't got nothin' to worry about. Just do like I tells yews and everything will be fine."

The moose quieted and The Eldest walked over to Mancun. Reaching down, he picked the unconscious warrior up by the nape of the neck and slammed him down on the moose's back. Humming cheerfully, The Eldest passed his hands over the length of Mancun's body, binding him to the animal's back with a sticky web-like substance.

"Yews should appreciate the ride home I got for yews, yews being an animal lover and all and this being one of your favorites," The Eldest said, picking up Mancun's head by an ear for emphasis. "When yews get back to that asylum yews lives in, yews tell that boss of yours that I'm thinkin' about him and I'll see him soon. Think yews can remembah all dat, moron?"

Mancun gurgled in assent and The Eldest slammed his head down against the moose's neck.

"Well, it was nice meetin' you, Sonny, but it's time yews was on your way. Maybe we can have us another little intelligent being to idiot talk sometime soon," The Eldest said, slapping the bull moose on his right haunch.

"Git along with yews, Dobbin, yews got a ways to go before yews can rest, so yews better get goin'."

The moose trotted north out of the clearing with Mancun webbed to his back, intestines dragging through the snow behind him. The Eldest stood watching until they vanished into the forest and then strode off toward his ship.

At dusk, the bull moose had charged up the stone slope below the Dark One's crèche. Five feet from the entrance, the animal locked his front legs and lowered his head. Mancun was catapulted ass-over-intestines into the cavern. Wheeling, the bull moose fled down the slope and escaped.

Rolling across the stone floor in a tangle of arms, legs, and digestive tract, Mancun came to a halt sprawled between his master's feet. Seizing him by the hair, the beast dragged over to the base of the throne. Turning him over on his back, the Dark One stuffed his intestines back into the incision and set him to heal.

The situation, The Wendigo reflected, wasn't looking any too spruce. The other Lapushtan were gone, destroyed past any chance of reanimation. When The Eldest killed something, it stayed dead, and Judgment Day itself wouldn't raise it again. When The Eldest wounded something, as he had Mancun, it was slow to heal, if ever. As for The Eldest's threat of a future confrontation, he'd worry about that if and when the time came.

And that, motherfucker, the beast seethed, smashing his feet down on the stone floor in fury, was the name of that tune. Still though, all wasn't lost yet. There was still a spoke or two left to turn before the prophecy rolled down on the final battle. Be patient, the Dark One counseled himself, and the weight of the prophecy will crush Redbird and his half-wit white friends to dust as it passed. Just be patient and wait for the tide to turn. It had worked for millennia, it would work now.

CHAPTER 55

THE GENERAL QUARTERS alarm on a maritime vessel whooped and reverberated through the room.

"Now heah this, now heah this, breakfast will be soived in thoity minutes in the dining salon on the promenade deck," The Eldest roared through hidden speakers. "Yews people make sure yews bathes before you come down, I ain't runnin' no hog farm heah. Dat is all."

Groaning, David tunneled under the covers, trying to escape the ear-piercing din. The alarm continued sounding, volume intensifying every second. Deciding to surrender rather than go deaf, he swung his legs over the side of the bed and the alarm silenced itself mid-whoop. Laughing a little, David walked into the shower to finish waking up. Emerging a few minutes later, he toweled of and dressed.

Trotting up, Susie thrust her nose into his face and whined as he was finishing tying his boots. As soon as the bedroom door was opened for her, she charged off down the hallway. Reaching the door to the dog run, she sat and barked, urging him to hurry. As soon as he opened the door a crack, she shot through and disappeared.

Stepping inside, David felt his feet sink into a thick carpet of grass. A vast botanical garden stretched away in front of him, containing everything from bonsai juniper trees to redwood giants stretching up to a clear blue sky far overhead.

As Susie trotted away after watering a bed of American Beauty roses, a cottontail rabbit erupted out of the grass between her paws and circled back toward David. Barking happily she launched into the chase, intent on running down her lifelong nemesis. Three feet away from David's legs the rabbit vanished mid-hop, bringing Susie to a skidding halt at his feet. She nosed through the dewy grass for a few seconds before settling on her haunches and glaring up at him.

"Don't blame me, it's not my fault they always get away," he said, laughing.

A soft chime sounded which David presumed was the breakfast bell. Stepping out into the hallway, he saw Rachel and Gina just starting down the stairway at the far end. Hurrying down the corridor, he and Susie caught up with the others at the bottom of the stairs.

"There yews are, sunshines!" The Eldest cheerfully called from the dining room. "Come on in. I gotta say, yews are an ol-factory delight this morning, which I know ain't easy considerin' yews anatomical inherencies."

Filing through the doorway, they saw that the formal dining room of the previous evening had been replaced by a glass-enclosed breakfast room decorated with flowering plants. A row of ornate silver chafing dishes stood steaming on a linen-draped table. Beverages, cereals, fruit, pastries, and condiments occupied another table.

After greeting their host, Charlie and the others walked down the buffet line and served themselves breakfast. As with dinner the night before, the food was strangely prepared and singularly delicious. After everyone had finished eating, they sat silently watching The Eldest, waiting for him to speak.

"Well, I guess this ain't gettin' it done," he sighed. "Let's adjoin to the conference room and get this here show on the road."

Rising, The Eldest led them into the living room and gestured at the sofa. When everyone was seated, he settled into a worn armchair and pulled a cigar out of his breast pocket. Striking a match with his thumb, he puffed on the cigar until its end glowed cherry-red. Exhaling a blue cloud of smoke, he smashed his fist down on the end table, startling his guests.

"Oyez, oyez," he roared. "Let the record reflect that present at this here meeting are Char-, hell, I know who's here, let's just get on with it."

Pausing to take a long draw on his cigar, he continued in a quieter voice.

"I gotta say, Redboid, that I don't like yews chances in this here frolic one little bit. I mean, lookit yews, shot through with the black cell disease in yews airboxes. Don't smell none too good either, lemme tell ya. All yews got goin' for yewsself is that Celtic mojo stick and I gotta say that ain't much given the current sit-u-ation. Ask me, it's kinda like huntin' a water buffalo with a pea shooter.

"And sheesh, lookit the rest of your merry band. A clinically depressed ambulance chaser in denial clear up to his eyeballs. A loony-tune librarian with bats in her belfry. A little girl who oughta be at home playin' with dolls and havin' tea parties. And a mutt that can't even catch a rabbit and wouldn't know what ta do with it if she did.

"Doan get me wrong, Redboid, I like yews, always have. I like yews friends, too, includin' the mutt. I ain't tryin' to be rude by strategically analyzin' dis here problem. It's just dat I doan think yews'll stack up very well in the clinches with His Ugliness and I'm afraid yews'll get hurt.

"Because I like yews all so well and I'm afraid of what might happen to yews, I'm gonna haveta help yews out and— What's da mattuh dare, Redboid, yews look all pale, like yews just sucked up the spit outta that nasty damn pipe you smoke?"

"I, I, ungh," Charlie stammered, groping for words.

"Yeah, yeah, I know, I ain't supposed ta upset the balance, that's one of Her commandments, THE commandment yews might say," The Eldest said, frowning and pointing his cigar at the ceiling. "But His-self has been gettin' sassy just lately and the balance has been improperly tilted in his favor. My job is maintainin' da balance and I'm gonna put it right by helpin' yews out a little. Got all dat, Redboid? I knows yews is a little slow on the uptake at times."

"Yes, Eldest, I understand," Charlie replied, "and thank you. I, we, probably wouldn't have gotten much further without your help. He would have taken us by sundown tonight at the latest."

"Yeah, well, that's okay. Yews is a bunch of incompetents, but nice enough, so yews deserves a hand. Besides which, I got no stomach for violence and turmoil and such and I'd just as soon yews took care of this little problem for me.

"Speakin' of TV, I knows yews has been worried about your grand-kiddie, whats 'er name, Ethel, Elaine, Eugenia, whatever. See, she's doing all right, but I doan know for how much longer. Another reason yews needs to hurry things up and settle his hash before things get any worse."

The Eldest pointed across the room at a console television in a dark walnut cabinet. An electronic crackling sounded as a small white dot in the center of the screen began slowly expanding as the set warmed up. The white clutter on the television screen vanished and a black and white image of Ellen Talltrees appeared. Head tilted back with her eyes closed, she looked tired and careworn. The camera panned back, revealing her nude to the waist, jets of water sluicing down her breasts and flanks.

"E-e-e-yow!" The Eldest roared, placing a huge furred hand over Rachel's eyes as the television went dark. "Jeez Louise, Redboid, I'm sorry, I woulda nevuh, I mean, holy cripes, in front of women and children. Damn cable company, wait 'til I get a hold of them! Da country's been goin' to hell ever since that damn Roo-se-velt took us off the gold standard. Jeez Redboid, I apologize, I woulda never, you know, on purpose, jeez, I'm sorry."

"That's all right, Eldest, accidents happen," Charlie replied, smiling. "Thank you for showing her to me, I've been very concerned about her safety."

"I'm glad yews ain't mad or nothin'" The Eldest said. "I've known yews all yews life, not that it amounts to much. Dat's a nice grand-kid yews got there, she seems like a nice girl, bathes regulah.

"Well, anyway, on dat note we is adjourned. I got yews some going away present ovah dare in da cornuh. Yews need to look 'em ovuh 'cuz yews'll be disembarkin' shortly. I ain't runnin' no roomin' house heah. Now if yews'll excuse me I'm needed on the bridge, this thing doan run itself I'll have yews know."

Standing, The Eldest walked out of the room, face still glowing red. Climbing the stairs, he vanished from sight into the upper reaches of the house.

"No questions until we leave in a few minutes," Charlie cautioned them with an upraised hand. "In the meantime, let's go look at The Eldest's gifts."

Walking over by the front door, they started sorting through the jumble of gear piled in the corner. At first, they thought The Eldest had somehow recovered and repaired the gear they had lost. Closer inspection revealed that while the equipment resembled that lost, it actually consisted of cleverly executed copies. In common with everything else The Eldest set his hand to, the gear was functional but utterly alien.

A bright flash of color on a backpack with his name on it caught David's eye. Reaching down, he pulled off a cartridge scotch-taped to the pack's side. A checked red, white, and blue pattern was etched into the brass just above the cartridge's rim. The letters "NSAA" were printed in bold black capital letters just above the checkering. Intrigued by the odd shell, David turned to show it to Charlie.

"Yews just put that bullet in yews pocket for the moment and fuhgit about it," The Eldest said deep inside his mind. "Yews keep it secret for now and we'll talk about it later."

Startled, David put the cartridge in the right breast pocket of his shirt and buttoned it closed. Looking up, he saw that the others were almost finished sorting through the pile of equipment.

"Please return to your seats if you are standing," a woman's voice said from hidden speakers in the ceiling, "and return your tray tables to the upright position and fasten your seat belts. We will be landing shortly and on behalf of your captain and crew, I would like to thank you for flying, for flying, ungh, that is all."

The floor beneath their feet began shaking and a muted roar filled the room, adding to the sudden pressure which had begun thrusting against their ear drums. Charlie hurriedly led them over to the couch where four seat belts, three for adults and one for a child, were laid out and waiting. Sitting down, they hastily buckled up while Susie cowered under David's knees.

"I didn't even know we were flying," David said, amazed and a little frightened.

"We have been since shortly after dinner last night," Charlie told him.

"This is yews Captain speakin," The Eldest said through the ceiling speakers. "We'll be landin' shortly. Because we may encounter some toib-u-lence, I strongly encourages yews to remain in yews seats wit dem belts fastened."

The living room pitched violently to one side and the engine's roar increased to a mind-numbing thunder.

"Hold on, she's a headin' for the barn," The Eldest roared, making the speakers crackle and distort. "Whoa mule, dammit, slow down! More power on the mid-starboard thruster! Whoa now!"

Negative G-forces gripped Charlie and the others, making it feel as if their stomachs were rising into their throats. Their arms and legs floated akimbo, pulled upwards by the forces exerted on them. The vessel suddenly slammed to a halt, throwing them down hard against the lap belts.

Tasting vomit, David swallowed hard and opened his eyes. Susie's shivering was beating a rhythmic tattoo against his calves. Charlie, seated to David's right, was resting his forehead on the backs of his hands which had a white-knuckled death grip on the staff. On the other end of the sofa, Gina was sitting with her eyes closed, trembling. Squeezed in between Charlie and Gina, Rachel was all smiles, convinced this latest experience beat the monster coaster at Busch Gardens *any* day.

"Jeez, I apologize for the rough landin'," The Eldest said as walked into the room. "Well, I hope yews all liked yews presents, I ain't much of a shopper. It's about time for yews to gather up your things and get ready to go. I ain't runnin' no hotel heah, I'll have yews know. All ashore dat's going ashore!"

The bass roar of a ship's horn boomed through the small room, the traditional fifteen-minute warning that a vessel was about to sail. Unlatching their seat belts, David and the others rose and walked over to the piled equipment. After putting on hats and coats and adjusting their new backpacks, they turned and saw The Eldest waiting by the front door.

"Well, now comes the hard part, the sayin' of the goodbyes," he sadly told them. "Yews has been uncommonly fine guests who bathes regular, even dat mutt dare. I'm gonna miss all of yews. I'd like to have a private woid wit each of yews and then I'll walk yews to my front gate like civilized folk do."

Stepping forward, The Eldest grasped Charlie's hands.

"Charlie, old friend, yews race is almost run," The Eldest said deep inside his mind. "Yews war is nearly over and the time of yews long rest is almost here. I know yews is tired, just this one last thing to do and you'll have the peace you deserve. Yews tell Mary I said hello when yews see her, she's a fine goil and I know yews've missed her somethin' awful."

Releasing Charlie, The Eldest kneeled and took Rachel's hands.

"Sweetie, I hope yews had fun whiles yews was here," he said into her mind. "I enjoyed havin' yews here and I'm gonna miss yews. Come back sometime and we'll play with the baby ducks and cook hamburgers again. Pay attention to what the grownups tells yews to do and yews'll be fine.

Drooping her hands, The Eldest started to stand but Rachel intercepted him with a hug before joining Charlie on the front stoop. Standing, The Eldest looked deep into Gina's eyes for a long moment before taking her hands.

"Gina Tolliver, yews is a sweetheart and a fine mother to that beautiful little goil," he told her. "Unfortunately though yews is very ill, which means yews road will be more difficult than that of yews friends. I'd help yews if I could, but da cracks in yews basement is too deep for even me ta fix. So instead, I'm gonna leaves yews a garden to walk in when the world goes dark for the last time. When that time comes and yews is afraid, just remember the garden, okay?"

Gina nodded and The Eldest released her hands. Walking out the front door to join Rachel and Charlie on the stoop, she had no memory of their conversation, just a radiant inner vision of a garden that Monet would have envied.

Dropping to one knee, The Eldest whistled softly. Susie trotted up, sat, and placed a paw in his outstretched right hand.

"Little Susie, smallest and bravest of all yews friends," he crooned into her mind. "Loyal even in the worse of time and yews asks so very little in return. Yews has taught me much, which ain't no small thing at my age. Keep an eye on David for me, he's gonna need all the help he can get. If yews comes back to visit, maybe I'll have a canine for yews to associate with instead of havin' to lissen to humans all day long. I know, bruddah do I ever, just how borin' that can be."

Giving Susie a final scratch, The Eldest dropped her paw, rose, and stood facing David. Reaching out, he placed David's hands between both of his.

"And finally yews, David Adam Garrison, counselor-at-law and staff-wielder-to-be," The Eldest said deep into his mind. "Seeker of things forever lost, unwavering even in the depths of blackest despair. I knows yews didn't ask for any of this to happen to yews, but yews gotta keep goin'. Much will depend on yews over the next few days.

"Dat bullit I gave yews is one of my special hand loads di-rect from the port powder magazine. Don't worry, yews'll know when da time is right to use it. One thing though. If for some reason yews don't use it or it might fall into the wrong hands, yews gotta dispose of it properly. Just load it into yews pistol and shoot it straight up into the sky. Make sure yews is outside when yews shoots it though, you wouldn't wanna be standin' inside a buildin' or under anything when it goes off. Dare's people who would give a lot to get their meat hooks on dat bullit. Yews can't allow that to happen, David. The woild just ain't ready for the technology contained in dat dare pro-ject-tile.

"And well, I guess dat's it. Yews is a good boy, David, a fine man. Just believe in yewself and put one foot in front of da other and everything will be fine, you'll see."

Dropping David's hands, The Eldest stepped aside and pointed him toward the others waiting out on the front stoop. Seeing them approach, Charlie led Rachel and Gina down the front steps, across the tiny yard, and out through the front gate. After David passed through, Charlie swung the gate closed and latched it. Standing in a tight group, they stood watching their host approach, feeling suddenly awkward.

"The time of parting is at hand," The Eldest said in the clipped, accent-free voice he used for formal occasions. "May peace find you and remain with you always and may our roads meet again soon."

Dropping to one knee, Charlie pulled Rachel, Gina, and David down with him before replying, "And with you, Eldest. Go with our thanks and wishes for a safe voyage, now and always."

Nodding once, The Eldest turned and strode up the cement sidewalk toward his ship. Rising, Charlie led the others off at a fast trot toward a small hillock about a hundred yards away.

Rachel, Gina, and David all tried to speak at once, but Charlie cut them off, saying, "Not now, first we must—"

"Be well," The Eldest bellowed from behind them, "and come back safe."

Turning in surprise, they saw a huge fur-covered creature waving at them from the house's front stoop. They waved back, and the creature somehow squeezed its huge frame through the front door and closed it.

"We need to get over on top of that little hill over there because The Eldest's navigation can be a little shaky at low altitude," Charlie said.

A minute or so later Charlie and the others reached the shelter of the hilltop. Hearing raised voices in the direction of the house; they turned to watch what happened next.

"All sail, lively now!" an amplified voice roared in the distance. "Put some sweat on that capstan, damn it, or we'll miss the tide. Yes, you Sonny, midships the helm, today, damn it, today! You there, put a reef in that fore tops'l or I'll kick your arse up around your ears!"

Thunder rapidly grew in volume until the earth was trembling beneath their feet. In the meadow below the house rose fifty feet into the air before suddenly tilting down and to the right. The structure slowly righted itself but slowly started drifting on a collision course toward the hilltop.

The house suddenly vanished and was replaced by a 17th century sailing ship. The vessel's bow name board identified her as *The Flying Dutchman.* Tattered sails hung from her yards and skeletal figures scrambled about her rigging. The Eldest shouted, "No, you dumb son-of-a-bitch, not Hologram One, turn the hologram projector OFF! Whattya, deaf or somethin'?"

The sailing vessel blinked out of existence, revealing the true nature of The Eldest's ship. Resembling a vast three dimensional arrowhead, it blotted out the late afternoon sun as it approached and cast the hilltop into sudden shadow. The craft's smooth lines were unmarred by any projecting control surfaces or hatches. The black hull seemed to both absorb and reflect light, confusing the eye and brain. It made a stealth bomber look as primitive as a Model-T Ford.

"We better run!" David said, backing up a step. "If that thing hits us—"

"Reef ahead, twenty-five yards hard on the port bow!" The Eldest's voice bellowed from the ship. "Hard a starboard! Reverse one hundred and ten percent of normal on the starboard engines, make bells for two-thirds ahead on the port engines and gimme thirty degrees positive angle on the bow! And turn the external communication system off, idiot! I ain't a carnival barker, ya know!"

Catching hold of his friends, Charlie somehow halted their flight after only a couple of steps. Standing on the back slope, eyes level with the hilltop, they stood watching as the vast ebony wedge pivoted gracefully on its axis and started climbing. Internal organs and teeth vibrating in sympathy with the vessel's propulsion system, they stood staring upwards until the ship suddenly vanished from sight at an altitude of about 750 feet. Three circles pressed into the snow, each twenty-five yards in diameter, were the only evidence that The Eldest and his ship had ever been there.

"It's getting late, so we are going to camp for the night at the bottom of this slope," Charlie said. "And then we can talk."

CHAPTER 56

LIFTING A SLAT on the blind covering the living room window, Ellen peered out through the misted glass. A rusty old Nissan Sentra was parked fifty yards away on the other side of the road, partially concealed by a stand of birch trees. Which was the same place it had been parked for the last four hours.

Squinting into the eyepieces of Charlie's beat-up old binoculars, she watched the man sitting in the Nissan mindlessly lick his lips while staring at the cabin. Although his face was obscured by a baseball hat, sunglasses, and a beard, she was certain of who he was. Or more accurately, what he had become.

Two hours earlier, Ellen had teetered over the raw edge of panic and decided to call Terry Thomas and beg for help. Picking up the telephone's handset, she had heard nothing at first, not even a dial tone. After a second, a raspy voice had crooned, "E-l-l-l-en, I'm gonna fuck—" Smashing the handset down on the receiver, Ellen had ripped the line out of the wall, opened a window, and flung the phone out into the backyard.

Since then, she had been pressed up against the wall by the front window, staring out of the gap in the blinds until her eyes teared. Sliding down the wall, Ellen hugged her knees to her chest, struggling not to vomit at the stench rising through the floorboards from the cellar. She had first noticed the carrion reek shortly after dawn, around six o'clock. In the hours since, the effluvium of rotting meat had slowly seeped into the cabin, permeating her clothes, her hair, even the soft tissues in her nose and mouth. The wet towel tied around her lower face wasn't helping; she could still taste the foul stench every time she breathed.

A car horn sounded outside and Ellen scrambled to her feet. Jerking the blind aside, she saw that the watcher in the Nissan had moved and was now parked in the front yard a few yards away from the living room window. The man was leaning out of the open driver's side window, body swaying sinuously, reptilian tongue flickering. Scenting her, Ellen realized, savoring her.

Dropping the blind with a crash, Ellen slammed her back against the wall, palms covering her mouth to keep the scream in, clenched fingers digging furrows in her cheeks. Think, she told herself, begging the panic gibbering in her mind for an answer. Run, it advised her, far and fast and never stop. Yes, she decided, run and keep running until she came to salt water, which ocean didn't matter, just cross it and then run some more. No one, she told herself, could or would blame her. And if they did, she really didn't care.

Yes, get her old backpack out of the closet in the spare bedroom and stuff it full of canned goods, anything with lots of carbs would do. Put her grandfather's ratty spare sleeping bag on top along with a couple of gallons of water. And don't forget the shotgun and the two boxes of shells sitting on the kitchen table. Open the little window above the sink and drop the pack out, then squirm through with the shotgun pointed out barrel first with the safety off. A quick sprint to her car, then get in and lock the doors. And then run and keep on running and never stop.

"NO, YOU MUST NOT!" A voice bellowed deep in her brain, dropping Ellen to the floor, arms wrapped around her head in reaction to the searing agony inside her skull. "YOU MUST REMAIN INSIDE THE CABIN. GREAT EVENTS DEPEND ON YOU NOW, SO YOU MUST STAY AND BE STRONG."

"I'm havin' a stroke," Ellen mumbled, psychedelic colors swirling across her vision. "Holy shit, a stroke that talks."

"Ellen Talltrees, hear me now," the woman's voice said, volume now reduced to a loud shout. "If you leave the cabin, they, the Dark One's pawns, will have you before you can reach your car. They want to flush you out where they can take you. The one out front in the car is not the only one, there are seven others scattered all around the outside of the cabin.

"This cabin is a place of great power, steeped in the old magic and they fear to enter it, are uncomfortable even being close to it. The cabin's power is why you can hold the thing downstairs so easily, why you were even able to capture it in the first place. This power, and your courage, is all that holds them at bay. You have only these two advantages, and if you leave the cabin, you will be surrendering the stronger of the two and they will take you."

"B-but I-I'm not brave," Ellen stammered. "I-I'm afraid and I—"

"Of course you are afraid, child, that's normal," the woman's voice soothed, becoming quieter yet. "The things outside are as afraid of you as you are of them, as is the thing imprisoned in the cellar. The only difference is that they can smell your fear and it makes them bold, able to torment you. That is how the thing in the cellar makes the graveyard stench. What you really smell is your own fear.

"So you must be strong, unafraid. Much depends on you yet, Ellen. This will all be over soon, no more than a couple of days. Until then, you cannot yield and you must endure. You must!"

And then the voice was gone. Ellen could hear the sudden silence echoing inside her skull along with the pounding of a world-class migraine. She had just managed to sit upright on the floor, head clutched in her hands, when the watcher parked outside blew the car's horn again. A bolt of white-hot agony flashed through the left side of Ellen's skull at the sound, and then the watcher blew the horn yet again.

"Strong, unafraid, unyielding!" She screamed. "I'll give you all that and more, motherfucker, see if I don't't!"

Rising, Ellen grabbed the shotgun leaning against the wall and jerked the blind up. Throwing the window open, she thrust the shotgun out and fired the left hand barrel without bothering to aim. The Nissan's left headlight exploded and the left front fender bulged out from the impact of the ten gauge shotgun slug tearing through the sheet metal. Taking aim this time, Ellen fired the shotgun's right hand barrel. The slug struck the upper windshield frame dead center, blowing in the glass and peeling the roof back in a ragged vee for three feet before deflecting downwards into the back seat and exiting through the undercarriage. The Nissan swayed on its suspension, rocked by the shotgun blasts, while the driver shrieked and ground the starter. On the third attempt, the engine kicked over and he slammed the car into reverse. Tires spinning, he backed across the yard.

Fumbling in a fresh pair of slugs, Ellen closed the breech and raised the shotgun again. The Nissan was already thirty yards away, still backing down the road and gathering speed every second. Lowering the gun, she ran to the kitchen to the kitchen window and peered out from behind the curtain. A young Poshto woman, no older than nineteen or twenty, was crouched next to the woodpile staring at the cabin. Moving with deliberate slowness, Ellen pulled the curtain aside and raised the window. Snarling, the watcher rose and charged toward the window. Shouldering the shotgun in one fluid motion, Ellen started to fire, but the watcher was quicker. Diving behind the woodpile, she started screaming, begging Ellen not to shoot. Taking careful aim, Ellen squeezed the shotgun's front trigger, blowing the top half of the woodpile apart. Lowering her aim, she pulled the rear trigger and felt something break deep inside her right shoulder. Crying out in pain, she dropped the shotgun, narrowly missing her feet.

Tears blurring her vision, Ellen watched the young woman jump out from behind the remnants of the woodpile and run toward the cover of the forest. Jagged wood splinters protruded from the back of the watcher's blood-stained denim jacket. Other figures, only half-seen through her tears, also retreated toward the safety of the deep woods. Smiling in grim satisfaction, she closed and locked both windows with her uninjured arm.

Sensing something was different, Ellen turned away from the window. The pervasive carrion stench was gone, replaced by the musty air of a sealed house with the acrid taint of gunpowder mixed in. Taking the wet towel off her face, she walked over to the kitchen sink.

Working with one hand, she knotted a pair of dish towels together into a makeshift sling. Her shoulder felt better riding in it, but there was a clicking-grinding sound felt more than heard every time she tried to move it. Not to mention the fact that it hurt like a son-of-a-bitch.

Picking up a bottle of Ibuprofen, she walked over to the refrigerator, took out a bottle of water, and sat down at the kitchen table. Counting out six tablets, she swallowed them by threes, chasing them down with long sips of water.

Sleepy now, Ellen walked over to the couch and lay down. Everything might turn out fine yet if the voice was to be believed. But just in case things went south, she was going to keep the shotgun and a box of shells close at hand. In fact, she was planning on sleeping with them. Because life was just full of surprises and lately none of them were worth a damn.

CHAPTER 57

"THE ELDEST," CHARLIE said as he stacked twigs for a fire, "is the oldest of the Great Mother's children. He was the first of all creatures to exist in our reality and brought the light with him when he came and he shall be the last to fall when the final darkness comes.

"The Eldest is a collective or multiple being, both male and female, flesh and stone, one and many and all things in between. Everything you saw, the house, its furnishing, the food, the ship at the end, were all part of The Eldest, but not the whole of him. Or more properly, not the whole of *it*."

Remembering the giant masseuse and the nude Japanese bath girl, David swallowed hard and visibly paled. Charlie, who had made an educated guess about what had happened to David, grinned large and fought hard to keep from laughing out loud.

"Why is he so rude sometimes?" Gina asked, sounding near tears. "He called me a loony-tune, and in front of Rachel. I can't help it that I'm sick. He's cruel, he—"

"I'm sorry he hurt your feelings," Charlie interrupted, reaching out a hand to calm her and trying to coax a flame out of the stacked twigs with a lit match with the other. "And you're right, he's very rude. The Eldest is a paradox, cruel and kind, generous and selfish, rude and polite. And as I'm sure you noticed, he is also obsessed with personal hygiene.

"His function, as he told you, is to maintain the balance between light and darkness for the Great Mother. The darkness is always here, always trying to overpower the light, always trying to upset the balance. Because the darkness is so persistent, The Eldest is always busy, always one disaster behind, which over time has driven him slightly mad. He believes impersonating humans makes it easier for people to relate to him when in fact his behavior is utterly bizarre. Although in his defense if he showed you his true form, at least when you first met him, it would scare you to death. That and I suspect that he also has a sly and very warped sense of humor.

"He uses, I guess you could call it ritual rudeness, to frighten away those seeking sanctuary because granting it distracts him from tending the balance. Even after he grants sanctuary, if you are rude to him in return, he will use that as an excuse to turn you out of his ship. That allows him to go back to tending the balance, which is his sole reason for existence.

"Normally, The Eldest will not interfere in human affairs and is very seldom seen by man. I have never heard of him giving sanctuary seekers a ride in his ship or giving them equipment. Given our current predicament, they were priceless gifts. Without them we wouldn't have lived very much longer."

"I guess, but I still don't like him," Gina said, swiping at her eyes with the back of her hand.

Nodding, Charlie concentrated on getting the fire lit, growing more aggravated by the second. He'd been lighting wood stoves and campfires for most of his life, often when failure would have meant freezing to death. So why in the hell couldn't he get a pile of dry kindling to fire on a calm afternoon? When the third match he lit scorched his fingers, he swore under his breath and slammed the butt end of the staff into the pile of stacked kindling. A ten-foot column of blue fire shot skywards, startling the others. The pillar of flame quickly receded and became a small pile of burning twigs.

"Oops!" Charlie said, throwing a couple of larger sticks on the fire. "Even us wise old shamans mess up once in a while."

Gina and David laughed, accepting his explanation. Kneeling with his back to the others, Charlie made a show of fussing with his pipe to cover his embarrassment at losing his temper.

"Grampa Charlie, can I ask you something?" Rachel asked.

Taking a deep breath to regain his composure, Charlie turned and faced her.

"Yes, Sugar, of course you can ask me a question," he replied. "What's the matter, you sound like something's bothering you."

"The man with the baby duckies in the space ship, is he like ET?"

"No, honey, he's not like ET at all. ET is make-believe and the man with the baby ducks, his name is The Eldest, is real."

After a moment's thought, Rachel said, "Okay, but I don't understand why if the man with the baby duckies is real, ET isn't. I'm hungry, are we gonna eat soon?"

"Yes, honey, we're going to eat right now."

Rummaging through his pack, Charlie found a strange looking red foil package. The unlabeled bag featured a smiling chef dressed in whites pointing a spoon at bold black print which read, "JUST ADD COLD WATER AND VIOLA!" Looking up, he saw that Gina and David were each examining one of the gaudy foil packages.

Deciding he was hungry and damn the torpedoes, David hunkered down and tore the foil package open along a dotted line at its top. Holding the opened bag by one corner, he filled it with cold water from his bottle. The water started simmering and quickly broke into a rolling boil. Startled, David dropped the bag and took a couple of hasty step backwards. Black smoke started spewing out of the bag, hiding it from sight. When the smoke cleared a few seconds later, a burger, fries, and sixteen ounce beverage were sitting in a cardboard to-go container on the ground.

"Ray Kroc would have loved this," David said. "Just add water and wham-bam, instant Value Meal."

Everyone stood looking uncertainly at the food until Rachel settled the issue by darting forward and stuffing some of the fries in her mouth.

"Good!" She giggled, french fries hanging out of her mouth. "Are we gonna eat now?"

The adults were hungry and after a few cups of water and some further pyrotechnics, dinner was served. Sitting knee-to-knee in the snow, they all ate with the silent attention of the truly hungry. No one commented on the food's strange appearance or how it looked out of the corner of their eyes. Instead they concentrated on filling their bellies.

Adages from The Eldest on subject of personal hygiene had replaced the usual corporate advertising logos on the food wrappers and containers. "Bathe twice a day with plenty of soap" one proclaimed in bold black letters. "Wear clean underwear" read another, and yet another decreed, "Wash your hands after using the toilet".

Laughing, David lifted his drink cup and examined the message printed on its side. "Love Yews Mother," it commanded below a fanciful image of Earth suspended in outer space surrounded by ringed planets, stars, and comets. As he watched, the globe morphed into a female fertility icon, belly gravid and breasts distended in the late stages of pregnancy. When the icon winked and waggled her breasts at him, David dropped the cup, soaking the front of his parka and jeans with ersatz Coke. Lusty female laughter pealed deep in his mind.

Scrambling to his feet, David tried to brush the sticky fluid off his parka and jeans. Rachel and Gina hadn't noticed anything out of the ordinary other than his apparent clumsiness. Charlie though was staring at him with the look David had come to think of as "The-Wise-Old-Shaman's-Thousand-Yard-Stare". Feeling self-conscious, he started gathering up the trash left over from the meal.

Sorting the trash by type next to the fire, David intended to burn the paper and cardboard now and bury the plastic drink cups later. When he threw the combustible trash on the fire, flames leaped high into the air. Startled, he stumbled backwards and fell. Rolling over, he brushed off the singed remnants of his eyebrows and slowly got up. The plastic drink cups were gone, presumably kicked into the fire during his clumsy retreat from the flames, and probably now smelted into a smoking, toxic mess.

Drawing in a deep breath, struggling but failing to assert self-control, he started to roar, "Am I the only one around here who can tend a fire?", but looked down in time to bite it off at "Am I—"

Instead of combusting or melting, the trash had somehow formed itself into multiple briquettes glowing an incandescent red. Noticing the toes of his boots starting to smoke, David hastily backed away from the fire before anything else could happen.

"You were saying, David?" Charlie asked.

"Ungh, nothing, Charlie," he replied. "But I would like us to sit down and talk later, if that's all right with you."

"Of course, whenever you like."

Rachel whispered into Gina's ear and they both stood up. Excusing themselves, they walked out of the ring of firelight toward a copse of fir trees about twenty-yards away. Wincing, Charlie stood and started setting up Rachel and Gina's tent. Pulling the tent out of its blue nylon carrying bag, he laid it on the ground and stared at it, trying to figure out how to open it. The folded tent was circular, about nine inches in diameter and three inches thick. There were no apparent tent poles, pegs, or guy ropes packed in either the carrying bag or the tent itself. After thinking for a second, Charlie flipped the tent over and grinned at what he saw.

"THIS SIDE UP, STUPID" was printed in large fluorescent yellow letters. Underneath were a pair of circles, each of which enclosed an arrow. The word "UP", again in fluorescent yellow letters, was written inside one arrow while the word "DOWN" was written inside the other. Reaching out with the staff, Charlie pushed the button labeled "UP". A muffled *pop!* sounded, closely followed by the hiss of compressed air as the tent rapidly expanded upwards and outwards.

Charlie backpedaled a couple of steps and realized too late that he was losing the race. Pivoting, he took a single step forward before the ballooning tent smacked him across the buttocks, sending him staggering forward. Catching his balance with the staff just before he would have fallen, he retreated a few more steps before turning and glaring at the offender. Blue fire pulsed up and down the staff's length as Charlie prepared to avenge himself on the culprit. A choking noise a few feet away distracted him in the instant before he would have incinerated the tent. David was sitting on the ground, one hand clapped over his mouth, the other hand clutching his belly, tears running down his face.

"Suh, suh, sorry, Charlie," he gasped in between whoops of laughter. "I, I know its aggravating as hell, but shit, you should've seen yourself. I, I, I'm sorry, I—"

"You're goddamn right it's aggravating!" Charlie roared. "As a general rule, I find that getting kicked in the ass aggravates the shit out of me! I—"

Closing his mouth, he quelled the staff's fire. Silent now, David looked worriedly at him, afraid that he had angered his friend. Lips pressed into a stern line, Charlie couldn't contain himself any longer and started laughing. Dropping the staff, he dropped to his knees, arms held against his belly, tears rolling down his face, roaring with laughter. When Rachel and Gina walked up a minute later, they found Charlie and David sitting side-by-side in the snow, gasping for breath.

"Are you two all right?" Gina asked.

"Yes, we're fine," Charlie replied, smiling. "David and I were laughing together and we got out of breath."

"Okay, I'm glad everything's all right. Well, I think we're ready for bed. Would you please help us set up our tent?"

"I already set up your tent because I thought you'd be sleepy when you got back. But you better let David and I check it out first. I wouldn't want the damn thing to ambush you and Rachel."

Ducking their heads, Charlie and David cautiously entered the tent. Soft white lights clicked on as they entered the spacious front room. Behind a solid door there was an enclosed bath cubicle complete with shower, toilet, sink, and The Eldest's patriotic motif toilet paper. Through another door there was a spacious bedroom with a pair of inflatable sleeping couches in the middle of the floor. A soft current of warm air brushed their faces and after a quick search they discovered a small thermostat attached to one of the interior bedroom walls.

Shrugging, Charlie grinned at David and led the way out of the tent. Concerned about the tent's lack of poles, pegs, or guy ropes, Charlie placed a palm against one of the outer wall and pushed hard. The wall didn't bulge at all, not even the slight give normal for a nylon tent wall. Satisfied, he turned and watched while David carried Rachel and Gina's gear into the tent.

After saying goodnight, David and Charlie walked over to the fire. The wood had burned down to grey ash, but the trash briquettes were still glowing red and emitting a furnace heat. Using their packs as seats, they sat side-by-side, keeping a safe distance from the fire's searing heat.

"David, I'm glad that you wanted to talk," Charlie said, fiddling with his pipe. "We may not get another chance to speak privately. I know the last few days have been hard on you, hard on all of us."

"It's not so much that its' been hard, it's just that everything is so weird and so dangerous and it just never stops, never lets up," David replied, struggling to frame his chaotic thoughts and emotions into coherent speech. "I don't understand any of this and it feels like I'm trapped in an evil fairy tale that started the day my wife and daughter disappeared."

"It is a frightening situation," Charlie told him, blowing out a long plume of smoke. "If you weren't scared, there would be something seriously wrong with you. Your lack of understanding has been caused by the prophecy which has created our current predicament. Normally, the staff heir begins preparing for his stewardship right after his puberty ceremony. When he assumes stewardship of the staff, usually sometime in his late-teens to late-twenties, he will have been preparing for anywhere from six to fifteen years to wield the staff.

"The prophecy commands that when one of the Celtic chief's descendants, that's you remember, takes possession of the staff after the death of the last Redbird shaman, that's me remember, he must do so unprepared and stand or fall on his own inborn talent. That's because the staff originally belonged to your people and it should respond to your blood immediately without any need of prior training.

"I have some very serious doubts about this. The staff is a complicated and powerful supernatural artifact, difficult to understand and even harder to use. There is no other choice, no help for it, this is the way things must be, have to be, in order to fulfill the prophecy and defeat our enemy. The truth is, you're a victim of circumstances, of your own genetics, plain and simple."

David sat wearily rubbing his eyes before finally looking up. "Goddamn, that's a real comfort, you know?"

"I know, David, I know, but it's best that you be told now. There are a couple of other things I need to discuss with you if it's all right."

After a long moment David nodded and Charlie continued.

"There are two things I would like to impress upon you. First, the danger of pride. You must always remember that you and the staff are separate entities. You are, or will be, only the guardian of a supernatural artifact. The true power lays in the staff, not in you. If you forget this and start to wield the power as if it's yours, a part of you like an arm or a leg, it will consume you and drag you screaming into the darkness beyond. You must never forget that you are the power's servant, not its master.

"Second, you must jealously guard the secret of the staff's existence and its true nature. There will always be a few people that have to know, but you must try to keep their number and what they know to a bare minimum. There are many people, including some in our government, who would covet the staff above all things if they knew of its power. Although the staff will sing only for you, and unfortunately for our enemy, they would not hesitate to coerce you by any means, including harming you or those you love, in order to have that power at their disposal.

"There are a few other people, collectors of arcane knowledge and such, who already know of the staff's existence and its probable location. There are probably no more than six of them in all, but they are extremely dangerous. Most are powerful shamans in their own right and you must be especially wary of them. The staff will tell you of them when the time comes and you must do whatever is necessary to defeat them and preserve your stewardship of the staff and your life."

Pausing, lost in thought, Charlie fumbled with his pipe and finally managed to get it relit.

"I shouldn't tell you this next part, David, because it may make you angry, but I'm going to anyway," he said, puffing furiously on his pipe. "You must beware your good heart, your pity, your compassion. The staff is not meant feed the hungry, house the homeless, or right the wrongs of the world. It is only a fortunate accident that you can heal others with its power provided that you are trained to do so. You are a decent man, David, a good man, and you will always want to help others. That will be your greatest danger once you begin your stewardship, wanting to do what is right.

"There, I am done lecturing now, a fact I'm sure you're glad of."

"Charlie, how much longer until we get wherever it is we're going, until the battle?" David asked, fear sounding in his voice.

"Now that The Eldest has helped us out by giving us a ride, it will be tomorrow or the day after at the latest. Don't worry, you'll do just fine."

"God, I hope so!" He sighed, face buried in his hands. "Because I am so fucking scared!"

"Just trust yourself and everything will be all right," Charlie said, putting an arm around his friend's shaking shoulders.

Long minutes passed before David finally regained his composure.

Looking up, he cleared his throat and said, "Thanks for telling me all this, Charlie; I appreciate your being honest with me. I think I'll go set up the other tent now. If it's all right with you, I'm going to sleep a couple of hours and then I'll keep watch 'til dawn so you can get some rest."

"That's all right, David, go ahead and call it a night, I'll be fine. Just like they say, us old folks don't require a lot of sleep."

Nodding, David rose and pulled the other tent off his backpack. Walking away to set it up, his head and shoulders were bowed by the weight of what lay ahead. Worried, Susie trotted whining at his knee, trying and failing to get his attention. After making sure David got the tent set up, Charlie sat staring into the fire, brooding on the magnitude of his duplicity.

"You are a lying, gutless old man," he told himself, recognizing the need for his deceit but hating himself for it nonetheless. *"Your friend thanked you for your honesty and you just sat there, Judas without the silver. He would not thank you nor call you friend if he knew that the staff rejected one out of every two prospective candidates. He would not thank you nor call you friend if he knew those rejected candidates die screaming, burning in blue fire when the staff's power flared in them for one terrible second."*

Reloading his pipe, Charlie thought of his younger brother Gerald standing in the sacred stone circle all those Octobers ago. Gerald, youngest of the Redbird boys, followed by Charlie, and then by their older brother, Robert. Gerald, reaching out and taking the staff with trembling hands from John, their father. Off to one side, Charlie stood praying for his success, wanting nothing to do with the staff and wanting only to be an artist.

For a long second nothing happened and Gerald started smiling, Charlie along with him. Then suddenly Gerald was gone, replaced by a screaming column of blue fire that burnt until nothing was left but a handful of ash. Weeping, John Redbird had thrust the staff into Charlie's hands. Charlie had felt the power sing in him and knew that his life would be forever altered. Looking up, he saw Robert glaring at him, teeth bared, and wondered why — Well, better not to think of any of that now, at least not during the hours of darkness.

"And what of the woman and the child, Gina and Rachel Tolliver? A mad woman and her six-year old daughter. Grampa Charlie!" He thought, shame twisting and eating at him.

Gina and Rachel Tolliver were here because they were available when he needed them to help fulfill the prophecy and easily led. So he had taken them, both helpless, both innocent, the human equivalent of plastic cigarette lighters, disposable people. And like David's, their probable deaths would be terrible when the time came. And like David, they were here because he had gently prodded them along with the staff's power from the moment he had met them.

"Then why don't you just tell them? Because," Charlie told himself, *"I cannot bear to. My wife, my children, my life died, and I thought I died, too. In my anger and pain, I thought I had become the perfect staff wielder, capable of making any sacrifice, bearing any consequence in my war against the Dark One.*

"But in the end I was all too human and glad of it. I came first to respect those I chose to sacrifice and then to love them as friends. I will not tell them all that lies ahead and what I fear will happen. I will not needlessly frighten them because in the end it will change nothing anyway and—"

Jaws clenched to keep from screaming, Charlie leaped erect, intending to smash the butt end of the staff down as an expression of his shame and rage. Searing pain roared through his chest as he reached the vertical, dropping him first to his knees, then to his belly. Something tore deep inside his chest as his upper body convulsed and he coughed out a fist-sized mass of smoking black blood.

"Good!" He thought even as he feebly choked and wheezed, struggling to clear the blood and mucus out of his airway. *"At last! I'm tired, been tired, and I am more than ready to go home to the Great Mother. Let's hurry up and get this done and over with!"*

Lying prone on his belly, Charlie waited for the final spasm that would kill him, waited for Old Man Death to carry him home. But the sly one must have had business elsewhere because after a few moments Charlie started feeling better than he had in days. Perhaps because he had purged himself of some of the poison or more likely due to the staff's influence. The time of his death had been determined long ago and he knew that the staff wasn't going to grant him peace a moment sooner.

Sighing in resignation, Charlie climbed back up onto the pack. Using the toes of his boots, he scuffed snow over the congealing puddle of blood until it was well hidden, glad that the others hadn't witnessed the indignity of his collapse. As calmness returned, he relaxed a little and his perspective returned.

Fate and reality, as he knew from bitter experience, were tangled skeins of webs stretched across time and space. Something as simple, as innocent, as picking late-season apples could change a life, lives, forever. The seemingly random events that had brought them all here had been ordained long ago and were beyond anyone's conscious control, his included.

Fishing a toothpick out of his top pocket, Charlie used it to impale one of the three dried seed pods lying at the bottom of the aspirin bottle in his right hand. Lowering his lips to the mouth of the bottle, he popped the seed pod into his mouth, near puking at the vile taste. Throwing the toothpick into the fire, he resealed the pill bottle, taking great care to avoid touching any of the inner surfaces. If he brushed his skin against one of the thunder pods or even against where they had rested, he would be comatose for up to seventy-two hours. And like it or not, and he didn't like it a damn bit, he still had things to do.

The seed pod quickly dulled the fire in his chest and Charlie's thoughts soon drifted into more pleasant channels. Pupils dilated by the whopping dose of narcotic he had just taken, he sat unmoving atop his pack, staring into the heart of the fire, thinking about Ellen, remembering.

Book III

Yesterday's Harvest

Memories are hunting horns whose sound dies on the wind.

Guillaume Apollinaire, *Cors de Chasse*

CHAPTER 58

SINCE BIRTH ELLEN had been Charlie's favorite grandchild. In short order she became his favorite person. She smiled and laughed often, delighted by all she saw. In her Charlie found renewal, a reason to keep going after so many bitter seasons of loss. Returning home the week after her birth, he walked straight to the lake and pitched in the last seven beers left in the cooler after the long ride up from the Cities. An hour and a half later, he dumped his still and eighteen fifths of high-octane moonshine in a hundred feet of water about a half-mile offshore. In the thirty-two years since he hadn't touched a drop of alcohol.

As she had grown Ellen's intelligence had become obvious. By the time she was six, their roles had reversed. Sitting in his lap, she would read her chosen bedtime story aloud until she fell asleep.

Charlie's only regret about Ellen, and it was a selfish one, was that she was a city girl and always would be. She had no real interest in wildlife or in the cycles of life on the Great Mother. He tried to instill his reverence, his awe of the natural world into her and failed. Although she tried to hide it, Charlie knew that she was frightened of the great northern wilderness. Frightened by its vastness, frightened by its dark spaces and deep hush, frightened by anything to do with it.

After a few attempts, Charlie yielded to Ellen's aversion to the wilderness, both saddened and relieved by the outcome. Saddened because despite how much they loved each other, there would always be a level on which they wouldn't be able to communicate. Relieved, because with the exception of a few short visits a years, Ellen's fear dictated that she remain in the city far from the dangers prowling the great woods. They spoke at least bi-weekly on the phone but it was usually Charlie that did the traveling.

Which wasn't to say that Ellen was perfect, a goody two-shoes that would have gladdened the hearts of right-wing conservatives everywhere. If she had been smug or arrogant or preachy-pious, it would have broken Charlie's heart along with his foot against her ass while he tried to cure her. Like most kids, she experimented with alcohol, drugs, tobacco, and sex. And like most kids, she got caught.

A series of minor traffic accidents and speeding tickets failed to lighten her lead foot. A roll-over crash at eighty miles an hour which she had walked away from unharmed, saved by the seatbelts and airbag, finally cured her wild driving habits.

And then there was the Big Kahuna, a first-place, blue ribbon fuck-up if ever there was one.

On a late August afternoon sixteen years earlier, Charlie had picked two dozen of his prize vine-ripened tomatoes and was turning them into Marinara Sauce when the phone rang. Picking up the receiver, he at first couldn't recognize who was speaking over the shouting in the background. After a moment, he recognized the voice of Ellen's father, Timothy, and the screamer in the background as Lisa, her mother. Wincing, he held the handset away from his ear before he got a headache. Lisa was his youngest daughter and he loved her dearly, but there was no denying that she could bitch the paint off the wall and Jesus, was she ever LOUD.

"Ellen," Timothy said before pleading with Lisa to calm down.

Guts churning, Charlie stood waiting to find out what had happened to Ellen. Usually the staff kept him well-informed about his loved ones. But sometimes when he was busy, like when he was making tomato sauce, the staff would store the information and tell him later, the supernatural equivalent of voice mail. Growing frustrated, and then angry, Charlie finally lost patience and bellowed at Ellen's father, demanding to know what had happened.

After a long silence, Timothy told Charlie that he and Lisa had come home early from a short vacation and found Ellen in bed with her boyfriend. Naked in bed, as a matter of fact, lying on top of the covers with their limbs intertwined. Not sleeping, but passed out from the effects of an empty bottle of wine next to the bed and a near-empty bag of pot on the night stand.

When awakened, Ellen had raged at her parents, saying that she was moving out of their house and in with Daryl, last name unknown. Forcibly restraining Ellen's mother, Timothy had told Ellen and her boyfriend to dress and come down to the living room where they could talk. Twenty minutes passed and Timothy had become concerned and went back up into her bedroom. All he found was a gentle breeze blowing through the open second story window. Ellen had fled with Daryl Last-Name-Unknown.

Cutting Timothy off mid-sentence, Charlie had asked if the police had been called. No, not yet, he was told, that's our next— Then don't, Charlie had ordered, knowing that the police would create more problems than they solved. Sit tight and wait for her to call, he had told them, and I will be there soon.

Hanging up on Timothy mid-squawk, Charlie turned and regretfully surveyed the fragrant tomato sauce simmering on the stove. When Old Man Winter laid his hand heavy on the land, he would thaw out a container of Marinara Sauce and dream of the summer sunshine that created it. Not this year though. Throwing the kitchen window open, he pitched the sauce, pot and all, out into the backyard. Slamming the window shut, he ran for his truck, remembering to turn the stove off as he passed.

The long hours spent driving down to the Cities gave Charlie plenty of time to mull over Ellen's latest escapade. Long ago he had peered deep inside her and discovered that the demon rum would never find a home there. So he wasn't particularly concerned about her pitching the occasional good drunk, considering it therapeutic for those not afflicted with the Drunkard's Disease.

Ellen's use of marijuana concerned him even less, except for the possible legal problems that it could create for her. A living pharmacopeia in his own right, Charlie openly scoffed at the myth of reefer madness perpetuated by the American government. It never ceased to amaze him how millions of people could be so easily deceived into believing that an innocuous plant which man had been smoking for centuries was the root of so many evils.

The sexuality involved saddened but didn't in any way shock him. At age twelve Ellen had started sprouting in all directions until now, at age sixteen, she was a knockout. Given a concert violin, it didn't surprise him that she had finally decided to fiddle. It grieved him though because it meant that his baby was now a grown woman, soon to marry and start a family of her own, leaving him behind.

By 2:30 a.m. Charlie was parked on a dimly lit street in one of the worst neighborhoods in the Cities. Despite the late hour, large numbers of people in varying stages of intoxication were streaming up and down the street. A black and white police car with two bored-looking officers sitting inside was parked at the end of the block next to a vacant lot. It was a typical late summer evening deep in the heart of any American inner-city neighborhood.

Climbing out of the truck, Charlie turned and carefully locked it. Leave a vehicle unlocked in this neighborhood and even the tire tracks would be stolen before you got back. Leaning against the front fender, Charlie closed his eyes and concentrated. Ellen and Daryl, last name Porter, were aimlessly walking the streets, waiting for the 4:00 a.m. bus to Chicago to arrive.

Their naiveté made Charlie laugh out loud. Ellen's chances of escaping couldn't have been any worse had she locked herself in a broom closet with a soup bone in her pocket and a starving pit bull for company. Still laughing, Charlie pushed off the truck and headed for the mouth of a dark alley across the street. Why, he wondered, were bus stations always located in such bad neighborhoods?

Fifteen feet into the alley he paused, certain that he'd heard something just ahead. Carefully picking his way forward through the pools of shadow, Charlie saw an emaciated Hispanic woman lying in a fetal curl between a pair of overflowing dumpsters. An empty syringe was lying next to her and the narrow belt she'd used as a tourniquet was still cinched around her left arm.. The woman's tiny breasts were exposed and her dress was hiked up around her waist, pearls of semen glistening in her sparse pubic hair. Even in the dim light, Charlie could see bruising around her throat where she had been strangled.

Squatting, he reached out and gently pressed his right index finger against the woman's clammy cheek. Her name was Gabriella Martinez, he learned, a twenty-nine year old prostitute, although she looked closer to fifty. A single mother of three, she was also a long-term heroin addict and alcoholic suffering from full-blown AIDS. The pulse Charlie felt was faint and irregular and becoming weaker by the second. Her breathing was tortuously slow, more of a liquid burbling than true respiration. The higher functions of her brain had already died, leaving only the involuntary functions barely ticking away. Charlie sensed her spirit dancing in the brown skin just under his finger, anxious to begin its long journey home to the Great Mother.

Knowing that it was far too late to heal her, Charlie stroked her cheek and clumsily straightened her clothes, trying to give her back some of the dignity that life had stolen from her. Looking down at her, he thought that no matter the circumstances, it seemed like it was always too late for the Gabriella Martinezes of this life. Reaching into a small leather pouch, he sprinkled a few grains of pollen over her body and wished her a safe journey. Reaching down Charlie gently grasped her neck, blue fire dancing around his fingers, and started Gabriella Martinez on her long voyage home.

Walking down the alley, Charlie felt his right foot connect with something soft hidden in the darkness. Looking down, he saw a blue vinyl tote bag printed with yellow daisies lying on its side, diapers and baby wipes spilling out of its open top. Charlie continued down the alley without stopping but he never forgot about that blue diaper bag.

Stepping out of the alley and into the middle of the street, Charlie stopped and listened, puzzled. Ellen was nowhere to be seen in this block of run-down tenements and seedy shops, yet he could sense that she was somewhere close and should be in sight. DANGER! the staff suddenly advised him, up half a block on the left, HURRY!

Breaking into a shambling trot, Charlie started up the street, damning his wooden legs and plodding middle-aged pace. Up ahead he saw a pair of shadows flow around a parked car and then he caught sight of Ellen. She and Daryl Porter were cowering between a pair of cement apartment stoops, their backs against a brick wall. Six young men were standing in a ragged semi-circle in front of them, drawn by Ellen's beauty.

The gang members' behavior reminded Charlie of timber wolves circling and pulling down prey, which was exactly what would happen here unless he got a move on. Braids flying out behind him, he ran on, legs aching. Charlie arrived just as the gang started moving in. All had guns, he noticed, and all were mesmerized by Ellen, wanting her.

Predator and prey were transfixed by each other, allowing Charlie to arrive unnoticed. Ellen was cowering into the brick work, crying, dreading what she knew lay ahead. Daryl Porter was so bug-eyed with fear that it would have been comical if not for his babbling offer of, "Take the girl, but LET ME LIVE, P-P-L-L-E-E-ASE!"

The alpha gang member, a rangy kid with a purple mohawk, pointed his pistol at Porter and said, "Say good night, cuz, 'cuz I'm gonna bust a cap in—"

"Hello, Blossom, are you all right?" Charlie asked, stepping forward into the dim spill of light from the apartment stoops.

"Grandpa?" Ellen mumbled, her mind not yet comprehending what she was seeing.

Confused, the gang members retreated a couple of steps and stood poised on the balls of their feet, not knowing whether to fight or flee. Their still watchfulness again reminded Charlie of the countless wolves that had lurked near his campsites over the years. Sensing their uncertainty, the gang leader attempted to rally his troops by stepping forward and pointing his pistol at Charlie.

"Grandpa Geronimo," he jeered, "you just fucked—"

Smiling, Charlie smashed the butt end of the staff down on the pavement, sending a shock wave rippling down the street, shaking it like a carpet. The gang members got airborne and tumbled back to earth, several landing with the dry, crunching snap of breaking bones.

"You broke my fucking arm!" the leader screamed, staring in horror at the grey-white splinter of bone protruding from his right forearm.

Despite their injuries, or maybe because of them, several of the gang members started reaching for their dropped pistols. Everyone has a dark room buried in their psyches where their darkest fears dwell, their nightmare terrors. When Charlie cracked open their doors, the gang members scrambled to their feet and fled screaming down the street, pistols forgotten, each pursued by his personal demons.

Hearing footsteps creeping along behind him, Charlie whirled and drove the staff deep into Daryl Porter's belly. The boy collapsed into a wheezing, retching pile while Charlie impassively looked on.

"Blossom, would you like to go home?" he asked.

Ellen hesitated for a few seconds, nearly giving her grandfather a coronary in the process. Much was at stake this night, far more than the lust of a beautiful teenaged girl and her cowardly lover. The skein of fate is far kinder if it is allowed to unravel gracefully in a single strand than if it is pulled tight into a strangler's knot, and it was up to Ellen Talltrees to make that choice.

"G, Grandpa, I, I wanna go home," Ellen wailed, sobs racking her. "I want to, but I can't. Mom and I fight all the time, and I messed up bad, I can't—."

"Of course you can go home if you want to, but it's up to you to choose, I can't decide for you."

"T, take me home, Grandpa, please?" Ellen said, smiling a little.

"Yes, Blossom, of course, let's get out of here. This is an awful place, even the air stinks."

Reaching out, Charlie took Ellen's hand, quieting her into docility with the staff as soon as their fingers touched. The events of the last few minutes had been too much even for this neighborhood and the whoop of approaching sirens could now be heard in the distance. Despite their need for haste, Charlie had one last piece of business to take care of.

Leading Ellen the few feet to the street, he commanded her to stand and wait for him. Turning away, he walked back and stood over Daryl Porter who was still on his hands and knees struggling to breathe, strings of vomit hanging out of his mouth. Swinging the staff in a blurring overhead arc, Charlie smashed Porter across the shoulders, knocking him face down into the pool of vomit.

"Look at me, boy!" he ordered, jabbing the staff into Porter's left kidney for emphasis.

Groaning, Porter rolled his face to one side until he was looking up at Charlie with one eye. Barely resisting the urge to kill him, Charlie squatted down, being careful not to step in the spreading pool of vomit.

"I name you coward, boy!" Charlie said, laying the staff across Porter's neck. "You will stay away from Ellen from now on or I will come for you and it will be terrible beyond anything you can imagine. Understand?"

Porter gurgled-coughed in assent and Charlie commanded, "You will remember this always but you are to never speak of it to anyone. Never!"

The staff flashed blue fire, smashing Porter's face down into the sidewalk. Grimacing in distaste, Charlie reached down and grabbed Porter's hair and dragged him a couple of feet so that he wouldn't drown in his own vomit. Ellen was standing where he'd left her, smiling dreamily, raptly watching the three glowing balls atop a pawn shop across the street.

The first police officer to arrive on the scene was certain that he saw a pair of figures, a grey-haired older man and a much younger woman, walking hand-in-hand down the dimly lit street. But when he looked again, they had vanished, swallowed by the shadows. After that, he was too busy tending the unconscious kid laying bleeding on the sidewalk to give the pair much thought.

Steering Ellen around the corner at the end of the block, Charlie halted and looked back down the street. The paramedics were just lifting Porter into the back of the ambulance on a gurney. Smiling in grim satisfaction, Charlie turned the corner and led Ellen back to his truck.

The hardest battle Charlie fought that night was with Ellen's mother, Lisa. As soon as they pulled into the driveway, she charged out of the house and started shrieking at Ellen. Timothy, Ellen's father, excused himself saying that he was tired and needed some sleep. Watching him walk away, Charlie wondered yet again how anyone could allow themselves to become so thoroughly beaten down, so whipped. And he wondered yet again how anyone could be so cowardly when the welfare of his child was at stake.

Once inside the house, Lisa's abuse toward Ellen became worse, cruel even, leaving wounds that no amount of time would ever heal. Waving her arms, she screamed that she was casting Ellen out of her home. With her dark hair flying around her face, Lisa's behavior reminded Charlie of an agitated raven and he wondered where the darkness in her had come from. She had always been bitchy, but never anything like this.

Sitting at the kitchen table, Ellen wept, begging for forgiveness. Sensing her weakness, thriving on it, Lisa cranked her invective another notch and started pounding on the table with both fists. Fearing for Ellen, Charlie smashed the butt end of the staff down on the linoleum floor and bellowed at Lisa to shut up. Make peace, Charlie told her, or he would take Ellen home with him and neither of them would ever darken her door again.

More importantly, Charlie told her, he would spread the tale of her cruelty toward Ellen throughout the close-knit Poshto community. For the Poshto, a dwindling people, love of family, especially children, was valued above all things. For her cruelty Lisa would become a pariah and be denied the interlocking web of familial relationships that defines Poshto culture.

Angry, Charlie rose from the table, intending to wait outside in his truck. As he walked away, Lisa started barking threats at his back. She would call the police, she would hire a lawyer to haul him into court, she would do this, she would do that, she would do the other. Stopping mid-stride, Charlie turned and walked back toward his daughter. With every step he took he grew until his shoulders were bent to protect his head from the ceiling. Cast in sudden shadow by his approach, Lisa cowered and squirmed in her chair.

"That is enough out of you, child," he said, hunkering down until he was at eye level with her. "Don't threaten me. Not now, not ever. Understand?"

Lisa shook her head, more of a spastic twitch than a nod and Charlie turned away, diminishing to normal size as he walked out of the room. Sitting alone in the truck, he slowly calmed himself. He didn't regret his harsh words to his daughter, they were years overdue, but the necessity for them grieved him terribly. He just couldn't understand how a child of his could be so filled with cruelty and hate.

Ten minutes later, Ellen walked out of the house with her shoulders slumped and her eyes downcast. Seeing her, Charlie felt his guts churn with fear. Although he would take her home with him if necessary, he really didn't want to. Events surrounding the prophecy were gaining momentum and his home would have been a terribly dangerous place for her to live.

Instead, Ellen surprised him by saying that she and her mother had made a tentative peace. Leaning into the window, she kissed him and thanked him for everything. Hugging him hard, she begged him to visit often and Charlie said of course he would. Releasing her grandfather, Ellen stepped back and watched him drive away.

Watching her recede in the rear-view mirror, Charlie started worrying, driving on auto-pilot. The Dark One was growing ever stronger, ever more clever. There were, he reflected, too goddamn many problems and not enough Indian, shaman or not. And this particular Indian was growing old, tired, and cranky.

By the time he arrived home late that night, Charlie felt like he had spent a weekend in one of the world's garden spots, say Beirut or the Korean DMZ. Collapsing into bed, he doubted that he would be able to meet all his responsibilities. Yet somehow he found a way.

Drawing heavily on the staff's power, Charlie managed to visit Ellen at least twice a month, sometimes more often. The sixteen hour round trip played hell on his old pickup and he wore out tires and brakes at a prodigious rate and burned enough oil to delight an Arab potentate. Even with the staff's help though he was fast approaching exhaustion. Soon he would have to either scale back his commitment to his granddaughter or to his calling, a no-win situation if ever there was one.

Finally, on a Friday afternoon in mid-May, Charlie couldn't get up off the couch to start the long drive down to the Cities. Just couldn't, he was too damned tired. Surrendering, he dragged his legs up on the couch and was on the edge of sleep when the phone started ringing. Ignoring it, he adjusted his pillow and rolled over on his side but the damn thing kept ringing.

Years ago he had read a magazine article about the Mennonites. The piece included a photo of a wooden kiosk located about twenty-five yards away from a farmhouse. The booth had an old rotary dial phone inside and was located away from the house so that its ringing wouldn't disturb the tranquility of the residents inside. At the time Charlie had thought it a ridiculous idea. Right about now though, he considered that kiosk a brilliant idea and decided to build one as soon as he got enough rest to make the effort.

On the twelfth ring Charlie gave up and stumbled across the room to answer the phone. With difficulty he reminded himself that he was a shaman, a healer, and the foremost elder of his people. No matter the provocation, he mustn't lose his temper even if he was pissed off enough to kick Godzilla's ass all over Tokyo.

Focusing on keeping the anger out of his voice, it took Charlie a second to realize that he was speaking to Ellen and that she was approaching hysteria. A full-boat scholarship, she babbled, to the School of Nursing at Griffith University in Southern Nebraska contingent on accepting an accelerated curriculum beginning the week after next. Did he think that she should accept it, she really wanted to go?

Yes, Charlie told her, feeling both proud and duplicitous in equal measures. Because she had so many preparations to make, so much shopping to do, would he mind canceling his visit this weekend? No, Charlie had said, he didn't mind at all, visions of his comfortable old bed dancing in his head. He was still coming to her high school graduation, wasn't he? Yes, he had assured her, of course he would be there. And he would come visit her in Nebraska, wouldn't he? Yes, Charlie had promised, he would visit at least once a semester. Goodbye and love you she said and Charlie was left with the dial tone buzzing in his ear.

Easing himself into bed, Charlie congratulated himself on his good fortune, jubilant at the turn of events. Ellen would be getting an excellent education at a private university and a free education at that. More importantly, she would be safe from the Dark One and her role in the prophecy, at least for a while. Best of all, he would get to take an entire weekend off, something that hadn't happened in years. Yawning, he fell hard asleep and didn't wake until seven the next morning.

The next few years had been among the happiest of Charlie's adult life. Added on to the short time he was married to Mary, those years totaled up to a little less than a decade. Not much time, not much happiness in the course of an average person's span of years, but they were all Charlie had, and he treasured his memories of them.

Ellen walking down the aisle in cap and gown, valedictorian of her high school class. Her father Timothy loading her last suitcase into the trunk while Charlie stood with his back turned, hiding his emotions. The many trips to Nebraska to visit her, watching his granddaughter mature into a beautiful, self-assured woman with dazzling academic skills. The long solitary walks on the prairie while she was in class when the tall grass would whisper to him, mourning his cousins passing, and foretelling of their eventual return when the weight of their passage would again shake the earth as of old.

Then in May 1993, the best day of all. Seated in the second row, Charlie watched as Ellen graduated second in her class with a Master of Science Degree in Trauma Nursing. After a lifetime of grief and hard choices,

Charlie wasn't much given to public weeping. But if his smile was any broader that day, the corners of his lips would have met at the back of his head and toppled the top of his skull into his lap.

On the trip back to the Cities, Ellen and Charlie talked of her hopes and dreams for the future. The only dark cloud on Ellen's horizon was the absence of her parents at her graduation. They were in the middle of an acrimonious divorce, Charlie explained, and sometimes other people, especially their children, got hurt. Despite his soothing words, Charlie was furious with Lisa and Timothy and intended to confront them about missing Ellen's graduation as soon as he returned to the Cities. But even though he made repeated efforts over the next few months, including calling the police, Charlie was unable to locate either of them.

Despite her parents' absence, or perhaps because of it, Charlie still thought of that slow trip back to the Cities with Ellen as the best of his many journeys. Once back, Ellen moved in with her maternal grandmother and started looking for work. Within a week she was hired as a trauma nurse at a newly built hospital on the north side of the Cities.

The next three years, 1994 through 1997, were the best of Charlie's golden decade. Gaining recognition both for her nursing and administrative skills, Ellen was soon promoted to Supervising Nurse of the Trauma Department. A primarily administrative position, it dictated that she work banker's hours, Monday through Friday. More importantly, it meant that she was able to schedule her own days off and vacations, many of which she spent with her grandfather.

In late 1997 things started changing. In early November, Ellen called and said that she was seeing a man named Marcus Taylor. He wanted her to meet and spend the Thanksgiving holiday with his parents. Would Charlie mind canceling his scheduled visit? No, he had said, go and have a good time and tell me all about it when you get back. We'll come and spend Christmas with you, Ellen had promised, and then said goodbye and hung up.

Putting the receiver back in the cradle, Charlie loaded his pipe and took a seat in front of the wood stove. Staring at the flames dancing in the firebox, he reflected that the day he had been dreading for so long had finally arrived. Ellen had spoken often of her desire to marry and have children and clearly that time was close at hand. Although Charlie had other grandchildren, as of yet he had no great-grandchildren, and he consoled himself with the thought that Ellen would soon present him with one.

Besides which, Ellen's unexpected absence would allow let him accept an invitation to Thanksgiving dinner from a pretty widow named Etta. Charlie knew he was an old dog, but given a flat field and a fair day, he could still hunt like a son-of-a-bitch. Feeling cheerful now, he picked up the phone again to seal the deal and ask her if there was anything he could bring.

December passed slow and dreary. Christmas week finally came, and so did Ellen and her beau, Marcus Taylor. Half an hour before they arrived, the staff informed Charlie, making his nerves twitch and dance. Pulling on his hat and coat, he stepped out onto the front porch. Engrossed in forecasting tomorrow's weather, he didn't hear their car until it was a hundred yards away. He watched as a new Acura churned and slid its way down the frozen dirt track. The driver barely made the turn into the driveway, narrowly missing the mailbox next to the road.

The passenger door opened and Ellen ran across the yard. Hugging her and listening to her chatter in his ear, Charlie watched over her shoulder as Marcus Taylor climbed out from behind the wheel of the car. He was somewhere around six-feet tall with styled brown hair and a salon tan. Charlie figured the clothes Taylor was wearing were worth more than the latest in his long line of used pickup trucks. Ellen had told him that Taylor was some sort of investment banker specializing in foreign stocks, bonds, and currencies. Investment Grade Asshole was Charlie's assessment of the man, a Moody's Triple-A Investment Grade Asshole to be precise. Worse yet was the darkness Charlie could see boiling and writhing just under Taylor's skin.

Lips downturned at the corners, Taylor paused and disdainfully surveyed his surroundings, as haughty as an aristocrat dismounting from a coach and six into a peasant's front yard. After introducing the two men, Ellen excused herself and left them to get acquainted. Taylor stuck his right hand out to shake, a look of contempt flickering across his face. Grasping the proffered hand, Charlie wasn't the least bit surprised when Taylor started exerting crushing pressure. It must be the health clubs and the steroids, Charlie thought, that have turned this moron's brain to shit.

"Careful, little man," he whispered into Taylor's mind, bearing down until he felt the bones grasped in his hand start to grind together, "or else I will hurt you."

Grunting in pain, Taylor tried to free his hand, but Charlie kept squeezing, wanting to make sure that the lesson had been learned. Hearing Ellen's footsteps approach the door, Charlie released his hand. Glaring at him, Taylor shoved his aching hand into his coat pocket and turned away. When Ellen called to him, Taylor entered the cabin with Charlie directly behind, chuckling into his ear.

That night was Christmas Eve and Charlie still thought of that night as being special, the last of the good times before the on-rushing darkness started seeping in. They all sat together on the couch, Ellen in the middle, talking mostly to Charlie about times gone by. Taylor even lightened up and socialized a little, although he made a point of sitting as far away from Charlie as possible.

At eleven o'clock, Charlie announced that he was tired and said good night, leaving Ellen and her pet baboon to make their own sleeping arrangements. To his surprise, Ellen said she was also tired, but offered to put sheets and blankets on the couch for Taylor before going to bed. Taylor's jaw dropped so far at the thought of sleeping alone on a strange couch that for a second Charlie could actually see his rear fillings.

Somehow managing to keep a straight face, Charlie said good night again and walked the few steps to his bedroom. Gently closing the door behind him, he hurried over to the bed and buried his face in a pair of pillows and roared with laughter until his guts ached. From out in the living room, he heard Taylor pleading with Ellen to let him sleep with her, which made him laugh all the harder. Maybe, just maybe, Charlie thought as he slowly sobered, his granddaughter had more steel in her than he had previously thought. He hoped so, because she was going to need all she could get in the next few years.

Christmas morning was a subdued and tense affair. When Charlie joined Ellen and Taylor in the living room, it was plain from their strained expressions and tense body language that they had been arguing. After they exchanged gifts, Ellen suggested brunch at a local restaurant.

Remembering Taylor's difficulty navigating the frozen dirt road the day before, Charlie led them over to his truck and climbed behind the wheel. Kicking her way through the snow drifts, Ellen opened the passenger door and seated herself next to Charlie. Taylor entered the truck last and sat erect as if afraid that something in the cab might rub off on him.

During the ride over to the restaurant, the mood lightened and Charlie even managed a short conversation with Taylor. By the time they walked through the eatery's front door, Taylor was as near jovial as Charlie had seen him. After they were seated and handed menus, Ellen excused herself and went in search of the ladies' room.

"Mr. Redbird, Charlie, I need to speak to you about something, if it's all right with you."

Charlie had been dreading this moment and now it was here. A black flash of hatred for Timothy Talltrees, Ellen's missing father, surged through him so powerfully that his hands shook. This should be his decision, his heartache, and Charlie should have been a neutral spectator watching events unfold. Instead, he was stuck with the decision and its possible consequences. Lowering his menu to the table, Charlie nodded at him to continue.

"Mr. Redbird," Taylor said, a smug smile spreading across his face, "I would like your permission to marry Ellen."

Blowing out his breath in a long sigh, Charlie thought that what he would like to do was strangle this silly fuck, but he couldn't. It was what old man Dennison, his chess partner, called a fork. Meaning no matter what choice he made, he was going to lose something.

For whatever reason, his granddaughter was smitten with this idiot. It was beyond Charlie why; the vagaries of the feminine heart had always eluded him. If he said no, Ellen would marry Taylor anyway. All that withholding his permission would accomplish was a lasting estrangement from Ellen with no change in the ultimate result.

The real decision though was made by the staff. For the last few months whenever Charlie peered into the future, Ellen was moving further away from the center of the web of probabilities surrounding the prophecy. Today when he had risen with the sun and looked long into what would be, Ellen had vanished from sight. Occasionally, the whirlpool of probabilities that swirled through time and space would seize an individual central to the prophecy and deposit him or her safely out of harm's way. Not often, but it did happen.

The maelstrom had swept Ellen from the epicenter of the prophecy and straight to Marcus Taylor. Any attempt to alter her current fate would drop her back into the whirlpool and on to places and dangers unknown. The only problem with looking gift horse in the mouth, Charlie thought sourly, was that they usually turned out to be jackasses with halitosis.

"I don't much like you, son," Charlie said after hesitating for so long that he got the satisfaction of seeing Taylor start squirming. "But you do have my permission to marry Ellen because if I refuse, it will hurt her deeply. In return for my permission, I want you to always promise to be kind to her."

"Then I have your blessing to marry her?"

"There is a difference between permission and a blessing," Charlie replied, "and I'm a man who chooses his words carefully."

Angry now, flushing red, Taylor snapped, "And if I'm not kind to her, just what in the hell are you going to do about it, old man?"

A tremor struck, rattling glasses and flatware and shaking the building down to its foundations. A few people screamed, someone shouted, "Earthquake!", and the stampede was on for the exits. Suddenly as it started, the tremor stopped and everyone froze before slowly returning to their seats.

Born and educated in California, Taylor was ready to flee, certain that the Big One had found him at last. The room quieted and he returned his attention to the table, becoming transfixed by the twin reflections of himself floating in the bottomless wells of Charlie's black eyes.

"Do not mock me, little man," Charlie said. "If you ever hurt Ellen, I will come for you and it will be terrible beyond anything you can imagine. You would do well to remember that and never forget it."

Gasping for air, certain that his lungs were filling with frigid water, Taylor leaned out in the aisle and retched but brought up nothing but a thin string of bile. Seeing him near collapse, Ellen rushed back from where she had been waiting near the ladies' room and started examining him. Wheezing, Taylor sat back up in the booth with Ellen's help. Resting his head against the padded banquette, he opened his eyes and found himself looking at Charlie.

Pleading Taylor's illness, Ellen told the waitress they were leaving, and asked Charlie to drive them back to the cabin. During the ride back, Taylor sat rigid in the passenger seat of the truck, staring out of the passenger side window to avoid looking at Charlie. Sensing the tension between the two men, Ellen remained silent, unsure of how to mend the situation.

When Charlie parked in the driveway, Taylor climbed out of the truck and started toward his car. Looking upset, Ellen hurried into the cabin to gather up their belongings. Halfway to the Acura, Taylor slipped on the icy driveway and fell hard on his back. Although Taylor's fall had nothing to do with him, Charlie grinned at poetic justice of it. Making sure Ellen was out of sight in the cabin; he walked over and jerked Taylor to his feet. Snatching the Acura's door open, he stuffed Taylor behind the wheel.

Kneeling down, he stuck his head in the car and said, "Never forget what I told you, because I won't."

Slamming the door shut, Charlie walked over to the bottom of the porch steps to wait for Ellen. A moment later she appeared carrying a heavy suitcase in each hand. Meeting her halfway up the steps, he took the suitcases and carried them over to the car. Closing the trunk, he turned and saw Ellen crying with her hands over her face.

Hugging her, Charlie kissed her on the forehead and said, "Now, Blossom, don't beat up on yourself, everything will be fine. You have a long drive ahead, so you better get going."

Sniffling, Ellen kissed her grandfather goodbye and got into the car. Climbing up the steps to the porch, Charlie watched Taylor fishtail down the icy driveway. Many women, he knew, were happily married to men filled with dark impulses. Watching the darkness inside Taylor boil out of the Acura and chase it down the frozen road, Charlie was certain that Ellen's marriage wasn't going to be one of them. Wishing for the first time in years that he could strap on a snorkel and submerge himself in a fifth of something high-proof, Charlie walked into the cabin to chew on his misery.

Filling the coffeepot with water and grounds, he set it on the wood stove to brew. Taking a seat in front of the firebox, he coaxed his pipe to life and sat thinking. There would be a price to be paid for today's flash of temper and he knew it would be a dear one when it came due. Pride and temper had always been his greatest faults but Charlie refused to condemn himself. There were limits beyond which he refused to be pushed, no matter the cost.

Winter dragged on while Charlie found endless trivial chores to stay busy with and stave off his increasing anxiety about Ellen's upcoming marriage. His few telephone conversations with her had been marked by an increasing frostiness and Charlie knew that he was starting to pay the price for his actions toward Taylor.

In late February, an ornate wedding invitation arrived announcing a wedding date of June the tenth. A schedule accompanying the invitation listed an interminable round of pre-wedding parties and rehearsals. Opening the envelope intending to put the schedule of events in for safe-keeping, he noticed a handwritten note stuck in the crevice down at the bottom. It was from Ellen and stated that "under the circumstances," she had decided that her Uncle Leonard would give her away at the altar and that she was sure he understood. There was no affectionate closing on the note, just the black slash of her signature.

Dropping the note on the table, Charlie buried his head in his hands, knowing that he would never understand. He had expected the price for his actions toward Taylor to be high, but not this high and never this soon. Looking back in years to come, Charlie marked this moment as when he departed from a hale middle-age into the twilight land of the elderly.

That night, despite the frigid weather, Charlie tramped for miles down frozen dirt roads and through towering forests seeking peace. But no matter how far he walked, he still couldn't find solace. Near dawn and near frozen, he returned to the cabin. Stoking up the wood stove, Charlie filled the coffeepot and waited for his toes to thaw out. About the time the coffee brewed and his toes started tingling, the sun started rising, a sight he was certain he'd be seeing a lot more of in the future.

Although tempted to skip Ellen's wedding, after some thought Charlie decided that he would go. Ellen may have been angry with him, but he wasn't angry with her and he wanted to see her walk down the aisle into married life. Also, he refused to be run off by someone as inconsequential as Marcus Taylor.

Early in the second week of June, Charlie braced himself for what lay ahead, and left for the Cities to attend the wedding. Driving down he was in a bittersweet mood, reflecting that he wouldn't miss the long ride at all. In the years since Ellen's birth he estimated that he had driven enough miles visiting her to circumnavigate the Earth several times over and the miles didn't pass as easily now as they once had.

Arriving in the Cities, Charlie checked into one of the generic chain hotels just off the interstate. Normally a gregarious man, he usually stayed with one of his children when visiting so that he could socialize with his extended family when Ellen was busy. Walking into the room, Charlie dropped his bag on the valet rack, thinking that he damn sure didn't feel like socializing or seeing anyone, family or otherwise. After a quick hunt through the Yellow Pages, he found what he was looking for and scribbled the address down on a piece of hotel stationary.

Closing the door behind him, he left the room without ever having taken the time to sit down.

Twenty-five minutes later, Charlie pulled up in front of the establishment he was seeking and felt his blood-pressure soar. The end of the business day was near, so he had no choice other than to climb out of the truck and enter the upscale store. A half hour later he walked out with a rented tuxedo and matching shoes, muttering under his breath about the clerk's attitude.

Arriving back at the hotel, Charlie showered and changed into casual clothes. Stopping first at the front desk to ask directions, he managed to drive across the Cities to his destination without getting lost. When he pulled into the restaurant's parking lot and saw the waiting parking valets, he sighed and finally surrendered to the fact that this was going to be a seriously shitty few days.

Leaving his battered pickup truck with a disbelieving valet, Charlie walked inside and caught sight of two of his cousins disappearing around a corner. He hurried to catch up, hoping that he wouldn't lose them in the restaurant's dim interior. Joining the end of the file, Charlie followed them into a private banquet room.

Rising from a table at the far end of the room, Ellen came over to greet them. Reaching Charlie last, she pecked him on the cheek and tried to step away. Holding her arm for a second, Charlie could sense her anger and her deep sense of hurt. To his surprise, Charlie also detected a tiny cluster of cells deep in her womb which were the embryonic beginnings of his great-grandson. Ellen was a few hours pregnant and although it was far too soon for conventional obstetrics to detect it, Charlie was certain of what he'd seen.

"I have missed you, Blossom," he said, leaning forward to bus her on the cheek.

Nodding and looking near tears, Ellen wriggled out of his grasp and crossed the room to rejoin her scowling fiancé. Looking around, Charlie saw a table placard with his name on it and took a seat in front of it. Picking up a menu, he was pleased to see that it was written entirely in French and offered an eclectic selection of continental cuisines.

"I can help translate that for you and help you order if you like," a voice said in his ear, startling him.

Looking up, Charlie saw a young man dressed in the traditional black and white garb of a waiter locked into a Michelin three star hover just aft of his right shoulder.

"Sonny, I've been reading, writing, and cooking French since before you were an itch in your daddy's pants," he replied, reflecting that petty as it was, sometimes being an asshole was its own reward. "And I'm capable of ordering my meal without your assistance. Now get your pad out and see if you can get my order right without screwing it up. You need help spelling anything, you let me know and I'll be more than happy to help you."

Speaking rapidly in fluent French, Charlie ordered a six-course meal while the flustered waiter struggled to keep up and write everything down. After making the waiter read his order back to ensure it was correct, Charlie let him escape back to the safety of the kitchen. A strangled giggle off to his right captured Charlie's attention and he turned to confront the source.

"Are you always this gracious with the servants," the blonde pixie seated next to him asked, "or are you trying to set a new standard for uncivilized behavior?"

Glaring, Charlie paused a second before answering to look her over. Twenty years old and no more than five feet tall, he guessed, maybe a hundred pounds, if that. A short helmet of blonde hair, too brassy to be anything but dyed, accented her pointed face. A hellion's grin was all that saved her from waif-dom. That, the tattoos, and the multiple rings and studs in her ears, nose, and tongue. Charlie thought that she couldn't have been any more thoroughly pierced had she tripped and landed face-first on a porcupine.

Never one to let a verbal jab go unanswered and still feeling cranky, he asked, "Can you drink fluids with all that metal stuck in your head or do you leak like a sieve?"

The young woman's face flushed red and Charlie winced, certain that he'd needled her a little too hard. Choked strangling noises issued from her throat and then suddenly she was hooting with laughter, her entire body shaking with the joy of it. Struggling to keep a straight face, Charlie finally surrendered after a few seconds and started laughing with her. After a while, he noticed that the other guests were staring at them but he decided that he didn't care and just kept on laughing.

"I'm Katie Henderson," she announced, sticking out one tiny hand and wiping her eyes with the other. "I'm Prince Peckerhead, that's the groom-to-be's, second cousin. I'm in poor odor at court because me and the girls took Princess Ellen, that's the bride-to-be, out for an unscheduled bachelorette party and we didn't get her home until five in the morning and now he's pissed off at me. What's your excuse? We get any further away from the head table and we'll be sitting on the toilets in the ladies' room and talkin' to each other through the walls."

"I'm Princess Ellen's maternal grandfather and I—"

"Oh-my-God, I'm sorry," she blurted out. "Shit, me and my mouth! I like Ellen a lot, I really do, it's just the way that he, they, carry on, I, I—"

"That's all right, it's about the best description of the situation I've heard so far," Charlie said. "I'm sitting way down here because I also pissed off Prince Peckerhead. Great name by the way, it fits him perfectly."

Katie sat thinking for a few seconds before telling him, "That night we went out, Ellen said there was a problem between you two, you and the prince I mean. But she didn't seem to know what was wrong. I wanted to talk to her some more about it because I could tell it was really bothering her, but then we drank some more Margaritas and the male strippers showed up and we got some dollar bills and, well, things kinda got out of control and we never did talk about it again."

Charlie's shock must have shown on his face because Katie blushed beet red and started fidgeting, beginning with her toes and reaching the crown of her head a second later.

"Well, don't look so scandalized," she said, sounding defensive. "Girls will be girls, you know. If you don't clamp your jaw shut soon, you're gonna start drooling."

Closing his mouth, Charlie just grinned.

"I'm studying Anthropology and Archaeology at the university," Katie rattled out, speaking as fast as she could. "Ellen said that normally you disapprove of academics prying into your culture, but that you might help me if you liked me. I mean, I hope you do, so far you've lasted two minutes and that's longer than most people, including my parents. Please? I'm not doing so well in school and I really need some help. If you don't want to, I'll understand and I hope we can still be friends."

Believing that Katie had arranged to sit next to him for the purpose of making her pitch, Charlie stiffened and started getting angry. Turning to snap at her, Charlie brushed Katie's shoulder and was surprised to discover she was guileless. And underneath all that brass, she was very intimidated by him. Gathering his thoughts, Charlie had a sudden flash of intuition and knew it was no accident that they'd met.

"You wanna be careful," she told him, "you're about to start slobbering again."

"Usually I don't like anthropologists and the like," he said, watching disappointment dance across her face. "But in your case, I'm going to make an exception provided that you do something for me."

"What's that?" she asked, suspicion and hope commingled in her voice.

"Ellen is my favorite grandchild, well, really my favorite person. Just because she's angry with me right now doesn't matter because no matter what, I'll always love her very much. I want you to continue being her friend; she will need your friendship very badly in the days ahead.

"Sometime soon, she is going to need me, her grandfather, just as bad. When that time comes, I want you to call and tell me. I don't mean spy on her or tell me every time she has a marital spat or you two go out to see the male strippers. I mean that sometime in the near future she is going to need me desperately and when it happens, I want you to call me. You're intelligent; you'll know when that time comes. In return, I'll teach you more about First American Anthropology and Ethnology than you ever wanted to know. Deal?"

"Deal!" she proclaimed, sticking out her hand.

They talked all through dinner, which amazed Charlie considering how much she ate. How anyone so tiny could eat so much and still manage to talk was beyond him.

"I could never live in one of those little eastern states like Delaware or New Hampshire," Katie confided during the fish course. "I'd start a famine for sure and thousands would starve. I may be little but I sure do like to eat!"

Impressed, Charlie sat watching her lay waste to the sea bass. In between courses and bites, he explored just how much she knew about her chosen field of study. To his surprise he found her quite knowledgeable for one so young. Katie's main problem, he surmised, was one that confronted many intelligent students. At least for now, she was incapable of warping her esoteric knowledge and exuberant personality into the channels desired by her professors and her grades reflected their displeasure.

Near the end of the meal, their roles were reversed and Katie started asking the questions. Digging deep into a lifetime's of accumulated knowledge, Charlie was able to answer most of them after some serious thought. But he was unable to answer a pair of related questions about matriarchal clan relationships, something that hadn't happened to him for a very long time. Ransoming off half his Black Forest Torte bought him two weeks to find the answers and mail them to her.

Over coffee, Charlie realized how much he had enjoyed his conversation with Katie and how much he had missed talking to Ellen. Looking around the room, he noticed how the other guests, especially the Poshto contingent, avoided meeting his gaze. Like any animal, humans can sense potential conflict and seek to avoid it.

Returning his eyes to his coffee, Charlie thanked the luck that had seated him next to Katie.

A few minutes later the party broke up. Standing on her tiptoes, Katie surprised him by planting a wet smack on his cheek. Would Charlie, she inquired, like to join her for an excursion downtown to listen to a post-punk-metal-thrash band? Flattered but wincing at the headache the featured entertainment promised, Charlie politely declined and thanked her for the pleasant evening. Grinning, he watched Katie break into a half-skip, half-trot into the dim recesses of the restaurant, certain that the floor joists would collapse under her feet from the weight of the ballast she had just taken aboard.

Outside, Charlie said goodbye to his relatives and handed the valet his ticket. Headlights flooded the parking lot and tires squealed as a car slid around the building's corner and accelerated toward the street. The small knot of remaining guests hurriedly stepped back as Taylor's Acura flashed by. The tension and anger in the car's wake washed over Charlie, making him frown in distaste.

"Asshole!" he muttered to no one in particular.

The clatter of lashing valves announced the arrival of Charlie's pickup and he stepped forward off the curb, eager to make his escape. The valet stepped on the brakes and the truck sailed by with the unmistakable grinding noise of worn brake pads before coming to a rocking halt about ten feet away.

Meeting the valet halfway, Charlie gave him a five-dollar bill and said, "Cheer up, son. Just think about all those yuppie chariots you drive night after night, Mercedes, Beamers, Caddies, whatnot. Must get kinda boring after a while. But this here pickup truck of mine is a one-of-a-kind American original. Consider yourself blessed that I let you drive her around the parking lot."

Laughing, Charlie climbed behind the wheel and clattered off toward the street trailing thin clouds of oily blue smoke. Tomorrow, he reminded himself, he had better pour a couple of quarts of thirty-weight into the old beater or else he'd be joining the ranks of the dreaded pedestrian tribe.

Walking into the hotel room, Charlie felt his earlier attempt at good humor drain away. Undressing and climbing into bed, he stared up at the spayed gunnite ceiling and listened to the semis roar by out on the interstate. When the alarm clock read 4:30 a.m., he gave up on all hope of sleep and got out of bed. Opening the room's only window, he dragged a chair over, lit his pipe, and settled in for a serious think.

Needing a break after a couple of hours, he hiked a few blocks to a convenience store and bought himself a large coffee. On the walk back to the hotel, Charlie considered the problem anew and still didn't get anywhere. Walking into his room, he sat down by the window again and kept thinking. Two hours later he finally conceded defeat.

Ellen was marrying the wrong man and she was estranged from him, two facts that weren't going to change no matter how much he disliked them. The long mental battle over and the war lost, Charlie slumped forward in his chair as fatigue toxins swept through him. Hearing a clattering just down the hall, he got to his feet and crossed the room. Opening the door, he hung the "Do Not Disturb" sign on the outside doorknob just in time to interrupt an irate looking maid mid-knock. Closing the door, he crossed the room, flopped onto the bed, and fell asleep without bothering to undress.

Five hours later, hunger woke Charlie. After showering and changing, he headed out to find something to eat. After feeding his truck a couple of quarts of oil, he drove down the street to a pancake house and ordered a large breakfast. After finishing a second cup of coffee, he looked at his watch and sighed. After paying his tab, Charlie walked out to his truck. Rush hour traffic was just starting and the drive across the Cities was tortuous. Pulling into the lot, he sat looking at his destination for a moment.

A dark stone Episcopal church stretched out for half a block on either side of his truck. Its soaring spire rose at least a hundred feet into the air above a gothic bell tower. Stained glass windows set inside deep recessed vaults pierced the church's walls at regular intervals. A host of ornate stone gargoyles looked down from the roof line above.

Climbing out of the truck, Charlie swept his eyes over the towering pile and muttered, "I wonder where that damn hunchback is."

Entering the apse, he paused to let his eyes adjust to the church's gloomy interior. Hearing a few tentative organ chords echo through the building, Charlie followed the music into the center of the church. When he arrived in the main chapel, the rehearsal had just gotten underway. Everything ground to a halt while he mumbled an apology and found his place in the proceedings.

Putting his mind in neutral and his feet in gear, Charlie eased along learning his place in tomorrow's festivities, which consisted of walking up the aisle and sitting in the right pew. Four repetitions later and just about the time he was certain brain damage was imminent, the rehearsal was over. Anxious to escape this gloomy mausoleum of a church, Charlie said his goodbyes and left. Outside in the parking lot, he sat in the truck breathing deeply, grateful for even the Cities' stale air after the stuffy atmosphere inside the church.

Cranking the engine over, Charlie pulled out onto the street. A pair of left turns took him to a mall about a mile away. Congratulating himself on his navigation, Charlie climbed out of the truck and went inside to browse the Borders store. A few minutes later he emerged with a pair of just-published detective novels. A quick stop at the art store next door for some new charcoal pencils and a heavy bond drawing pad and he was ready to leave.

Four blocks from the hotel he saw it, a neon oasis floating in the summer twilight. Almost of its own volition the truck glided over to the curb and stopped in front of the liquor store. Just inside the door, perfectly aligned rows of bottles stood glittering under the harsh glow of the overhead fluorescent lighting.

Neural synapses fired up and down the length of Charlie's body. Gastric juices started churning and his mouth went dry with the craving, the need for release, for oblivion. Just one pint, he decided, just one pint of vodka to take the edge off. He'd more than earned it, today and every other goddamned day as a matter of fact. His fingers touched the door latch and the staff smashed down on his right elbow. Grunting, Charlie leaned forward, cradling his injured elbow with one hand.

"Fuck you!" he spat, eyes tearing with pain.

Snarling, determined, Charlie reached for the door handle again. This time, the staff flew across the cab and lanced him in the short ribs. Slammed hard against the door, Charlie grunted and wheezed, fighting for breath.

"All right, I give," he gasped after recovering enough to speak.

The agony racking his ribs and elbow vanished as if they had never been. Pulling away from the curb, Charlie drove back to the hotel. Parking in the lot, he sat thinking about that pint of vodka he had wanted so badly. The thirst was gone now, leaving him feeling washed out and tired. Starting to drink again after all these years would have been an unmitigated disaster. Still, he didn't like having his choices dictated to him, no matter how ill-considered.

Gathering up his purchases, Charlie walked back to his room. Tossing his packages on the desk, he climbed into the shower. Emerging in a billowing cloud of steam twenty minutes later, he pulled on a pair of sweat pants and a tee-shirt and prepared for the long night ahead.

Throwing the paperbacks on the bed, he tore the complimentary bookmark in half, putting half inside the front cover of each novel. Picking up the drawing pad, he laid it out on the desk after making sure that the light was passable. Taking the charcoal pencils out of the box, he laid them on the pad and got a small pencil sharpener out of his bag. Placing the small wastebasket between his feet to catch the shavings, Charlie carefully sharpened the expensive pencils, using his pen knife to put the last fine point on.

Lying down on the bed, he was soon lost in the desert world of Jim Chee and Lieutenant Leaphorn. A half-hour or so later, he marked his place at the end of a chapter and stood up. After a bone cracking stretch, he sat down at the desk and began sketching a hen and drake wood ducks, his personal favorites. Forty-five minutes later he was back on the bed, working a homicide case with Harry Bosch.

Rotating between the bed and the desk, Charlie read a couple of hundred pages and completed three excellent sketches of wood ducks in different postures. At three-thirty in the morning, he yawned, signed the last sketch, and put the charcoal pencils back in their box.

Climbing under the covers, Charlie drifted off almost immediately but didn't sleep well. Mocking bass laughter chased him down endless identical corridors without any doors. Every time he dared a glance over his shoulder, a vast dark shadow was closing in, nearly engulfing him. He didn't have the staff, couldn't find it, and knew that he was helpless without it. The taunting laughter formed words, a mindless chant, "Staff's mine, staff's mine, staff's mine..."

"You in there, shut the fuck up!" a man's voice bellowed from the room next door as he pounded on the wall for emphasis.

Charlie's eyes shot open and he heard a wailing shriek of utter panic. Realizing that he was the source of the awful noise, he slammed his jaw shut. Struggling back to full consciousness, he discovered that he was lying in a pool of sweat and that his heart was beating dangerously fast for a man well into his sixties. Laying still and concentrating on his breathing, Charlie slowed his pulse until he was sure that he wasn't going to die of a coronary in the next few minutes. Taking his time, he levered himself upright on the third attempt and swung his legs over the edge of the bed.

Feeling better now that he had escaped the clammy sheets, Charlie looked around and was relieved to see the staff leaning against the bedside table. Standing up, he headed for the shower. The hot water sluiced away the last of the nightmare and Charlie decided he wanted two things and he wanted them as soon as possible. Food and coffee, in great quantities, and the sooner the better. Stepping out of the shower, he hurriedly dried, dressed, and headed for his truck.

Five minutes later he pulled into the parking lot of the pancake house. Driven by his appetite, he climbed out of the truck and hustled across the asphalt. Once inside, he ordered a huge breakfast. Breakfast had always been his favorite meal of the day, tasting best at dawn when the day was new and free of care. Finished eating, Charlie pushed his plate back and sat drinking coffee. Paying his tab, he walked out to his truck with a great deal less enthusiasm than he'd demonstrated on the way in.

Walking into the hotel room, Charlie sighed and set to work. He shaved with care, going over his face twice. After some truly inspired cursing he managed to get the tuxedo on and looking right. Carefully braiding his hair, he bound the end of each tress with an engraved silver band well over a century old. Mindful not to break the delicate clasp, he hung a turtle shell amulet with amethyst and turquoise spacers hung around his neck. A pair of engraved solid silver hoop earrings were added next. Slipping a heavy amethyst ring in a silver setting over the third finger of his right hand, Charlie turned and preened in front of the mirror, vain as any peacock and just as proud. Beyond question, Charles Lantot Redbird was the most stylish First American in the State of Minnesota, maybe on the entire continent, this beautiful June morning. Well pleased, Charlie fired up his pipe and sat smoking, stealing the odd admiring glance at the mirror now and then. Too soon, the tobacco was spent and it was time to go.

Parking next to the church, Charlie crossed the parking lot and joined the rest of the wedding party standing in front of the doors. The steeple clock struck eleven and the wedding party started into the church. After some initial confusion, Charlie and the rest of the party sorted themselves out and found their seats. A few minutes later, the resonant chords of Hayden's Wedding March slowly gathered volume and filled the chapel.

Stunning in an ivory wedding gown with a long train, Ellen walked down the aisle on her Uncle Leonard's arm. As she stood at the altar, the darkness inside Marcus Taylor boiled out and enveloped Ellen, hiding her from Charlie's sight. Hanging his head, Charlie wept in black despair, trying to console himself with the thought that at least she was safe from a far greater evil. Tried, but failed miserably.

An interminable time later, Charlie shuffled out with the rest of the wedding party, leaning heavily on his staff. This was the first moment that he felt truly elderly, the first time that he knew in the depths of his soul that he was old.

Getting into his truck, Charlie sat waiting for the procession of vehicles to form up. During the drive across town, his composure returned. In the course of a long and difficult life, he had suffered much and always endured. While it couldn't be said the Charlie was a ray of sunshine, he was hanging in there.

Pulling into the country club parking lot, Charlie had a sudden flash of memory. Several months earlier one of the local television stations had run an expose on the club's membership policies. No African-Americans had ever been granted membership, no Jews, no Asians, and for damn sure no First Americans. Sighing, he got out of the truck, wishing that the day would hurry up and get over with.

As he stood at rear of the crowd waiting in front of the glass doors, someone pinched him on the ass, HARD.

Caught by surprise, Charlie yelped and came close to exiting his rented shoes. Hearing an ever increasing giggle behind him, he turned to confront the individual that had assaulted him. Katie Henderson, his dinner partner from the night before last, was standing with both hands locked over her midriff, trying to stifle her laughter.

"I'm, I'm, I'm suh, suh," she gasped.

Unable to speak, she stood laughing helplessly while Charlie glowered down at her.

"I, I'm sorry," she giggled, undeterred by his wrath. "I, I couldn't help it, you have such a nice butt for an old guy."

After an initial snort, Charlie started laughing. After a few seconds he was leaning on the staff to avoid ending up on the sidewalk.

Taking the arm he proffered, she asked, "Wanna take a lady to a wedding reception?"

"If I could find one I would," he replied.

Passing through the entry doors, they started down the reception line. Marcus Taylor offered Charlie a limp hand to shake and Ellen gave him a dry peck on the cheek. She murmured something inaudible in his ear and then they both turned and walked away.

Arriving at the gift table, Charlie fished a flat, gift-wrapped package from his pocket and added it to the rapidly growing pile. He had chosen antique First American silver jewelry for both of them. Turquoise earrings and a necklace for the newly minted Mrs. Taylor and matching cufflinks and a tie tack for her husband. Deeply hurt by Ellen's behavior, Charlie decided that he should leave before things got any worse. Turning on his heel, he almost tripped over Katie.

"I'm really sorry," she said, and not about nearly tripping him. "Please don't go, I don't have anybody else to sit with except my Aunt and Uncle."

Touched by her concern and startled by her prescience, Charlie allowed himself to be led to a table at the rear of the room. After seating Katie, Charlie sat down and prepared himself for an extended exercise in misery. As soon as she sat down, Katie had started chattering in his ear. At first, he considered it a transparent effort to jolly him along, but then he realized that she was thoroughly enjoying herself.

She had it all going on. The other wedding guests. Personal hygiene. Ethnicities. Sexual foibles. If it had something to do with the human condition, Katie Henderson had something, usually several somethings, to say about it. Blessed with a bawdy sense of humor, Charlie was delighted with the unexpected wealth of new material.

When the time came, Charlie squired Katie through the buffet line and was again amazed at her appetite. Scanning back through his memory, he was certain he'd never seen anyone so little eat so much at one sitting. While the toasts were being said the buffet line was taken down by a small army of service help. Seeing Katie's disapproving frown, Charlie leaned over and whispered that he would take her out to eat later if she was still hungry.

When the band started playing, Charlie asked Katie for the first dance. Leading her out onto the floor, he was surprised at how well she danced.

"Fooled you, didn't I?" She said, smiling up at him. "Mrs. Gracini's School of Dance for Young Ladies and Gentlemen, Fall 1992, blue ribbon in the waltz. Right after that I got expelled for punching that fat bastard

Eric Rimes in the eye for pinching my left tittie. The way my parents carried on, you'd a thought I'd cold-cocked His Holiness the Pope and got kicked out of Harvard Divinity School."

Laughing, Charlie glided her across the floor, swept away by the majestic music. They danced the entire set before returning to their table *via* the bar.

Eying the fish bowl goblet Katie was carrying, Charlie said, "If that glass was any bigger, you'd be able to swim in it."

"Just watch this," she laughed. "Take two shots of premium tequila, one shot of Triple Sec, some sweet and sour mix, shake well, and *voila*, instant social *faux pas*."

Taking a sip, she smiled, and then started choking. The staff thrummed in Charlie's hand and an electric tingling pulsed through his skull. The tableware rattled as he jumped to his feet and Katie barely kept her margarita upright. Guests at the surrounding tables gaped at the sight of a distinguished-looking Native American man standing wreathed in a nimbus of blue fire. A heartbeat later he was just an elderly man leaning on his stick and the onlookers were certain they'd been deceived by the room's dim lighting.

"Hello, Blossom," Charlie said, "You startled me."

Ellen Talltrees Taylor looked perplexed, not understanding how she had startled her grandfather from over ten feet away. The real reason for Charlie's alarm was holding his wife's left hand with a malicious smile on his face. Black tentacles were writhing out of Taylor around Ellen and the fetal cells in her belly, making Charlie's flesh crawl. Feeling pressure on his left leg, he looked down and saw Katie clutching at his leg like a frightened four-year old.

"Ch, Ch," she stammered, wide-eyed with fear.

"She is a seer," he thought, surprised, then whispered deep into her mind. "Don't fret yourself, child. All will be well."

"Grandfather, will you please bless our marriage?" Ellen asked and Charlie knew why Taylor was smiling and whose idea this had been.

For decades Charlie had presided at countless weddings. Since Ellen's birth he had dreamed of the day when he would sing the ancient song and bless her way into married life. And now he couldn't, unwilling to betray the power he had been entrusted with for any reason.

"No, Blossom, I'm sorry, but I cannot bless your marriage," he sadly told her.

Great crystalline tears filled Ellen's black eyes as she turned and fled across the room, hands raised to her face. Smirking, Marcus Taylor took a long step forward.

"Leave here, old man!" he snapped. "Leave right now and take this pint-sized piece of shit with you!"

Stepping forward, he grabbed Charlie's arm and froze, unable to move.

"We're going," Charlie said, freeing himself. "Remember our earlier conversation, little man, and how it tasted?"

Finished speaking, Charlie took Katie's arm and the two headed toward the exit. Behind them, Marcus Taylor was down on all fours spewing up cold, metallic tasting water from a lake hundreds of miles to the north. A pair of uniformed security guards, one male, one female, hustled toward them from across the room.

"Peace, palefaces," Charlie said, striving for a little humor in a very unfunny situation. "We surrender."

To his surprise, both of the guards smiled and took up flanking positions on either side of them. Once through the exit and out of the sight of the guests, they relaxed even more.

"That Taylor is a complete fucking asshole!" the female guard blurted out. "Whatever it is you did to him, I hope he chokes to death on it!"

Brushing up against her arm, Charlie caught a quick flash of sexual violence, of rape, with Taylor at its center. Squeezing his eyes shut, Charlie silently wailed in grief for Ellen. Pretending to stumble, he jostled Katie into the male guard. A vision followed of a fifty dollar bill floating to the ground. As the guard bent down to pick up the bill, a foot smashed him in the face. Marcus Taylor was standing over him, laughing, rimmed in red from the blood running into the guard's eyes. Arriving at the truck, Charlie boosted a still-crying Katie into the cab.

Turning to the two security guards, he said, "I'm sorry, my Ellen isn't—"

"Please," the male guard sighed, sounding weary and defeated, "it would be better for all of us if you just left. Please?"

Nodding, Charlie climbed behind the wheel and started the old Chevy. Clattering out of the county club parking lot, he noticed that Katie was staring blankly out the windshield into space. A few blocks later, Charlie found what he was looking for and pulled into the parking lot of a donut shop. Ignoring the stares caused by their formal wear, he led Katie over to a quiet corner.

It took a pot of coffee and well over an hour for Charlie to make Katie understand what had happened and the depth of her talent. When she started eating a fourth chocolate covered donut, he figured that she was pretty much recovered.

"I can't help it," she said, noticing his stare. "When I get upset or nervous I like to eat."

"I've noticed you also like to eat when you're perfectly calm."

"Yeah, well, there's that too," she laughed, eying the last donut in the box. "Lucky for you, donut, I'm full and it looks like you'll survive until breakfast, maybe even lunch. You better drive me home now, Pops. It's getting late and I wouldn't want an old geezer like you to get overtired."

"Yeah, yeah," Charlie grumped, relieved by the return of her insouciant good nature.

Forty-five minutes later, he dropped her off at an upscale home out in the southern suburbs.

Before getting out of the truck, she surprised him by saying, "Charlie, please be careful, there's something dangerous going on, I feel it. Promise?"

"There's nothing to worry abou—"

"Oh, horseshit!" She said, bussing him on the cheek. "You be careful. I'll call and I'll be up to visit."

And with that she was gone, a running pixie in a flowing blue evening gown. Charlie was saddened by her leaving; meeting her had been the only bright spot in an otherwise shitty few days. Driving back to the hotel, he decided that it was time to go home. Right then and not a second later. He was bone-weary of the Cities' stench in his nostrils and its taste in his mouth. Between the day's events and the coffee he knew that he wouldn't sleep anyway.

Walking into the hotel room, Charlie stripped out of the tuxedo and took a quick shower. A few minutes later, he roused an irate-looking desk clerk and checked out. The woman's attitude brightened considerably after

Charlie tipped her twenty dollars to return the rented formal wear.

It was early afternoon when Charlie pulled into his driveway. Seldom, if ever, had he been happier to get home after one of his many journeys. Seldom, if ever, had he felt lonelier. Not even in the terrible days after Mary was taken all those years ago.

These were hard days and worst nights for Charlie. He became irritable to the point of rudeness, something unheard of in a Poshto elder and healer of his stature. The long walks which had started with his growing distance from Ellen became even longer now that they were estranged. Often he would hike through the dark forests until his legs failed and he collapsed into sleep wherever he dropped. Depending on his mood, which was always some varying degree of angry, these hikes could go on for two or three days, sometimes even longer.

At the beginning of October of that first year of Ellen's marriage, events took a decided but not unexpected turn for the worse. Charlie should have been alarmed by the timing, but its significance escaped him. Despite the power he wielded he was still human and prone to error.

That late fall afternoon Charlie's troubles fell away and he was just an angler pursuing a trophy fish. For the last five years he had caught and released a monster smallmouth bass. Every year the fish grew a little larger, a little craftier, and a little harder to catch. This year, he knew, would be the bass' last. The fish's life cycle had run its course and now he intended to harvest it. Directly after that, he was going to take his trophy to a taxidermist friend for modeling. And directly after that he was going to fire up a fish-fry of epic proportions.

"Yo, Moby!" He called out over the still afternoon water. "You got lucky this morning, fish, and spit the hook. Now though you are mine. So why don't you surrender because I'm getting hungry."

Despite his confident words, Charlie was getting worried. The afternoon was wearing on and if he didn't catch the bass today, it would swim off into deeper water to meet its fate.

The first time the phone rang up in the cabin, Charlie was so engrossed in fishing that he failed to hear it. When it started ringing again fifteen seconds later, he did hear it. Swearing under his breath, he ignored the intrusion and remained focused on the flat, calm water. After a full minute, the phone finally stopped ringing.

"'Bout time, ain't it?" he muttered, concentrating on working the rattletrap lure over a gravel bar.

Five seconds later the phone started ringing again.

"Goddammit, give it a rest!" he roared.

Turning his head, Charlie glared up the slope at the cabin and that was the moment the fish chose to smash the lure. Taken by surprise, Charlie jerked the pole back as the great bass engaged full power astern. The ten pound monofilament line split the difference and the fish swam off to meet its death in the cold depths of the lake. Enraged, Charlie slammed down the pole down on the ground and opened his mouth to roar, but no sound came out.

"Ellen!" he finally croaked, all thoughts of fishing now gone.

Whirling around, he started running up the slope toward the cabin. Halfway there, the staff somehow found its way into his hand and his speed doubled. Even before he picked up the phone, he had a pretty fair idea about what had happened.

"What has happened to Ellen and the baby?" he demanded. "Quickly, child, tell me, all of it."

"I've been trying to call since early this morn— how did you—" Katie said before Charlie interrupted her.

"It doesn't matter how I know. Now take a deep breath and tell me what happened."

A long inhalation sounded in Charlie's ear and Katie began speaking.

Ellen had called her about three-thirty in the morning, crying, and said that she had just suffered a miscarriage. Katie had told Ellen to call an ambulance, stay still, and wait for it and her to arrive. On the drive over, Katie had time to wonder where Marcus Taylor was and why Ellen had called her. When she had pulled into the parking lot of the Taylor townhouse, there was no ambulance, no emergency vehicles, no sign of the dog and pony show associated with a late-night medical emergency. Concerned, she had hurried across the parking lot and found the townhouse's door ajar. Entering without knocking, she had found Ellen lying in a fetal curl on the marble floor of the entryway. Between sobs, Ellen said that she had fallen down the stairs and miscarried.

Katie had immediate doubts about her story because Ellen's right eye was swollen almost shut. When Katie had said that she was going to call an ambulance, Ellen became hysterical. Fearing further damage to Ellen's health and nearing hysteria herself, Katie had reluctantly agreed not to call.

Calming down a little, Ellen had said that she wanted to go upstairs and change clothes. After a struggle, Katie had gotten Ellen up off the floor and up the stairs to the master bedroom on the second floor. Helping her clean up and change, Katie had seen that which she had feared most. An ugly, foot-shaped bruise was centered low on

Ellen's belly. When Ellen had noticed Katie staring, she had hung her head and wept.

"Ch, Ch, Charlie, all that blood," Katie had wailed. "And the other stuff, I've never seen—"

"Easy now, just tell me what happened next."

After helping Ellen into bed, Katie had excused herself and gone downstairs on the pretext of locking the front door. What she had really intended to do was make a long overdue 911 call. By then, Katie hadn't cared about Ellen's wishes. She was frightened and had planned on screaming into the ear of an emergency operator until help arrived. Halfway down the stairs, she had run into Marcus Taylor and three other men. Before she could utter a word, Taylor and one of his associates had seized her arms and hustled her down the stairs.

When she had finally croaked out that Ellen needed a doctor, Taylor snapped, "You just passed two of them on the stairs, genius."

Reaching the first floor, the two men had lifted her off the floor by the arms and started toward the front door.

"You're hurting me, leggo!" Katie had yelled. "Fucking jerks, I'm gonna call the cops!"

"Lemme save you a quarter, genius," the man crushing her left arm had said, flashing a badge wallet in front of her face. "Unless you wanna go to jail for breaking and entering and whatever else I can dream up, I'd suggest you shut the fuck up."

Carrying her out to the top of the front steps, the two men had released her and stood there laughing. Arms windmilling for balance, Katie had stood teetering on the edge of the steps. As she had started falling, Taylor had lashed out with his right foot and kicked her in the ass. Three steps below her flight ended in a jumble of bleeding knees and elbows on the concrete sidewalk.

"A-n-n-n-d then he called me a runt cunt and a, a," Katie sobbed. "I'm gonna, gonna—"

"You will do nothing," Charlie said, compelling her with the staff's power, "it is far too dangerous. And no matter what happens, you must stay away from Ellen in the future."

It took a few minutes, even using the staff's power, before Katie reluctantly agreed. After making sure that she was physically unhurt except for scrapes and bruises, Charlie hung up. He awoke from a deep fugue state sometime later just before he, the cabin, and a few acres of prime northern waterfront property would have lifted off into a geo-synchronous orbit. Concentrating hard, he brought the staff back under control just in time.

Sprawling back on the sofa, he closed his eyes and concentrated on breathing the tension out of his body. Feeling better after a few minutes, he stood intending to pack and then leave for the Cities. Two steps later, he halted and stood thinking.

Events were now balanced on a razor's edge. One misstep and the bleeding would begin in earnest. If Ellen was drawn in any closer to the web of events being spun around the prophecy, she would be snared, perhaps fatally. The baby was lost now and nothing could change that. Still, the bastard had hurt her, could've even killed her. In the end though it was Ellen who made up Charlie's mind for him.

Marching back to the telephone, Charlie snatched up the handset and held it to his ear without benefit of dialing. A second later a woman's voice sounded in his ear.

"Taylor residence, Ms. Robinson speaking. How may I help you?"

Freezing her in place, Charlie sorted out the images. Flowers, curtains, a window, no wait, it was a mirror. The reflection showed a large woman dressed in white and yes, there it was, she was a private nurse named Janine Robinson. She liked soap operas, crossword puzzles, and most of all, inflicting her version of order on everyone and everything.

"Nurse Robinson, this is Dr. Crowley," Charlie said, his voice mimicking an upper class, east coast, Harvard Medical School graduate, practice solely confined to Obstetrics and Gynecology accent, "I forgot to ask Mrs. Taylor something when I was just there. Put her on the phone and then please leave the room."

"But Doctor, I thought you were downstairs, I just saw you—"

"Damn it woman, don't argue with me!" the nasal Yankee voice roared. "Get Mrs. Taylor on the phone! Do it now!"

Grinning, Charlie watched in the mirror as the nurse set the phone down and ran into the adjoining bedroom. He had always believed that the minds of those inclined to inflict order on others resembled a line of dominoes stood up on end. The controller perceived his or her place in the line and bullied all of the dominoes below. Convince the bully that you stood somewhere in the line above and could knock him or her down and you had it made.

"Hello, Dr. Crowley?" Ellen mumbled, voice slurred with sleep and painkillers.

Charlie hesitated a second until he caught a flash of Nurse Robinson's double-wide posterior double-timing it out of the room.

"Blossom, this is your grandfather," he said, desperately wanting to heal the rift between them. "I heard you've been sick and I was worried about you."

"I'm fine, Grandpa," she told him, voice icy. "I just fell on the stairs, that's all. Now if you'll excuse me, I'm supposed to be resting."

The empty electronic hum of the dial tone buzzed in his ear and he put the handset back on the cradle. Leaning on the staff, Charlie shuffled over to the couch and sat staring at the wall. He was still sitting there, staring at the wall, when the sun rose ten hours later.

One positive aspect of Charlie's anger and hurt was that season's battle with the Dark One. Filled with rage, he was as the Charlie Redbird of old. Aided by an extended spell of foul weather that kept all but the hardiest home and dry, he had roamed the great forest locked in battle with his ancient foe. From the aches and pains he suffered, Charlie knew that it would be the last time he had prevented the Trickster from feeding. After all the suffering the monster had inflicted on him, it filled Charlie with black satisfaction to hear its hungry whining.

By the end of November though, Charlie was suffering. Missing Ellen, he rose early every day and fought the creeping darkness within. Deep winter set in early that year, denying him all but the shortest healing forays into the great forest. In the second week of December, Charlie stared at his haggard reflection in the bathroom mirror and knew that the battle was almost lost.

Walking into the living room, he sat down on the couch and picked up a mug of coffee sitting on the end table. A slight twitch in his hand increased to a violent tremor, slopping coffee out of the cup. Charlie watched as his traitorous hand lost its grip and let the cup fall and shatter against a corner of the end table. It was only an old ceramic coffee cup with a white glaze long since stained brown from many decades of use. Mary, his late wife, had given it to him on their first wedding anniversary. The shattered cup had been one of his prize possessions, one of the few things he had left that she had given him.

Slamming back against the couch cushions, Charlie's back and neck arched as he fought to keep his jaws clenched. His jaws shot open with a wet, smacking sound. Mary, his sons, the innocents lost to the Dark One, Ellen, it all came howling out.

Charlie screamed until his vocal cords gave out and only inarticulate grunts issued from his mouth. He watched in horror as his spittle splattered up against the ceiling above. Time passed, and when Charlie regained consciousness he was lying on the floor, soaked in sweat. Moaning softly, he crawled up onto the couch. A hard rap on the pine coffee table sounded and he opened his eyes. Encased in blue fire, the staff was tapping itself against the tabletop, gaining power with each down stroke.

"All right, you win," he said, relieved now that the decision had finally been made. "New Year's Day right after sunrise, okay? I want to see the dawn of one more year before I go and then we're quits. After fifty years, you owe me at least that much."

The staff hovered motionless in midair, blue fire pulsing up and down its length. Then suddenly it was gone, vanished. Just as abruptly it reappeared, resting as usual against the side of the sofa near his right hand as if to say, "Done!" Decision made, Charlie shuffled into the bedroom and slept for the next twelve hours.

Finalizing his affairs took up the following days and weeks. After organizing everything, Charlie was amazed at the variety of goods he had collected over the course of a long life. Much of the collection was purest dreck. A small plastic figurine of a bare-breasted girl in a hula skirt intended to wiggle and shimmy on a dashboard. A battered postcard touting Miller's Tourist Cabins which had burned to the ground in July 1965. A single beverage coaster extolling the 1967 World's Fair in Montreal which he'd never visited, neither city nor fair.

Some of the collection though was very valuable, near irreplaceable. First American jewelry, much of it dating back at least two hundred years, whose value Charlie estimated at around a hundred-thousand dollars. An extensive collection of First American pottery worth approximately the same amount.

Nearest to Charlie's heart though were his many sketches and paintings of North American wildlife, especially birds. For years he had intended to leave the entire portfolio to Ellen and had never sold even a single drawing. Nevertheless, he was positive the collection was extremely valuable. This wasn't the unfounded conceit of an untalented hack but rather the calm certainty of a great artist.

The hardest part was deciding what to leave to whom. Kitchen trash can sitting at his knee, Charlie attempted several formulations for the final disposition of his estate. When the wadded up sheets of yellow legal paper overflowed the trash can onto the floor, he threw the pad and pen down on the table in exasperation.

Walking outside, he copped a lean against one of the porch columns and lit his pipe. Blue tobacco smoke coiled in the cold winter air as he fussed over the problem. A minute later Charlie had his solution, which was the same one he had started with five hours earlier.

Ellen and Katie would split his estate fifty-fifty, share and share alike. He wasn't angry with Ellen, but he did want Katie to know how much he had valued their short friendship. Each would be directed to award such gifts to his other surviving relatives as she saw fit. Putting down the pen, Charlie smiled through the black fog of his depression, imagining the effect Katie would have on his strait-laced Poshto relatives.

Estate disposition finished, there was nothing left to do now but say goodbye. The next few days passed in a series of short hikes and drives as Charlie visited his favorite places one last time. On December 27th he left on a four-day camping trip to the most special spots of all.

Charlie spent the 27th atop a high hill camped among the skeletal remnants of an apple orchard. Sitting cross-legged in front of a small fire, he stared out over the frozen expanse of the lake. This hill, crowned by the then great orchard, had been his and Mary's special place when they were courting all those long years ago.

On the morning of the 28th, Charlie rose with the sun. Coaxing the fire back to life, he filled the coffeepot and set it on the coals to brew. Facing the sun, he said a brief prayer for Mary and scattered a handful of dried wild-flowers in her memory. Done praying, he sat and had a quick breakfast. After loading his pack basket, he strode away to the south, snowshoes crunching on the icy snow pack.

A half-hour later, he stopped at the edge of a grove of fir trees and stood looking down into a bowl-shaped valley a quarter of a mile wide. A small stream, flowing fast enough to still be ice-free this early in the season, steamed past banks lined with shattered pieces of basalt and the bones of small animals. There were no trees in the valley and the ground was thickly covered with yellow-green vines that seemed impervious to the cold. The thin snow cover was interspersed with large patches of mud bubbling up a foul, sulfurous gas. It was a blighted wasteland, a toxic anomaly in the midst of the great northern forest. For the better part of an hour Charlie stood looking down, remembering. The staff thrumming under his hand eventually dragged him back to the present.

"Shut up!" he barked, rapping the staff hard against a convenient tree. "You own a piece of this and you goddamn well know it!"

Leaning hard on the now quiet staff, Charlie started zigzagging down the slope. Given the forces that had once been unleashed here and still remained, a fall, regardless of injury, would be fatal. Arriving safely on the valley floor, he paused for a deep breath and braced himself for what lay ahead.

Stepping carefully, he started toward the center of the valley. No matter how cautiously he walked though the cancerous looking vines would whip around his lower legs and dig their thorns into his flesh. Despite the pain they were causing him, Charlie wielded the staff with a light touch, driving the rapacious vines back but not killing them.

Each time the staff's fire brushed against a vine, the wind's voice cried a little louder. Keening voices, amongst them children and infants, wailed down a thirty-knot gale. Reaching the geographic center of the valley, Charlie drove the staff deep into the foul earth. Clenching both hands around the staff's intricately carved runes, he leaned forward and rested his forehead against the carved headpiece.

A thin blue fog crept out of and hung over the stagnant ground as Charlie began singing. When the mist had completely filled the valley, he altered the timbre and speed of his song. The fog began accelerating, swirling in toward the center of the valley. Horizontal chain lightning danced down the plasma currents, thunder rolled, and the ground shook underfoot.

After two hours Charlie conceded defeat. In common with his many other efforts over the decades, this one had accomplished nothing. Despite the sorcery he commanded the task was beyond him.

He pulled the staff out of the ground and the valley quieted. The accusing voices of the dead returned though, howling down the frigid gale. Nauseous from the charnel stench filling his mouth and nostrils, he started walking eastwards toward a low hill. Wielding the staff, he fended off the thorns as they struck at him. Despite his care, some of the thorns still managed to pierce his flesh. Ignoring the pain, Charlie increased his pace to a near jog. Without breaking stride, he started uphill, climbing hard. As soon as he left the valley floor, the wind and the voices quieted and became still again.

Reaching the top of the slope, Charlie started forcing his way through a dense stand of fir trees, wanting only to escape this terrible place. Branches whipped and scratched his face as he fled. A quarter-mile later his snowshoes crossed and he went down hard on his face. Gasping for air, he rolled over on his back and lay staring up at the clear blue sky. After a few minutes the cold started creeping in and he sat up, arms splayed out behind him for support. By pulling on the thighs of his woolen trousers, Charlie hitched himself forward and started struggling out of the snowshoes.

"Damn things!" he swore, finally managing to free his left foot from its binding after an extended battle.

Free of the snowshoes, Charlie scooted over a couple of feet and rested his back against a birch tree. Working with both hands, he brushed the sticky fir needles out of his hair and off his clothes. The painless part of the job done, he finally dared a closer inspection of his lower legs, dreading what came next.

A dozen or more long yellow-green thorns protruded from his lower legs. Many more had been driven into the thick leather of his boots and into the ash snowshoe frames. Rummaging around in his pack basket, Charlie pulled out a pair of forceps and a large sealed plastic bottle. Grimacing in anticipation of the pain he knew was coming, he started plucking out the thorns with the forceps. Decades before he had learned at cost of slit fingers never to handle the razor-edged thorns with his bare hands. Working quickly but carefully he pulled out the thorns and dropped them in the snow. Writhing and smoking they lay on the snow for a few seconds before dying. As usual at least half of the daggers snapped off in his flesh and immediately started burrowing inwards.

Knowing that he had to be quick or face certain infection, Charlie unscrewed the top of the plastic bottle and set it down next to his right calf. Eyes watering and nose running from the salve's fumes, Charlie rolled up his pants' legs. The thorns had already disappeared, leaving bloody puncture wounds behind as they tunneled in straight toward his marrow. Gritting his teeth, Charlie used a putty knife to spread the pasty-white salve all over his lower legs. A high-pitched screaming filled the air as the thorns backed out of their burrows as they tried to escape the salve. Hissing in pain, he brushed the points off into the snow with the forceps before they could re-entrench themselves in his flesh.

Thorns finally removed, Charlie sagged back against the tree. Staring out into the mid-distance, he ignored the injuries inflicted to his lower legs. After a minute or so, he looked down at his calves and shins. Even though he knew what he would see, it still saddened him and weighed on his spirit. The bloody punctures sat atop old scar tissue that completely banded both of his lower legs. Physical evidence, as if he needed any, of his failure. Evidence too of the limits of the staff's power, of its inability to heal wounds which it was responsible for inflicting. Worse yet though were the faces on the thorn points screaming in agony as they died in the snow. Charlie could have named each of those faces and recited their degree of kinship to him.

It was growing late and this place was too close to the valley for safe camping. Anxious now to be gone, Charlie hurriedly pulled the thorns out of his boots and snowshoes. If not removed now, the toxic points would lay dormant until the first opportunity arose to attack him and poison his flesh. Finished at last, he reloaded the pack basket, strapped on the snowshoes, and set off.

Five miles later Charlie stopped in the middle of a maple grove to smoke and watch the sun set. Finished smoking, he walked out to the edge of the grove and pitched camp.

The next two days, the 29th and the 30th, were spent on a long ramble back toward the cabin. Berry picking spots, hillsides where rare medicinal plants grew, and favorite fishing holes were all visited in no particular order.

Charlie arrived back at his cabin around noon on the 31st. The only tracks in the yard were those made when he had left days earlier. Entering the cabin, he froze, sensing an intruder's presence. A second later his shoulders sagged as his cognitive functions caught up with his instincts.

For the prescient time is fluid, sending temporal currents eddying through the past, present, and future. Stepping through the door, Charlie had stepped into a rip swirling forward from the past and mistaken it for the here and now. Depressed and distracted, he had sensed Ellen's presence and for a second had believed her here. Realizing his error, he shambled over to the couch and collapsed.

"Be over soon now," he whispered to the cabin's stillness.

Exhausted, Charlie levered himself to his feet with the staff's help and shuffled off to the bedroom. Considering what lay ahead he slept well. Long before dawn though he was up and stirring, making his final preparations.

After a long shower he braided his hair and dressed with care. Depression may have laid him low, but Charlie intended to meet his death with as much dignity as he possessed. For a long while he sat drinking coffee and smoking until the air in the cabin was thick with blue smoke. Sensing that dawn was near, he rinsed the cup out and left it in the sink. Picking up a pencil, Charlie tended to the last remaining detail.

"Gone camping in the breaks," he wrote on the yellow pad next to the phone. *"Back January 2 by dark. CR"*

The breaks were just that, broken ground that rose to four-thousand feet in a stair-step series of crumbled granite ledges with a maze of alder swamps covering what little horizontal ground there was. Charlie figured that it was an excellent place to explain the mysterious disappearance of an eccentric elderly man.

Stepping out onto the porch, he lit his pipe again. A last lingering look up and down the dirt road that had launched so many journeys and then he was off. Walking around the side of the cabin, Charlie started up the path without looking back, picking up speed as he went. He wasn't eager by any means but rather anxious to be done with it and be at peace.

A hundred yards later Charlie stepped out onto the snow covered stone circle. Walking carefully on the slick stone, he advanced to the circle's center and faced eastward. Dawn started racing across the lake and he rapped the staff against the granite beneath his feet. Blue light flickered across the circle, vaporizing the snow into a thick fog which quickly dissipated on the gentle morning breeze. The dying of Charles Lantot Redbird had begun.

Pausing for a moment, Charlie swept his vision in a 360 degree arc around the land and water which had shaped his life. Soon he would be returned to the atoms from which he came, the only evidence of his passing the echoes in the memories of those he had touched in life. An instant later the staff would find David Garrison no matter where he was. Unschooled and unprepared, the staff would probably immolate him on contact. If somehow he survived, Garrison would have to wield the staff against and keep it from The Wendigo, a near impossibility.

Garrison's probable fate and the consequent loss of the staff weighed on Charlie's spirit, but not enough to deter him. Caught by the darkness within after a lifetime of struggle and sacrifice, he yearned for release at any price. All things wrapped in flesh and bone have their limits and Charlie had reached his. David Garrison would just have to take his chances with the staff as had all those who had come before him. It was a hopeless solution, a bitter harvest after a lifetime's unceasing effort.

Kneeling, he took the tanned deerskin bag off his shoulder and untied the drawstring. Reaching inside, he pulled out three mason jars, each containing a different color pigment. Picking up a jar of ochre pigment, Charlie walked out to the edge of the stone circle. Taking a handmade deer bristle brush out of his breast pocket, he painted a thin ochre line around the circle's circumference. Earth, the Great Mother, now girded the site.

Returning to the center of the circle, Charlie put down the jar of ochre dye and balanced the soiled brush on top of it. Picking up a jar of bright yellow pigment, he walked out to the reddish-brown line banding the outer edge of the circle. Taking a fresh brush out of his pocket, he drew four large circles at the four cardinal points of the compass, each neatly intersecting the ochre line at its top.

In the eastern circle, he drew a yellow orb representing the sun, bringer of warmth and light. In the southern circle he made three long narrow strokes representing rain, bringer of life. In the northern circle Charlie drew a slashing lightning bolt for the great storms of fall and winter which revitalized a fallow world after harvest. To the west he left the circle empty for the dark that comes at the end of every day and at the end of every human life.

Walking back to the center of the circle, Charlie set the jar of yellow dye down and put the soiled brush on top of it. Picking up a jar of blue pigment, he walked back to the yellow circles he had drawn. Taking the third and last paint brush from his pocket, he scribed a circular blue line which touched the bottom of each of the yellow circles. Father Sky, who looks down upon all things upon the Great Mother, was now present.

Backing up now, he drew a straight blue line. Four feet from the center of the circle, he traded colors and started painting a yellow line back out to toward the outer edge of the circle. Finished, he put down the yellow dye, picked up the ochre, and drew another straight line. Now the inner circle of blue was evenly divided by spokes of blue, yellow, and ochre pigment running back toward the center of the circle. At the end of each of the spokes, Charlie painted arcs of color that were different than those of the spokes they connected. Finished painting, Charlie rose and stood for a moment in the multicolored inner circle.

The short hairs on his neck bristled and his nerves tingled as the magic began gathering power. The granite vibrated beneath his feet and blue ball lightning shot around the perimeter of the stone circle. Loading his pipe and taking a deep draw of smoke, Charlie began inspecting his handiwork. Stepping on the bare stone to avoid defacing the sacred drawing, he walked out to the edge of the stone circle in a slow corkscrew pattern. A grey wall had attached itself to the outer edge of the circle. Reaching out, he gently rapped his knuckles against the solid barrier, surprised by the absence of any resulting sound.

Afraid now for the first time since entering the circle, Charlie walked back to the center of the circle with his eyes locked on his feet. Once there, he took a deep breath and looked up. The grey barrier extended many thousands of feet upwards as would the eye-wall of a hurricane. In the far distance at the top of the well, Earth hung suspended in starless midnight space.

Snapping his head down, Charlie squeezed his eyes shut and smoked until his pipe bubbled cold. Putting the pipe into his pocket, he knelt and completed the rune. Using the colors and brushes sitting on the stone by his right knee, he painted a tri-colored pictograph of a man leaning on a staff.

The last brush stroke joined the pictographic shaman's left leg to the tri-colored inner circle and the forces which had bounded his life. The sorcery Charlie had unleashed exploded, violently pitching the circular granite slab from side-to-side. Screaming in fear, he was knocked flat on his belly as the slab surged skywards. When the upwards acceleration abruptly halted, Charlie kept flying up for another second or so before crashing back down hard on the granite.

Hammered breathless by the fall, he lay gasping for a few seconds before struggling up to a sitting position. Feeling warm fluid on his hands, he looked down. Both of his hands were thickly coated up to the wrists with the yellow, blue, and ochre pigments. Wiping the colors off on his coat front, Charlie looked down and noticed a perfect pair of tri-colored hand-prints framing the pictographic shaman. The three colors in the hand-prints hadn't bled together and were delineated into vertical bands at the index and fourth fingers. The jars of pigment and the brushes were gone, apparently blown off during the meteoric ascent to wherever this was.

Drawing in a shaky breath, Charlie surveyed his surroundings. The slab was hovering in a black abyss. In the distance, a blue-green marble hung suspended in the void. There were no icecaps and the continents were different, but it was still recognizable as Earth.

"Bad idea," he mumbled, locking his eyes back down on the pictographic shaman.

Suddenly he began choking and realized that he couldn't breathe. Ice crystals were rapidly accumulating on his flesh and on the insides of his nose and mouth. Whatever atmosphere had been transported with the slab was almost gone and Charlie was in danger of dying of anoxia and exposure.

The deerskin bag, he realized, he must find the deerskin bag or else he would die and his soul would be trapped forever in this terrible void. Lashing his head about searching for it, Charlie knew, was certain, that the bag had blown off the slab along with the jars of pigment and the brushes. A carbonic tingling spread through his body as his blood started boiling in the vacuum of space.

The staff found its way into Charlie's hand just as he opened his mouth to scream. Clutching the staff with one hand, he felt something brush against his free hand. Flailing, he caught the tied bundle of sticks just before they would have floated out of reach. Panicking, he slammed the bundle of sticks down on the pictographic shaman. The lack of gravity caused his feet to fly up over his head and started him on a fast drift toward the edge of the stone circle. Blue fire licked out from the headpiece of the staff, igniting the bundle of sticks. The oxygenated atmosphere immediately returned and with it, gravity.

Belly-flopping down on the stone for the second time in less than a minute, Charlie grunted in pain. There was no air left inside his lungs so he lay wheezing and gasping, struggling to re-inflate them. The warm atmosphere melted the accumulated ice crystals, flooding his airway with moisture, making him cough and gag all the harder. Even as he lay coughing and wheezing, Charlie took a quick inventory and decided that except for some impressive bruises, he was unhurt.

Except for his lower legs, he suddenly realized. There was no sensation below his knees, just a cold aching numbness. Looking back over one shoulder, he saw that his lower legs were hanging off the edge of the stone slab. Stiff as a pair of kindling logs, they were wreathed in a rapidly expanding cloud of frozen blood and tissue.

Knowing there were only seconds left to save his legs and his life, Charlie started scrabbling forward away from the slab's edge. Whatever gravity existed on top of the slab didn't extend beneath it. As soon as he shifted an elbow, the slab's equilibrium was disturbed and it began tilting. Feeling himself slide backwards a couple of inches, Charlie clawed at the stone and finally made it back to the center of the circle. After wobbling for a few more seconds, the stone slab slowly returned to the horizontal plane.

Rolling over, Charlie looked down the length of his body, fearing what he might see. The denim covering his lower legs was stained red and frozen solid. Although his legs were lying flat, his left foot was lying on its side and his right foot was upside down with the sole pointing up. Lowering his head, Charlie started shaking as shock took him.

A cold aching throb started slowly advancing down his shins. When the ache reached the breakwater of his toes, it reversed direction and raced up his legs and body as a roaring wave of white-hot agony. Throwing his head back, Charlie screamed and pounded the stone.

A persistent tapping under his chin prodded him back to consciousness. Moving the staff away from his jaw, Charlie lay staring up into the abyss, thinking. The pain in his legs was gone now, replaced by a deep, tingling itch. When he looked down, he saw that his feet had resumed their normal positions at the bottom of his legs and the blood-soaked denim was now clean. The fear remained though, rooted deep inside of him.

"If I knew dying was going to be such a pain in the ass," he said aloud, "I'da stayed home and watched TV instead."

While true, nothing about Charlie's feelings had changed. Still resolved to die, he just wished that it was easier, less of a production. The stone was warm now and he stretched out and yawned, hovering on the edge of sleep. A sharp rap on the crazy bone of his right elbow jarred him awake.

"Bitch!" he grumbled.

Slamming the staff against the rock, he sat up and rubbed his bruised elbow. Pulling the deerskin bag over with one heel, he turned it upside down and shook out a buckskin loincloth, leggings, shirt, and moccasins. Stripping off his clothing, Charlie put on the traditional buckskins. On his chest the same circular hieroglyphic design that he had drawn on the stone slab was repeated in smaller scale. Stuffing his street clothes into the deerskin sack, Charlie whipped it around by the drawstrings and flung it off the slab into the void.

Bending forward, Charlie untied the bundle of sacred sticks. Hands impervious to the dancing blue flames, he arranged the sticks into a four-sided pyramid. Apple, maple, spruce, and birch, the trees that had helped shape his life, stood waiting. Easing himself into a cross-legged sit, Charlie whistled softly. The blue flames whistled back at him and slowly began combusting the sacred sticks. Time to begin, time to finish.

Singing softly in Poshto, he began reciting the epic of the Redbird shamans and their long struggle against the

Dark One. Every time he finished a verse and paused for breath, the flames crackled and devoured a bit more of the sacred woods. When the last verse of the saga was sung, the sacred sticks would be totally consumed as would Charlie Redbird's life.

CHAPTER 59

PUSHING HIS BLACK horn-rimmed glassed up on his nose a little, the young man glanced at the speedometer and frowned. Tapping the brakes, he slowed the ancient Dodge Caravan, keeping it five miles-per-hour under the posted speed limit. Even though unmarried and childless, he'd purchased this battered symbol of American family life, "Because it was a good deal, below Blue Book."

Glancing in the rear-view mirror, he noticed an errant hair lying over his right ear. Correcting the problem, he promised himself a haircut at the earliest opportunity. Looking down, he frowned again and picked a piece of lint off his white button-down shirt.

The young man's name was Gilbert Mason, age twenty-four, a resolute member of that most peculiar of tribes, the Nerds. In any pool of eligible single males, Gilbert would be one of the least likely candidates to be Katie Henderson's new *amour*, yet here he was. Depending on the observer's point of view, it proved yet again that love, if not blind, is at the very least myopic; opposites attract; the creator has a strong sense of humor; or all of the above.

The love of Gilbert's life was currently occupying the seat next to him. Occupying, not sitting, because that part of her anatomy was in a state of ever-increasing nervous fidget. Starting in early December, Katie had tried repeatedly to contact Charlie. Unable to reach him by phone, she had even tried sending him a registered letter but still couldn't reach him. Then it was Christmas and time for the new couple to make the holiday rounds.

Her family had been delighted. Their wayward, tattooed, body-pierced daughter had hooked herself an MBA, soon to be a CPA, and heir to a chain of nine hardware stores. His family, a clan of proud hardware-selling nerds, was appalled. Their friends loathed each other. But as is usual in such cases, the moonstruck couple ignored it all and kept on spoonin' and cuddlin'.

By the evening of December 31st though, an intravenous drip of pure estrogen couldn't have eased Katie's concern for Charlie. Enough, she had decided, was enough. It was time, past time, for the mountain to visit Mohammed. Throwing a change of clothes into a small duffel bag, she paused long enough to scribble a short note to her parents. One last quick look around, one final check of the house locks, and it was time to go.

Tossing the duffel onto the rear seat, Katie climbed behind the wheel and started her Subaru. Gillie, she reminded herself, gotta call Gillie from that truck stop about halfway to Frechette or else he'd worry. She didn't want to think about what he'd say or do about getting stood up at the last minute on New Year's Eve.

"All right, then," she said aloud, pushing in the clutch, "ready, steady, go!"

And so she did, for about ten feet until the timing belts in the Subaru blew. Yelping in alarm, Katie stomped on the brakes and the clutch, slamming herself back hard against the seat. The instrument panel was lit up like a tilted pinball machine; displaying idiot lights that she hadn't even know existed. Switching off the ignition, she held her breath for a few seconds and tried to restart the engine.

Laboring, the engine turned over without firing as the pinball lights on the dash lit up again. On her next attempt, the low-battery light began strobing as the grinding engine slowed, then stopped. Pulling the key out of the ignition, Katie squeezed her eyes shut and battled competing urges to cry, scream, curse, pound on the dashboard, or do all four at once.

"Charlie," she said, gaining conviction as she spoke the words, "Charlie's gonna die, he—"

"HUSH, CHILD," a voice roared deep in her mind with such force that it snapped her skull back against the headrest. "YOU MUST HURRY. MUCH DEPENDS ON YOU NOW."

"Who— who are you?" Katie whimpered, hands clutched around the agony pulsing in her skull. "What depends on—?"

"YOU MAY CALL ME MOTHER," the voice boomed, pounding Katie into a sobbing ball against the car door. "YOU ALREADY KNOW WHAT YOU MUST DO, SO HURRY UP AND GET A MOVE ON!"

Then silence, blessed silence. Sitting up, Katie released the sides of her skull. The voice and the pain were gone now, leaving only a muted ringing in her ears as a sign of their passage. Feeling something wet, she looked down and saw a pair of bloody streaks running down her top. A glance in the rear-view mirror showed twin streaks of blood running down her face from a heavy nose-bleed.

"Gross!" She muttered. "Where are those damn wetnaps I—"

A horn honked behind the Subaru and the pain proved that it wasn't gone, only hiding. Silver pinwheels whirled across Katie's vision and her skull felt as if it would explode. Gilbert, her knight in shining armor, had arrived mounted in his 1988 rust-speckled, $500.00-below-Blue-Book Dodge Caravan of a steed for their New Year's Eve date.

By the time Gilbert reached the Subaru, Katie was balled up against the door frame with her eyes squeezed shut. Seeing the blood on her face and top he became concerned, or more honestly, scared shitless. When he jerked open the door, Katie rolled out. Squatting to catch her, he lost his balance and they both ended up down on the asphalt with him on the bottom.

"Gillie honey, would you please get me the wet naps in the center console so I can clean up this nosebleed?" she asked.

Wiggling out from under her, Gilbert stuck his arm into the car and reached into the center console.

"Gillie, my car's broken down and something's wrong with Charlie and I gotta go to Frechette and make sure he's all right," she said as he handed her the wet naps.

What ensued next was a classic All-American male-female argument.

"You need to see a doctor." Gilbert told her.

"No I don't, it's only a nosebleed and I've gotta leave for Frechette just as soon as I can," she replied.

"You should at least lie down and rest awhile before you go."

"Well, my car's broken, so I won't be driving and I can rest on the way up."

"Who's going to drive you" Gilbert asked, getting annoyed.

"Oh, I dunno, I'll think of something, I always do."

Trailing along behind, Gilbert followed her into the house, objecting every step of the way. After three or four more volleys, he did what all intelligent males do when dealing with an intractable lady love: he struck his colors and surrendered.

"He's such a sweetie," Katie told her reflection in the bathroom mirror. "I feel like I'm taking advantage of him, but I gotta get to Frechette no matter what."

When she walked out into the living room, Gilbert was standing by the front door with her favorite quilt rolled up under one arm and her favorite pillow under the other.

"You should get some rest on the drive up," he said, looking stern.

Knowing how easily scratched male pride can fester; Katie stood on her tiptoes and kissed him on the chin.

"That's a real good idea, Gillie, I still don't feel very well."

Taking her by the hand, Gilbert led her outside to his seriously used chariot. Stretched out full-length on the back seat, Katie had a change of heart and decided that she loved the old rust bucket. And its owner. Definitely its owner.

As Gilbert accelerated up the ramp onto the interstate, she asked, "Gillie, do you think that God could be a woman, female I mean?"

Surprised by the question, Gilbert started rooting around in the memories of his Hard-Shell Baptist upbringing. But by the time he was ready to answer her question, Katie was already asleep.

Three hours or so later she woke up, climbed into the front passenger seat, and started doing the left cheek-right cheek fidget. Her certainty that Charlie was in terrible danger was growing by the mile. Sneaking a peek, she saw that the speedometer read nearly ten miles-an-hour below the posted speed limit of seventy miles-per-hour. Time, she decided, for a touch of Significant Other encouragement.

"Gillie, are you tired?" she asked.

"Yeah, kind of," he admitted. "It's a long drive and I didn't get much sleep last night."

"I can drive if you like, I'm feeling a lot better now. There's a rest area up ahead a couple of miles where we can switch and I need to pee anyway."

Posture suddenly relaxed and limber, he replied, "Ungh, no, that's all right, really. I'll just get out and stretch at the rest area and I'll be fine, honest."

As Gilbert was well aware, riding in a car with Katie behind the wheel could put the fear of God in a seasoned Formula One driver. Looking straight ahead, she glanced out of the corner of her eye and saw the speedometer read seventy-seven miles-per-hour.

"Gilbert, are you driving faster just because I want to drive?"

Striving for a look of pained innocence, he said, "No, I wouldn't do that."

"Not much you wouldn't!" She snapped, glaring at him.

The two didn't speak for the next few miles until they reached the rest area. After visiting the facilities, they sat and ate a quick vending machine dinner while watching the traffic stream by on the interstate.

"Love you, sweetie," she announced, surprising him with a big smooch on the mouth. "And I can too drive!"

Arriving back at the van, there was a silent moment of conflict when both of them ended up at the driver's door. Opening the door, Gilbert bowed low and with a grand sweep of one arm gestured for Katie to enter. When her butt touched the driver's seat, he cleared his throat, loudly. Seeing his look, sensing his mood, Katie decided to quit while she was ahead and yielded the command seat without further comment. Grinning, Gilbert climbed behind the wheel and started the engine.

Three hours later, a little after dawn, they arrived in Frechette. A couple of navigational miscues later they turned onto the rutted corduroy road leading to Charlie's cabin. Braking hard, Gilbert stopped and climbed out of the van. Looking down the road, he stood with his nostrils flared as if sampling the chill dawn wind. Shivering, he got back into the van.

"Listen to me!" he said, twisting in the seat to face Katie.

Believing that he was angry about something, maybe about their tiff earlier, she said, sounding hurt, "What?"

"Something here is very wrong," he continued. "We're going to have a quick look around for your friend and if he's not home, we'll leave him a note, get a hotel room, and try again later."

Afraid, Katie realized, Gilbert was afraid, near terrified. A quick internal review revealed that she too was frightened, very frightened.

"Yes," she replied, trying to hide her fear. "Let's get this done and over with. All of a sudden this place is giving me the weirds."

Nodding, Gilbert put the van in gear and started down the road. Getting this trip done and over with and getting back to the Cities, he concluded, was a real good idea. In fact, it might be the best damn idea he'd ever had.

Anxious and driving too fast for the conditions, Gilbert almost overshot Charlie's cabin. Finessing the brakes, he turned hard into the drive and parked as near to the road as he dared. They sat without speaking, looking at the unlit cabin.

On her other visits, Katie had found the cabin to be a warm and welcoming place. Now though the cabin seemed dark, frightening even. Gilbert had no reservations about the log structure whatsoever: it creeped him out clear down to the bone marrow.

Reaching for the key intending to shut the engine off, Gilbert instead changed his mind and flicked on the high beams instead. He didn't know why, but the thought of light, no matter the source, was suddenly very comforting. Leaving the engine running, he climbed out of the van and joined Katie in the front yard. Holding hands, they climbed the front steps together, looking like two frightened children daring the approach to a haunted house. As they stepped up onto the porch the front door swung open of its own accord.

"It's probably just the wind," Katie said, not believing it for a second.

Neither did Gilbert, digging in his heels, preparing to turn and run like hell.

Releasing Gilbert's hand, Katie stepped through the door and he took a reluctant step forward. Patting the wall, Katie started searching for the light switch while Gilbert made sure she stayed within arm's reach in case he had to pull her out in a hurry. Her fingers brushed against a switch plate and she turned on the overhead living room light.

"Charlie, you here?" she called.

Feeling a little safer now that the light was on, Gilbert let out a long sigh of relief. Even though he was uncomfortable about invading a stranger's home, he stayed on Katie's heels while she searched the other rooms. Finding them empty, they returned to the living room. Seeing the yellow pad next to the phone, Gilbert picked it up, read Charlie's note about camping in the Breaks, and showed it to Katie.

"No," she told him, hoping that she was right, "that's not it. He might have meant to go there, but that's not where he is now."

Short hairs tingling and wishing that he was elsewhere, anywhere but here, Gilbert said, "Katie, let's get out of—"

"Hush, sweetie," she interrupted, head cocked as if listening. "Would you please wait outside and turn out the lights and shut the door when you go. I need to be alone for a few minutes. I'll explain later, I promise."

Inclined to argue, Gilbert opened his mouth to speak, and then thought better of it. Doing as he was asked, he turned off the living room light and walked out the door wearing an expression composed of equal parts fear and irritation.

Closing her eyes, Katie summoned Charlie's voice from the depths of her memory.

"Like many things of the mind," he had told her, "the sight is complicated only if you make it so. To use it, just empty your mind and concentrate on what you want to see. It's that simple."

Leaning back on the couch, she tried to picture Charlie's face. Previous efforts to use her gift had succeeded only about ten percent of the time and this attempt was faring no better than those that had preceded it.

Images of having sex with Gilbert flashed across Katie's consciousness. Next came a vision of her Subaru parked in her parents' driveway. After that another image of having sex with Gilbert. Following that, a chocolate sundae topped with fresh strawberries floated in her mind's eye.

"Oh man!" she sighed. "It's Katie Henderson, the pedestrian, chocolate sundae eatin', nymphomaniac psychic."

Try as she would, her thoughts kept wandering down the same mental ruts: sex with Gilbert, food, and the Subaru.

Frustrated now, Katie yelled, "Goddamn it, Charlie, you have to help me! I can't do it by myself! I just can't! Simple my ass!"

Emotions vented, Katie took a break, and although she wouldn't have thought it possible, fell asleep within seconds. Mind cleared, distractions now absent, the sight came to her just as Charlie had foretold.

He was sitting, she saw, in front of a small fire in the center of a stone circle. From the design painted on the stone and the traditional clothing he was wearing, she knew he was performing a ritual of some sort. Though she didn't know why, she was positive that he didn't have much time left to live.

On a previous visit in late September, Katie had discovered the granite circle on a short hike while Charlie was napping. Curious, she had stepped onto the circle. An unpleasant electric tingling had surged up her body, making her hair stand on end and crackle with static electricity. Frightened, she had jumped off the circle and retreated down the hill to the cabin.

Arriving breathless back at the cabin, she had found Charlie sitting on the porch smoking. Observing her condition, he grinned and kept on smoking. Collapsing into the rocking chair next to him, Katie had sat trying to catch her breath.

After thirty seconds or so she couldn't stand it any longer and had asked, "What's so funny?"

"You know, it's a strange thing," Charlie had said, simultaneously laughing and talking while blowing a smaller smoke ring through a larger one. Impressed with his feat, he waited for the rings to dissipate before continuing. "A woman could have the entire North American continent to wander around in, but if there was a matchbox in the middle of Kansas with something in it, she'd have to fool with it until she got it open and found out what was inside."

"That's a sexist remark," Katie had protested, "and besides which—"

"The circle is many things. At times a door, a window, a communications system, or sometimes, all three at once. The granite, the circle's essence, is part of the Great Mother's breastbone. The circle's shape, its circularity, represents the great wheel of life of all things which live upon her."

"I am not nosy!" she had said, annoyed. "All I did was stand on the damn thing and it shocked me!"

"Your gift activated it, that's all. In time you'll get used to the circle and learn how to use it. It's no different than learning how to use one of those computer contraptions."

"Ungh-huh, and why is that you aren't the proud owner of one of those computer contraptions?"

Realizing that he had just stuck his foot into a conversational bear trap, Charlie had grinned, bore it, and replied, “Because I don’t like the damn things, that’s why.”

“Yeah, well I feel the same way about that creepy piece of rock,” Katie had sputtered. “And I have no intention of learning anything more about it because it scares the ever living shit out of me.”

Still smiling, Charlie had relit his pipe and said, “A man of my vast intelligence and experience knows better than to argue with a woman.”

True to her word, Katie hadn’t been back to the stone circle since then. There was no choice for her now though but to revisit the circle or else Charlie would soon die. Launching herself off the couch in a manic whirl or arms and legs, she exploded out of the cabin’s front door, desperate to reach the stone circle.

Sitting alone in the van for thirty minutes had finally exhausted Gilbert’s considerable store of patience. Even though it was just after dawn, it was growing darker by the second and he’d decided that it was time to leave, NOW. Having made his decision, Gilbert had sallied out of the van intending to take Katie back to the Cities one way or another and by force if necessary. When he started climbing the cabin’s front steps, Katie had just started sprinting down them.

“Gillie honey,” she said, “we gotta hurry, there isn’t much time.”

“Now you just wait a second,” he told her, sticking out an arm as a barricade, “we’re leaving right—”

Concentrating on the slippery boards under her feet, Katie shoulder-faked left, ducked, and ran under Gilbert’s arm. As she passed, her shoulder slammed hard into his hip. The blow sent him reeling backwards off the steps, arms windmilling. Three staggering steps later, he tripped and fell backwards into a puddle of snowmelt.

As he sat in the puddle with freezing water assaulting his balls and seeping up the crack of his ass, something snapped deep inside of Gilbert Mason. The Associate Youth Pastor of the Galilee Free Will Baptist Church, past President of the State of Minnesota Young Republicans Clubs, and current Secretary of the University of Minnesota chapter of the Future Business Leaders of America underwent an internal quake that was clear off the Richter Scale.

"Son-of-a-bitch!" he roared. "Goddamn it, Katie, you come back here this second!"

Already around the corner of the cabin, Katie heard the tone but not the content of Gilbert's words. Grimacing, she took a bead on the grove of fir trees at the top of the small hill just ahead. Minding her footing on the icy path, she started climbing, praying that her vision was correct. If it wasn't, her relationship with Gilbert would probably end after what had just happened. For a young woman with marrying on the mind, that would be a disaster of the first magnitude.

Reaching the top of the hill, Katie dug deep and increased her pace a little. Raising her hands in front of her face, she bulled forward through the dense grove of fir trees. Breaking out into a clearing, she skidded to a halt where the stone circle was supposed to be, or where she thought it was supposed to be. Near panic, she whipped her head around searching for it. Five feet ahead and slightly to the left she noticed a shimmering anomaly in her field of vision. The terrain in front of, behind, and on either side of the phenomena was visible, but not the anomaly itself. Every time she tried to look at the shimmering curtain of light, her eyes slid away and locked onto the surrounding fir trees.

Feeling dizzy and nauseated by the visual effect, Katie closed her eyes and slowly started walking forward. Four steps later she stopped and opened her eyes. The shimmering haze had transformed into a vertical vortex of whirling blue fire suspended seven or eight feet above the ground. A great roaring noise, distant but still very loud, filled the air and shook the earth beneath her feet. Stars and planets swirled and danced, trapped by the forces in the anomaly.

"It's a wormhole," she thought, filled with wonder, "a time-space wormhole!"

Curious, Katie reached a hand up towards the beautiful cyclone of whirling blue fire and it snared her. The flesh and bone of her hand, then her arm, then the rest of her body, plasticized into a flowing stream of atoms as she was sucked screaming upwards into the mouth of the vortex. A millisecond, or an hour, or a week sooner or later, she was deposited mid-scream on the granite slab in front of Charlie. Although his lips weren't moving, she could hear him singing deep inside her mind.

"Charlie, what are you doing?" Katie asked, feeling something snap underfoot as she stepped forward. "Shit, I'm on fire!"

Stumbling out of the ceremonial fire, Katie slammed down hard on her butt and stared in shock at the blue flames encasing her lower legs and boots. Bending forward, she beat at the flames with her bare hands. To her amazement, she discovered that the flames were cold and extinguished easily without burning or charring her hands, jeans, or boots. Nearing panic, she pushed off hard and stood, tilting the slab.

Belly-flopping back down on the slab, she hugged the rock and held her breath as the rock slowly righted itself. Left cheek pressed against the cold stone, she opened her eyes and beheld the blue-green jewel of Earth hanging in the starless void.

"I'm not seein' this, I'm just not!" she said aloud, snapping her eyes down and staring at the rock at the end of her nose.

Elevating her vison a few degrees, Katie locked her eyes on Charlie's moccasins and started crawling forward. Arriving at his feet, she reached up and shook his leg without receiving a response. Irritated now, she pinched his calf hard and got the same result. Easing up into a sitting position, she felt the slab shift a few degrees before settling back to the horizontal. Suspicious, she leaned forward and examined his pupils.

"Jesus, Charlie!" she wailed, a breath away from full-blown panic. "This isn't the time to be gettin' wrecked!"

Truth be told, Charlie Redbird was lit enough from the herbs he had been smoking since stepping onto the slab to—take your pick—fire up a 1967 Grateful Dead concert or any half-dozen new millennium techno-raves.

"Wake up!" she screamed, shaking him hard.

Steadying Charlie before he tumbled over backwards, Katie shook him and yelled until her shoulders ached and her throat burned. Charlie just sang on, oblivious to all but what lay ahead. Winded and frustrated, Katie released him and sat thinking.

"I'm sorry for this, I really am," she said. "But I'm really scared, and we've gotta get out of here."

Leaning forward a little, Katie shook her hands a little to loosen up and swung for the fences. Once, twice, a short pause, then three and four times she struck him with ringing, open-handed slaps. Oblivious, Charlie sang on while Katie sat cradling her bruised hands, listening to his song whisper down the corridors of her mind.

Staring down, Katie strained to see her aching hands and realized that it was becoming darker by the second. And cold, terribly cold. Hearing steam hiss, she shifted her vision a few degrees to the right and watched as ice first engulfed, then froze, the flames in the ceremonial fire. Ice crystals began rapidly scaling on her face and hands.

Blurs of motion caught her attention and she wiped the rime out of her eyes with both hands. Colored spheres the size of fifty-cent pieces were hurtling out of the void and attaching themselves to the outer surface of the slab's atmosphere. Blinking, Katie leaned forward and stared. The spheres' faces were jet black with yellow jack-o-lantern eyes demarcated by vertical pupils. Fangs protruded from their upper and lower jaws. Barbed stingers an inch long hung down from the posterior end of their bodies.

"Crawl in and eat you inside out, bitch!" they howled at Katie, each voice-word-sentence laid over the other in a deafening howl.

The spheres hadn't fully enveloped the slab's atmosphere yet but it wouldn't be long before they did. Once it did, Katie was certain the bubble would implode and the monsters would slaughter her and Charlie. Opening her mouth to scream, Katie gagged, unable to breathe or utter a sound. Ice had filled her breathing passages and she was starting to suffocate.

Reaching up, Katie clawed at the frozen mass filling her mouth and started falling forward. Her head came to an abrupt and painful halt against Charlie's right kneecap. One of the carved runes on the staff and the last two fingers on his left hand lying atop it filled her field of vision.

The day before she had stepped onto the stone circle for the first time, Katie had picked up the staff while Charlie was out back picking the last of his tomatoes. The instant her hand had curled around the intricately carved wood, the staff had jolted her hard enough to send her chair sailing into the wall three feet away with the back of her head in hot pursuit. Which was why Charlie's lecture on nosiness a day later had stung so much. She knew somehow that he was aware of her trespass, but hadn't dared 'fess up. Not to mention her own assessment of "Once bitten, twice goddamn stupid!" If she touched the staff again, Katie was certain that this time it would shock her into unconsciousness and she and Charlie would both die.

Reaching up, Katie placed her hand on top of Charlie's. Using his hand as a cat's-paw and his knee as a fulcrum, she raised the staff an inch above the granite and released it. Expending the last of her strength, she tapped the staff twice more against the stone. Face flushing dark blue, Katie collapsed and lay staring at the soles of Charlie's boots.

Oxygen deprivation concentrates high volumes of carbon dioxide in the bloodstream, causing mental states ranging from mild euphoria to psychosis in those afflicted. Images of family and friends flashed across the frontal lobes of Katie's brain as the CO^2 level in her blood soared. The cerebral slide show paused often on Gilbert, filled with aching regret for what might have been.

The atmospheric bubble surrounding the stone slab imploded at its apex. Thousands of the howling spheres swarmed down toward the unconscious figures lying on the stone below. Slowing, they braked and hovered as if awaiting further instructions. One of the creatures, twice the size of its kindred, descended and lit on the staff. A delicate thread of blue fire licked out and vaporized it, but others were already dropping down to replace it. Charlie twitched, startling the monsters off his body and back into flight. Enraged, the spheres darted around his head, not quite daring to recommence their assault on him.

Blue plasma began pulsing out of the staff and into the granite. In response the stone began emitting a faint blue luminescence which rapidly spread outwards. Reaching the edges of the slab the radiation began rising, cocooning Katie and Charlie in its protective glow. Both began gagging and wheezing, spewing up melted water and mucous from their breathing passages.

The blue radiation continued rising until it made contact with the bottom of the sphere-swarm and began incinerating them. Chittering in terror, the creatures clogged the narrow breech in the atmospheric bubble as they tried to escape and died in flames by the hundreds as the blue glow continued rising.

The rock slab began gently trembling which rapidly increased to a violent shaking. The blue radiation flared into blinding brilliance as it matched its amplitude to the ever increasing tremors. The violent quaking and flaring blue light abruptly ceased as the wormhole supporting the circular stone slab imploded. Slowly at first, then with ever increasing acceleration, the slab began tumbling down the center of the maelstrom, an insignificant pebble gripped by the gravitational forces that underpin the universe.

Adhered to the rock's surface by the power of the staff, Katie and Charlie tumbled through the decaying anomaly. Above them the spheres milled about in panic, trying to escape the tidal pull of the collapsing wormhole. Finding escape impossible, they reversed course and swarmed after their prey. Thousands of the creatures had been incinerated by the staff's power, but thousands still remained to take up the chase. Many thousands.

CHAPTER 60

GILBERT WAS STANDING next to the cabin staring up at the hill when Katie was sucked screaming into the wormhole. Although startled, he wasn't really surprised. Ever since turning into Charlie's driveway, a sense of impending epiphany, of dramatic change, had filled him.

Taking a deep breath, he began humping it up the hill, struggling to keep his footing on the icy path. Reaching the top of the slope, he dropped down on his hands and knees and started crawling under the fir trees. Emerging from under the trees a few yards later, he stood for a moment, then dropped down flat on his belly.

After watching the center of the clearing for a full minute, Gilbert rose and unzipped his parka a few inches. Proceeding with great deliberation, he removed his glasses and polished them on his shirt front. Lifting the glasses up against the weak morning sun, he carefully inspected the lenses. Satisfied, he put the glasses back on, zipped up his coat, and focused his vision on the center of the clearing.

One of the wonders of human perception is that two people can interpret an identical event differently. Gilbert was perceiving something entirely different in the center of the clearing than Katie had. Taking a step forward, he tilted his head back, waited a few seconds, then returned his vision to the center of the clearing. Shaking his head, he looked up yet again. And still he couldn't believe. Squeezing his eyes shut, Gilbert gave it a slow ten count before reopening them. Sighing, he conceded the reality, or unreality, of the situation.

"Holy shit," he mumbled, remembering one of the major frights of his early childhood. "It's Jack-n-the-Beanstalk!"

A vast green plant stalk, or what Gilbert perceived as a plant stalk, was occupying the center of the clearing. Thirty feet wide at the base, it climbed skywards until vanishing in the grey cloud cover a couple of thousand feet above. Blue energy pulsed up and down the immense stalk, gently shaking its branches and leaves. Small brown creatures resembling a cross between a flying squirrel and a dwarf pterodactyl glided chattering through the branches. The ground under his feet was vibrating from the subterranean rumbling the plant was emitting.

Unlike Katie, Gilbert was a solid bus stop or six away on the rational side of the tracks. He had about as much intention of getting any closer to the monster plant as he did of shoving his arm into a commercial sausage grinder. Turning away, he started back towards the fir trees intending to hide and watch what happened next.

A hurricane blast of wind caught him square in the back and sent him staggering into the trees. Freeing himself from the grip of the interlocking fir branches, Gilbert tangled his feet and fell hard. Scrambling to his feet, he heard something a few feet behind him. Certain this couldn't be good news; he risked a glance over his shoulder as he started retreating through the spruce grove.

The bean stalk was gone, replaced by a circular stone slab. Katie and a decrepit-looking old native man dressed in traditional buckskins were sitting on the rock, coughing and retching. Coming about, Gilbert charged toward Katie. A deep tingling, almost an ache, raced through him when his feet touched the slab. Stopping, he looked up and saw a fast moving black cloud at the outer limits of his vision. Somehow, he knew the cloud was coming for them.

"Ji-ji-ji," Gilbert stuttered, dread tying knots in his tongue, "giant coming! Run!"

When Gilbert reached Katie, she had risen to her knees. Reaching down, he grabbed the collar of her coat and hauled her upright. Getting one arm around Katie's shoulders, he dropped the other behind her knees, intending to pick her up and run. An unbearable howling filled his mind, a noise so terrible that it had a color: black.

Tilting his head back, Gilbert watched the swarm pass through one-thousand feet and arrow down toward the slab. Death was coming, death was here. As he picked Katie up, he caught a flash of motion out of the corner of one eye and turned to look. Charlie Redbird was up on his hands and knees, runny strings of vomit hanging from his mouth and nostrils.

Settling Katie in his arms, Gilbert took a step and dared another quick look up. The diving black cloud was now at five-hundred feet and he could see that it was composed of individual components. Hearing a cough, Gilbert snapped his eyes down and watched Charlie crash down hard on the stone. Swiveling on one foot, Gilbert tried to run and found that he couldn't move, just couldn't do it. In that moment, Gilbert Mason, *nudnik* supreme, sprouted a pair of big hairy brass ones the size of honeydew melons. Shifting his grip, he threw Katie toward the dense cover of the fir trees.

"Run!" He screamed even as he reached down for Charlie. "Run, get in the cabin, hurry!"

Barely conscious, Katie started crawling toward the spruce grove, knowing only that she had to get away and hide. Kneeling down, Gilbert maneuvered Charlie into a sitting position. Even in his old age, Charlie Redbird was a big man, easily fifty pounds heavier and six inches taller than Gilbert. Straining, getting his knees into the lift, Gilbert hoisted Charlie in a shaky Fireman's Carry. Something deep in Gilbert's back snapped and he nearly fell, but somehow he staggered on. Three years from now, almost to the hour, day, and minute, two ruptured disks in his lower back would have to be surgically repaired.

The first echelon of incoming wasps missed and smashed themselves to smoking pulp against the granite because Gilbert was moving forward. Had he fallen or remained stationary, the monsters would have slaughtered him and Charlie.

"Hurry," Charlie said, startling Gilbert, "get us off this rock or we are both going to die."

The second wave of wasps wounded Charlie deep in the flesh of his upper right arm, hammering him as if he'd been shot. The next two insects, if that's what they could be called, lanced Gilbert in the right palm and in the back of the left thigh and smashed him down on the granite.

At first, Gilbert thought it was some sort of dart or projectile until he saw the creature's wings fluttering. Some of the pain was caused by the barbed stinger that had been driven deep into his palm. The rest was caused by the wasp trying to chew its way through the palm of his hand.

"Howyadoin', Gil," the monster said as it chewed, somehow managing to wink a faceted eye at him. "Thanks for havin' us all over to dinner, beats shit out of Prince Spaghetti Night! Woo-ooo-ooo-eee!"

Unaware that he was screaming and crying, Gilbert tried to tear the wasp out of his hand and failed. Changing tactics, he raised his right arm and smashed his hand down until the insect was nothing more than a gelatinous smear on the grey stone. Despite the pain and the fear, he somehow kept crawling toward the edge of the slab with Charlie riding on his back. Finally though, three of the wasps stung him deep in the back of his right thigh just above the knee. Sobbing, he collapsed.

"C'mon now, crawl!" Charlie grunted, stirring on top of him. "Crawl off the stone or we are done for! Not much further now!"

A corona of blue fire danced around Gilbert's head and he began crawling forward again, dragging Charlie with him. Suddenly, he fell off the edge of the stone slab with Charlie still on top of him. The wasp swarm burst into blue flames, screaming as they died, leaving behind fetid black ash and nightmares yet to come.

An intricately carved black staff that Gilbert hadn't noticed before was pressed up against the side of his nose. Twisting his head, Gilbert eased the pressure on his schnoz but still couldn't free himself from Charlie's weight.

After struggling in vain to free himself for a few more seconds, he asked, "Ungh, are you all right? Can you move?"

Charlie replied, "I'm badly hurt, but if you'll get your knee off my balls, I think I can stand up. We have to hurry, those wasps are as poisonous as cobra snakes and we've been bitten enough times to kill us many times over."

The men disentangled themselves, Charlie standing first with the aid of the staff. Reaching down, he hooked one hand under Gilbert's arm and hauled him up, grunting with the effort. Leaning to one side, Gilbert started falling and was only kept upright by Charlie's arm around his waist.

Fuzzy black spots spun across Gilbert's visual fields and exploded into flaring novae. Blue fire flickered and danced at the edges of his vision but it wasn't strong enough to drive back the encroaching darkness. A freezing chill swept through him and he began shivering uncontrollably.

"Mr. Redbird, I—" Gilbert mumbled and started vomiting out great arcs of black bile that lay smoking on the snow.

Out of any given group of envenomed victims, a small number will be violently allergic to the toxin and be at far greater risk of death or permanent injury. Sixty seconds after being bitten, Gilbert's face flushed a terrible dark purple color as the neuro-venom he had absorbed began shutting down the respiratory functions in his brain.

Already feeling the effects of the poison, Charlie was hard up against it. Their wounds had been struck by the hand of the Dark One and the power of the staff alone could not heal them. If he could reach his pharmacopeia in the cabin, Charlie knew he could treat their wounds. Yet he was too ill and lacked the strength to carry Gilbert down the hill. But if he left Gilbert behind while he tried to reach the cabin, the young man would die.

Charlie hadn't walked and survived all the dark roads of his life by being afraid of doing the hard thing, the difficult thing. Even though he was certain that he would die in the attempt, Charlie wrapped both arms around Gilbert and started bulling his way through the spruce trees. He fell almost immediately, but got up and kept on moving, dragging himself and Gilbert forward through the fir branches. After what seemed like hours, Charlie became aware of two things: he was lying in a pool of weak sunlight at the edge of the spruce grove and it had been at least thirty seconds since he'd last heard Gilbert breathe.

Kneeling, Charlie rolled Gilbert over on his back and pulled up his shirt and parka. Raising his right fist high above his head, Charlie smashed down on Gilbert's solar plexus. Twice more he struck, but Gilbert lay still, chest unmoving. Desperate now, Charlie summoned the power of the staff and sent a finger of blue fire arcing into Gilbert's sternum. Body convulsing, touching the earth only at the head and heels, Gilbert hung suspended on a thread of blue lightning for a full five seconds but still he didn't breathe.

Calling the power back into the staff, Charlie collapsed down into the snow. The thought of having to tell Katie that Gilbert was dead, and dead because of him, was unbearable. So Charlie decided he would sit here up to his ass in cold snow and wait for the wasps' venom to finish its work.

Wanting one last smoke, he started patting his pockets down searching for his pipe. Gilbert coughed hard and puked up a near-solid mass of stinking black vomitus. Shallow and uneven, his breathing would have provoked alarm in a well-seasoned emergency medicine department, but it was there, if just barely.

Grabbing Gilbert, Charlie pulled hard for both of their lives. The pause while he sat in the snow had been long enough for the wasp venom to seep deep inside of him and begin its work. Three steps later, he collapsed face down in the snow, body numb from the hips down and battling for breath. The cabin was close now, he could see it down at the bottom of the slope, but Charlie knew he couldn't go any further.

Dragging an arm forward to clear the snow away from his face, Charlie's knuckles dragged across something hard. Pain exploded under the nail of his little finger and he jerked his hand back. A drop of blood was hanging from a small wooden splinter lodged deep under the nail. It wasn't until he pulled out the splinter with a drawn-out hiss of pain that he realized where it had come from.

The beat-up old toboggan he used to haul firewood with during the winter was lying next to him in the snow. If asked, Charlie would have said that the toboggan was stored in the garden shed where it belonged and where he had left if after using it last. No matter though, he was happy to see it.

"Thank you, Mum," he mumbled, rolling Gilbert onto the toboggan and then climbing on top of him.

For one terrible moment, Charlie thought that the sled was too heavily laden for him to move it. Legs paralyzed by the wasp toxin, he clawed at the snow and the toboggan finally lurched forward. The front of the sled teetered over the edge of the slope until Charlie shifted his weight forward and started it sliding down the hill.

Slowly at first, then with ever increasing acceleration, the toboggan sped down the hill, firmly in the grasp of Newton's law.

Peering up over the curved headpiece, Charlie could see that they were traversing the slope on an angle away from the cabin. Rolling over on one hip, he changed course a few degrees, but not nearly enough to reach the cabin. On this heading, they would crash into a small copse of sugar maples at the base of the hill.

Rolling back on his belly, Charlie looked up again and saw the berm bordering the icy track that led up the hill looming dead ahead and knew they were going to come a cropper. The toboggan began climbing the snow bank and then slammed into a solid outcropping of ice. The curved headpiece snapped off as the sled slewed violently to the left and took flight. Feeling his body soar, Charlie wrapped his arms around Gilbert and braced for the impact he knew was coming. Instead of the expected crash and tumble, Charlie and Gilbert ended up back on top of the toboggan where they had started. Trapped between the knee-high snow banks lining the icy path, the old toboggan was flying downhill as straight and true as a two-man bobsled bound for Olympic gold. Reaching the bottom of the slope, the toboggan took a home team bounce and ran out its momentum along the side of the cabin. The sled coasted to a halt near the front of the building just as Katie came charging around the corner.

Reaching out with the staff, Charlie froze her in place and said, "Quickly now. There is an old leather satchel in my bedroom closet. Inside there is a large brown bottle with a cork stopper and an eye-dropper attached to the side with a rubber-band. Bring me that bottle. Hurry now, Gilbert and I are going to die soon unless we get treated with that medicine."

Without questioning or hesitating, Katie was off and running. Sprinting through the cabin, she pulled open the door to Charlie's bedroom closet. Dropping to her knees, she started patting her hands across the dark floor searching for the satchel. Something soft brushed against her fingertips. Taking a firm hold, she backed out of the closet and dragged the heavy satchel out into the bedroom. Pushing it upright, she started struggling with the antique brass latches.

The dust from the closet floor caught up with her just then, bringing on a violent sneezing attack. When her head cleared the bag lay open by her knees. The interior of the satchel was filled with assorted bottles, surgical paraphernalia, and a mortar and pestle. Katie's hands started dropping down and then stopped as she was racked by a third-degree brain cramp. Had Charlie said the bottle was brown or blue? It was supposed to be sealed with a cork and there was something about an eye-dropper and—

"Smarten up and think!" she said aloud, closing her eyes and focusing on her breathing.

Clarity returned and with it, memory. There it was in the middle of the satchel, a large brown glass bottle with a cork stopper and an eyedropper attached to the side with a rubber-band. Lifting the bottle out of the bag, Katie got up and ran toward the front door. Sprinting down the porch steps, she rounded the side of the cabin and suddenly stopped.

Charlie was lying on his belly in the middle of a large puddle of snowmelt. Gilbert was curled up on his left side on the toboggan. Their faces were pale with an underlying purple tinge and neither showed any sign of respiration.

The quiver in her hands deepened to a violent trembling and Katie's fingers lost their hold on the medicine bottle's smooth glass surface. The bottle fell in an upright posture, spinning slowly on its axis as it fell. Without thinking, which would have doomed the effort to failure, she bent down and plucked the bottle out of midair just as it reached her toes. Drops of moisture clung to the bottle's bottom from where it had kissed the snowmelt puddle at her feet.

A memory came unbidden from an afternoon's channel surfing the week before.

On the Food Channel, a French sommelier had proclaimed, "To open zee champagne, you tilts zee bottle at a forty-five degree angle, and holding firmly zee cork, you twist only zee bottle, and *voila!*, the bottle, she opens!"

Getting a good grip on the cork, Katie tried twisting only zee bottle but the cork refused to move. Deciding that taking advice from a foreign sommelier in an emergency was a losing proposition, she tightened her grip and gave the bottle and cork the All-American-New-Year's-Eve-Cheap-Bottle-of-Champagne-Two-Handed-Counter-Torque-Twist. A slight tremor was the only warning she got before the cork exploded out of the bottle and sailed off for parts unknown. The bottle began percolating, releasing a clear vapor which was somehow both fragrant and astringent at the same time. Although barely audible, she could hear Charlie singing from somewhere down inside the bottle.

Dropping to her knees, Katie shoved the medicine bottle into a snow bank. Pushing hard, she managed to roll Gilbert over on his back. With her knees framing his head, she reached over, picked up the bottle, and sucked up a dose of medicine into the eyedropper. Bending forward, she discovered that she couldn't coordinate keeping her balance, Gilbert's mouth open, and the medicine dropper upright all at the same time.

"Sorry, Honey," she said, grimacing as she hooked Gilbert's nostrils with a pair of fingers and pulled his mouth open.

Shoving the eyedropper into his mouth, Katie squeezed the rubber bulb. Finished with Gilbert, she scrambled over to Charlie and immediately ran into a problem. Lying face-down on his belly, there was no way that all two-hundred and five pounds of Charlie Redbird was going to be moved by all ninety-five pounds of Katie Henderson. Grabbing his right ear, she tugged until his face was resting on its left cheek. Refilling the eye-dropper, she forced it between his teeth, pushed it as far back into his mouth as she could, and squeezed the bulb.

Refilling the dropper again, she moved back to Gilbert, intending to treat the wounds in his thighs. Kneeling, she parted the shredded fabric and froze, staring. There was *stuff* in there, flaps of torn skin, clotting blood, globules of yellow fat, and strings of red muscle tissue. A great roaring filled Katie's ears and her vision narrowed to dark pinpoints as she started pitching forward.

"Can't-can't-can't!" she shrieked-chanted, fighting off the faint.

Avoiding looking at her hands too closely, Katie repeatedly filled the dropper and jabbed it deep into their wounds, ignoring the awful squelching noises it made. Although she was trying to hurry, it felt like the faster she tried to move, the slower she went. Finally though, she was through medicating their wounds. Shoving the eye-dropper back through the rubber-band, she pushed the bottle back into the snow bank. Two minutes passed and still neither man breathed.

"Please," she begged, face tilted up to the grey sky. "Please."

Another minute passed without either man showing a sign of life. Crying, deciding there was nothing left to lose, Katie picked up the medicine bottle again. Tilting the bottle to one side, she filled the eye-dropper. Walking over to Gilbert, she knelt intending to re-medicate the wounds in his thighs.

"That's enough now," Charlie said. "That's not baby aspirin you're pumpin' there."

Shrieking, Katie went vertical and didn't regain Earth again for a solid five feet.

"Don't-fuckin'-do-that!" she yelled. "Are you all right, I thought—"

"Yes, Katie, we'll be fine in a couple of days," he replied, muffled by her hug. "Easy there, you'll squish me flat. Gilbert will wake up in a minute and then we can go inside before I freeze to death in this goddamn puddle."

It took longer than a minute for Gilbert to regain consciousness and longer yet before Charlie escaped the icy puddle. Racked by his violent allergy to the wasp venom, Gilbert was still extremely ill. An hour later though Katie had them both in bed and the cabin's wood stove roaring.

Exhausted, she spent the night catnapping on the couch in between checking on Charlie and Gilbert and stoking the wood stove. Near dawn, a metallic clatter woke her from a nightmare of icy strangling amidst a swarming cloud of terrible black shapes. Looking pale and wasted, Charlie was battling a birch log into the stove while the enamel coffeepot perked away on top.

"I didn't mean to wake you," he said. "It's getting so I can't sneak around worth a damn."

Getting up off the couch, Katie crossed the room and hugged him.

"You're lucky you're still here, sneaking or not. You should be in bed resting."

"Coffee," Charlie told her, "can cure most everything that ails you."

"And what it doesn't, the magic medicine in the brown bottle cures, right?"

Deciding to let that remark lay, Charlie took a pair of cups down off the shelf and filled them. They sat drinking coffee, comfortable with each other's silence, watching the flames weave yellow tapestries in the stove's firebox. Feeling that it needed raising before it could fester, Katie broached a delicate subject.

"I, well, when we first got here, and later when I was running up the hill, I thought you were going to commit suicide," she said. "I've always believed that people should be allowed to make their own choices. I, I didn't mean to interfere or anything."

"Now don't fuss yourself. I'm getting old and I'm ready to go home now. But my employer had other ideas on the subject, so I will be here until my natural end, which isn't all that far away. I'm just sorry that you and Gilbert got caught up in my problems and got hurt."

Letting the conversation sink in, Katie refilled their cups and sat watching the fire, thinking.

"Charlie, will Gilbert be all right?" she asked after a few minutes.

"Yes," he replied, "the fever will break in a couple of hours and he should be up and around by early afternoon. But it may take several days, perhaps as long as a week, for him to fully recover.

"You need to be very careful with him the next few days. Gilbert is very conservative and he's had an experience which is alien to his world-view. If you aren't patient with him, what happened yesterday could scar him forever."

"Yeah, well he ain't the only one," Katie said, making Charlie smile. "And I'm going to be very good to him. Do you think he—"

"I think he will make you a fine husband. You will probably never meet a better man or a braver one," Charlie told her, getting to his feet and leaning heavily on the staff. "You should let him do the asking though. Poor Gilbert's had enough shocks to last him a while and you don't want to scare him off."

"I'm not going to, how did you—"

"Because despite my recent shortcomings," he replied, looking over one shoulder and laughing as he entered the back hallway, "I am still a wise old man sometimes."

Still sleepy despite the coffee she had drunk, Katie took the pot off the stove and lay back down on the couch. Waking a couple of hours later, she checked on Gilbert and Charlie and found them both sleeping. Leaving the bedrooms, she walked into the kitchen and disaster struck. Charlie had shopped carefully for his premature exit. The cupboard, along with the refrigerator, were bare, and one of the most voracious appetites on the continent was awake and on the prowl.

"This isn't gonna get it," she announced, shutting the refrigerator door.

After writing a quick note, Katie took Gilbert's keys out of his coat pocket and left the cabin. As she backed down the icy driveway, the van began sliding sideways. Startled, she slammed on the brakes, which only accelerated the slide. The slide stopped three feet later when the van smacked into Charlie's mailbox, snapping the two-by-four post it was mounted on cleanly in half.

Hanging on the edge of sleep, Charlie heard the impact and grinned, thinking of the numerous times the women in his life had run down the mailbox. *"Must be a law of nature or something,"* was his last thought before drifting off to sleep again.

"Oh-man-oh-man," Katie sighed, looking down at the battered mailbox laying in the snow next to the van's dented left-rear quarter panel, "am I ever gonna catch a ration of shit about this."

Popping open the Caravan's lift gate, she bent down to pick up the mailbox but found that it was too heavy. The large aluminum box was stuffed full of unopened mail, at least a couple of weeks' worth. Grabbing a double handful of mail, Katie carried it over to the van and shoved it up against the back seat. Two trips later, the box was finally emptied of mail. Squatting down, she got the mailbox up on one shoulder and held it there with the remaining stub of two-by-four attached to the box's bottom.

"Cities student starves to death in cold after freak collision with a rural mailbox," she grunted, heaving the mailbox into the back of the van because it was too heavy to carry back to the porch. "Read all about it in the Inquirer."

Between the icy roads, getting lost on both legs of the trip, a monster fast-food attack which demanded immediate gratification, and long checkout lines at the grocery and drug stores, it was nearly four hours before Katie arrived back at the cabin. Lugging the first armful of groceries through the door, she found Gilbert and Charlie sitting at the kitchen table. Both men looked pale and tired, but they were *here*, alive if not yet kicking.

Setting the groceries down on the kitchen counter, she bent down and hugged them both.

"How are you two doing?" she asked. "I'm surprised that you're up and around."

"Pretty good," Gilbert replied. "We were getting worried because you'd been gone so long."

"We were going to call the police and get an APB put out," Charlie said, using his pipe as a microphone. "Calling all cars, calling all cars, be on the lookout for a short white female driving a rusty baby blue Dodge Caravan with a large mailbox in the back belonging to Mr. Charles Lantot Redbird. Calling all cars, calling all cars."

"Stop it!" Gilbert begged, fighting hard not to laugh and losing the battle. "It hurts just to breathe, never mind laugh. You're, you're killin' me here!"

"I, you," Katie began, face red. "I don't want to talk about that damn mailbox!"

Dignity punctured, she retreated out the front door to the sound of muted male laughter. Five trips later the van was emptied of groceries, mail, and the mailbox.

"So," she asked, stacking cans on the pantry shelf, "what else have you two been discussing other than your gender-based prejudices?"

"Reality," Charlie answered, "and its various interpretations in different cultural systems."

"Oh," Katie said, "guess maybe I'll stick to lighter stuff like making lunch."

"Take cover!" Gilbert mumbled, ducking his head and hoping that she hadn't heard his tongue slip a gear.

"What was that, Gillie?" she asked, turning around with her hands on her hips. "Did you say something?"

"N-no, I didn't" he replied, struggling not to laugh.

A column of blue tobacco smoke was alternately rising then disappearing back into the bowl of Charlie's pipe, duplicating his respiratory battle with mirth. First Gilbert, then Katie, became mesmerized by the dancing plume of smoke. The battle was finally lost on the exhalation stroke of the cycle. Burning tobacco embers cascaded out of the pipe in a volcanic shower as Charlie coughed out an amazing volume of smoke and started laughing. Unable to stifle himself, Gilbert joined in.

"All right, damn it," she began and then gave up as the two men continued laughing.

Humor is contagious and eventually Katie caught the bug. Laughter eluded her, but she did manage to smile. After thirty seconds or so, she licked the first two fingers on her right hand, stuck them in her mouth, and loosed an ear-piercing whistle.

"All-right-all-ready, I give," she said, raising her hands in mock surrender. "So maybe I'm not the world's greatest driver or cook. Could we please talk about something else, maybe even express some appreciation for the heroine of this piece, yours truly?"

An awkward moment passed into uncomfortable silence until Gilbert took her hand and declared, "I love you completely, even though your driving would scare a kamikaze pilot and you couldn't burn water with a six-week head start."

"As do I," Charlie said, taking her other hand. "Although I'll be able to love you longer if you let me do the driving and the cooking."

"Well, at least I'm loveable," she told them, smiling a little.

With some much-needed advice from Charlie, Katie prepared them a large brunch. By the time the cooking, eating, and clean-up were finished, it was late afternoon and both Charlie and Gilbert were tired. Shooing them off to bed, Katie collapsed on the couch for a well-deserved rest.

Hours later she awoke from the same nightmare she'd had the night before. Crying out, she sat up clutching her throat, shivering and coughing.

"Easy now," Charlie soothed from the kitchen table, "it's only a bad dream."

Leaving the couch, Katie walked over and sat down. Taking a sip of the coffee he'd poured for her, she tried to stretch the couch-kinks out of her neck and back.

"No, it wasn't a bad dream," she said. "It was a memory."

Looking up from loading his pipe, Charlie nodded and waited for her to continue.

"It's going wrong, isn't it?" Katie asked. "That special part of me, the clairvoyant, feels like everything is spinning out of control, like we're a millisecond away from something terrible happening. Do you know what I mean?"

It took Charlie so long to light his pipe that Katie was in a state of full-tilt fidget by the time he spoke again.

"Yes, Katie, I know what you mean. There are no proper moments to speak of things like this, but the hours of darkness are worse because this is when evil things are strongest. So you must listen carefully because I want to be brief."

Wrapping both arms around herself, Katie shivered and glanced out the window. The season, the lake, the endless forest, and especially the deep dark all weighed heavily on her. Suddenly, she wanted to be somewhere, anywhere, but here.

"Steady now," Charlie said, "there's nothing out there tonight but your own fears. If there were anything, I'd know and so would you."

Managing a wan smile, Katie nodded and sipped on her coffee.

"Events are now spinning toward the millennium like a whirlpool, making evil things especially strong. That is what the clairvoyant part of you feels and senses. Your feelings are normal; all millennial times are like this.

"Everyone, whether they know it or not, is trapped in this whirlpool to one degree or another. Unlike most people, you can sense the whirlpool's power, its pull, and it frightens you. All we can do now is wait and see where the current takes us. That's all, nothing more, nothing less."

"Hot damn," Katie said bleakly, "that's a cheerful state of affairs, isn't it?"

"It is what it is," Charlie replied, sweeping his hand through the tobacco smoke as if dismissing the subject. "Now I'd like to talk about something that directly concerns you."

"Ungh, what might that be?" she asked, trying to sound innocent while at the same time racking her brain for past misdeeds both major and minor.

Pulling a piece of paper out of his pocket, Charlie unfolded it and laid it on the table facing her.

"I," he said, tapping a forefinger on the sheet of paper for emphasis, "have been offered a teaching position in the Art Department of your university based on my submission of a dozen sketches and watercolors of wood ducks and other aquatic birds. Since I didn't submit those sketches and paintings and you know where I keep them up in the attic, I believe you are responsible."

Groaning, Katie squeezed her eyes shut and lowered her head onto her crossed forearms.

"Smooth busted," she said, voice muffled by her arms. "*Mea culpa.* I did it because I was worried about you being up here all alone after Ellen, I shouldn't have, I'm sor—"

"You were right, although your methods leave a lot to be desired. Ends and means and so forth."

"Well, it's not exactly a ringing endorsement," she said, raising her head and looking at him, "but I'll take it."

"As will I, the teaching position I mean. When I was young I wanted to go to college but She had other ideas. Now I'm finally going to get to go, except as a teacher, not a student."

"I'm so glad!" she told him in a garbled rush. "I've been so worried about you, especially after yesterday."

"I'm glad also," Charlie said, standing up, "a change will do me good. Right now though, I'm a beat-up old man who is feeling his age and needs his rest. Good night, sleep well."

After waiting a few minutes, Katie checked on her patients and found them both sleeping soundly. Unwilling to risk waking Gilbert, she got an extra blanket out of the closet and resigned herself to spending another night on the couch. Making herself comfortable, she lay staring up at the ceiling, thinking about everything Charlie had told her.

"Sleep well, you gotta be kidding," she mumbled just before falling into a deep, dreamless sleep.

CHAPTER 61

THE NEXT DAY, and the following two, Charlie and Gilbert both ran high fevers. The fourth day they spent packing and preparing for the drive down to the Cities. On the fifth day they left Frechette in a two vehicle caravan with Charlie's smoking old pickup truck bringing up the rear.

Finding a rental in the University District and setting up house occupied Charlie for the next week. After an exasperating few days he settled on a well-worn three-bedroom ranch house and signed a lease. By urban standards the house was in a quiet, well-tended neighborhood. By Charlie's standards his new digs were in a crowded, noisy neighborhood whose only attraction was its close proximity to the university.

At 10:00 a.m. on the first Monday in the second week of January 1998, Artist-in-Residence Charles Lantot Redbird stood leaning on his staff at the front of a classroom and began teaching the intricacies of drawing avian wildlife. As he had hoped, Charlie loved teaching, loved helping others learn and hone artistic skills.

A guest lecture for the Anthropology Department on First American creation myths led to an accepted offer of teaching a graduate seminar on the same subject. Suddenly, Charlie Redbird was a very busy man. In short order he became a familiar part of the university community, well-liked and respected by both his colleagues and students.

Katie and Gilbert were frequent visitors both at his university office and at his home. Coming together at first, they soon began stopping by separately and Charlie began worrying. Those worries were confirmed over dinner in early February when Katie announced that "Gilbert and I are going to spend some time apart." Wailing inside, Charlie said nothing and kept eating.

A knock on the front door a few minutes later surprised them both. While Katie went to answer the door, Charlie finished clearing the table and started a pot of coffee. An ordinary person would not have been able to hear the irritation in Katie's voice from the other side of the closed front door. But Charlie was far from ordinary and he clearly heard the veiled anger in her voice.

Exercising his prerogative to be nosy, Charlie hot-footed it for the master bedroom and peeked through a slat in the venetian blind. Shoulders hunched against the cold, Gilbert was standing in a spill of light looking thoroughly dejected. The edge of a shoulder and upper arm were all that Charlie could see of Katie, but it was enough for him to sense her mood, her hurt.

"Ah-h-h," Charlie said, suspicions confirmed.

As he had suspected, Katie's statement "Gilbert and I are going to spend some time apart" should have been phrased "I have decided...." The shadow that Katie had been casting across the yard changed aspect as she turned away toward the house. Charlie, an avid Minnesota Twins fan, made a long-shot prediction on the game in progress.

"Bottom of the ninth, tie score, bases empty," he whispered aloud. "C'mon, Gilbert, faint heart never a fair lady won."

Dropping to one knee on the cold cement sidewalk, Gilbert took a small blue velour box out of his pocket. In a moment that would have been comical in other circumstances, he struggled to open the box for so long that even Charlie, normally unflappable, was getting nervous. With the box finally open, Gilbert called out to Katie's retreating back. She stopped, turned, and walked back to Gilbert.

"He winds up," Charlie intoned.

Gilbert began speaking to Katie.

"The pitch: a slow, sinking knuckleball."

Head cocked, Katie stood listening.

"The batter waits."

Shifting her position a little, Katie took a half-step to the left.

"She swings!"

Delighted, Katie leaped into Gilbert's arms, carrying them both back into a snow bank.

"A-n-n-d it's outta here!" Charlie crowed, pumping his fists in celebration.

When the newly betrothed couple walked into the kitchen a minute later, Charlie was seated at the table sipping coffee and smoking his pipe. Thrusting her ring-hand into a pocket, Katie bent over and stage-whispered in his ear, "Wanna know a secret?"

"Always," he replied.

"If you're gonna peek through the blinds, make sure they stay still and that you're not backlit by the hall light."

"Smooth busted!" Charlie said, standing up and hugging them both. "Congratulations! You two had me worried there for a minute."

"You should of been there," Katie commented, extending her ring finger for Charlie's admiring approval.

"Oops!" Gilbert cracked, trying to look abashed, but failing by grinning.

The engagement party went until midnight and would have lasted longer had Charlie not pleaded fatigue. Knowing his friends were tired, he offered them the use of the spare bedroom. No good deed goes unpunished and Charlie's reward for his hospitality was being serenaded by their lovemaking until dawn began creeping around the treacherous venetian blind.

With the exception of his estrangement from Ellen, these were good days for Charlie. He loved teaching and his classes and seminars were over-subscribed. Several exhibitions of his art work were held, two of which attracted national media attention. At the end of his life Charlie got a brief sweet taste of what could have been had he not been called to wield the staff all those Octobers ago.

On a beautiful morning in early July, Charlie and Gilbert were standing in an apple orchard atop a hill overlooking the Cities. Taking Gilbert by the arm, Charlie led him on a walk around the hilltop while they waited for Katie to arrive.

"Are you nervous, Gilbert?" Charlie asked.

"N-n-not really."

"Know what?"

Gilbert didn't answer, but rather just shook his head and kept walking.

"You're full of shit!" Charlie said, laughing and hugging his friend.

Murmuring voices rose from the trees off to their left and the two men stopped and stood listening.

"Well," Charlie told him, "it sounds like the bride and her co-conspirators have arrived. Come along, Gilbert, your moment is at hand."

Taking him by the arm, Charlie led Gilbert into the center of the orchard. Dropping him off with the rest of Clan Mason, Charlie walked up to a bower draped in fresh flowers. The wedding guests were gathering in rows of folding metal chairs a few feet away. The rose petal-covered aisle between the Henderson and Mason families set his mind churning in search of a word. Bi, de, di, yes, he decided, dichotomy was the word best describing the scene unfolding a few feet away.

On the left, the Henderson family sat beaming, showing more sparkling teeth than a toothpaste commercial. Katie's younger relatives and friends were seated behind them, sporting enough dyed hair, body piercings, and tattoos to frighten a tribe of New Guinea headhunters.

Across the aisle the Mason family sat rigidly upright, unsmiling, as if awaiting collective root canal surgery *sans* anesthesia. The only dyed hair and earrings in sight were worn by women of appropriate age. And no tattoos, at least none visible. There were crew cuts though, lots of them, a few even spruced up with butch-wax and accented with whitewalls. Somewhere out there on the right side of the aisle Charlie was certain, just positive, that someone was wearing a pocket protector. He just hoped that it wasn't Gilbert.

The wedding march began playing out of a hidden stereo system as the bride and groom and their entourages started walking up the aisle. The looks exchanged between the two families as they craned their heads back to watch the bride and groom pass promised many interesting family holidays in the years ahead. Resplendent in his best ceremonial clothing and jewelry, Charlie stood smiling as the bride and groom approached the bower. Five minutes later the simple wedding ceremony was over and Katie and Gilbert were Mister and Missus.

Desiring to end his public duties on a happy note, Charlie had previously announced his retirement as shaman of the Poshto people. Despite many pleas to reconsider, he had stood firm and insisted upon stepping down. Now, as he circulated among the wedding guests, he was certain that his decision was correct. After decades of service he was weary of the never-ending ceremonial and healing duties which devoured so much of his time, so much of his life. With the exception of some black looks from the older members of Clan Mason, he couldn't have picked a happier or a prettier day to bow out on. Well pleased, Charlie went searching for Katie to ask for a dance.

Retirement from his ceremonial and healing duties could not alter Charlie's servitude to the staff. Nor could his love of academia, of wildlife art, or of anyone or of anything halt the slow wheel of the seasons. Too soon gone it was October time and Charlie was driving north with dread in his heart.

CHAPTER 62

TURNING INTO THE cabin's dirt driveway, Charlie parked and let the environment seep in through the driver's side window. Satisfied after ten minutes that no danger was near, he got out of the truck and stood with his head bent, listening. Again sensing no danger near, he reached back into the cab and pulled out a pack basket loaded with enough supplies for a frugal ten days. That was the length of the emergency leave-of-absence he'd taken from the university. If he wasn't back in a ten days, Charlie knew he probably wasn't coming back at all.

"Probably my ass," he bitched out loud, feeling pessimistic despite his own best efforts. "If I'm not back in ten days, they're not even gonna find my footprints, never mind the rest of me."

Reaching the foot of the porch steps, Charlie stood looking up at the cabin, thinking how forlorn and neglected his home looked. He had been gone for nine months now, his longest absence since moving here shortly after the death of his wife almost a half-century ago. After her death, he'd wanted only to escape his guilt and—

"That's enough now," Charlie told himself as he climbed the porch steps. "An unhappy warrior is a dead warrior and that would ruin my day for sure."

Once inside, he laid a fire in the wood stove and chased the chill out of the cabin. After a simple dinner of canned beef stew, Charlie lay down on the couch and slept surprisingly well. Just before dawn the staff awakened him by rapping him hard on the head.

"Cut the shit, I'm awake!" he roared, stumbling to his feet and kicking the coffee table out of the way.

Rotating on the balls of his feet, Charlie dragged the staff across the floor until he was standing in the center of a blazing pool of blue fire. Bringing his pulse and breathing under control by a conscious effort of will, he stood listening to the gale lashing the trees behind the cabin. The Wendigo was here, held at bay only by his fear of the staff's power and the man who wielded it.

"Come on in, Trickster," Charlie said, knowing that the creature outside could hear him, "and let's have an end to this nonsense. I've got better things to do than chase your dumb ass all over hell's half-acre for the next week."

Enraged, the monster changed tactics and attacked the cabin. The log structure groaned and for a second Charlie could see stars shining through the gaps in the roof as The Wendigo started tearing it off. The assault suddenly stopped and there was silence for a long moment before the monster roared off to the northeast, snapping trees off at the base as he went.

"Jesus!" Charlie said, trying to get his fear under control. "Old bastard's already huge and he hasn't eaten for going on two years!"

Extinguishing the protective ring of blue flames, Charlie sat down to a quick breakfast of cold cereal and coffee. Five minutes later, he shouldered his pack basket and walked out the front door into a new dawn. Reaching the tree line, he stood peering into the great forest for long minutes.

"Enough already!" he snapped at himself, voice echoing in the stillness of the forest. "Stop being such an old woman and go do what must be done!"

Taking a course parallel to the tangled blow downs the Dark One had left behind, Charlie started hiking northeastwards into the forest. The staff thrummed and pulsed in his hands, eager to bring its ancient foe to battle. Hanging on tight, Charlie staggered along behind it looking like a small owner being towed along by a very large and unruly dog that never tired. Every couple of miles or so, he would lean the staff against whatever was handy and take a few minutes of much-needed rest. If the break lasted any longer than ten minutes, the staff would begin bouncing, signaling that a sharp crack in the ribs was imminent unless he got moving. Late that evening, long after midnight, they camped for a few short hours until dawn. Other than these short breaks, man and staff pursued their enemy around the clock.

At sunset on the evening of the second day, Charlie was standing atop a small hill, gasping for breath. Though he drew great strength and stamina from the staff, the thirty-nine miles he had traveled over rough country had exhausted him. Last year's victory over the monster seemed a distant and irrelevant memory now. Catching his breath after a few minutes, he limped over to a maple tree and sat at its base. The erratic breeze extinguished the first two matches, but on the third try he got his pipe lit. Eyes closed, he sat enjoying the smoke and pondering the Dark One's latest stratagem.

The beast had repeatedly drawn near, then fled, leading Charlie ever further north. More puzzling yet, the monster had passed up at least five easy opportunities to feed, a behavioral anomaly in a creature of such insatiable appetites. Just then the staff began bouncing, which as usual aggravated Charlie no end. Opening his eyes, he continued smoking and watched as the staff began circling around him.

"Lookee here now, Stick," he said, sounding weary. "My geriatric self isn't marching off this lump of rock until dawn tomorrow. You can jump up and down until you pound yourself into splinters or beat me like the Wednesday wash but I'm still not gonna move."

The staff hung suspended in midair for a moment and uttered a series of pealing bell tones. Silencing itself mid-knell, it laid down on the ground next to his right leg. The staff's unexpected obedience to his wishes while on the hunt combined with the strange bell tones filled Charlie with a vague unease.

Rising, he gathered some wood and started a small fire. Digging around in his pack basket, he pulled out a can of pork-n-beans and a small blue enamel coffeepot. Opening the beans and filling the coffeepot, he set them in the fire and waited for the boil that would signal dinner was ready.

Rubbing at the kinks in the small of his back, Charlie took inventory of his assorted aches and pains. Finding the list too long, he changed tactics and focused on those parts of his body that felt well and came up with hair and teeth. Every other part of his body felt wind-burned, strained, blistered, cold, or a combination thereof.

"Redbird," he said aloud, "you have become a soft, fat, out-of-shape, town-living Indian." A second later he added, "And before that, you were a soft, fat, out-of-shape, country-living Indian."

Laughing and groaning at the same time, he knelt and slid dinner out of the fire. Taking a seat against the maple tree, he ate quickly. Finished, he stood, buried the trash, and reloaded the pack basket. Using a small trenching tool, Charlie pulled the edges of the fire in until the glowing coals were stacked in a neat circle. Covering the coals with a thin layer of moist soil, he added a layer of small sticks, then another layer of moist soil, and a final layer of small sticks.

Satisfied that the fire would burn until at least dawn, Charlie laid down next to it. Wrapping both arms around the staff, he fell into a light doze. The moon was setting in the small hours of the morning when the staff awakened him with strident bell tones and a sharp rap under the chin. Scrambling to his feet before he was fully awake, he summoned a ring of protective fire. Snatching up the pack basket, he shoved his arms through the shoulder straps. Holding the staff at waist level with both hands, he stood listening and waiting.

In the distance, trees snapped and fell as The Wendigo raged forward on the attack. From the base of the hillock pealing bell tones were sounding. Confused, Charlie pivoted, keeping the fast approaching Trickster at his right hand and the strange bell tones at his left.

A gentle breeze parted the ring of protective blue flames. The flow of air teased and tickled around Charlie's ankles for a second before accelerating itself into a spinning whirlwind. A muted roar interspersed with pealing bell tones issued from the cyclone as its rotational speed increased. Anchoring himself to the ground with the staff, Charlie struggled to avoid being knocked over by the whirlwind. Thought caught up with fear and became reaction as he raised the staff, intending to cut his way out of this impudent little tornado. As if sensing its imminent doom the cyclone died of its own volition. The only evidence of its brief existence were red rose and pink Impatiens petals floating to the ground in the chill October air. That and a lovely floral scent that he recognized as an expensive perfume, although for the moment he couldn't put a name to it.

"Hi, Grandpa," Ellen tearfully said from behind his left shoulder. "I'm sorry, Marcus fooled me, he—"

Yelling in fright, Charlie leaped forward, slipped, and almost fell down the hillside. Whirling, he held the blazing staff at port arms, believing this was a new and particularly malicious ploy by The Wendigo. A quick look later and he was sure it really was Ellen and he knew then why she was here. Panic began gobbling away deep in his brain.

The little whirlwind that foretold her visitation. Impatiens and roses, her favorite flowers. The other floral scent had been *La* something-or-the-other, her favorite perfume. The mournful bell tones mimicked those of one of her favorite poems, Sandberg's *For Whom the Bell Tolls.* The rapidly fading blue glow that rimed and permeated her figure. Ellen was seconds away from death and he had never even seen it coming.

"Grandpa, my head hurts!" the Ellen shade wailed, hands cradling her skull. "Marcus hit me, it hurts!"

A vertical maelstrom of whirling blue-white light appeared off to the left and rapidly increased in size. Long trailing filaments of blue matter began tearing away from Ellen's figure, making her scream in terror.

The doorway between here and the Great Mystery was open and now it was Ellen's time to pass through.

During his long career as a healer Charlie had attended numerous deaths and seen the gateway vortex many times. The doorway between the two planes of existence, life and death, would open only for the deserving and never for the non-deserving. Those unfortunates trapped on this side of the divide became the ghosts, haunts, and night terrors that populate the myths of all cultures. Planting his feet, Charlie took a ball park swing with the staff and made solid contact with the side of the vortex. The whirlpool stopped and then collapsed in on itself with a soft hiss before vanishing. Charlie was committed now; if he failed to heal Ellen, her spirit would be trapped here until time itself ended.

Reaching out, Charlie wrapped his left arm around Ellen and shuddered in revulsion. The spirit resting in the crook of his arm was neither ethereal nor solid, neither warm nor cold, neither completely dead nor completely alive. Touching her was as alien and as unpleasant as shoving a bare arm into a barrel full of live eels.

Three feet of Ellen's severed *slar*, the silver cord which binds body and spirit together, hung down from its attachment point at the base of her skull. Hearing the pressing tick of seconds in his mind, Charlie hurriedly coiled the remnant around his left hand. The remainder of the *slar*, the part attached to Ellen's dying body hundreds of miles away in the Cities, lay on the ground rapidly shrinking and fading away to nothing. Swinging the head of the staff down, he welded it to the fading *slar* with an eye-watering flash of blue fire and sent a preliminary healing charge surging through it.

"Grandpa, what?" Ellen cried, squirming around to face him. "My head hurts so, I—"

"Hush and be still, Blossom," Charlie said, struggling to keep a firm grip on her amorphous form, "I need to concentrate."

A hurricane blast of wind roaring up the rocky knoll heralded The Wendigo's arrival. A granite boulder the size of a Volkswagen Beetle sailed by inches from his head and Charlie knew that he was out of time. Raising the staff a couple of inches, Charlie dropped it back to the ground and he and Ellen vanished in a flare of blue light.

A second later The Wendigo reached the top of the knoll and found the bag empty. Enraged, the monster raised his arms and roared until lightning blasted the rocky hilltop and softball-sized hail pounded down. Calming himself after a few minutes, he sat down on a boulder to think.

A little later he started laughing. Redbird and that cunt granddaughter of his still had some surprises in store, oh indeed they did! Overcome with glee, the Trickster raised his head and howled until lightning lashed the hilltop and hail battered down again.

CHAPTER 63

ROCKETING DOWN A roller-coaster tube of blue-white light, Charlie clung to the staff as it reeled in Ellen's *slar*. The revenant in the crook of his left arm was growing ever more diaphanous and he knew that the race, and Ellen, were nearly lost. Desperate now, he demanded more, all the power the staff possessed.

Never having performed this particular sorcery before and having only rarely called on the staff's full power, Charlie had no idea what to expect. Time-space tore, leaving him suspended in a blue-white void that hurtled by and through him. Dizzy, near unconscious, he heard and felt Ellen's shade fading away, screaming as she went.

Without warning or transition, Charlie crashed *inside* the ambulance carrying Ellen's body without benefit of having entered from the *outside*. He slammed down hard on top of a kneeling paramedic who had just announced, "Flatline!" Working with both hands, Charlie quieted the paramedic and the driver with the staff in one hand and guided Ellen's spirit back into her body with the other.

The second paramedic, a stern-looking woman in her forties, he ignored for the moment. She had fainted dead away at the sight of a wild-looking native man materializing near the ceiling and crashing down on her partner.

Cradling Ellen's skull in his hands, Charlie probed her injuries. Contrary to the paramedic's opinion, there was a flicker of life deep in her brain. It wasn't much, not even a weak spark, but it was there. When the gateway vortex had opened, Ellen had been dead, yet now she was alive, if just barely. When Charlie smiled, he had to ease the cramp out of his clenched jaws first. The race wasn't over yet but he'd gained a couple of long steps. Done with the moment of self-congratulation, he began the long task of healing her.

Laying the staff down along Ellen's side, he placed the headpiece against the three-inch wide dent in the side of her skull. Burying his forefinger up to the great knuckle in the wound, Charlie felt-sensed fragments of shattered bone suspended in gelatinous matrix of hemorrhaging brain matter. Withdrawing his finger, Charlie sat with his head bent and his eyes squeezed shut. In the course of his long career as a healer he'd never seen or treated a worse head injury.

"Goddammit, old man, move!" he snapped at himself. "This is not the time for self-doubt!"

Cradling Ellen's head in both hands, Charlie began crooning in a language that was ancient when Rome was nothing more than a few rough huts sitting next to a muddy crossroad. A gossamer web of glowing blue threads began encasing Ellen's skull. The electronic monitors hanging on the bulkhead began beeping and flashing as they detected increasing signs of life. Feeling the quickening pulse under his hands, he deepened the timbre of his voice.

Without breaking the rhythm of his song, Charlie dared a quick look out the windshield. Two blocks away, the yellow glare of massed sodium arc lights outlined the towering monolith of Mercy Hospital. Not yet, he decided, way too soon. Taking one hand away from Ellen's skull, he reached out and lightly gripped the driver's shoulder. Alarms began sounding as Ellen's vital signs crashed.

"Pull over and stop," Charlie ordered, "then turn off all the outside lights. After that you will sit without moving until I tell you what to do next."

Releasing the driver's shoulder, he gripped Ellen's skull again and resumed his song. The alarms quieted as her signs stabilized and the monitors again resumed their steady beeping tones. Sunk deep in concentration, Charlie didn't hear the electronic commotion blaring a foot above his bent head. Twelve minutes later, he stopped singing but didn't remove his hands from Ellen's head. Eyes closed, he sat listening, sensing.

The life fluttering just beneath his fingers slowed and then steadied. Probing with a finger's feather touch, Charlie reexamined the wound. The shattered bone was solid now, although covered with a fine tracery of fine blue lines like a much mended piece of fine pottery. There were things now that only a major medical center could do for her and Charlie decided that it was high time they were doing them.

Tapping the paramedics with the staff, he commanded, "Tend to your patient, but see nothing else, remember nothing else."

Climbing into the front passenger seat, he told the driver, "Take us to the hospital now, but see and remember nothing but your driving."

The driver blinked, shook his head, started the engine, and turned on the lights. When force of habit caused him to glance across the cab, he saw nothing, not even a shadow. Putting the ambulance in gear, he stomped on the accelerator and sent the vehicle roaring down the busy four-lane street. Cloaked in the glamour, Charlie hung on for dear life and considered the possible irony of him and Ellen ending up as statistics two blocks from her place of employment.

The driver cut the wheel hard left into the hospital parking lot and backed into the Emergency Room loading zone. The back doors of the ambulance opened and Ellen was wheeled inside the building with Charlie walking unseen next to her. One hand pressed against the side of her head, he softly began singing again, continuing the healing process. While all the bells and whistles of modern medicine descended upon her, Charlie sang on, unseen and unheard. Medical personnel, many of them friends of Ellen, came and went. Through the small part of his mind not preoccupied with healing her, Charlie began learning what had happened.

Around 1:45 a.m., neighbors had heard Ellen and her husband, Marcus, quarreling. Shortly after, Ellen had started screaming for help and then suddenly stopped. Concerned, a neighbor had gone to check on her. Finding the front door ajar, she had walked in and found Ellen lying in a pool of blood in the foyer. Terrified, the neighbor had rushed home and called 911. When the police arrived, they had found Ellen near death, a bloody claw-hammer lying next to her. Marcus Taylor, her husband, was the only suspect. As the information filtered down through his consciousness, Charlie began considering possible courses of action. Just after dawn his concentration was shattered by two events.

The first was The Wendigo ravening down on a hiking party of three female college students. The women all suffered agonizing deaths with Charlie a helpless witness hundreds of miles away. Horrified, he stood rimmed in blue fire, fighting hard not to scream.

The second was the unexpected arrival of porter Baxter Benson. One look at the fierce-looking native man alight with blue fire and he fled screaming down the hall. Drawn by his cries, medical and security personnel began pouring into the room.

"Right there, I tell you!" Benson said, pointing into the room but refusing to enter it. "I saw a fuckin' ghost right there!"

Like any good magic trick, a glamour only works if it isn't too closely scrutinized by too many eyes at once. With this many people staring into the room, Charlie had to step lively to avoid being seen or heard. Eeling his way through the crowd, he slipped out into the hallway. Already fretting about being away from Ellen, he leaned up against a wall and impatiently waited for the crowd to disperse.

Charlie's problem was solved when a nurse wheeled a gurney into the room. Five minutes later she wheeled Ellen out into the hallway and turned right. Taking up a station near the foot of the gurney, he walked unseen down the hall with them and onto the elevator. Three stories below, they got off and started walking down an interminable series of hallways.

When the nurse started wheeling the gurney through a door marked "Radiology", Charlie pulled up short and broke formation. There was no way he could tend to Ellen and still remain concealed during the diagnostic procedures. Besides which, he badly needed to take a leak. A sign proclaiming "Bathrooms" with an arrow pointing down the hall promised relief. The water from a nearby fountain and the jerky in his pocket would provide a quick meal afterwards.

Eyes closed in the ecstasy of a man long denied, Charlie was almost pumped out when the short hairs on his neck began bristling and his ears began ringing. From its spot leaning against the door of the stall, the staff fetched him a sharp jab in the small of the back. Fearful, he zipped up, grabbed the staff, and rushed out of the cubicle.

Reaching the hallway, Charlie put on a turn of speed that would have been the envy of many a gym-loving thirty-something. Skidding around a corner, he saw a figure at the far end of the hall. Unable to determine whether the figure was advancing or retreating or whether it had reached Radiology yet, he somehow managed to increase his pace a little. Passing Imaging, he sensed Ellen safe inside. A few more steps and he stopped, staring at the dark figure twenty feet away down the hallway. To Charlie's eye, Ellen's husband Marcus looked no more human than a coiled rattlesnake.

Darkness roiled inside Taylor so violently that lashing tendrils of it extruded from his body. His pupils were vertical slits that glittered red under the overhead fluorescent lighting. The tip of a forked tongue repeatedly flicked out of his mouth and dripped smoking saliva which burned holes through the linoleum floor tiles when it landed. When he opened his mouth to speak, only a reptilian hiss came out.

Unimpressed, Charlie stood watching, waiting. Deciding on a change of tactics, the monster cloaked itself more fully in the *persona* of Marcus Taylor. Except for the blood and tissue spatters on his expensive Italian suit, Taylor now looked pretty much normal.

"Well, old fuck, we meet again," the Taylor creature mocked, taking a long step forward. "Just wanted to tell you how much me and my boy Marcus here enjoyed fucking Miss Ellen. Beautiful tits on that girl, just beautiful. Unfortunately, she also has a skull like a cinder block or else we wouldn't be having this conversation. Now if you'll excuse us, we have unfinished business with our wife."

Even though he'd been near certain for the last few hours, confirmation of his worst fears hit Charlie hard. He'd been gulled, conned, hoodwinked, fooled, had. BIG TIME. In doing so, he'd allowed the person he loved most to be terribly injured. He had failed, again. A lance head of blue fire erupted out of the staff and began charring the paint on the right-hand wall. Recognizing the danger, the creature wisely back-pedaled a couple of hasty steps as Charlie brought the staff under control.

"Whattsa matter, Sunshine, truth hurt?" the monster spat. "I've always been stronger, always been one step ahead of you. Always. Every hour now I grow stronger while you grow older, weaker, and closer to death.

"And I have always been smarter, cleverer. Not that I'm proud of it, mind you. Out-thinking you is about as challenging as winning an IQ contest against the village idiot. Christ hammered on a cross, you are some kind of stupid, you know? Taylor has been mine ever since he was six and drowned his cute little next-door neighbor in her cute little wading pool. And you're so goddamned stupid you couldn't even see him for what he is, although I have to admit, I did help him out a little bit. Well, actually a lot, but who's counting.

"And your daughter Lisa, now there's a piece of work. Fuck anything she would, man, woman, child, animal, mineral, vegetable, anything. A little quickie with me and my boy Marcus here and well, you know the rest. If you'd like to pay your respects to her and that limp-dick husband of hers, take a shovel and go out to the end of Shelbourne Point down on the river and dig. You might want to take along some Vapo-Rub and a mask because I imagine they're still pretty ripe.

"And Mary, your precious Mary, Mrs. Charlie Redbird herself. How I have enjoyed knowing her, biblically and otherwise. Even though they're not related those lovely big brown nipples of hers remind me of Elle—"

Unable to bear hearing anything further, Charlie roared and sprang forward, swinging the flaming staff in an overhand arc. The creature leaped ten feet backwards, never taking his eyes off Charlie. Laughing, he started to speak then paused, listening. A moment later the unmistakable crackle of a two-way radio sounded in the hallway.

"Gotta go, sweetums, but I'll be seein' you soon," the Taylor creature hissed as it ran toward the fire stairs. "I'll stick my best into Mary and tell her you said hello."

Charlie was starting toward the stairs when he heard the slap of running footsteps in the corridor behind him. Cloaking himself in the glamour, he moved a few feet away and waited. A pair of Cities cops came charging up the hallway, hands on their sidearms. Stopping near where Charlie stood hidden, they surveyed the hallway, looking puzzled.

"I'd a swore that I saw—" the younger of the two officers said, sounding confused.

"Yeah, me too," the older, grey-haired officer interrupted, "not that it really matters. Let's just find Mrs. Taylor and we'll worry about what to put in the report later."

Falling in behind, Charlie followed them as far as the doorway into Medical Imaging. Once there, the sergeant explained to the nurse that he and the younger officer were a security detail assigned to protect Mrs. Taylor. Her husband had been seen on the hospital grounds and was considered armed and dangerous. For the next few days, Mrs. Taylor would be under twenty-four hour a day police protection until her husband was arrested. Concerned, the nurse asked the officers to wait in the hallway and said she would call them when Mrs. Taylor's MRI was finished. Collapsing into an uncomfortable plastic chair, Charlie sank into a brown study. Ellen, Mary, Lisa, he—

"Worry about Ellen now," he told himself, *"and cry for the dead later."*

When he looked up, Ellen, the nurse, and the two police officers were turning the corner at the far end of the hallway. Hustling along in pursuit, Charlie squeezed in unseen between the closing elevator doors just in time to avoid being left behind. Once back on Ellen's floor, the nurse wheeled her into the room while the younger police officer remained posted just outside the door. After a confused few minutes of medical staff coming and going, the room finally quieted. Taking up his station at the head of the bed, Charlie resumed the healing ritual. With the exception of three very short breaks, he remained there as the hours spun out and day became night and then day again.

So slowly that it nearly drove Charlie bug-eyed with impatience, Ellen began waking from her coma. Finally at 11:27 a.m., thirty-six and a half hours after she was attacked and thirty-six hours and twenty minutes after he began the healing ritual, Ellen opened her eyes. For the first few seconds Charlie feared that she had suffered brain damage that was beyond his or anyone's ability to heal. Unmoving, she lay staring up at the ceiling without blinking. A deep, hacking cough gripped her and she began looking around for something. After a few seconds her eyes locked onto the bedside table. Feeling dense, Charlie grabbed the plastic bottle of ice-water off the table and squeezed a few drops into her mouth. Ellen stopped coughing and he added a few more drops.

"Hi, Grandpa," she croaked.

"Hello, Blossom," he said, bending over to kiss her on the forehead. "How are you feeling?"

"My head hurts," Ellen replied, sounding confused. "Marcus, I dreamed of you in the woods, you were singing and—"

"I know all about it. You're going to be as good as new in a little while. Right now though, I want you to get some rest so you'll get better."

"'Kay," she mumbled, nearly asleep. "Are you coming back, Grandpa? I'm afraid Marcus will hurt me again.

"Yes, Ellen," Charlie said. "I'll be in and out and when you're better, I'll take you home. And don't you worry about Marcus; he won't ever hurt you again."

"'Kay," she mumbled again before falling into a deep, natural sleep.

Hearing footsteps rushing down the hall in response to Ellen's elevated vital signs, Charlie cloaked himself in the glamour and slipped out of the room. His only regret, and it was a very small one, was the white lie he had just told her.

Ellen would never be as healthy as she had been before the attack. For the rest of her life she would suffer from dizzy spells, blinding migraine headaches, blurred vision in her left eye, and short-term memory loss. Most importantly though, at least to her grandfather, she was still alive. A mended vessel perhaps, but still here. And for this moment on this day that was enough.

Feeling claustrophobic from the sickness and misery pressing in from all sides, Charlie fled the hospital as fast as his legs would carry him. Five minutes later the brown baggers eating lunch in the park across the street from the hospital were treated to the unlikely sight of an elderly First American man dancing a spirited jig with a huge grin on his face. Feeling his legs getting weak, Charlie plopped down on a bench to the muted applause of the onlookers. Bowing, he sat waiting for his breath to catch up with the rest of him.

After a few minutes, he started rummaging through his pockets. Looking rueful, he stopped and lit his pipe. There was no point in searching for the truck keys when the truck was parked several hundred miles away. Which begged the question of how he was going to get across town to the University District.

Ten minutes later, Charlie's problem was solved when a city bus pulled up and stopped at his bench. Dropping $1.25 in the fare box, he asked for a transfer and took a seat. An hour and three buses later, he got off at a stop three blocks from home. Leaning on the staff he trudged up the street, bone-weary but happy.

The rented ranch house had always seemed a little down-at-the-heels to Charlie, a hurried rental that satisfied an immediate need. Now though the house had never looked better to him. In order of appearance, he planned to bathe, eat, and sleep for at least eight hours. Had he not been so preoccupied with the pleasures waiting on the other side of the front door, he wouldn't have been taken by surprise.

Stepping through the door, he turned and closed it without bothering to turn on the living room lights. A metallic clank sounded from the center of the darkened room and Charlie's heart started pounding. He knew that sound well, anyone who had ever hunted did. It was the unmistakable ratcheting of a pump-action shotgun slide being cycled. Were he young and in his prime, Charlie knew that he would have had a fair chance of coming out on top. Now though, shaman or not, he was a weary old man in a dim room with a shotgun aimed at his back. Closing his eyes, he prepared to die.

The living room lights came on and a voice snapped, "Put your hands up and turn around very slowly. Do it!"

Raising his arms, he began turning, but before he was halfway around a woman's voice asked, "Charlie?"

"Gee-fucking-hose-a-fat, Gilbert," Charlie sighed as his legs collapsed and he slid down the door until his ass bumped hard against the floor, "what are you doing in here with that moose shooter?"

"Oh jeez, Charlie, we're sorry," Katie said as Gilbert pointed the shotgun at the ceiling. "You scared us!"

"You should've been there," Charlie told her, trying to smile and hoping that his crotch was still dry.

"Ellen's been, she was," Katie began, not knowing quite how to proceed.

"I know, I've just come from the hospital."

"Ellen ha, hasn't, she, she didn't," Katie stammered, not wanting to voice the awful word.

"No, no, Ellen will recover, it's just going to take some time, that's all. Not that I mind, but what are you two doing here? And what are you doing with that howitzer?"

"We knew you'd gone up north," Gilbert said, leaning the shotgun in a corner. "So we called there, but you weren't home. So we thought maybe you'd already heard about Ellen and driven back, so we called you here and still didn't get an answer."

"So next we decided to come over here and check," Katie continued, "because we all know how much you love answering the phone, especially when you're sleeping."

"When we got here," Gilbert told him, "Taylor was parked in the drive. We didn't know if you were home or not and we were afraid he might have done something to you, so we got out of the van and—"

"You what!" Charlie said, touched by their concern for him but horrified by their folly. "You know how dangerous he is, yet you—"

"Yes, we did," Gilbert said with conviction, "but we were real careful. There were three students from the university walking down the street plus the mailman, so I wasn't too worried. As soon as we got out of the van, Taylor started screaming that he'd see us later. Then he got back in his car and took off and almost ran the mailman down when he was backing up."

"We wanted to follow him, but we had to come in here and make sure everything was all right," Katie added. "Besides which, the van is too slow to keep up, ungh, I think I better shut up and quit while I'm ahead."

"I wanted to call the police then," Gilbert said, sounding aggrieved, "but Katie talked me out of it. After that we went to see Ellen at the hospital, but they weren't letting anyone in but immediate family. So we went back to our apartment and that damn Acura of Taylor's was parked outside, but he was nowhere to be seen. I wanted to call the police again but—"

"But I talked you out of it again because I thought we should still talk to Charlie," Katie interjected. "I just think it's real important to keep the police out of this if we can."

"Well, after seeing Taylor's car parked at our apartment, I got really worried," Gilbert continued, anxious to finish the chronology of events, "so I borrowed a shotgun from my dad. Since Taylor seems to have it in for all three of us, this seemed like the best place to wait. We had just put the van in the garage and sat down when you got here. And, ungh, well, you know the rest. Charlie, I'm really sorry, I didn't mean to scare you, I feel terr—"

"That's all right, Gilbert, these things happen sometimes," Charlie said, lifting his arms. "Now how 'bout giving an old fart a tow up. My tired elderly ass sits here much longer, I'm just gonna roll to one side and sleep where I land."

Once up, Charlie headed toward the bathroom for a much-needed shower. Although he would have never admitted it to Katie and Gilbert, he was still a little rattled. Staring down the business end of a twelve-gauge shotgun will do that to a body.

As the last of the fear melted away under the pounding spray, Charlie realized just how hungry he was. It had been days since he'd consumed anything but venison jerky and water. Counting back, he calculated that it was just shy of forty-eight hours since he'd eaten the campfire warmed beans atop the rocky knoll on the Canadian border. Toweling off, he dressed quickly and headed for the kitchen at a fast trot.

Halfway down the hallway, Charlie stopped and groaned aloud. Before leaving for Frechette he'd used up most of the groceries in the house. The remainder he'd thrown in a box and taken up north. Which left, if memory served, a can of sardines and a handful of uncooked elbow macaroni. Poor fare for a man who currently felt like his stomach was welded to his spine.

Resigning himself to a delay that would probably end in a fast-food hamburger, Charlie started toward the kitchen again. To add insult to injury, he'd have to bum a ride just to end up with a grease-burger. Walking into the kitchen, he whooped with delight. A large pizza and three foot-long sub sandwiches, all wrapped in the distinctive yellow packaging of his favorite delicatessen, were sitting on the table.

"I thought you'd be hungry, so we ordered take-out from Sam's," Katie explained. "My girlfriend Karen works there now and she brought our order over after her shift ended."

"You're a lifesaver," Charlie said as he sat down next to Gilbert. "If I weren't so hungry and you weren't a married woman, well...."

Laughing, Katie started handing out sandwiches and slices of pizza. Minutes passed as they ate in silence. Finally though the meal was finished. Charlie got up to make coffee while Katie and Gilbert cleared the table.

Sitting on the couch in the living room, legs stretched out in front of him, pipe in one hand and coffee cup in the other, Charlie sighed happily. Walking into the living room, Gilbert sat down on the sofa. Although he liked Charlie a great deal, Gilbert still found him a mysterious, even intimidating, figure.

"Ungh, Charlie, can I talk to you about something," he asked after a long minute of screwing his courage up.

"Of course, Gilbert," Charlie said, already certain which channel the conversation was about to steer into. "What would you like to talk about?"

"Don't you think we should call the police?" he said, a note of desperation creeping into his voice. "Taylor's really dangerous and I just think it would be a good idea to call the cops."

Since meeting Katie and later Charlie, Gilbert's conservative view of life and reality had been forcibly altered forever. More than anything, he wanted a safe and happy married life with Katie. Invoking the power of the criminal justice system was the only way he knew how to achieve this happiness, the only way to make life normal again. It was Gilbert's last best hope and he was clinging to it desperately.

Well acquainted with the personal trauma caused by fear and uncertainty, Charlie both pitied and understood Gilbert's distress. Despite his compassion though he had no intention of letting Gilbert call the police.

"The police are already looking for Taylor," he said. "It would be best not to call them if we can avoid it."

"Charlie," Katie asked as she sat down next to Gilbert, "what are you going to do?"

"Do you really want to know?" he replied, making and keeping strong eye contact with them.

After a long moment and to Charlie's great relief, they both nodded their heads and mumbled "no". Compelling them with the staff would have bothered him, but he would have done so if necessary. Dealing with Taylor and the symbiont inside of him would be a delicate and dangerous undertaking. Interference from any quarter, no matter how well-intentioned, was something he would not tolerate.

"It would be best if you stayed here tonight," he told them. "But you can go home in the morning, just be very careful and keep that shotgun handy. This will all be over within twenty-four to thirty-six hours."

Katie and Gilbert both tried to speak at the same time. Raising his hands, Charlie smiled and waited until they both hushed.

"I will be fine, don't worry. The only reason I want you to go home in the morning is because you cannot tell that which you don't know."

This last statement silenced them for so long that Charlie feared he had lost their friendship.

"Okay, Charlie, if you say so," Katie finally said with Gilbert nodding his agreement. "Promise you'll be careful? Please?"

"I promise," Charlie replied, glad they were all still friends. "Now if you'll excuse me, I'm going to bed before I fall asleep sitting here and you have to carry me back to the bedroom."

After a quick hug from Katie and a handshake from Gilbert, Charlie walked back to the bedroom. Undressing, he slid in between the sheets. Even though he started thinking about Mary and Lisa, he fell deeply asleep within seconds.

CHAPTER 64

A FULL BLADDER combined with the aroma of fresh brewed coffee chased Charlie out of bed nine hours later. Stepping out of the bathroom, he stuck his nose in the air and inhaled deeply, a human pointer hot on the scent. Yes, he decided, the delicious aroma was that of sweet rolls. Nothing else smelled quite so good this early in the morning.

Walking down the hallway, Charlie grinned thinking about Gilbert's plight. The wonderful odors wafting down the hall had to be the result of his labors because Katie was incapable of creating such culinary delights. The way Charlie had it figured, Gilbert must have run up the white flag and taken over the cooking duties rather than face certain starvation. As a man who had done most of his own cooking for decades, Charlie was sympathetic but still found the situation funny. Walking into the kitchen, he was amazed to see Katie icing sweet rolls with Gilbert nowhere in sight.

"Good morning," he said, pouring himself a cup of coffee and taking a seat at the table. "Everything smells wonderful this morning."

"Yes," Katie snapped, "I'm sure it does. After two weeks of lessons with Gilbert's mother, Mrs. Cleaver herself, it goddamn well better."

"You and Gilbert's mother?" Charlie asked in amazement, so surprised that he spoke without thinking. "I'd a liked to have been a fly on the wall, ungh, maybe I should hush up."

"That would be a real good idea," she said, placing a plate of sweet rolls on the table and giving him a hug, "especially if you plan on eating."

"What's a good idea?" Gilbert asked as he walked into the room grinning from ear-to-ear.

Turning, Katie glared at her husband as he sat down at the table. As he poured a cup of coffee and reached for a sweet roll, she continued glaring. After a small introductory bite, he devoured the pastry in two large bites.

"Shuts my mouth," he said after swallowing the last bite, a look of ecstasy on his face.

"Well, hot damn!" Katie said. "Victory is mine and pigs will fly and all that other kind of good stuff."

When the laughter died down, she looked at Charlie and moistened her lips, a sure sign that a difficult question was imminent.

"Charlie, where's your truck?" she asked. "Did you teleport here or something from up north? Or is this a part of our new don't ask, don't tell, don't know policy?"

"Yup," he elliptically answered.

Knowing from his reaction that she had guessed somewhere near right, Katie smiled and let the subject drop.

"Speaking of," Charlie said, trying to hide his irritation at being a pedestrian, "could one of you kind young people please give a senior citizen a ride to the hospital so that he can visit his sick granddaughter?"

"I'll drive you," Katie told him, "but we gotta hurry, I have a class in an hour and a half and the hospital is way across town."

Walking into the bedroom, Charlie opened the closet and pulled an old rucksack down off the shelf. Opening the top, he threw in a spare shirt, a light jacket, some pipe tobacco, four packages of venison jerky, a pair of sunglasses, and a bush hat with a floppy brim. Carrying the pack into the bathroom, he filled and sealed a pair of quart water bottles. Placing the bottles inside, he tied the rucksack shut. Gripping the pack with both hands, he gave it a good shake and nothing shifted or rattled. Satisfied, he headed for the living room.

Finding the house empty, he hurriedly turned on a few lights. Stepping outside, he pulled the door shut and locked it. The van was idling in the driveway with Gilbert behind the wheel and an irate-looking Katie seated next to him. Grinning and swallowing hard so that he wouldn't laugh out loud, Charlie climbed into the back.

Before long though his good humor faded as he contracted a bad case of the Backseat Driver's Blues. Katie's driving was enough to frighten a root vegetable. But Gilbert putted along so slowly on the surface streets that Charlie figured they would arrive at the hospital just in time for him to expire of natural causes and end up in the morgue. As the blocks dragged by, Charlie caught himself bearing down on the floorboard with his right foot in an unconscious effort to hurry Gilbert along.

By the time they reached the hospital Katie was in a state of high squawk about the possibility of missing her class. Telling them both to be careful, Charlie got out and watched them drive off. Katie was running her gums at a prodigious rate while Gilbert, unperturbed, rolled down the hospital's drive at his normal funerary pace. Finding it funny now that he was finally at the hospital, Charlie laughed and entered the building.

Just inside the front doors, he stepped aside and made a pretense of studying the lobby directory. Gripping the staff, he scanned the building for any sign of Marcus Taylor but found nothing. Crossing the lobby, he waited by the bank of elevators and rode the first available car upstairs.

Rounding the last corner, Charlie saw there was still a police officer posted outside Ellen's room. As he approached, the officer assumed a stiff upright posture, what Charlie thought of as the "Smokey-The-Bear-With-Corncob-Firmly-Lodged-Stance."

"You must be Mr. Redbird," the officer said, surprising him by smiling and opening the door. "Mrs. Taylor has been asking for you. Enjoy your visit."

"Thank you, I will," Charlie said as he walked through the door, relieved by the officer's sudden change of attitude.

Skull swaddled in thick pressure bandages, Ellen lay sleeping, pale but otherwise serene. A clear plastic drainage tube ran down behind her left ear to a bottle hanging off the bed frame. After a long moment of staring at the IV lines, urine catheter, and other personal indignities attached to her, Charlie had to turn his back and regain his composure.

Calming himself with a couple of deep breaths, he walked up to the head of the bed and cradled Ellen's skull in his hands. As he had hoped, her natural healing processes were ticking along just fine. Time spinning its slow eternal thread could heal her now. Well pleased, he dragged a chair over to the bed and sat holding her hand.

Waiting for Ellen to wake, Charlie reflected on how much she resembled his late wife, Mary. Although one was dead before the other was born, the two could have easily passed as sisters. Ellen was a little taller and rounder and—

"Hi, Grandpa," Ellen mumbled, barely awake.

"Hello, Blossom, you snuck up on me, I thought you were still asleep."

"I told them you were here yesterday," she said, her voice a little stronger now, "but they said I was imagining things."

"Never mind them," Charlie said, getting up out of the chair and kissing her on the forehead, "we know better. How are you feeling?"

"A little better, I wanna go home."

"Not yet, Blossom, you need to stay here and get better. Now I have something here for you"

"Present?" she mumbled, falling asleep with a smile on her face.

As Charlie's fingers brushed the top of the rucksack, a look of dismay crossed his face. Yesterday he had intended to tie his medicine bag around Ellen's neck to protect her from Taylor's evil, but somehow he had forgotten. Remembering only when he was riding home on the bus, he'd decided to make her a new one before returning to the hospital today. It was a simple magic, one of the first he'd ever learned, and it only took a minute or two to complete. But in his rush to get to the hospital this morning it had somehow slipped his mind. So now it was a day later and he was still a medicine bag short.

Hooking his thumbs under the leather thong, he pulled the beaded medicine bag out from under his shirt and passed it over his head. Working with a feather touch, he draped the bag around Ellen's neck.

"Ellen, hear me now," he commanded, speaking to her sleeping mind. "See how pretty?"

"Pretty," Ellen murmured, dreaming with her eyes open. "Mine?"

"Yes, Blossom, it is just for you," Charlie crooned, tucking the bag out of sight beneath her hospital gown. "But you must promise to never tell anyone about it and you must always wear it, even when you're in the shower."

"Promise," she sighed, eyelids fluttering.

"Good, sleep now and I'll be back to visit you soon."

"'Kay, Grandpa," Ellen said, falling into a deep sleep.

Leaning back in the chair, Charlie sat watching her sleep and collecting his thoughts. Certain that she would sleep for several hours; he stood and kissed her goodbye. Picking up the pack, he turned and left the room. Exiting the hospital by the main entrance, he crossed the street to the park where he had danced the day before. Walking to the far end, he sat down on a wooden bench. Putting the rucksack between his knees, he untied the top flap and flipped it out of the way.

Twisting his braids into a loose bun with one hand, he pulled the floppy bush hat out of the pack and set it firmly on his head with the other. Groping around in the cargo compartment, he found the sunglasses and put them on. It wasn't a perfect disguise, but it would fool anyone who didn't know him well.

As Charlie reached for the top flap to tie the pack closed, his eyes strayed across a plastic bag in one corner that didn't belong there. Tugging it out into the light, he discovered that it was a zip lock bag containing the last two sweet rolls from breakfast. The note taped to the side of the bag read, "Better late than never. Love, Katie." Charlie had no idea how she had gotten into the pack without him seeing her, but he was happy to forgive her the trespass.

"Hands of a goniff," he thought as he opened the bag's seal and the delicious aroma began tickling his nose, *"and the heart of an angel."*

As he sat eating the sweet rolls and sipping water, Charlie revisited his decision about Marcus Taylor. On the loose, Taylor and the thing inside of him were a danger to everyone Charlie loved or cared about. Unacceptable.

If Taylor was arrested, Ellen would have to suffer through the trauma of testifying at his trial. Even if he was convicted, she would live in constant terror of the day he was released and came hunting her. Unacceptable.

Making Taylor disappear would only further complicate matters. Years would have to pass before Ellen could seek a divorce or have him declared dead. Unless Charlie confessed his malfeasance to her, and he had no intention of doing so, she would always live in fear of his possible return. Still unacceptable.

Meting out an obviously violent death to Taylor, tempting as it was, would create other difficulties. A murder investigation would focus on Ellen and those closest to her, bringing her yet more grief and putting Charlie in danger. Unacceptable yet again.

Which left only one viable alternative. Marcus Taylor had to die in circumstances that were above suspicion by the authorities. Acceptable solution.

Satisfied that yesterday's decision was still correct today, Charlie shifted from the what of the matter to the how of it. Blowing smoke rings into the chill air, he sat smoking and thinking for long minutes. By the time his pipe gurgled empty, he had the rough outline of a plan in mind.

First though Charlie had to find him. Gripping the staff with both hands, he leaned back on the bench, closed his eyes, and began an odd rhythmic humming. For ten minutes he sat concentrating and humming, looking to passersby like someone's grandfather out enjoying the weak autumn sunshine. Taylor's tracks formed a tangled skein that crossed and re-crossed the Cities metro area. Sweat beaded on Charlie's forehead as he unknotted the tangle and slowly crafted a single thread that led straight to Marcus Taylor.

"Ah!" he finally exclaimed. "Got you now! Good!"

Getting up off the bench and shouldering the pack, Charlie strode off across the park. If Taylor had fled the Cities it would have only delayed the inevitable. Marked as he was now, Charlie could find him no matter where he went or what he did.

Three blocks later Charlie found the drugstore he was looking for. After pulling his hat brim down and pushing the sunglasses up on his nose, he walked inside. Reading the overhead aisle signs, he walked back to the stationary section where he selected a cheap legal pad and a roller-ball pen. Paying for his purchases with a small bill, he took his change and left the store, just another faceless customer, or so he hoped. Setting off down the street, he stopped after a few blocks and dumped the legal pad and pen into the pack. Double checking that the receipt was still inside, he wadded up the plastic drugstore bag in a tight ball and stuffed it deep inside a bus-stop trash can.

Closing his eyes and cocking his head to one side as if listening, Charlie consulted the staff. Taylor was now in the center of the East Side, "Deep East", the baddest part of the bad part of the Cities, the worst of the worst. Taylor was moving, which wasn't surprising, but his creeping pace was. Puzzled, Charlie stood thinking for a few seconds, and then suddenly grinned.

Taylor, he realized, had abandoned his car because the police were looking for it. Forced to rely on shank's mare and public transportation, Charlie had worried that Taylor would run him in circles, even if unconsciously. It wouldn't have altered his fate, but it could have delayed it for as long as a couple of days. Now both men, if Taylor could still be called that, were on foot and Charlie felt that gave him a considerable edge.

Putting yesterday's experience to good use, Charlie climbed aboard a city bus and took a seat. An hour and a quarter and four transfers later he debarked into the alien landscape of Deep East.

Vacant brick factory buildings, abandoned by an industrial revolution that had moved on two or three turns ago, lined one side of the street into the far distance. Empty sockets gaped in their facades where doors and windows had once hung. Sagging chain link fences surrounded each building, fronted by gates that either hung askew or had been knocked flat.

Squalid wooden shotgun shacks, employee housing before the late great revolution departed, occupied the other side of the street for an equal distance. Some of the houses, with steel security grilles hung on their windows and doors, were presumably still occupied. Most though were in various states of decrepitude up to and including total collapse. Three lots up on the left there was nothing left but a charred front wall with the message, "Wellcum to Oz motherfuker," spray-painted in garish yellow letters.

The few pedestrians on the street, mostly members of various ethnic minorities, were divided into two distinct groups. One group walked on the uneven sidewalks with their eyes downcast, seeing nothing. The other, smaller group, mostly male, prowled the entire width of the street with confident strides and predatory eyes.

A low-slung sedan pulled out onto the street a couple of blocks up. The bass line pounding out of its stereo was annoying even at this distance. The pedestrians on the sidewalk hastened their pace and vanished into the shotgun shacks. Most of the street predators fled for cover behind something bulletproof. Two of them though walked out into the road and held a lengthy conversation with the driver as traffic piled up behind the stopped vehicle.

Conference finished, the two young men walked away and the low-rider started rolling toward Charlie. Wrapping both hands around the staff, he stood waiting. As the car pulled abreast of him, it stopped and the windows facing him all glided down. Five young Latino men stared out at him. Holding his ground, Charlie returned their stares. The driver's right hand dipped down out of sight and Charlie began amping up the staff, preparing to strike. Raising his hand, the driver pointed and fired an imaginary pistol.

"Bang!" he yelled, flooring the low-rider and sending it roaring down the street.

"Best mind who you starin' at, Pops," a voice said from behind Charlie's shoulder. "Next time dem punks bust a cap in you for real."

Startled, Charlie turned and saw a tall pregnant black woman wearing an abbreviated bikini top and a matching miniskirt that would qualify as a belt in conservative company. A prostitute, he realized, embarrassed even though he had done nothing to encourage her presence or conversation.

"Looks like somebody already busted one in you," he said, staring at the gravid swell of her bare belly.

"Right idea, wrong kind of hole," the woman laughed, flicking an emery board over a red-lacquered nail. "If I'd a had some latex body armor, I wouldn't be in this mess. You lookin' for some fun later, I'll be around. Bye now, sugar."

Laughing, Charlie watched the woman sway off down the street leading with her belly, stiletto heels clicking on the pavement. This was easily the worst neighborhood he'd ever been in. But he couldn't have asked for nor found a better hunting ground. The people in this community would hear nothing, see nothing, and report nothing. The coming of the Rapture itself wouldn't elicit a phone call to the authorities from these environs.

Taking a bearing on his quarry, Charlie found him moving diagonally away at about three-quarters of a mile distance. Calculating an intercept course, he stepped off in pursuit, grimacing when his foot came down on the shards of a broken beer bottle. Fifty minutes later he had closed to within an eighth of a mile of Taylor. Ten minutes after that Charlie caught sight of him in the next block.

Taylor was no longer the dandified yuppie prince that Charlie had met all those months ago or even of yesterday. Unshaven, suit filthy, he looked furtive even from a block away. Unseen by anyone but Charlie, black tentacles from the symbiont residing inside Taylor extruded and violently lashed the air before retracting back inside his body. Seeing Taylor turn his head, Charlie cloaked himself in the glamour and kept walking forward.

The day wore on with Charlie remaining a few yards behind Taylor but always keeping him in sight. On multiple occasions Taylor turned and stared behind him for up to a minute but saw nothing. Yet he was positive someone or something was behind him, following, watching. Finally his paranoia grew so great that he took to walking backward and nearly undid Charlie's carefully laid plans.

At an intersection Taylor's right heel caught the curbstone and he staggered backwards into the path of an oncoming police car. Seeing the black and white squad car out of the corner of his eye, he jumped back on the sidewalk, yelled an apology, and started walking toward Charlie. The cruiser's loudspeaker blared as the officer in the passenger's seat ordered him to stop. Releasing his seat belt, the officer started getting out of the car. The radio squawked and the driver ordered his partner back into the squad car. Slamming the cruiser into gear, the driver turned on the roof lights and siren and roared off up the road.

A long, whistling sigh of relief escaped from Charlie as he watched the police car race away. If Taylor had been arrested, it wouldn't have been an insurmountable obstacle to his plans, but it would have been a very difficult one.

Unnerved by his close encounter with the law, Taylor changed his gait to a sideways crab sidle and kept sweeping his eyes up and down the street. When the streetlights started coming on his last nerve gave out.

Veering across the street, he entered a small liquor store. While Charlie stood cloaked and watching through the front window, Taylor bought a gallon of cheap vodka in a plastic jug, a half-gallon of orange juice, and three packs of cigarettes.

Leaving the store, Taylor passed out of the grey country of paranoia and into the black realm of fear. Hugging his purchases to his chest, he broke into a shambling run and fled into the darkness without looking back. Unconcerned, Charlie remained motionless and watched him go.

"Fly away home, boy," he whispered aloud, certain that Taylor was near his final destination for the day, "you won't get far."

And he didn't. A half-hour later, Charlie was standing concealed in the deep shadows at the rear of an abandoned factory building. According to the faded metal sign on the chain-link gate he'd squeezed through, it was once the home of something-or-another and Sizemore, Textile Manufacturers. In a large top floor room at the end of the building, Taylor was pacing, chain smoking, and swilling screwdrivers as fast as he could pour them down his throat.

Walking to his right a few yards, Charlie eased down and sat with his back against the end of a crumbling concrete loading dock. Placing the rucksack between his knees, he untied the top flap and took out a package of venison jerky and a water bottle. As he sat eating and drinking, Charlie mulled over what came next. Two problems, both related, concerned him at the moment.

One problem was time. It was now 8:30 p.m. and he had been away from Ellen and on the hunt for almost twelve hours. Finishing Taylor quickly was an urgent priority for both of their sakes.

The second problem was maintaining the element of surprise. Under no illusions about what he was facing or the dangers involved, Charlie knew that striking first was crucial to his chances of success. If Taylor or the symbiont inside of him sensed his presence the final outcome would be a very nearly run thing.

Linking the twin problems of time and surprise was the factory building itself. Four stories tall with a deep basement and two sub-basements, it was a city block long and nearly half again as wide. From scanning with the staff Charlie had learned that the interior spaces were a rabbit's warren of interconnected rooms and hallways filled with abandoned textile equipment and other industrial debris. Unwilling to expend the time necessary to pick his way through the maze and knowing that he would lose the critical element of surprise if he tried, Charlie was left with only one alternative. And he wasn't happy about it, not one bit.

Loading a short bowl, he sat smoking and thought the whole thing through a second time, and then a third. Each time he reached the same conclusion. There was simply no other way to get it done. Putting his pipe away, Charlie stood and put the rucksack back on. Staying in the deep shadows, he began walking along the back side of the building. Arriving at the far end, he craned his head back and looked up at the fourth story some eighty feet above. Whipping his head down, he clung to the staff with both hands, nearly hyper-ventilating.

"Asshole couldn't hide out in a one story building," he muttered. "That'd be just too goddamn easy."

Short distance flight was one of the staff's gifts and many of the Redbird shamans had made extensive use of it. Charlie though was acrophobic, afraid of heights, and had been since he got stuck in an apple tree for hours when he was eight years old. Even changing a burned-out light bulb in a ceiling-mounted fixture was difficult for him at times. And now he had to ascend this brick monstrosity of a building in the dark.

Bringing his breathing under control, Charlie walked away from the building a few paces and looked up again. In a corner window up on the fourth story, a dim glimmer revealed that Taylor had lit a candle or other weak light source. The next bank of windows a few yards to the right were dark and he selected those as his target.

Keeping his eyes open, Charlie tightly gripped the staff with both hands and emptied his mind of everything but an image of the bank of windows far above. A soft blue glow enveloped his body and for a long second nothing happened. Slowly at first, then with increasing speed, he began lifting into the air. Reaching the fourth floor he stopped, suspended motionless in midair with a marked starboard list.

Easing in toward the darkened bank of windows, Charlie noticed too late that he was on a collision course with the last intact panes of glass in the center casement. Squeezing his eyes shut, he braced himself for impact, injury, a rough crash landing, further injury, and immediate combat with Taylor. Instead, the staff neatly side-slipped him through a glassless window on the left. Opening his eyes, Charlie found himself suspended an unknown distance above the floor in a pitch black room. Without warning, the staff withdrew its support and he started falling through the dark. Three feet later his boots slammed down hard on the concrete floor. As landings go, it wouldn't have made first string with the

Bolshoi but it was quiet and he climbed up off the floor unhurt.

Looking around to orientate himself, Charlie's nostrils flared as he inhaled the faint but unmistakable odor of carrion. The air currents inside the building shifted a little and the faint odor became a pervasive stench.

A faint spill of artificial light at the far end of the room caught his eye. Leaning on the staff he started toward it, picking his way around and through abandoned textile machinery and loose piles of assorted junk. As he drew closer to the light the fetid stench of rotting meat grew ever stronger. The sound of Taylor's ringing footsteps and his muttering voice were clearly audible now even without benefit of the staff's power.

Arriving at the edge of the spill of light, he paused for a couple of deep breaths. Gathering himself up, he charged forward into the dimly lighted room, swinging the flaming staff in long, horizontal arcs that crackled and hissed in the cold air. Three steps into the room Charlie skidded to a halt, head whipping around as he sought answers.

On the top of a blue milk crate a few feet away a boom box was broadcasting the sound of Taylor's pacing footsteps and his muttering voice. A battery powered florescent camping lantern was sitting on the crate next to the boom box. The vodka, orange juice, and cigarettes were piled unopened at the base of the crate. What captured and held Charlie's attention though were the dead bodies.

The corpses were those of two teenaged girls, two women, and one man. Or at least that's what Charlie thought they were, between the decomposition and the dim light he couldn't be certain. Bound with their hands overhead, the cadavers were all hanging on chains attached to the steel I-beam rafters far overhead. Split down the centerline, each corpse's viscera was piled between its feet with its severed head sitting atop the pile.

Two of the chains held photographs instead of dead bodies attached to their ends. One picture was of Ellen on her wedding day, the other showed Charlie walking out of a university building. Biting down hard until his jaws ached, Charlie managed to keep his teeth from chattering. The staff thrummed a warning under his hands but he was oblivious, transfixed by the dead bodies.

"Charlie me fine boyo," Taylor mocked in a fine Irish brogue as he jumped down from one of the rafters high above, "sure'n I didn't think ye slow movin' self would ever get here, ye geriatric fuck. Ye didn't think that children's magic trick of yours kept me from seein' ye now, did ye?"

Coming out of his funk, Charlie broke right but it was too late. Taylor slammed into his shoulders, smashing him down hard on the concrete floor and pinning the staff under his body. Winded and bruised, he lay helpless with Taylor on top of him.

"Got you now, motherfucker!" the Taylor creature shrieked, baring a fearsome pair of fangs. "Got you at last! Give me the staff! Give it to me!"

As the fangs touched his skin, Charlie was strangely calm, even smiling a little. A second later he shrieked in agony as the twin daggers lanced deep into his right forearm, scraping against the ulna and delivering a massive dose of venom. The medicine bag that Charlie had been relying on to protect him, the one that should have orbited Taylor, was tied around Ellen's pretty neck miles away. Terrible as the pain was, it saved Charlie and proved Taylor's undoing. As agony racked him, the staff detonated under Charlie's body, lifting him to his feet and sending Taylor flying across the room.

"You've killed me!" Charlie said, looking down in disbelief at the terrible wound in his forearm. "I don't believe it, you've killed me!"

Howling in delight, the Taylor creature began swinging on and between the suspended chains, turning the corpses into macabre marionettes. Any second now he expected Charlie to die from the massive dose of venom he'd just injected. The venom had worked that quickly on his other five victims who were all young and in the prime of their lives, so why should this old Indian, no matter how powerful, be any different?

In time, the venom inside Charlie would fester into lung cancer and then metastasize. Unlike the wasp bites, this wound had been dealt directly by the hand of the Dark One and it would be fatal without hope of a cure. But not for at least a year's time, the staff would see to that. Shiny new scar tissue had already formed over the gaping puncture wounds and full feeling and mobility were rapidly returning to his lower arm. But that didn't mean Charlie was the least bit sanguine about his upcoming demise in the near future indefinite.

"You forget yourself, little man," he roared, amping up the staff until the concrete floor quaked and cracked beneath his feet, "and whom and what you are dealing with!"

Sensing that his plans were somehow miscarrying, Taylor waited until the chain he was on reached the apogee of its swing and leaped for the door. A twenty-foot long rope of blue fire flicked out, coiled around his torso, and slammed him down on the floor.

"You're supposed to be dead! Die, you worthless old fuck, die!" Taylor screamed, speaking first to Charlie than to the symbiont. "You promised he would die! You promised!"

Ignoring him, Charlie concentrated on slowly increasing the staff's power. A violent seizure racked Taylor and he vomited up a truly amazing volume of foul-smelling bile. A black eight-legged creature resembling a shell-less crab reared up in the vile mess. Hissing and chittering, the Trickster's symbiont scuttled forward, covering ten out of the twenty feet that separated it from Charlie in a blur of motion. Reacting without direction from Charlie, the staff split its fire and began incinerating the creature. Writhing and screaming, the symbiont kept charging forward then suddenly vaporized in a flash of blue fire. Far to the north, a wild thunderstorm lashed the forests outside Frechette as the Trickster shrieked from the pain of the unexpected amputation.

"Ch-Ch-Charlie, Mr. Redbird, listen to me, please," Taylor begged, crying now. "It made me do all these things, honest, it made me. Would you like to be rich? I've got a lot of money, just let me go. I'll never tell, I—"

"Shut up!" Charlie ordered, compelling him into silence with staff's power. "If you are innocent, you have nothing to fear from me."

This last statement galled Charlie no end, but it was a true. He didn't like Taylor, had loathed the man since the second they'd met. But if Taylor was innocent, he would do everything he could to help him, including salvaging his marriage to Ellen. And even the thought of having to do that was giving Charlie a world-class case of red-ass. But he'd do if he had to.

Walking up to Taylor, Charlie tapped him on the left temple with the staff and commanded, "Sleep". Resting the staff on Taylor's shoulder, Charlie began listening to his innermost thoughts and memories. Scowling in revulsion, he abruptly broke the connection and backed up a couple of hasty steps.

The symbiont had spoken truthfully when it claimed that Taylor had been killing since childhood. Birds, cats, mice, dogs, men, women, children; it didn't matter to Marcus Taylor as long as he could kill it. He had been a broken vessel long before The Wendigo's symbiont had arrived to fill him. Even now, Taylor was contemplating how to escape from Charlie and finish killing Ellen. Walking back over to Taylor, Charlie fetched him a sharp rap on the skull with the staff.

"Wake up!" he ordered. "You are going to do what I tell you when I tell you. Now get up off the floor and walk over to the milk crate. Take everything off the top and then sit down on it."

When Taylor started protesting, Charlie compelled him into silence and onto the milk crate with the staff's power. Placing a noose of blue fire around Taylor's neck as a precaution, Charlie backed up a few steps and took off the rucksack. Opening it, he reached inside and took out the legal pad and the pen using the first two fingers of his right hand as a pincher. Dropping the pad and pen to the floor, he tied the pack closed and put it back on. Kneeling down, he picked up the pad and the pen, again using the insides of the first two fingers of his right hand. Walking back to Taylor, he dropped the paper and pen between his feet. Walking around behind him, Charlie released the compulsion and tightened the noose of blue fire.

"Pick up the pen and the paper," he ordered. "On the first page you will write that you can no longer bear what you have become. Do as you are told and I will let you drink and smoke. Fool with me or even think about it and I will teach you things about pain that even you never dreamed possible. Understand?"

After mixing a screwdriver and lighting a cigarette, Taylor wrote a couple of lines on the first page.

"Finished," he said, sounding pleased with himself. "Happy now?"

"Nothing about you makes me happy," Charlie snapped. "Now pay attention. Next you are going to write that you are sorry for all the pain and suffering you have inflicted on others."

"All right," Taylor agreed, pen scratching across the pad resting on his knee. "But you know I don't mean it. Actually, I enjoyed every second of it."

"Believe me, I know. Next you are going to write down everything you can remember about your victims. Names, dates, how they were killed, where you hid their remains, everything that you can remember. Make sure you include my daughter, Lisa, and her husband. Ellen deserves to know and it is the least you can do for her."

"I don't think so!" Taylor laughed, taking a long sip of vodka and lighting another cigarette. "A confession? *Moi?* You're out of your—"

Taylor twitched, sending the screwdriver, the lit cigarette, the pen, and the paper flying. Clutching his skull with both hands, he screamed helplessly.

"Do as you are told," Charlie said, "or I will boil your brain inside your skull like an egg inside a shell."

Without attempting to speak, Taylor picked the pen and the pad up off the floor and began writing. And kept writing. Over an hour passed and still he wrote. Finally, a couple of hours before dawn and just about the time Charlie began despairing of him ever finishing, he stopped writing.

"That's it, I can't remember anything else," he said, keeping his eyes forward and his tone polite. "May I please mix another drink and smoke a cigarette?"

"Yes, in a minute" Charlie replied. "Now write a quick note to Ellen saying that you are sorry that you hurt her and that you have decided to go away. Then sign your name and put today's date underneath."

Picking up the pen again, Taylor did as he was told and finished in less than a minute.

"Now tear off the pages you have written on, fold them in thirds, and put them in the plastic liquor store bag by your feet," Charlie directed. "Then put the bag in the breast pocket of your jacket."

Working methodically, Taylor tore off the pages he had written on, stacked the loose sheets and then folded them into thirds. Shaking out the plastic liquor store bag, he placed the folded sheets inside and wrapped the excess bag around them. Opening the left breast pocket of his jacket, he stuffed the bag inside and zipped it closed with a flourish.

"Well, now what?" he asked, voice slurring. "Where are we going? Cities police? State Police? County Sheriff maybe? FBI? Or maybe you'd like to wait for the state or federal DA's office to open. It really doesn't matter because if you think this confession is admiss—"

"Shut up, fool!" Charlie said, forcing him into silence again. "Your days of going anywhere are just about over. Now have another drink and let me think in peace."

While Taylor sloppily mixed another drink, Charlie stood behind him reviewing what came next one last time. Nothing had really changed. Taylor was still the

Trickster's creature and always would be. Even if convicted and imprisoned for the murders he had committed, it was certain that he would escape with his master's help. There was only one person capable of imprisoning him but Charlie had no intention of getting into the incarceration business.

"Get up!" Charlie ordered, wanting this done and over with.

Morphing the noose's tether into a rod, Charlie compelled Taylor to stand and got him moving forward. Dodging around derelict textile equipment and the piles of trash, Charlie picked his way through the dark factory while keeping a wary eye on his prisoner. Ten minutes later they arrived at the center of the building.

A broad yellow warning stripe bordered an elevator shaft that ran all the way down to the building's sub-basements. Estimating twenty feet a floor times four plus another twenty feet for the main basement plus ten feet each for the two sub-basements minus ten feet for the elevator car and cables at the bottom of the shaft, Charlie calculated the drop at one hundred and ten feet, give or take a couple. At any rate, a bitch of a long ways down and more than enough to do the job.

Knowing that a thing well-dreaded is a thing best done soon, Charlie lifted Taylor and centered him over the elevator shaft, a human balloon on a tether of flaming blue plasma. Then for some reason he didn't understand, Charlie let him speak one last time.

"Charlie, please, don't," he begged, crying, voice echoing in the vast room. "I'm sick, you're a healer, help me—"

"There is only one cure for what ails you," Charlie said, compelling him into silence and granting him one final mercy. "Sleep deep and do not awake under any circumstances."

Waiting until Taylor's eyes were closed for a few seconds, Charlie spun him around until he was hanging head down over the center of the elevator shaft. Drawing in a deep breath, Charlie reined in the staff's power and let Marcus Taylor fall to his death. Although it seemed like forever to Charlie, it was over in a little more than three seconds. Not knowing quite what to expect, he had supposed the only sound would be a distant thud or maybe a distant clang or two. Instead, what echoed up the elevator shaft was a wet concussive noise akin to a dropped watermelon hitting a sidewalk.

Nausea unexpectedly gripped Charlie and he stood hunched over with his hands on his knees, struggling not to vomit. Feeling a little better after a few seconds, he straightened up and took a deep breath. Suddenly, he wanted out of this awful place and he wanted it NOW.

Trotting up to a glass-less bank of windows, he commanded the staff to take him down. Gripping it tightly with both hands, he leaped up into the cold air and was through the window casement and smoothly descending before he had time to think about it. Nearing the ground, he slowed and flared out into a running two-point landing that would have done a Special Forces paratrooper proud.

Cloaking himself in the glamour mid-stride, Charlie rounded the back corner of the building and headed for the street fifty yards away. Squeezing through the sagging chain-link gate, he turned right and started retracing his steps. For six city blocks he set a cracking pace for a man who was first eligible for AARP membership early in Reagan's second term. Finally though the years and the past day caught up with him.

Staggering over to a bus-stop bench, Charlie sat with his head down, glamour forgotten, wheezing in great draughts of cold air.

A car braked to a halt in front of him, tires squealing. The young ghetto wolves in the low-rider had returned, he was certain of it. Too exhausted for subterfuge, Charlie decided to take them out with one flaming sweep of the staff and worry about escape later. Keeping his eyes closed and his head down, he began powering up the staff.

"Hey, old timer, mama throw you out and now you cribbin' on that bench?" a woman's laughing voice asked. "You lookin' for some fun by any chance?"

Calling back the power surging through the staff, Charlie raised his head and opened his eyes. The pregnant prostitute he'd spoken with earlier was smiling at him from inside a battered Honda. Too winded to speak yet, he shook his head in response to her questions.

"Damn and I wonder why I can't make the Fortune 500," she sighed, turning on the dome light and checking her makeup in the rearview mirror. "You sure there's nothing I can do for you? I'm a full service rent-a-squeeze and I kinda like you old guys. In fact, I'm kinda likin' you more by the second."

"A ride," Charlie croaked, expending his meager oxygen surplus.

"A ride, huh?" the woman sniffed, sounding offended. "Well all right, I guess. But Vice has been around all night and I ain't made a dime. I ain' got no heart of gold or I'd pawn it and put the take in the tank. Less'n you got some gas money, I ain't goin' anywhere but home and you ain't going' any damn where."

Fishing down in the right front pocket of his jeans, Charlie pulled out a crumpled twenty dollar bill and waved it in the air.

"Wh-o-o-oh, sugar, you're on!" she cried in delight, reaching over to open the passenger side door. "Climb your handsome self in here and let's go!"

Knees and back protesting, Charlie squeezed into the front seat of the sports coupe. Settling the staff and the rucksack in the cramped space between his knees, he pulled the door shut and put the seatbelt on.

"Esmeralda Anne Parker," the woman said, offering her hand, "and I'm very pleased to meet you."

Turning to face her, Charlie quickly looked away in embarrassment. Save for a few strategically placed leather straps and a triangle of see-thru fabric, Esmeralda was near enough naked. What she had on, or didn't have on, would have gotten her arrested in Oklahoma. It probably would have gotten her arrested here in the Cities except that it was five in the morning and too dark outside to see much.

"Charles Lantot Redbird," he replied, shaking her hand, "and it is very nice to meet you too."

Unable to resist, he added, "Aren't you cold driving around naked at this time of year?"

"No, sugar, I'm warm-blooded year round. Now you hang on, Jezebel here is dinged up, but she still runs good. Where we goin' anyway?"

"I live over by the south side of the University"

Letting out the clutch, Esmeralda sent the Honda flying down the road. Within a block Charlie was hanging on for dear life and sorely missing Gilbert's driving. Staring straight ahead, he tried to ignore all that naked female skin seated next to him as the speedometer climbed past eighty miles-per-hour. After

Esmeralda blew through a third red light in as many blocks, he could stand it no more.

"You got something against the color red?" he asked, trying to keep his eyes of her now bare breasts. "Or do you always drive like this?"

"No, I like red just fine, else you wouldn't be sittin' where you are," she laughed. "And no, I don't always drive like this. You know how us pregnant ladies are, if we're not peein', we're thinkin' 'bout peein', and right now I gotta go. There's a convenience store up on the left a couple of blocks with the best gas prices in town and a nice clean bathroom with yours truly's name on it."

A blur of light barely registered on Charlie's tired eyes before the car veered left, radial tires howling. An uphill driveway loomed through the windshield and Esmeralda hit it dead center, bottoming out the suspension. Cutting the steering wheel hard right and locking the brakes, she brought the car to a halt next to the gas pump closest to the store and six inches behind the rear bumper of an F-150 pickup truck.

"Sorry, nature calls," she announced, pausing only long enough to reload her top hamper. "Be back in a few minutes."

Blowing out a long whistling breath, Charlie sat watching her charge toward the store, all wiggle, jiggle, and belly mounted on stiletto heels. Grinning, he pried himself out of the car and pumped in $12.50 worth of gas. Entering the store, he paid the clerk but there was no sign of Esmeralda.

Walking back outside to the pay phone, he called the hospital. Ellen was sleeping now, the duty nurse told him, and scheduled to be moved out of the Intensive Care Unit later in the morning. Relieved, Charlie thanked the man and hung up. The distinctive click of high-heels on pavement signaled Esmeralda's return.

"Much better," she sighed. "Buy a workin' girl a cup of coffee and a donut?"

"You're on. We gotta keep that blood of yours warm or else your naked self will freeze to death for sure."

Laughing, Esmeralda followed Charlie inside the store and over to the coffee urns. Finished mixing her coffee and selecting a pastry, she walked up to the front of the store. Seeing him approach after a minute or so, she walked up to the check-out counter.

"You can ring it all together," she told the clerk who was attempting and failing to keep his eyes locked on her face. "My husband will pay for it all."

Opening his mouth to speak, Charlie thought better of it and just paid the clerk. Walking outside, he followed Esmeralda's pealing laughter back to the car.

"'Scuse me," she gasped, still giggling even after they were both back in the car. "But those ears of yours are somethin'. Those big ole dudes must have extra blood vessels in them or something because when you get embarrassed, they turn r-e-e-e-d!"

Smiling, Charlie just shook his head and stared out the windshield. Pulling back onto the street, Esmeralda stayed near the posted speed limit and obeyed traffic lights and signs.

"You can unclench then big ole gnarly knuckles of yours from around your stick," she told him after a few blocks. "My bladder is directly connected to my right foot. When one gets full, the other gets heavy, and right now I don't have to go.

"That's good, but for my sake just don't drink that cup of coffee too fast."

Two blocks later, Charlie found what he had been looking for.

"Pull over to the curb, please," he said, compelling Esmeralda with the staff, "and leave the engine running. I'll be right back."

"'Kay," she said, eyes dreamy.

Hoisting himself up out of the car, Charlie walked over to the payphone and punched in the number, being careful not to leave any fingerprints.

"9-1-1 operator," a woman's voice immediately answered, "how may I help you?"

"There are five dead bodies up on the top floor of the old Sizemore Textile Building down Deep East," Charlie said, masking his voice with the staff's power. "And there's a dead guy in the basement. Hurry!"

"Ma'am, please stay on the line," the operator directed, but Charlie had already hung up.

Climbing back into the car, Charlie tapped Esmeralda with the staff and said, "Drive, please." A few blocks later he tapped her again and said, "Wake up now, Esmeralda."

"Whoa!" she said, yawning and shaking her head. "I must have dozed off for a second."

Twenty minutes later they were in the University District a few blocks away from Charlie's home.

"Pull over there by the curb," Charlie directed, "and park, please."

"We're not goin' to your place?" she asked, disappointment plain in her voice. "A girl has hopes, you know, and I really do like you a lot."

"I like you too, Esmeralda, but I'm sorry, it can't be that way," he said, compelling her again with the staff. "Listen to me now and remember."

"'Kay, I will," Esmeralda replied, eyes vacant.

"This is for you," he told her, pressing his last few bills into her hand.

"Thank you," she mumbled, stuffing the money into her small clutch purse.

Reaching for the door handle, Charlie paused, thinking of Gabriella Martinez dying in that alley all those years ago and the blue diaper bag with the yellow daisies printed on it. Releasing the handle, he sat composing his thoughts for a few seconds.

"You're very welcome. Now hear me again and remember again. First, you are to stop working as a prostitute and do something worthwhile with your life. Second, you are going to forget that you ever saw or met me. Now repeat what I just told you and remember it."

"First, gonna get out of the life, don't like it anyhow," she parroted. "Second, gonna forget I ever saw or met you. Doan want to though, like you."

"I like you too, but you will forget about me."

"Yes, forget," Esmeralda agreed, sounding sad, "right now."

"That's good, now you just be still for a minute."

Cloaking himself in the glamour, Charlie lowered the Honda's passenger side window. Checking to make sure the street was still empty, he climbed out and shut the door behind him.

"Wake up and drive home now," he ordered, putting the staff in through the open window and tapping her on the shoulder, "but remember what we talked about."

"Goodbye, miss you," Esmeralda said, putting the car in gear and pulling away from the curb.

Worried, Charlie stood watching her drive away. Some memories and emotions were so precious that the staff could not completely erase them. For whatever reason, Charlie was one such memory for Esmeralda. Little could be done about it though; compelling her further would permanently damage her mind.

Stepping off down the street, Charlie started toward home, aware of how weary he was now that he was walking again. Taking it slow and easy, he turned the corner onto his block twenty minutes later. Pausing, he scanned the block for any sign of something amiss, but sensed nothing. Still cloaked in the glamour he proceeded down the street, serenaded every step of the way by the howling of the neighborhood dogs. Reaching his front door, he checked the street again and found it still quiet. Unlocking the deadbolt, he slipped through the door. Cautious after his near-miss with Gilbert, he scanned the house and found it empty but for himself.

Stripping off all of his clothes, Charlie untied the top flap of the rucksack and stuffed them inside. Walking across the living room, he leaned the pack against the rear wall of the fireplace. Stepping back, he lowered the staff then hesitated.

The pack had been a birthday gift from Ellen when she was a little girl and it was one of his favorite possessions. Now though it was potential evidence of where he'd been and what he'd done. Powering up the staff, he incinerated the pack until the only thing left was an iridescent blue scar on the fireplace brick.

Walking into the bathroom, Charlie stood under the pounding shower jets until the water ran cold. Remaining in the stall, he cleaned and trimmed his nails with extra care. Finished, he flushed the parings down the drain and chased the water down with a flicker of power from the staff. Stepping out of the shower, Charlie toweled off and put on a pair of sweat pants. Returning to the living room, he placed the towels, washcloth, and bath mat into the fire place and dealt them the same fate as the rucksack.

Walking to the center of the room, he tapped the staff against the carpeted floor. A soft blue glow flowed along every interior surface in the house, destroying any traces that might have remained. Leaning on the staff, Charlie closed his eyes and tried to think of any evidence he might have overlooked but came up with nothing. Satisfied with his precautions, he walked back to the bedroom and climbed in between the sheets.

Hours later in early afternoon he woke and lay staring up at the ceiling, too comfortable to move just yet. After a few minutes though a full bladder and an empty stomach chased him out of bed.

Standing in the bathroom, Charlie flexed and rotated his lower right arm. Other than a little stiffness which could have just as well resulted from laying on it in his sleep, the limb seemed fine. But the twin circles of fresh scar tissue on his forearm didn't permit him the luxury of denial. He could already feel the venom doing its slow, inexorable work. Since the end result was already a foregone conclusion, he left worrying about it for another day.

Entering the kitchen, Charlie stopped dead in his tracks and groaned aloud. There were still no groceries in the house and he was still a pedestrian. Resigning himself to a six block hike to the neighborhood mini-mart, he walked over to the refrigerator to get a drink of water before he left. Opening the door, he found that Katie and Gilbert had stocked a few essentials during their last visit.

Grinning, he set to making himself an impressive pair of sandwiches. Going back to the refrigerator, he added potato salad and sweet pickles. Taking a seat at the kitchen table, he ate steadily for fifteen minutes. Finished, he stood up, put his dishes in the sink, and started a pot of coffee. A look of consternation began spreading across his face as he patted his pockets down.

Heaving a sigh of relief as memory caught up to deed, Charlie went into the living room and found his tobacco pouch and pipe laying on the coffee table. For a moment he had feared that they were incinerated along with everything else inside the pack. Loading and lighting the pipe, he returned to the kitchen and poured himself a cup of coffee. Walking back into the living room, he took a seat in the recliner next to the coffee table. Finding the remote control wedged in its usual spot down between the cushions and the side of the chair, he turned the television on and began channel surfing.

Nothing but soap operas, talk shows, and the usual daytime pablum was on the Cities channels. Getting a bad case of surfer's thumb, he blew by CNN and had to back up a couple of channels to find it. A wide-angle shot of the Sizemore Textile Building filled the screen with the words "Breaking News" flashing on top. Cursing under his breath, Charlie fumbled with the remote control and finally got the mute function turned off. By then the picture had changed to that of a weary looking man standing in front of a lectern. A caption at the bottom of the screen identified him as Detective Jeremy Lundgren.

"...Acting on an anonymous tip," Detective Lundgen began, "Cities police entered an abandoned factory building on the East Side early this morning. In a sub-basement they found the body of Mr. Marcus Taylor who apparently committed suicide by jumping down the building's elevator shaft. On Mr. Taylor's person was a suicide note claiming responsibility for a large number of unsolved homicides and disappearances dating back —"

Having gleaned what he needed, Charlie hit the mute button on the remote and sat watching the silent screen. In a face-to-face conversation, the staff could always detect when someone was lying to him. The staff was less accurate, sometimes to the point of confusion, about the veracity of statements which weren't directly addressed to him.

Sorting through the sensory impressions the staff had shown him, Charlie decided that Detective Lundgren probably wasn't lying during the press conference. The lack of certainty made him uneasy, but "probably not" was as close as he could get. The press conference ended and the detective's image was replaced by a photo of Ellen and Taylor on their wedding day. In turn, that was replaced by a picture of Ellen taken when she had graduated from college.

"Assholes," Charlie grumbled as he turned off the television, annoyed by the media's invasion of Ellen's privacy even though he had been expecting it.

Getting up out of the recliner, Charlie returned to the kitchen. Rinsing off the few dishes he had dirtied, he loaded them in the dishwasher for a future wash. Sitting down at the kitchen table, he reviewed the errands he needed to run.

Standing in the living room a few minutes later, he glanced at the recliner, wishing that he was still in it. One way or another, he consoled himself with a little gallows humor, there would be plenty of time to rest and probably sooner than he liked.

Pulling the front door closed behind him, Charlie headed for the bus-stop a few blocks away. Once there, he caught a bus almost immediately and was downtown forty minutes later. After paying a quick visit to the ATM across the street from the bus station, he was on his way again within a few minutes. Getting off again at Belle Springs Mall, one of the Cities' largest, he spent a hurried hour shopping before resuming his travels. A block from the hospital, he debarked for the last time, at least on this leg of the journey. Ten minutes later he was finished shopping and ready to visit Ellen.

Turning into the hospital's driveway, Charlie froze, unable to believe what he was seeing. Vans and satellite trucks from every major American television network plus a host of foreign media outlets were parked everywhere. Reporters and technical support crews were crowded onto the large patio in front of the hospital's main doors. Somehow he doubted they were all here to report on the weather.

Changing course, Charlie walked away from the assembled media crews. Turning a corner, he cloaked himself in the glamour and slipped into the hospital through the ambulance sally port. Dropping the glamour, he rode an elevator up to Ellen's floor. Exiting the car, he turned the corner into the corridor where her room was located. Two hospital security officers were posted just outside the door. Seeing him approach, they stiffened their postures and frowned. Inwardly tense, Charlie just smiled and kept walking forward.

"You must be Mr. Redbird," the female officer said, smiling and opening the door to Ellen's room for him. "Mrs. Taylor has been asking for you."

"Please don't worry about the media vultures outside," the male officer added. "If there's anything we can do for you or Mrs. Taylor, please let us know."

"Thank you," Charlie said, chiding himself for always being suspicious of uniformed authority figures. "You're very kind."

Standing at the foot of the bed, looked down at Ellen. Although sleeping, she still looked harried and sad. Placing his gifts on the bedside table, he pulled up a chair and waited for her to wake.

"Hi, Grandpa," she mumbled a half-hour later. "I didn't hear you come in."

"Hi, Blossom," he answered, standing up and bending over to kiss her on the forehead. "That's because I didn't want to wake you up."

"Marcus," she said, staring at her blanketed feet, "and Mom and Dad. The police were here and they said—"

"Yes, Ellen, I'm afraid it's true," Charlie replied, calming her a little with the staff before she upset herself further. "I'm sorry."

"I was going to divorce him anyway," she said, black eyes shiny with tears. "If he did what they say he did, it's just as well that he's dead. It's the best thing for everybody involved, including him."

Surprised by her strength and clarity of perception, Charlie took cover behind the first instinctive male reaction that came to mind. Handing her the box of tissues on the night stand, he cleared his throat and searched for something appropriate to say. Ellen's next remark didn't just surprise him; it scared the hell out of him.

"Thank you, Grandpa," she said, reaching out and squeezing his hand. "It was the right thing to do, especially after what he did to Mom and Dad."

Startled, Charlie sat there thinking for long seconds. Out of the corner of one eye he could see Ellen looking at him, near laughter over his discomfort. Although Charlie couldn't be certain, he was pretty sure that she had discovered his role in Taylor's death. Two-way communication was possible with the staff and the Redbird blood ran strong in her. While he healed her, she had been unconsciously listening to his innermost thoughts and plans.

As life experiences go, Charlie found that being hoisted on his own *petard* ranked right up there with slamming a hand in a car door for sheer enjoyment. One thing was certain though, he damn sure wasn't going to ask her if or how she knew. Since this was the only time that the subject of Marcus Taylor's death would ever be raised between them, his best guess would always have to do.

"For me?" Ellen asked, eyes lighting on the dozen red roses as she reached over to put the box of tissues back on the night stand. "Oh, thank you!"

Relieved by the change of subject, Charlie got up and placed the vase of roses in her arms.

"These are for you, too," he said, placing a pair of plastic bags on the bed next to her.

Opening one bag, Ellen pulled out a medium-sized grey teddy bear. Opening the other bag, she pulled out a volume written by Maya Angelou, her favorite poet.

"I hope the presents make you feel better, I was worried about you."

"Oh, Grandpa, don't be. Marcus and I were finished months ago, almost before we got started. Everything is wonderful, but you'll spoil me rotten and go broke in the process if you're not careful."

"It's a rough job, but somebody's gotta do it. And I never thought I'd die rich anyway."

"Grandpa," Ellen said, sounding suddenly shy and unsure of herself, "when I get out of here, can I come and stay with you for a while? I'll understand if you say no, but I'd really like to if it's all right with you."

"Of course you can come visit, Blossom, and for as long as you like. I've been very lonely and I'm looking forward to having you come visit."

"Good, I'm glad," she mumbled, eyelids fluttering. "They keep me pumped full of medication and now I'm falling asleep again."

"The more the better," he said, taking the flowers and book out of her arms and placing them on the bedside table.

For the next few minutes, Charlie sat and watched Ellen sleep. Satisfied that she was well on the mend, he rose and kissed her goodbye. Turning away he left the room, happy to be on his way home.

For the next eight days, Charlie visited Ellen every morning. During the afternoons he wrapped up his affairs in the Cities, including resigning his teaching position and canceling a pair of scheduled art shows. On the ninth day he returned to the hospital in the early evening.

With the help of the nursing staff Ellen had dressed in dark clothing. Under protest, even though she knew the rationale for the rule, she was helped into a wheelchair and rolled downstairs. A few minutes later she emerged into the same ambulance sally port Charlie had slipped through over a week earlier. With a nurse holding each arm, she was helped out of the wheelchair and into a makeshift bed in the back of Gilbert's van.

A member of the hospital staff had "leaked" to the media that the widow of the "Cities Ripper", as the tabloid press had dubbed Taylor, was being released early the next afternoon. This subterfuge gave them an eighteen hour head start, more than long enough to escape the prying eyes of the press.

Two hours later they stopped at a motel for the night even though Ellen insisted she was fine. With Charlie and Gilbert holding her arms, Ellen walked across the parking lot while Katie looked worriedly on. Once inside the motel room, she collapsed on the bed, face pale.

"Guess I was a little shakier than I thought," she said, breathing hard. "But I'm all right, honest I am."

The following day they drove the rest of the way to Frechette with Gilbert behind the wheel the entire way. Every time Charlie found himself growing impatient at their slow progress, he thought about Esmeralda Parker's driving and grinned. Up in the front passenger seat, Katie was doing the left cheek-right cheek fidget, which tickled him even more. Ellen adopted an even more effective tactic: She dozed off and on for most of the eight hour ride north.

Arriving at Charlie's cabin in late afternoon, Ellen surprised everyone by climbing the front porch steps leaning only on Charlie's arm. By the time Katie and Gilbert left late the next morning, Ellen was moving around the cabin unassisted. Over the weeks that followed she grew stronger but suffered frequent migraine headaches and extended bouts of dizziness. At first two or three times a week, but less often as time went on, she would have days where she wouldn't say much. Usually at the end of those blue days Charlie would hear her crying late at night. Overall though he was encouraged by her steady progress.

In late December, Ellen and Charlie traveled back down to the Cities for the holidays. Three days after they arrived Charlie got an early Christmas present. Searching for Ellen after returning from doing some last minute shopping, he walked into her bedroom and found it empty. Turning to leave, his eyes flicked across an official looking sheet of paper lying on the dresser. Although he wanted to respect her privacy, he couldn't help noticing the document's title.

Already feeling guilty, he picked the piece of paper up and read it. In the good judgment of the County Medical Examiner, the late Marcus Taylor had committed suicide with the official cause-of-death listed as related trauma (jump). Putting the Death Certificate back exactly where he had found it, Charlie left the room feeling as if someone had taken the weight of the world off his shoulders.

In early January, Ellen and Charlie returned to Frechette. With the exception of three quick trips to the Cities to keep Ellen's medical appointments, they remained there throughout the winter and early spring. By mid-May though things had started changing.

The venom The Wendigo's symbiont had lanced into Charlie's arm was beginning to affect him. The symptoms weren't too bad just yet; a dry, hacking cough some mornings and bone-deep fatigue at night no matter how easy he took it during the day. Still, Charlie knew it wouldn't be long before he couldn't hide his illness from Ellen. And although she denied it, he also knew she had begun missing her life in the Cities.

After a long discussion that verged on an argument, Ellen finally admitted that she wanted to move back to the Cities. The next day, Charlie drove her back for the last time. Dropping her off at her paternal grandmother's house, he left after making repeated promises to call and visit. Three blocks later he pulled over to the curb and parked. For long minutes, he sat with his forehead resting on the steering wheel and his eyes squeezed shut.

Pulling back on the road, Charlie drove to a nearby motel and checked in. Rising early the next morning, he was back in Frechette by early afternoon. Walking into the cabin, he dropped his overnight bag on the sofa and started a pot of coffee brewing. When it was finished, he poured himself a cup and started back toward the couch. Changing his mind, he instead walked outside.

Taking a seat in his favorite rocker, Charlie put his feet up on the porch railing. There was nothing to do now but wait. Wait for the ill woman and the little girl he had seen in his dreams to arrive. Wait for David Garrison to return from Arizona. Wait to see what happened first, the last stage of a terminal illness or next October time. Wait, wait, and then wait some more.

Taking a sip of his coffee, Charlie settled in to do just that.

Book IV

A Song for Charlie Redbird

Not lost, but gone before.

Lucius Annaeus Seneca, *Epistles, 63, 16*

CHAPTER 65

FAR AWAY AND not long ago, Charlie Redbird sat dozing in the weak light of a late autumn dawn. Cold, pain, and a vague sense of unease slowly prodded him awake. Someone was there, close, he was sure of it. Raising his head, Charlie blinked several times, trying to clear the clotted mucus out of his eyes. Rachel and Susie were standing about two feet away staring at him.

"Grampa Charlie," she worriedly asked, one hand twined into Susie's ruff, "are you all right?"

As Charlie inhaled to speak the cold air bit deep into his cancer-raddled lungs. White-hot agony flashed through his entire body as a steel band tightened around his chest, cutting off his air supply. The scar tissue over the twin punctures on his right forearm ruptured, spewing out smoking black pus which burned through his clothing and dripped down between his thighs. Wheezing, unable to breathe, his face flushed bright scarlet, then blackened as he went into respiratory arrest. Raising his right arm, he smacked the butt of the staff down on the frozen ground, but it remained dormant. Gurgling, he collapsed face first into the ashes of last night's fire and lay still.

Not knowing what to do, Rachel stood crying while Susie whined anxiously. After a few seconds though the instincts of a threatened six-year old took over.

"M-ah-ah-ah-me," she shrieked, running toward their tent a few yards away, "M-ah-ah-ah-my, wake up!"

CHAPTER 66

DAWN ALSO CAME hard for Ellen Talltrees. A sleepless night spent on the couch had exacerbated her mental and physical exhaustion. The repeated trauma of firing Charlie's shotgun had left her right arm aching from shoulder to fingertip. That was small beer though compared to the excruciating migraine headache that had struck in the small hours of the morning and still remained.

The left side of Ellen's skull was in agony, especially the area around the recently healed fractures. The vision in her left eye was blurry and her left nostril ran freely. The left side of her mouth drooped down and twitched in an involuntary half-frown. Most of the feeling on the left side of her body was gone, replaced by a numb tingling feeling.

The floorboards beneath Ellen's feet groaned and strained against their fasteners as the creature imprisoned below threw itself upwards in a blind fury. A searing bolt of pain exploded in the center of her head. Leaning over the side of the sofa, she vomited into a small trash can. Wiping her mouth with a towel, she leaned back and closed her eyes. Grasping a quart plastic spray bottle wedged between her thighs, Ellen opened her eyes and forced herself upright on the third try. Limping around the living room, she started spraying the floorboards.

One of Charlie's weekly rituals was sprinkling salt around the base of the cabin's interior and exterior walls. When Ellen had asked why, he had replied that the salt "kept bad things away" and refused further comment. For some reason, Ellen had remembered that brief conversation all those years ago and had filled a spray bottle with a strong solution of salt water.

During the night, she had sprayed the living room floor every time the creature started smashing up against the boards. Even though the salt water never physically touched the monster, its mere presence or scent was enough. Every time she sprayed the floorboards, the creature would retreat, hissing and muttering. But it always returned and at ever shorter intervals.

Finished spraying, Ellen lifted the bottle up to her good eye and saw that only about a cup and a half of the salt water solution remained. Holding on to the wall for support, she walked into the kitchen. Picking up the box of salt, she gave it a good shake. A handful or so left, if that, plus whatever was in the shaker on the kitchen table.

Walking back into the living room, Ellen stood listening for a few seconds. Satisfied that the creature had been driven off, she set the spray bottle down on the coffee table and picked up a claw hammer. Just get it done, she told herself, just get it done and then you can rest. Clumsy because of the lack of sensation on her left side, Ellen knelt and began hammering down the nails the creature had pounded up. Each blow of the hammer against the floor sent an excruciating bolt of pain roaring through her head. Despite missing the nails as often as she hit them, Ellen kept hammering away. Finally finished, she rested for a moment on all fours with her forehead lying on the floor.

"Get up!" she silently raged at herself. *"Get up and sit on the couch or that thing down there will come up through the floor and kill you for sure! Get up!"*

When she tried to rise, Ellen discovered that she couldn't stand. Supporting most of her weight with the right side of her body, she crawled across the living room floor. Reaching the sofa, she levered herself up using her right arm. Afraid to lie down because she might fall asleep, Ellen sat upright with her eyes squeezed shut, pain clanging through her head.

Down below, she could hear the creature moving around again. Years ago, way back in eighth grade, her best-friend Sharon had a three-foot long boa constrictor that sounded like that when it slithered around its cage. A dry, paper rustling kind of sound. Except that the monster imprisoned below sounded much bigger, one hell of a lot bigger. And it seemed to grow larger with every hour that passed.

The creature's voice was familiar to Ellen, very familiar. No, she had decided, she would not listen to that voice. The sound of that voice haunted her dreams enough already. No matter what, she wouldn't listen to it.

A hard rap under her right foot signaled that the monster was resuming its assault on the floorboards.

"Grandpa, you gotta hurry," she muttered, words slurring from the involuntary droop on the left side of her mouth. "I don't have long, I really don't."

CHAPTER 67

THE WENDIGO WAS standing in the rough stone doorway of his crèche watching the sun rise. The sweet odor of Redbird's death carried to him on the weak morning breeze. Across the divide of time and space, he also sensed the dwindling life-force of Redbird's bitch granddaughter, Ellen. Better yet.

All that was left was for Mancun to slaughter Redbird, if he lived that long, the whites, and bring the staff back here. The outcome of that particular battle was in no doubt whatsoever.

The Dark One was certain that Mancun would try to keep the staff and use it against him. But the outcome of that battle was in no doubt either, whether Mancun knew it or not. And that left, let's see, why, that was all she wrote.

"Today, it will be today!" The Wendigo shrieked, voice rolling out over the snow covered hills below.

Roaring with laughter, he pounded the walls until stone chips ricocheted around the interior of the cave and struck up sparks. Calming himself, the monster stood lost in thought. Ah yes, he'd almost forgotten.

"Mary Redbird and Jennifer Garrison," he bellowed, "come here! Gonna keep you ladies n-i-i-i-ce and warm, oh yes I am!"

CHAPTER 68

ONE OF THE great advantages of his peculiar existence, Mancun reflected, was that physical hardship left him untouched. Neither cold, nor hunger, nor wounds could harm him, at least not for long. Even The Eldest, that fuck, had been unable to kill him. And with every day that passed his strength and cunning increased, along with his skill at killing. Being half-dead and half-alive, he concluded, was an entirely satisfactory state of affairs.

Directing his attention to matters tactical, Mancun examined the surrounding environment. The gentle slope of the land, the scattered trees, the underbrush, the sun, the breeze, all were perfect. The ambush would be sprung and done before Redbird and the whites knew what hit them.

Raising his head, Mancun focused his vision on a low line of hills a few miles away. The thin wisp of smoke was still there, floating down the gentle breeze before dissipating. The fools deserved to die for such carelessness. And so they would, and soon too.

The males, Mancun reminded himself, take the males first. If Redbird was still alive, which was doubtful, slaughter him first. Even in his old age and near death, Redbird was still dangerous. The master's venom might slow or weaken him, but it wouldn't render him harmless. Only death would do that. Yes, kill Redbird first and be quick about it. No sense in taking chances with success this close.

Gar-ri-son, the soft white man, would be next. No threat, no contest there. Slaughtering him would be easier than killing a week-old fawn since the fool would probably be too frightened to even run. No matter if he did though, it would only slightly delay the inevitable.

The woman and the little girl would be saved for later. Future plans revolved around them, especially the child.

And then the staff would be his. A short run back to The Wendigo's crèche, a shorter battle, and then he would be the ruler instead of the ruled. The Dark One would cower at his feet and he, Mancun the Great, would stride across worlds slaughtering all that lived. First on the agenda would be The Eldest for having hurt — The Dark One's cry of joy roared down the valley, startling Mancun so badly that he dropped his stone tomahawk.

"Shut up!" he hissed. "Just shut the fuck up!"

Picking up the flint tomahawk, Mancun settled back into his hide. To pass the time, he envisioned the woman's screams as he cut the liver out of her living daughter, roasted it on a spit, and fed it to her. Yes, today was going to be a good day. Indeed, a great day.

CHAPTER 69

FROM DAVID'S POINT of view, things were going to hell in a hand basket with the afterburners lit. Hugging herself, Gina was wandering an erratic circle around the two men while holding an animated one-way conversation with someone or something named Jillian. Crying, Rachel was sitting cross-legged in the snow hugging Susie.

"It makes no difference," Charlie told him, voice barely audible. "The Dark One's venom has me now and there is no cure, no anti-venom. If we turn back, I will still die today. Then Ellen, then the rest of you, and soon. If we continue on, I will still die, but all yet may be well. We must keep going forward, we must!"

Exhausted from the effort of speaking, Charlie closed his eyes and rested, breathing tortuous. As David opened his mouth to speak, The Wendigo's fierce cry of joy rolled over them, rattling leaves and branches as it passed.

"Jesus!" David muttered, gooseflesh breaking out all over his body. "What the hell was that?"

"It wasn't the Jehovah's Witnesses or the Avon lady," Charlie replied, voice sounding a little stronger. "That was His Nibs celebrating, let's hope a tad prematurely. Now how 'bout it, handsome, you in or out?"

Although David had no previous experience with terminal illness, he didn't think Charlie could even get up, never mind hike through rough country. Thin runnels of dark blood ran freely from each of his nostrils and dripped down from the corners of his mouth. His corneas had turned a strange yellowish-red color and his normally black pupils had bleached out to a muddy brown color. Hemorrhaging buboes had broken out on his face and seemed to be growing larger by the minute.

Last night, Charlie had been fine. Tired, as any elderly person would be, but otherwise healthy. And now this. People didn't get this seriously ill this fast, they just didn't. On top of everything else, Gina was falling apart and Rachel was nearly hysterical about it. Clenching his fists, David threw his head back, a thought away from screaming his fear and frustration to the sky above.

"Calm yourself, David, please," Charlie said, groaning as he pushed himself up into a sitting position. "All that lives eventually dies, and this is my time and nothing can change that. But if you'll help me, I can still go on and we can finish what we started. It's only three or four more miles, and I know I can make it that far if you'll help me. If we don't, Ellen will die, I—"

"All right, Charlie, we'll go on. But only because I don't see any other alternative and only on condition that once we kill this thing, we march day and night until we get out of here and get you into a hospital."

"Yes, David, of course," Charlie replied, knowing that was one journey he would never have to make. "I'm just going to lay here and rest while you get ready to go."

Nodding, David walked the few yards over to Rachel. She and her mother weighed heavily on his mind. Leaving them here, wherever here was, while he and Charlie went on was out of the question. Somehow, he knew that defeating the monster without them would be impossible. If they tried to run, he also knew that the monster would hunt them down and slaughter them before sunset. Gina was past consulting about anything, so he chose for her. Although he hated the idea, mother and daughter would continue on until the end.

"Hi, Honey, how you doin'," he asked, kneeling down in the snow and hugging Rachel. "I want you to stop crying and listen to me now. We're getting ready to leave, so I want you to put all your clothes and your sleeping bag in your pack. Nothing else, just your clothes and your sleeping bag. We've got something to do this afternoon and then we're going to start walking home."

"We're going to kill the monster, aren't we?" Rachel asked, swiping at her eyes with a grimy coat sleeve. "Maybe the nice man will give us a ride in his spaceship because I want to go home. I miss going to school and cartoons and my new best friend, Carol."

"I hope so," David said, out of practice with talking to children and not knowing quite what to say. "Now you go get ready. I want to leave in a few minutes."

Standing, David lifted Rachel to her feet and started her toward the tent with a gentle push. Sweeping his eyes across the small clearing, he spotted Gina wandering a crooked course off into the forest. Swearing under his breath, he sprinted after her before she could wander out of sight. When he had closed to within a few yards, David called out for her to stop but Gina ignored him and kept on going. When he was only a couple of steps away, he called out again and again she ignored him. Exasperated, he ran another couple of steps and reached out and seized her left arm. Shrugging him off with surprising ease, Gina kept walking without even bothering to look back, muttering to Jillian all the while. Running a couple steps ahead of her, David turned and stood with his arms outstretched. Without slowing or altering course, Gina slammed hard into his chest and knocked him flat on his back.

"Goddamn it!" he wheezed. "Stop!"

Getting back to his feet, David caught up with Gina just before she would have vanished into a thick stand of fir trees. Taking no chances this time, he rushed up behind and threw his arms around her. Lifting her off the ground, David turned until they were facing back toward the camp. When Gina's feet stopped pumping after a few seconds, he set her back down on the ground. Releasing his hold, David walked around in front of her. Through it all, Gina kept up her conversation with Jillian.

"Gina," he asked, a premonition warning him that he wouldn't like the answer, "who's Jillian and why are you talking to her?"

"Walking home from school when we were eight, Jillian got ate and never was seen again," Gina sang, sounding eerily like her daughter. "I'm going over to her house and play dollies this afternoon. Your wife Jennifer says hello and that she loves you and will see you soon."

"What did you just say? What do you mean my wife—"

"Would you like to fuck me, David?" Gina asked, voice hard and brassy as she snatched up her sweater and bared her breasts. "Do you like these? You can do anything you want to me, I won't mind. I love to fuck, I really do."

Repulsed and frightened, David backed up a couple of steps in a hurry. Understanding dawned and he charged forward with both fists raised. Reaching Gina, he grabbed the sides of her head and bent down until they were standing eye-to-eye.

"Get out of her head!" he screamed, so enraged he could barely speak. "Get out of her head and run, because when I catch you, you are going to die!"

The monster inside Gina Tolliver's mind laughed once, spat in David's face, and fled. Unaware that it had gone, David continued shaking Gina's head and shouting into her face.

"David, stop it, you're hurting me!" Gina cried, struggling to break his grip on her skull. "It got inside my head and made me say those things! It did!"

"I know," David said, releasing her head and turning his back while she adjusted her clothing. "I'm really sorry, I, I didn't mean to hurt you or scare you or anything. I, I'm so sorry, I—"

"Th, that's all right," she stammered, crying now which made him feel even worse. "I could feel and hear that thing talking, but I couldn't make it stop or go away. I was thinking about my friend Jillian, she disappeared when we were both eight, and somehow it got inside of me."

Wiping the spittle off his face, David risked a quick glance over his shoulder. Finished adjusting her sweater, Gina was standing with her hands covering her eyes, swaying back and forth as she wept.

"Easy now," David said, reaching for her elbow to steer her back to camp. "We need to get going, I want to leave as soon as possible. Bring only your clothes and your sleeping bag, I'll take care of the rest. I'm going to kill that damn thing today and then we're going to start home and travel day and night until we get there.

Charlie needs to be in a hospital and the sooner we get started, the sooner we can get him to one."

Instead of answering, Gina took a step forward, wrapped her arms around David's neck, and kissed him on the mouth. Although he could never say why later, David kissed her back. And then he kissed her again.

"Ungh, we should be getting back," he finally said, taking a step back and releasing her. "It's getting late and we need to get going. I'd like to be miles away from here and well on our way home by dark."

Stepping up next to him, Gina took his hand and they started back toward camp. Once again, although he couldn't say why, David let her hand remain in his.

"David, I really like you a lot," she told him, sounding perfectly lucid. "When we get home, could we start seeing each other?"

David started to tell her that he was a married man who was very much in love with his wife. After considering what was happening though he thought better of it.

"Now's not a good time to be making personal decisions," he said. "Right now, we need to concentrate on what lays ahead and on getting out of here. After we get back, we'll find a sitter for Rachel and go out to dinner and talk about things."

"Does it bother you that I'm, you know, schizophrenic," Gina asked, sounding near tears again. "When things are normal my medication takes care of it and I'm pretty much stable. But I get really lonely and—"

"No, it's not that," David assured her, although he had serious doubts already. "It's just that right now, and especially with Charlie being so sick, I have to keep my eye on the ball. When we get back, we're going to have that talk."

"Good," she said, wrapping her arms around his neck again. "I was afraid it would ruin things before they could get started."

After a moment's hesitation, David kissed her again. Sliding one hand down, he gave the left cheek of her ass a long, appreciative squeeze. Unzipping her coat, he reached up under her sweater and began fondling her right breast. Nice, very nice.

Something banged into the back of David's left knee and Gina violently started. As she backed away, his watchband somehow snagged on her sweater and the two spent a comical moment getting disentangled from each other. Turning his head to look to follow Gina's line of sight, David saw Susie and Rachel standing a couple of feet away. One looked puzzled, the other madder than hell.

"Don't back up any further," Charlie said from behind him, "or else you'll step in the fire."

Moving forward out of harm's way, David watched as Rachel took Gina's hand and towed her over to their tent. He just couldn't understand it. One second he and Gina had been out of sight in the woods and the next they were in the middle of the campsite. A private man, David never carried on like that with a woman in public, especially one that the barely knew. He never even behaved like that in private with his wife if his daughter was awake, never mind standing there watching. The whole episode didn't just revolt and embarrass him, it deeply frightened him.

"David, be careful what you do," Charlie counseled from down on the ground. "Time and space are different here and it can affect your judgment pretty quickly. Plus we are drawing close to our enemy and he is endlessly sly and full of evil mischief. Just bear it in mind, okay?"

"Ungh, yeah Charlie, thanks, I'll do that," he said, embarrassed. "I'll hurry up and finish packing and then we can get going. We've lost too much time as it is."

Trotting over to their tent, David unzipped the fly and crawled inside. Rolling up his sleeping bag, he strapped it onto his backpack. Opening the pack's top, he threw in a few items of clothing. Crawling back outside, he threw in their few remaining provisions and cinched the pack shut.

Standing, David walked over to the tent and a pushed a three-inch wide fluorescent yellow button next to the door with the word "DOWN" stenciled in block black capitals beneath it. Remembering Charlie's experience the previous day, he hastily backed up a few steps to watch what happened next.

Whistling like a boiling teakettle, the tent collapsed and lay flat on the ground. Emitting an odd series of rhythmic clicks, the tent folded itself in half, then in half again, before rolling itself into a tight cylinder. Walking over, he slid the tent into its carrying case and strapped it to his pack. Putting on the pack, he paused a second to review his preparations one last time.

Gina and Rachel would share a sleeping bag, Charlie would use the bag Gina was carrying, and he had his own bag plus the tent they would all share. Their meager food and water supplies, enough for two lean days, were resting on top of his clothes in his backpack. Everything else they would leave here and pick up on the way home if possible. They were ready, or at least he hoped they were.

Watching David approach, Gina smiled and blushed, obviously still under the influence of the passion that had gripped them both earlier. On the other end of the spectrum, Rachel glared down at his feet, still furious.

Lying on the ground, Charlie looked up at him, face pale and lined with pain. Taking it all in, David decided that it was shaping up to be a bitch of a day and it was barely seven o'clock in the morning.

"Okay, Charlie," he said, "let's get you on your feet and then we're out of here."

Straddling Charlie, David grasped his wrists and started backing up. Prepared for a heavy lift, he was surprised when Charlie came up off the ground with no more resistance than an oversized bundle of dried sticks. Digging in his heels, David caught his balance just before he would have toppled over backwards and taken Charlie with him. Releasing him, David backed up a half-step and stood with his arms outstretched.

"I'll be all right," Charlie said, breath gurgling in his chest. "Just lend me an arm and we can get going."

Leaning on David's arm, Charlie took a few tottering steps and paused to rest. Moving in on his other flank, Gina offered him her arm and his gait improved.

"Thank you, Gina," he wheezed, "that's much better."

With Rachel and Susie bringing up the rear and told to stay close, they entered the forest. Almost immediately, the terrain began sloping uphill in a series of ever higher benches connected by short but steep hillsides. Thick stands of fir trees and the dense underbrush prevented them from walking three or even two abreast.

For long stretches David was forced to carry Charlie on his back while Gina carried his pack. The benches weren't too bad because at least he could set Charlie down and rest if he had to. The hillsides though were pure hell; he didn't dare stop on the slopes and the footing was treacherous on the snow-covered ground. Charlie never complained, but David could tell from his tortured breathing and occasional muffled groans that being carted over hill and dale was causing him considerable pain.

On one particularly steep slope, David carried Charlie to the top and left him lying concealed in the center of a dense alder thicket. Climbing back down the slope, he picked up Rachel and carried her up the hill. Leaving her hidden in the alders with Charlie, he descended the slope yet again. Putting on his pack, he helped Gina up the hill, thankful that he didn't have to carry her. Leading her to the clearing inside the alder thicket, David arched his spine and kneaded the aching muscles in the small of his back. Easing himself down on the ground, he lay back with an appreciative groan.

"Da, da, dat's all folks," he said, arranging his parka hood so that snowmelt wouldn't run down his neck. "Garrison the mule that walks like a man needs a break. If I drift off, would somebody please wake me up in twenty minutes or so."

Closing his eyes, David immediately fell asleep. Too soon, something wet, cold, and foul smelling prodded him awake. Susie's nose, and her breath, were roaming over his face.

"Wake up, Mr. David," Rachel said, laughing at the dog's antics. "Mommy says lunch is almost ready."

Stretching a couple of times, David rolled over on his belly then got up on his hands and knees. Creaky and sore, he climbed to his feet and again tried to ease the kinks out of his lower back.

"I'll be back in a few minutes," he told the others, picking up his pack and heading off into the alders.

Thirty steps later, David stopped just short of the edge of the thicket. Dropping the backpack, he relieved himself and changed out of his wet socks and jeans. Putting the wet clothes in a plastic bag in the cargo compartment, he closed the pack and left it lying on the ground.

Walking on the balls of his feet, he slipped out of the alder thicket. Cat-footing it twenty yards out into the forest, he took cover behind a large maple. Standing perfectly still, he swept his senses through the forest, looking, listening, smelling. Nothing stirred, nothing to be afraid of. And yet he was, terribly so.

Dread so powerful that it made him tremble set in and for one awful moment David thought he was going to lose control of his bowels. Leaning into the rough bark of the tree, he willed himself to be still and silent, invisible. As swiftly as it came the terrible fear departed, leaving behind a feeling of malevolent watchfulness.

Pushing off the maple tree, he sprinted for the cover of the alder thicket a few yards away. Mocking laughter, whether from deep inside his mind or from somewhere in the surrounding forest, pursued him every step of the way.

Reaching the alder thicket, David lowered his head and started forcing his way through the wall of saplings. More by luck than by design, he arrived back at the spot where he had left his backpack. Snatching the pack up off the ground, he thrust his arms through the straps and ran on. A few steps later, his right foot caught on a root and he would have fallen, but was stopped halfway to the ground by the springy wall of alder saplings. Flailing his arms, David struggled upright and started running again. Two steps later he tripped again, but this time there was a break in the alders and he slammed down hard on the snow-covered ground. Rolling over on his back, he stared up at the clear blue sky.

"Stop it, stop it right now!" He ordered himself aloud, not knowing how but certain that he was right. "This fucking thing feeds on fear, it needs it! If you let if frighten you, you and everyone else are going to die!"

Closing his eyes, David took six deep breaths. Climbing to his feet, he scanned the ground and found his back trail. Following it to where his backpack had laid, David examined the ground again and spotted his boot prints in the faint trace leading back to the clearing at the center of the thicket. Concerned about the amount of time that he'd been gone, he started double-timing it down the trail.

Approaching the clearing, he dropped back to a walk to avoid frightening everyone. Stepping out of the trees, he saw Rachel and Gina scrubbing out the lunch dishes while Susie watched. Next to the fire, Charlie lay sleeping with the staff cradled in his arms. Watching the smoke plume from the fire rise high in the still air, David felt a stab of alarm and just as rapidly dismissed it. The monster already knew they were here so there was no point in doing without a fire.

"I was getting worried, you were gone for so long," Gina said, getting to her feet and walking over to kiss him. "Rachel and I got real scared a few minutes ago and we wanted to run away and hide, but we couldn't leave Charlie. Then there was all this noise off in the bushes right after and we didn't know if it was you or not and—"

"Sorry, it was me," David interrupted, squeezing her waist and stepping away before he lost control of himself again. "You're right, the monster has been sniffing around and I got scared and crashing around out in the toolies. I didn't mean to scare you or anything."

"That's all right, you didn't mean to. This whole thing is scary and I really want to get out of here. The other thing is Charlie. He keeps drifting in and out of consciousness and talking to someone named Mary. That was his wife's name, wasn't it? He's going to die, just like he said, isn't he? I, I—"

"I don't know if Charlie is going to die, but he is very sick and we need to get him out of here and into a hospital. So let me get something to eat and then we can get going."

Walking over to the fire, David picked up a bowl and a spoon sitting by the edge of the coals. Stirring the stew, he examined the alien looking meat and vegetables floating in the gravy. Deciding that he was better off not knowing, he concentrated on eating and found the strange looking concoction delicious. Finished eating, he scoured the dirty dishes with snow and reloaded them in his pack.

"Rachel and I need to powder our noses before we get going," Gina said, reaching for Rachel's hand. "We'll be right back."

Nodding, David watched them walk away then started to put the fire out. Suddenly, he stopped and stood thinking. Grinning, he threw the few remaining pieces of dry wood on the fire and watched them burst into flames. Grabbing the small hatchet off the back of his pack, he ran a few steps and cut down an armload of small alder saplings. Throwing them onto the fire, he continued cutting and hauling until the pile of saplings on the fire was waist-high.

The cut alders were green, which meant they wouldn't burn. But the saplings would smoke for hours and that was the object of the exercise. To anyone watching it would appear they had camped for the day after struggling through a rough morning. It wasn't a great diversionary tactic, but it might buy them some time to maneuver undetected. More importantly, it made David feel as if he was doing something besides stumbling along to an uncertain fate.

Kneeling, he strapped the hatchet back on his pack and watched Gina and Rachel walk back into the clearing. Seeing them both staring at the rapidly expanding plume of white smoke, he explained his plan.

"That's really smart," Gina said, making him smile with pride. "Would you please help Rachel with her pack? She keeps saying it's too loose and I can't seem to adjust it right. While you're doing that I'll see if I can wake Charlie up."

"What's the matter with your pack, honey?" he asked. "Bring it over here and I'll see if I can fix it."

"It hangs down too much on one side and it bounces all over," Rachel said, lifting the backpack, "and it—"

"Oh God, David, come quick!" Gina cried, sounding a thin hair away from hysteria. "Charlie, he, he won't wake up! I, I think he's dead!"

"Rachel, you stay right there and don't move," David ordered. "Gina, why don't you go stand with Rachel, she's really scared."

By the time David knelt down next to Charlie, his eyes were open.

"Sorry 'bout that, didn't mean to scare everybody," Charlie said, voice weak. "I'm winding down like an old clock and it's real hard for me to wake up now. Now that I'm up, I'm ready to go when you are."

This time, David didn't waste time finding out how well Charlie walked. Hoisting him to his feet, David turned and hunkered down. Slumping forward, Charlie leaned against his back and wrapped both arms around his neck. Locking his wrists behind Charlie's thighs, David straightened up, wincing at the stench of rot rolling off his friend, and they were off.

"That-a-way, please," Charlie said, pointing his left forefinger and making a strange rasping noise that took David a second to recognize as laughter. "I think there's only one hill left to climb, but it's a beaut."

Pushing his way through the last of the alders, David stepped out into the forest beyond. Following Charlie's directions, he followed a faint path that would through stands of silver birch and maple trees. Staying close, Gina, Rachel, and Susie brought up the rear. Noticing a large shaft of bright sunlight a hundred yards or so ahead, David increased his pace a little. A minute later they broke out of the deep woods and stood looking up at the last hill.

"Kiss a pig," David groaned, heart sinking. "How are we ever going to climb that thing?"

Most of the slope wasn't as steep as those they had climbed earlier in the day, but it was far taller with fewer trees and bushes to use as handholds. The last twenty-five feet below the summit was a near vertical collar of bare stone.

"It gets easier after this," Charlie said, which for some reason set David to laughing.

"Said Mallory to Irvine," he replied, laughing so hard that he had to set Charlie down before he dropped him. "Th, thanks, Charlie, I needed that. Everybody sit tight for a few minutes and I'll be right back."

Still laughing, David started picking his way across the base of the slope, searching for a safe route to the summit. The trees and bushes were thickest on the left side of the slope and there was a ravine eroded into the rock that extended all the way through the vertical collar of stone just below the summit. The route looked dangerous, but it was the only way up and over that he could see.

The first part of the climb went far better than David could have hoped. Moving in short stages, they easily ascended the first two-thirds of the slope. The last third though more than made up for the easy going and then some.

Craning his head back, David scanned the few yards remaining to the summit. The granite was sheer, near vertical, worn smooth by eons of rainfall and snowmelt. Not possible, he decided, they would have to climb down a find a way around this bitch of a hill. Peering down, he suddenly froze, muscles cramping as he clutched at the unyielding stone.

If they tried to climb back down, David knew they would all fall to their deaths. How or why he knew such a thing he couldn't say, but David was certain that he was right. Drawing in a deep breath, he closed his eyes and rested his forehead against the cold stone.

"Charlie," David asked, feeling foolish for not having thought of it earlier. "Can you use the staff to help us out here?"

"I'm sorry, David, but no," Charlie told him. "All the power in the staff is being used just keeping me alive. I'm getting near the end and I no longer have the strength to control it. The staff is on autopilot now, doing what it wants, when it wants. I'm sorry, David, I truly am. I'd help you if I could, but I can't."

"Guess that settles that," he sighed, trying to force his cramped muscles to relax. "Let's get you in your sleeping bag before you get any colder."

Working carefully, David eased Charlie into his sleeping bag. Picking up Rachel, he set her against the innermost face of the ravine in the crook of Charlie's left arm.

"You stay right there and don't move," he told her, hoping that his next statement was true, "and I'll be right back down to get you."

"Yes, sir," Rachel replied, yawning and curling up in the crook of Charlie's arm.

"Board! Going up!" David called, reaching down and pulling Gina to her feet. "Top floor, ladies' lingerie, men's haberdashery, perfumes and notions, board!"

"David, I can't, please!" Gina begged, clinging to him so tightly it was painful. "I'm really scared, I—"

"You can, you will, you must," he said, wrapping an arm around her waist and pulling them up a couple of inches before he lost his nerve. "I know you're scared, we're all scared, but if you'll help me, I know we can do this."

"Okay, David, if you say so, I'll try."

"I'm going to keep one arm around you," he explained, hoping that it would work, "and we're going to climb up together like a giant spider."

Creeping upward, they arrived at the vertical band of rock just below the summit ten minutes later. The face never exceeded an angle of seventy degrees, but to Gina and David it felt nearly vertical. Drenched in sweat, they lay stretched out on the cold stone, gasping for breath.

"Oh no, David, help me!" Gina moaned, starting to cry. "It's Jillian, she wants to talk to me, and she won't leave me alone!"

"Tell her to go away, you're busy right now," David said, worried that Gina might become delusional and wander off again, this time to her death. "Tell her that you're busy, but that you'll come over later today and play dolls. Tell her that and try to focus your mind on something, anything, but her."

"Okay, I will," Gina replied, remembering now the garden The Eldest had given her. "I did and she's gone, at least for now!"

"Good. If she tries to come back, tell her the same thing and keep your mind focused on something else. Come on now, let's get you up on top and then I can go back for Rachel."

The ravine they had been climbing narrowed as it passed through the vertical collar of rock just below the summit. Unable to crawl two abreast in the narrow fissure, David put Gina in the lead and spotted her from behind. Just short of the summit, the ravine terminated in a vertical stone wall five feet tall.

"David, I don't think I can climb that," Gina said. "I'm only five foot three tall and I can't even stand up to catch hold of the top."

"Walk up the wall on your hands until you reach the top," he told her, afraid this might be an obstacle they couldn't overcome, "then jump up. I'll be right behind you and I won't let you fall, I promise."

Creeping up the wall using her hands, Gina reached the top and stood frozen, waiting for David to join her.

"Take off your pack and throw it over the top," he said, reaching up from below and steadying her. "Just take your time, I've got you."

Moving with great care, Gina eased her arms out of the pack's shoulder straps. Raising the pack over her head, she heaved it over the wall, grunting with the effort.

"Good job!" David exclaimed. "Now just be still and let me get up there with you."

Mindful not to disturb her balance, David walked his hands up the wall until he was standing behind her. Moving slowly, he placed his right hand, then his left, on her waist.

"On the count of three," he said, aware that he wasn't standing on much more than thin air, "you're going to jump and I'm going to lift. Ready? One, two, three, jump!"

Boot toes scrabbling for purchase on the smooth granite wall, Gina hoisted herself up while David lifted with all of his strength. Supporting her weight on her forearms, she clawed at the stone shelf and began inching forward. A metallic scraping noise sounded and her forward progress stopped.

"Shit! I'm stuck!" she said, voice muffled by the intervening rock. "It's my belt buckle, I'm hung up on it and I can't move!"

Deciding this wasn't the time or the place for propriety or for half measures, David did the first thing that came to mind. Placing his hands on the twin globes of Gina's ass, he pushed, HARD. Yelping in surprise as her hips lifted, she started moving forward again. As she struggled to pull the rest of her body up onto the stone shelf, one of her boots slipped on the slick stone and she kicked David in the chest. Arms windmilling for balance, he cried out once and fell away from the stone parapet.

"David? David?" Gina called, crawling to the edge of the drop-off and peering down. "Day—"

"I'm right here, don't worry," he said from the mouth of the ravine a few feet below. "By the way, that's a really nice butt you got there, lady."

"I, thank you, are," she stammered, smiling as relief set in, "are you all right?"

"I'm fine," he replied, grinning as he rubbed at the newest additions to his collection of bumps and bruises. "My kingdom for a Three Musketeers bar and a cold Coke though."

"Me too," she sighed, smile gone now. "David, I'm not being whiney or anything, but could you please hurry? I'm real scared being up here by myself, so could you please hurry so that we can all be together again?"

"Yeah, I know, we all need to get off this damn rock. Let me throw my pack over the top and I'll be on my way back down. Just remember what we talked about and you'll be fine."

"Okay, I will," she said, sounding tense and frightened. "Just hurry please, I'm really scared."

"Yes ma'am, I aim to please," he told her, scrambling up to the stone parapet and throwing his backpack over the top. "Be back in a minute."

Descending the face, David found himself in a classic hominid quandary. His eyes were set wide, providing excellent binocular vision for an animal utilizing bipedal locomotion. In other words, he couldn't see a damn thing except the rock in front of his nose. Deciding it would take hours otherwise; he took a deep breath and pushed off. Keeping his feet raised, he started sliding down, using his hands to brake to a halt every ten feet to fifteen feet. Five minutes after leaving Gina, he slid to a stop next to Rachel and Charlie and took a seat on the small ledge.

"Cool!" Rachel enthused, clapping her hands. "That looks like fun! I'm glad you're back, Mr. David, because I'm ready to go now."

"Why's that?" David asked, enjoying the luxury of sitting on something solid. "You miss your mom?"

"Yes, sir, and I have to go to the bathroom real bad."

"Okay, we'll get going," he agreed, standing up and positioning himself in the ravine. "Now you come over here and we'll—"

Before David could stop her, Rachel was by him and starting up the slope. Possessed by the confidence of the very young she didn't bother crawling up the slope, but rather ran upright bent over in a slight crouch.

"Rachel, get down on your stomach or you'll fall!" David shouted, climbing in pursuit as fast as he dared.

"No, Mr. David, I can't," she shouted without even bothering to look back. "I really gotta g-o-o-o-o!"

"Son-of-a-bitch, will you look at her go, like a goddamn monkey goin' up a banana tree," he seethed, pounding the rock in frustration. "I swear to God those two will be the death of me yet!"

"David, you have no idea," Charlie said from a few feet below, laughing so hard that it triggered a coughing attack that left him gasping for air.

By the time David had climbed another five yards up the face, Rachel had arrived at the parapet wall and was reaching up for her mother's hands. Yielding to the obvious, David lay prone on the rock and watched Rachel scramble up and over the parapet with her mother's help. Mother and daughter waved, then walked away from the edge and disappeared. Swearing under his breath, David slid the few yards back down to Charlie.

"Sometimes," Charlie observed, "a little girl does what a little girl's gotta do."

"Well, I just wish she'd find a way to do it that didn't give me heart failure," David said, smiling a bit as the humor of the situation sunk in. "Undo your belt, Charlie. I'm going to join yours to mine, strap you on my back, and then we're out of here."

Wedging himself against Charlie, he joined their two belts together. Bending forward a little, David waited while Charlie tied the sleeping bag to the back of his belt.

"Damn it!" Charlie muttered, struggling to tie a solid knot with his hands behind his back. "Ah, there, got it!"

"Okay then, we're off," David said, stepping down off the ledge into the bottom of the ravine.

"Holy moly!" Charlie exclaimed, squeezing his eyes shut after daring a quick look down. "I sure hope you favor quality leather accessories."

"If I don't, you're going to be among the very first to know."

"That's very comforting, honest it is."

Laughing, David began the ascent to the summit. Climbing steadily, he dragged himself and Charlie up to the collar of stone ringing the summit. Keeping his fingers wedged into cracks in the rock, David rolled over on his left side and tried to ease his cramping muscles.

"All right," he told Charlie, "one more big push and we're there."

At first, David didn't think they would both fit in the narrow fissure leading up to the summit. With some creative wiggling though, he maneuvered them into the mouth of the shaft and started climbing. The fit was tight enough that the sides of the shaft helped support their weight. Finding this part of the climb far easier than he had expected, David reached the top of the fissure ten minutes later.

Pinning Charlie against the wall, David fumbled with the belts joining them together and finally got them unbuckled. Reaching around to the small of Charlie's back, he tried to untie the sleeping bag but the knot was cinched impossibly tight. Pulling his hand back, David fished around in the left-hand cargo pocket of his parka and pulled out a folding lock-blade knife. Opening the blade, he reached around Charlie's back and started groping for the strap.

"Eeyow!" Charlie yelled, starting so violently that he began sliding back down the ravine.

"Whoa boy!" David said, pinning Charlie against the rock wall after he had slid down a few inches. "What's the matter?"

"Don't quit your day job and take up a career in surgery," he replied, laughing. "You just stabbed me in the ass."

"Jesus, I'm sorry! Are you going to be all right?"

"I'll do, but I sure would like to get off this goddamn rock and get on with it."

"You and me both," David agreed, finally locating the strap and cutting the sleeping bag free.

Climbing the few feet to the parapet wall, David threw the sleeping bag up and over the top. Unable to keep his balance any longer, he slid down the parapet and came to rest sitting upright at its base. Fatigue was setting in and David knew that he had to get off the rock face soon or else die on it.

"I'm gonna bring Charlie up in a minute, so get ready to help haul him up," he called up to Rachel and Gina. "How're you two doing?"

"About the same," Gina told him. "I'll be really glad when you get up here."

"Okay," he said, concerned for her but unable to do anything about it, "I'll be back with Charlie in a minute."

Pushing off, David started sliding back down the ravine. Weary, he missed handholds as they flashed by and began accelerating. Rachel, Gina, and Charlie's voices all blended into an incoherent shouting babble. Just before he would have knocked Charlie of the face, his left hand jammed in a crack and halted the slide. Inertia took him, lifting his body up off the rock. For a moment David hung suspended in space, attached to the rock face only by the four fingers of his left hand. Gravity kicked in and he slammed back down on the granite, fetching Charlie a solid kick in the head as he landed.

"Oh man!" David groaned, left arm feeling as if it had just been torn out of the socket. "That felt so good I oughta do it again.

"Let me get my head out of the way before you do," Charlie said, rubbing at a goose egg on his right temple. "Are you going to be all right?"

"Yeah, I think so; I just wrenched my left arm and shoulder pretty good. Give me a second and we'll get going."

Feeling his arm stiffening up, David decided to start climbing immediately. Wrapping his right arm around Charlie, he crept up the fissure to the base of the parapet wall. Getting a shoulder under Charlie's torso, David hoisted him up until Gina and Rachel could catch hold of his arms.

"On three, I lift and you pull," David told them. "One, two, three, go!"

Gina and Rachel pulled on Charlie's arms as hard as they could while David grabbed the waistband of his jeans and lifted. For a moment nothing happened, then suddenly Charlie was rising up and over the parapet wall. Releasing his hold, David slid down until he was seated in the mouth of the fissure.

"I'll be up in a minute," he called to the others. "Just let me catch my breath."

"No, Mr. David, you can't!" Rachel cried, leaning out over the edge of the parapet. "Susie's down there. You can't leave her! You can't!"

Squeezing his eyes shut, David took a deep breath and tried to remain calm.

"David, you can't, you just can't," Gina said, hauling Rachel back from the edge by the hood of her parka. "Your arm is stiff and you're really pale. Susie's really smart; she'll find another way around and catch up with us later."

"You're right," David admitted, hating the necessity of what lay ahead. "But I just can't leave her, I'm not made that way. There's a spare long-sleeved flannel shirt in my pack. Would you throw it down here please, I'll need it to make a sling for her."

"David, you—" she began.

"The shirt, Gina, please," David interrupted, using a peremptory courtroom voice that he hadn't used in years. "The sooner I start, the sooner I get back, so hurry up please."

The flannel shirt came flying down a few seconds later and landed within six inches of him. Opening his parka, David tied the shirt around his chest then zipped the coat shut. Overhead but unseen, he could hear Gina's muffled crying.

"Gina, listen, I'm sorry," he called, regretting his curt tone toward her. "I'll be fine, I promise. We'll talk when I get back in a few minutes."

Gina shouted something down to him, but David couldn't make out the words over the sound of fabric rustling and tearing as he slid down the fissure. Cautious after his earlier near miss, he spread his arms and legs and succeeded in controlling the slide. Still though, it was a wild ride. Six stops later, David found Susie standing on the ledge everyone had started out from hours before.

"Hey there, Toots," he said, reaching out to give her ears a scratch.

Whining, Susie climbed into David's lap. Wrapping both arms around her, he closed his eyes and fell into a half-sleep. It would be so easy and so nice just to sit here on this comfortable ledge with Susie in his arms and wait for whatever. No more magic, no one dying while he watched, no more amorous crazy women, no children who thought they were monkeys, no more fear, none of it. Just he and Susie sitting together in the afternoon sunshine. Pretty soon the hours would tick by and he and Susie would get to be with Jennifer and Allison and everything would be all ri—"

"Ain't gonna happen," David snapped, coming fully awake and squeezing Susie so hard that she yelped in pain. "Get out of my head, asshole, and stay out of it."

Thunder rolled out across the hills and underneath the tumult David heard cold, mocking laughter.

"Go ahead and laugh, motherfucker!" he screamed, pounding on the granite in his fury. "I hope you're still laughing when I rip your goddam heart out! I am coming and you are going to die!"

Jerking down the zipper of his parka, David untied the flannel shirt wrapped around his chest. Passing the shirt under Susie's body, he knotted the end of the sleeves together. Picking Susie and holding her against his chest with one hand, David put the sling over his head and zipped his parka halfway shut with the other.

Stepping down off the ledge, he started climbing back toward the summit with Susie whining in his ear. Adrenalin carried David back to the stone collar, but no further. Collapsing on his side, David stared up at the narrow fissure leading up to the summit. The sun had moved a couple of degrees and the narrow cut was now dark. Somehow, he knew that death was close and he began shaking.

"We're so close," he whispered, tears pricking at the corners of his eyes, "and I can't go any further. I just fucking can't!"

For long minutes, David lay shaking on the cold granite. Eventually though the shaking stopped and he lay still. Feeling confined and frightened, Susie whimpered and licked his face until she got a response.

"Okay, okay, I get the idea," he said. "Well, we'll either be at the top or the bottom pretty soon. Either way, I want to get it done and over with."

Moving so slowly that it was barely perceptible; David began inching his way up the narrow ravine. At times, he slid back more than he advanced, but somehow he kept battling upwards. When he was halfway up the chute, Gina and Rachel began shouting encouragement, but David didn't hear them, trapped in his private war with the rock face.

Reaching the parapet, he clawed his way up the wall until he got one arm up over the top. Six fumbling attempts later he managed to get his parka unzipped. Pinning Susie up against the wall so that she wouldn't fall, David eased the sling over his head using his sore left arm. Reaching down, he grabbed Susie by the nape of the neck and lifted her toward the shelf.

"Don't drop her, honey," he begged Rachel as she reached down for Susie. "Please don't drop her."

"I won't, Mr. David, I promise," Rachel said, reaching down and grabbing Susie's collar. "I got her! C'mon, Susie, c'mon!"

Pulling hard with an assist from Gina, Rachel got the front part of Susie's body up on the shelf. Feeling something solid under her, Susie engaged all-paw drive and scrambled up onto the shelf.

"Come on, David," Gina said, reaching down and taking hold of his hands. "You're next and then were done."

"Not just yet," David lied, knowing that he was too spent to climb over the parapet and that Gina and Rachel weren't strong enough to pull him up. "I'm just going to slide down the wall and rest for a few minutes."

"No, David, stay where you are," Charlie ordered, slowly crawling to the edge of the parapet, "and listen to me very carefully."

Lifting his head, David looked at him in disbelief. Charlie's appearance was worse than ever, yet his voice was the strong, vibrant baritone of a few days ago.

"Take hold of the head of the staff," Charlie directed, thrusting it over the lip of the parapet, "and empty your mind. You have to help me, David, because I am too sick and too weak to do it by myself."

Reaching up, David grasped the staff and for the first time felt its immense power. Closing his eyes, he imagined a blank white screen. Suddenly he was floating, a drifty-dreamy feeling as if he was in the grip of a high fever. Charlie screamed in agony and he fell a couple of inches down onto the stone shelf. When he awoke sometime later, the others were all staring down at him.

"Greetings, Earthlings, live long and prosper," David said, closing his eyes because staring up at them was making him dizzy. "What happened and how long have I been out?"

"You fainted," Gina replied. "You were only out a minute or so."

"Climbing up and down mountains all day always gives me a case of the vapors. Speaking of all day and I hate the thought of it, but we probably ought to camp here. I don't know what time it is, but it's getting late and we don't want to be stumbling around in the dark."

"It's really funny, but it's not late," Gina told him, sounding puzzled. "It seems like it should be, but it's not."

"Can't be," David said, fumbling with his coat sleeve to expose his wrist-watch. "Its gotta be at least four o'clock. We've been climbing around on Mt. Everest here for hours."

Raising his watch to eye level, David read it once, then twice, then thrice. Exactly thirty-two minutes had elapsed since they had left the alder thicket. Closing his eyes, David let his arm drop and breathed deeply until everything stopped spinning.

"My watch must be broken," he reasoned, pleased at finding a logical solution to the conundrum. "It's the only—"

"Your watch is fine, David," Charlie interrupted, fishing around in his pocket. "Time and space are different here. That doesn't mean that a lot of time hasn't passed since we left the alder thicket because it has. It just passes differently here, that's all. The sun will not set today until our business with him is finished one way or the other."

"Thank you, Mr. Wizard," David sighed, groaning as his left calf spasmed into a vicious cramp. "Oh son-of-a-bitch, that hurts!"

"Here, chew this, I'm past needing it," Charlie said, handing him a wad of resinous organic material about the size and shape of a jelly bean. "Be warned though, it doesn't taste very good. Chew it like gum and swallow the juice until nothing is left. Then sleep for ten minutes or so and you should be good for another twelve hours. Try and not puke it up, it's all I have left."

"That's encouraging," he commented, sniffing at the resinous mass with a dubious look on his face. "Something tells me I really don't want to know what's in this."

"You sure don't," Charlie said, sounding weak and sick again. "Rachel, will you please get David a water bottle out of the pack over there, he's probably going to want it. You'll have to excuse me everybody, but I'm going to lie down and rest until we're ready to go again."

Waiting until Rachel handed him the water bottle, David popped the resinous mass into his mouth and started chewing. A vile medicinal taste flooded his mouth and he swallowed hard to avoid vomiting. Unscrewing the top of the water bottle, he took a long sip and kept on chewing. The agonizing cramp in his leg eased almost immediately. Impressed at least with the results, he kept chewing and sipping until both the medicine and the water were gone.

"Please don't let me sleep too long," he said to Gina, yawning and suddenly unable to keep his eyes open, "no more than twenty minutes or so."

Waking on his own a little later, David was amazed and a little frightened at how rested and well he felt. His fatigue and assorted aches and pains were gone, replaced by a numb tingling feeling that permeated his entire body. While David could sense that his various aches and pains were still there, he couldn't feel them. It was as if he had received a systemic Novocain injection.

"Are you sure you don't want to sleep a little longer?" Gina asked. "You only slept for a couple of minutes and you must still be exhausted."

"No, I'm fine," he replied, so full of energy that he no longer felt like laying down. "Let's get ready to go, I want to get this done and over with."

Walking over to Charlie, David knelt and tried to wake him. Groaning in his sleep, Charlie stirred a little but wouldn't wake up."

"He's been like that since he laid down" Gina said. "I think getting you up and over that ledge took an awful lot out of him."

"Let's get him out of the sleeping bag and then I'll get him up on my back and he can sleep for as long as he wants."

While David lifted him, Gina tugged the sleeping bag out from under Charlie and rolled it up. Lifting Charlie up on his back, David felt a stab of fear at how much lighter he was then when they had scaled the rock face together. Whatever was inside of Charlie was devouring him at a frenetic pace and David felt a renewed sense of urgency about getting him into a hospital.

"Stay close and make sure you hold Rachel's hand," David said, walking toward the forest a few yards away.

"Are you sure you're going the right way?" Gina asked, crowding in close behind him. "With Charlie sleeping we could get lost, couldn't we?"

"I don't think it much matters anymore," he replied after a little thought. "No matter where we go now, we're going to end up where we need to be. Besides which, there's only one path so we're going to take it."

A few yards down the trail, the vegetation thinned out and the terrain became level with the exception of a few gentle slopes. Pausing to look around, David was reminded of rolling English parklands he had seen on a vacation years before. Pleased with the prospect of increased speed, he congratulated himself on catching their first break in an otherwise shitty day.

`"Mommy, what's that?" Rachel asked, pointing ninety degrees off to the left.

Looking where Rachel's finger was pointing, David saw a vintage 1930's washing machine standing in the midst of a grove of birch trees. A wet pair of denim overalls was hanging in the exposed wringers and a box of Boraxo laundry soap was sitting on the ground in front of the machine.

Laughing David walked over and examined the machine with Rachel and Gina. "No tickee, no takee, extra starch please."

A short green hairless creature with large, almond-shaped black eyes and three long, spatulate fingers on each hand popped out from behind a tree. Startled, David backed up in a hurry, almost tripping over Rachel and Susie. Gina reached out and steadied him just before he would have fallen. They retreated together as the creature continued advancing, chittering and shaking one of its odd looking fingers at them.

"It's called a Collector," Charlie said, nearly earning himself a trip to the ground when David jumped in fright, "and they're mostly harmless, except that they'll steal anything that isn't nailed down and then arrange it. Just step forward and shake your fist at it and it'll take off."

"It's ET," Rachel giggled, delighted and certain that she had been right all along, "but he's mad!"

Angry with the creature for startling them, David took a step forward and shook his fist at it. The Collector ducked behind a birch tree, chittered once, and vanished from sight.

"That was too strange," he said, not knowing quite what to make of the encounter. "It looked like one of those aliens in those abduction stories you see on TV."

"They don't abduct people," Charlie told him, chest gurgling as he spoke. "But they do steal their dreams and nightmares. The people they steal from somehow subconsciously remember the experience and it traumatizes them."

Hearing someone crying, David turned and saw Gina sobbing into her hands while Rachel clung to her waist.

"Gina, what's the matter?" he asked, setting Charlie down and propping him against a tree. "What's wrong?"

"It's, it's everything," she wailed, hugging David with one arm and holding onto Rachel with the other. "I, I can't take any more! Trees that kill things and climbing around on mountains and, and aliens! I, I just want to go home and be left alone! I, I—"

Unable to speak further, Gina collapsed into full-blown hysteria. At a loss, David stood holding her. A pair of unpleasant memories surfaced and suddenly he knew what to do.

"Let her be," David said, taking Gina's chin in his hand and staring deep into her eyes. "Get out, foul thing. We are coming to kill you no matter what you do, so just give it up and get ready to die."

Thunder boomed again, but this time there was a note of frustrated fury underlying it.

"Th, thank you, David," Gina sobbed, upset but no longer hysterical. "I was thinking about my garden and he snuck up on me and, what are you smiling about?

"Because he's afraid," David replied, "and that makes me very happy."

It took another ten minutes to get Gina and Rachel calmed down enough to get underway again. Fifty yards further on, they found a child's inflatable pool float shaped like a sea monster lying in the center of the path. A face-mask and snorkel were strapped to the monster's head. A full set of scuba gear was stacked neatly inside the ring.

"Jesus," David muttered, unsettled by the strange collage, "that is just too strange for words.

There was no sign of the Collectors in the immediate area, but he could somehow sense they were near. The creatures were small enough to hide behind almost anything and trees lined both sides of the path. Feeling Gina's hand start trembling on his arm, David hurriedly led them on.

A few minutes later, two people walked around the corner of a small log cabin a hundred yards ahead and vanished. There was something odd about the two figures but they had vanished so quickly that David couldn't say what it was. Turning off the path, he hurriedly led Rachel and Gina behind a small stand of fir trees.

"Now what," David said, annoyed by this latest delay. "I didn't think anyone lived—"

"They don't live, they haven't since 1955 when I killed them all, even the children and the babies," Charlie wept, frightening his friends. "Go ahead and follow the path into the village, they won't hurt you, they can't. I need you all to witness something so that I can end my life in peace. Please, it won't take very long and then we can be on our way."

With Charlie's tears dripping cold down the back of his neck, David started walking down the path toward the village. As they approached the outskirts, three of the villagers wandered out of the trees and he felt the short hairs on his neck bristle. The villagers were specters, cocooned inside transparent veils of blue fire. Realizing what the source of that fire must have been, David shuddered but kept on walking.

As they drew closer, more of the village and its inhabitants became visible. From the number of cabins,

David estimated the population at somewhere between one hundred to one hundred and fifty people. Walking into a large open area in the center of the village, he watched uneasily as the spectral villagers congregated around them.

"Set me down please, David," Charlie said. "I have to stand on my own to do this. Just look after Rachel and Gina and listen. Hear what I say, David, and remember it always."

Bending his knees, David eased Charlie down off his back. Turning, he stood with arms outstretched until he was sure Charlie wasn't going to fall. Stepping back, he gathered up Rachel in one arm and put the other around Gina's waist. After looking at the crowd of villagers for a few seconds, he decided they were more forlorn than menacing. Curious, Rachel stared wide-eyed at the crowd of ghosts surrounding them.

"Hear me!" Charlie called out, tapping the staff three times against the ground. "I, Charles Lantot Redbird, staff bearer, wish to confess my crimes to these, my dear friends, and to you, my beloved people."

"Angered by what I perceived as your indolence, your sloth, I started ruling you with the power of the staff. In time you came to hate me and led by my older brother Robert, you came under the sway of the Dark One, him whom we call Wendigo or Trickster.

"Seeking to wrest the staff from me, my brother Robert and four others came to my home on the edge of this, our village. I was away on an errand, but my wife Mary was out back picking late season apples. Seizing her, my brother Robert and the four other men raped her then passed her onto Mancun and the Lapushtan. They in turn delivered my Mary to The Wendigo, who has raped and tormented her ever since.

"Sensing what was happening, I started for home, but I couldn't get here quick enough to save her. When I finally arrived, I found that our cabin had been burnt to the ground. Our two young sons, John and Michael, burned to death when their Uncle Robert, my older brother, caught them and threw them into the fire which he had started.

"In my grief and my rage at murder of my family, I unleashed the full power of the staff upon you, my people, condemning you to eternal half-life in this awful place. I made no effort to determine who amongst you had wronged me or why. Instead, I lashed out, killing all of you, e, e, e, even the children and the babies.

"As soon as I acted, I regretted it. For decades now I have searched for you and endured the poison thorns you left behind, trying to put right the terrible crimes I committed against you. Now, with the hours of my life almost gone, I have found you at last. Forgive me, please, so that I may die in peace and my spirit can reside among you for all time."

Seconds passed, then a minute, and still nothing happened. A sizzling electric noise swept through the crowd of revenants and David felt the earth tremble beneath his feet. The specters began advancing, tightening their ring. Suddenly, the crowd stopped as if on cue. One of the spirits, an older male near Charlie's age, stepped forward and touched the staff. Blue fire flared and the specter vanished, released by the power within the staff. One after another, the revenants stepped forward, touched the staff, and were freed. Within two minutes all but five of the spirits were gone.

The five remaining specters huddled together at what had been the furthest edge of the ring a short time before. Raising the staff, Charlie tapped it against the ground and the shades slowly came forward, obeying the summons. As they neared, David could see a family resemblance between the tallest revenant and Charlie. But where Charlie was a kindly looking man, the shade of his brother Robert exuded purest malice.

"I cannot forgive any of you, especially you, Robert, for what you did to me and mine," Charlie said, sounding tired and used up. "But it is not up to me to judge you, that is for She That Waits, The Great Mother. Step forward, touch the staff, and let us have an end to this nightmare that started so long ago. If it is any comfort to you, brother, and I'm sure it is, I will die soon, and then it truly will be over for all of us."

The five revenants stood glaring, unmoving, and Charlie tapped the staff against the ground once again. One by one, the specters were dragged screaming forward until their bodies made contact with the staff. The first four spirits met the same fate as their neighbors and were released from further torment. Robert Redbird though resisted the staff's power. Teeth bared, he stood glaring at Charlie.

"Come, Brother, I have neither the strength, nor the time, nor the patience for any more of your nonsense," Charlie told him. "Step forward, touch the staff and be judged, or try and walk away from the swift hand of the Great Mother. It's up to you; there are no other choices now."

"Weakling! Coward! You and your magic stick!" Robert spat as he turned and started walking away. "I was first-born, oldest, smartest, and I should have been chosen to wield the staff! Me, not you! I—"

A cloud of glowing blue mist materialized around Robert and suddenly he could no longer be seen. His one scream was muffled as if heard from a great distance.

And then there was nothing but a couple of handfuls of fine black ash drifting down the light afternoon breeze.

"I tried to tell him," Charlie said, weeping, "but he wouldn't listen to me. From the time we were children he would never listen to me."

Preoccupied with Rachel and Gina, David didn't see Charlie wobbling on his pins. Rachel yelled a warning and he looked up just in time to see him slam down hard on the ground. Fearing what he would find, David ran over and knelt by his friend.

"You know, David," Charlie said, exasperated, "this dying stuff is getting to be a major pain-in-my-ass."

"Well, you're not dead yet and maybe you won't end up that way if we can hurry up and get out of here. Are you all right?"

"Good as I'm gonna get," he sighed, coughing hard a couple of times and wiping a thin trickle of blood away from the corner of his mouth. "I'm ready to go when you are."

"Right now then," David said. "Let's get you up on Old Paint and then we're out of here."

Settling Charlie on his back, David paused and looked around. The wind had picked up a little and was whispering and crying around the deserted cabins. A rocking chair, set in motion by the fickle air currents, creaked back and forth on a porch a few yards to the left. Next to another cabin, an axe was leaning against a neatly stacked woodpile. A few feet away, a child-sized baseball bat was lying in the center of the path.

Without understanding why, David suddenly started running. Gina and Rachel called for him to stop, but he just kept running, desperate to escape this awful place. Reaching the outskirts of the village, he stopped and waited for them to catch up. Turning, he took one last, hard look back at the village. He never wanted to forget what had happened here or why it had happened.

"David, why did you run away?" Gina asked as she trotted up, crying again, which truth be told was getting on David's nerves something considerable. "You scared us, we were afraid we'd lose you."

Ready to bite, David saw how frightened they were and relented. "I'm sorry, I just couldn't stand being in that place any longer," he said, hoping they hadn't noticed his flash of irritation, "and I lost it and started running. We're all here now, so let's just keep moving."

Gina nodded and they started walking up the path again. But they didn't get far.

Two hundred yards after leaving the village, David's eyes slipped across and then returned to a flash of dark red about seventy-five yards ahead. Never taking his eyes off the splash of color, he tacked a few yards to the left for a better look.

For seven years he'd searched for this color, this shape. For seven years he'd literally scoured the Earth, devoting thousands of hours of his time and spending a few dollars short of a million searching for it. And now here it was, no more than seventy-five yards away. Here! At last!

When David started running this time, nothing was going to stop him and nothing short of a professional athlete was going to catch him. With every step he grew more certain, more sure that at last he had found it. Charlie said something urgent and yanked on his neck, but David was past hearing, past caring about anything except the dark red shape that was becoming clearer with every running step he took. At ten yards he was certain and loosed a fierce cry of joy. Lowering Charlie to the ground, he ran on, near certain now.

"David, wait, please!" Charlie called, fear plain in his voice. "Something here isn't right!"

Rushing around to the back of the vehicle, feet skidding on the snow, David knelt and checked the last confirming detail. Minnesota CH 5893 the license plate read and he knew that he had found it at last, the model year 1992 black cherry Toyota 4-Runner registered to his wife, Jennifer. He had gotten the SUV for her as a birthday present and she had been driving it the afternoon she and Allison had disappeared.

Sprinting up to the driver's door, David jerked it open and scrambled into the Toyota. The scent of the perfume Jennifer loved so much still hung faint in the vehicle's interior. A Raggedy Ann doll lay on the passenger side floorboards, his daughter Allison's favorite toy because her mother had made it for her. A brown leather purse was resting between the bucket seats and David fumbled it up onto his lap. Groping around in the bag, he pulled out Jennifer's wallet.

The hundred dollars or so in cash that he'd always insisted she carry was still there as were her credit cards. Removing the driver's license from the card pocket in the wallet, David held it up to his face and stared at it. A beautiful woman looked back at him. Her name was Jennifer Aubrey Garrison the license proclaimed, Age: 29, Height: 5'4", Weight: 118 lbs., Eyes: Blue, Hair: Blonde, Address: RR 3, Frechette, MN..

Reaching down with his free hand, David picked up the Raggedy Ann doll, crushed it to his chest, and wept. After all the long years of searching, he had found them, he was certain of it. They were here somewhere close, alive. He would not believe otherwise, he couldn't.

"Don't cry, David, everything is going to be fine," Jennifer said, her voice sounding from all around him.

"We'll be seeing you soon and there's so much I want to tell you."

"Daddy, would you come get us please?" Allison cried. "I'm scared and I wanna go home!"

"Jen, Allie, where are you?" David screamed, whipping his head around searching for them. "Where are you? Tell me and I'll come get you!"

The stereo, he realized, he had heard Jennifer and Allison's voices through the Toyota's stereo system. Reaching out, he put a finger on the stereo's power knob, uncertain about what to do next.

"Don't cry there, Davey-boy, you sniveling piece of shit!" The Wendigo howled as black smoke began pouring out of the stereo's CD slot. "Here, let me give you something to really piss yourself about."

The Toyota's power door locks activated and David yelled in fright as something smashed down on the front passenger side roof. A huge native man dressed only in a loincloth, buckskin leggings and moccasins leaped down onto the hood, rocking the vehicle on its suspension. The giant turned and faced the windshield and David got his first look at the monster; the red eyes, the scalp lock, the filed teeth, and the flint tomahawk. From Charlie's description, he guessed this must be Mancun and his heart quailed. Whatever it might take to kill such a creature, David was sure that he didn't have it and he wasn't likely to get it any time soon.

Spinning around one hundred and eighty degrees, Mancun began jumping up and down on the hood with a feral smile on his face. A few yards away, Rachel and Gina were trying to retreat into the safety of the forest, but the trees were too sparse to conceal them.

"Go ahead and run, you dumb cunts!" Mancun roared. "You'll just die tired!"

"Lemme out, lemme out!" a high-pitched voice called from David's shirt pocket. "Jesus tits, I gotta do everything around here myself? Look the fuck out, com-m-m-in' through!"

A spot the size of a fifty cent piece began smoldering on the front of David's parka. The pistol round that The Eldest had given him tumbled out of the hole and landed upright on his thigh.

"Just don't sit there, numbnuts, we got work to do," the cartridge said, face set in a scowl. "Now hurry up and get yews pistol out."

"Huh?" David managed, not believing what he was seeing and hearing.

"Whaddya mean, huh!" the bullet yelled, the top of its head glowing an incandescent red. "Your gun, your piece, your roscoe, heater, gat, pistola, shooter! Get it out, we ain't long on time here!"

Shoving his hand inside his parka, David wrapped his fingers around the butt of the 40 caliber Glock as the driver's side of the windshield exploded in his face. Howling in rage, Mancun jerked his tomahawk out of the passenger compartment, taking most of the steering wheel and the steering column with it. Swinging the tomahawk back across his body in preparation for a backhand decapitation stroke, Mancun grinned in savage triumph while David sat frozen with fear, certain somehow that his pistol would be useless.

"Got your priorities confused, don't you?" Charlie mocked, holding himself upright by leaning into the wedge formed by the passenger-side mirror and door. "But then again, you always were a dumb son-of-a-bitch."

A look of dismay spread across Mancun's face as the truth of Charlie's words sunk in. A thin filament of blue fire arced out of the staff's carved headpiece and struck Mancun in the chest. Compared to the power Charlie had once commanded, it was nothing, not much more than a static spark on a dry winter's day, but it was enough.

Screaming in pain, Mancun was blown off the hood, the center of his chest a blackened smoking ruin. The blast lifted the Toyota high on its left side wheels, sending Charlie sprawling to the ground. Seeing him fall, David tried to get out and help him, but discovered that the power door locks wouldn't release.

"Never mind that now," the cartridge commanded, rapping David smartly on his right forefinger knuckle. "Lock the slide open so I can climb in and we can get this show on the road. Today, David, today!"

Knuckle stinging, David grasped the butt of the Glock with his right hand and pulled back and locked the slide open with his left. The cartridge stuck its head into the open ejection port, but the rest of its body was too large to pass through.

"Think you could a got a smaller piece, say maybe a twenty-two or a BB gun?" the cartridge bitched, groaning as it slowly squeezed into the Glock's firing chamber. "Christ on a crutch, this is worse than trying to squeeze a fat lady into a size four Versace gown!"

Slamming down hard on his back, Mancun slid a couple of feet then kicked his knees up and executed a perfect backward somersault. Rolling to his feet, he back-pedalled a couple of steps until the force of the blast was exhausted and he was standing still, chest already healed. Throwing his head back, he howled until the cords in his massive neck throbbed and danced. Raising the stone tomahawk above his head, he started charging back toward the Toyota.

Something banged against the front passenger door and as David turned his head to look, Charlie's head slowly rose above the door. Bleeding from a deep gash in his left temple, he clawed at the mirror and slowly pulled himself upright.

"Yo, pay attention, we got things to do," the cartridge said. "Now push the cutesy little slide button by your right thumb and we're in business. DO IT, WE'RE ALMOST OUT OF TIME!"

Using his right thumb, David pushed the release lever and the slide ratcheted forward an inch and stopped. Looking out the hole where the windshield had been, he saw Mancun starting to charge, tomahawk raised high. Grabbing the gun's barrel, David slammed the slide against the dashboard, locking it shut. Flipping the gun back around so that he was holding the butt, he pushed the safety lever to the "fire" position and started aiming at Mancun.

"E-e-e-yow, the fuck are you doin' pinchin' my fat pad, moron?" the cartridge screeched, its voice echoing up the gun's barrel and sounding like it was emanating from the bottom of a deep well. "And put the safety back on and get your goddamn finger off the trigger. How'd you like it if I tried to kick you in the ass? Just put us up on the dash, cover your ears, and hang on. HURRY UP! YOU THICK OR SOMETHING?"

Startled, David dropped the pistol into his lap and from there it bounced off his right thigh and down onto the floorboard. Frantic to retrieve the gun, he started groping around his feet and pushed it under the driver's seat. A few yards away, Mancun halted and drew the tomahawk back past his ear.

"Goddamn it!" David raged, groping around under the seat. "Where is it? Gimme a break here!"

"Whattya, think I'm a paratrooper or somethin'?" the cartridge yelled from under the seat. "Now don't get your nutbag in a knot, you've almost got us. There, that's it, you've got us! Now put us on the dash! HURRY UP, TIME IS VERY SHORT NOW!"

Slamming the Glock down on the center of the dashboard, David started climbing out of the windshield hole intending to help Charlie. Shrieking, Mancun started whipping the tomahawk forward in a perfect overhand throw. Already halfway out onto the hood, David saw the blur of motion and knew what it portended. Pushing himself back in the passenger compartment, he ducked down behind the dash, nearly disemboweling himself on the jagged stump of the steering column.

"Ten, nine, fuck it, no time," the cartridge intoned, "one, fire-in-the-hole, blast-off!"

Altering his swing a little at the last second, Mancun threw the tomahawk with all of his might. Watching the tomahawk fly toward him, Charlie tried to duck and found that he couldn't move. Looking down, he saw that the staff had pinned him in the angle between the right front passenger door and the right passenger-side mirror. The succession was at hand and Charlie's time was almost up.

Throwing his head to the left, Charlie listened to the tomahawk sing by his ear. For a long second he thought he'd escaped unharmed, but then he felt the deep stinging in the right side of his neck and knew otherwise. It wasn't a long cut or a wide one, but it was perfectly placed and more than deep enough. Grabbing the side of his neck, Charlie slid down the side of the truck to the ground.

"You heartless fucks," he muttered, addressing both Mancun and the treacherous staff, "you've killed me."

Raising his hand, Mancun plucked the stone tomahawk out of midair on its return flight without even bothering to look at it. Certain that he had mortally wounded Charlie, he whooped with joy and charged toward David, intending to slaughter him and then collect the staff. After that, there'd be time for a quick snack of *Liver Bonne Femme* before dealing with his employer. Yes, things were shaping up nicely.

Crouched down on the driver's side floorboards, David crossed his arms over his face as a great roaring and shaking seized the Toyota. The few intact pieces of glass and plastic left in the vehicle began shattering. As he watched from behind his crossed arms, the Glock pistol began shaking itself apart. There was a final *pop!* and the cartridge flew out of the end of the barrel at a leisurely walking pace.

"Hoo-boy, am I ever glad to be outta there, worse'n bein' strapped in a whalebone corset, lemme tell ya," the cartridge said, winking over its sloped shoulder at David before turning its attention to Mancun. "And you, shut yer yap, you brayin', motheaten, snaggletoothed piece-of-shit!"

Calculating that the projectile would miss him by several feet, Mancun veered left but kept on coming. Blue smoke and the sound of screeching tires filled the air as the cartridge turned to intercept him. Wrinkling his nose in distaste, David swore that he could smell the stench of overheated asbestos brake pads.

Seeing the cartridge's maneuver, Mancun halted and stood waiting with an evil leer on his face. After all, he was Mancun the Great and this small, slow-moving bullet couldn't possibly hurt him. When the cartridge was about five feet away, he took a half-step forward and started swinging the flint tomahawk in an overhand killing stroke.

"Is the big strong man gonna hit me?" the cartridge jeered, altering neither its course nor its speed. "Oo-oo-oo, I'm scared, I'm scared! Go ahead and swing that stone-age toy, you overgrown, muscle-bound moron, and watch what happens!"

Shrieking in rage, Mancun struck the cartridge dead center on its point, intent on cleaving it in half. Sounding akin to an ice pack breaking up in the spring, the flint tomahawk shattered into hundreds of small pieces, leaving its owner holding nothing but an intricately carved handle with a few buckskin thongs hanging down from the top. The weapon that had slaughtered thousands in the centuries since its master first spelled it whole out of the earth was now nothing but a pile of stone chips lying on the snow covered ground.

A look of fear spread across Mancun's face as he finally realized that a mortal peril was almost upon him. Feet churning up clumps of snow, he tried to leap to the left. A three-foot long rooster tail of flame exploded out of the cartridge's round base, accelerating it into the center of Mancun's torso.

"On no ya don't, Chuckles, not this time. I got some-thin' just for you," the cartridge announced, anchoring its pointed nose in Mancun's belly. "I am the Seismic Sonic Hammer and you, junior, are my nail. Say goodbye because you're all done, son."

A subterranean roaring sounded, shaking the ground and throwing the battered Toyota SUV a couple of feet up into the air. An ear-shattering wave of sound closely followed the earthquake, throwing the vehicle back an equal distance before letting it fall to the ground. A millisecond later the cycle started again as the Seismic Sonic Hammer set about its work.

Seeing the trees and other debris being hurled about by the sonic hurricane, David stopped trying to get out of the Toyota. Grunting in pain as he banged his short ribs on the transmission shifter, he crawled over onto the front passenger-side floorboards before the vehicle's violent shaking impaled him on the jagged stump of the steering column. Sticking his head up over the dash a few inches, he risked a quick look.

Fifteen yards away, Mancun stood with his head thrown back and his jaws locked open in a scream that was lost to hearing in the gale. Where his torso had once been there was now a perfect circle, a clear window to the landscape beyond with the Seismic Sonic Hammer lodged at its exact center. Nothing remained now of Mancun except his head, lower arms, and lower legs. It was as if he was being erased with perfectly circular strokes.

A flash of motion out in the maelstrom caught David's eye and he ducked down behind the dashboard. A fifteen-foot long white pine tree shot through the space occupied by his head the second before. The ground shook and thunder rolled once more, and then suddenly it was quiet.

Squeezing between the pine log and the passenger seat, David climbed out the hole where the right front passenger door had once hung. Reaching up, he put both hands on top of the fender and pulled himself upright. Except for being dizzy as a child who has overindulged in a game of the Spins, he was unhurt. Raising his hands a couple of inches, he snapped his fingers. Although his ears were ringing a little, his hearing seemed unaffected by the sonic assault.

The dizziness started fading after a few seconds and with it the blear in his vision. Blinking rapidly, he started scanning the area around the Toyota. The earth had been scoured bare of trees, vegetation, and snow in a fifty yard circle around where Mancun and the Seismic Sonic Hammer had battled. There was no sign of either of them, which didn't bother David in the least. Growing anxious, he repeatedly swept his vision around the edge of the debris field, but still couldn't find what he was looking for. Double checking his bearings, he started trotting around the edge of the circle, peering under the blow-downs and piles of debris.

"I'm sorry, Davy, but this is all I can do for yews," The Eldest said deep inside his mind. "I can bend da rules, but I can't break 'em, that is for Her alone. The rest is up to yews now."

"Thank you," David replied aloud, unfazed by The Eldest's method of communication but deeply frightened by what it inferred. "I'll do my best."

"I know that, Davy, I never doubted it," The Eldest said, vanishing from his mind in a crackling burst of white noise.

An irregular shape a few yards away caught David's eye and he started running toward it. As he drew closer, the shape gained definition and became a boot. Dropping to his knees, he started pulling debris off Charlie. Frantic, he threw a pair of tree limbs aside and lifted the Toyota's right-front passenger door off him.

At first, David thought Charlie was lying in a patch of oddly colored mud. Then he noticed the wet stain soaking the right shoulder and arm of Charlie's coat and knew the truth. It wasn't possible, it just couldn't be. One elderly man couldn't possibly have that much blood circulating around inside of him. Some of it, maybe a lot of it, was blood. But the rest, the majority, was snowmelt and moisture from the recently exposed soil. Had to be, must be.

"Day," Charlie mumbled, stirring a little, "D-a-a-y—"

"I'm right here, Charlie," David said, reaching out and taking his hands, shocked at how cold and lifeless they felt. "Now you just lay still while I try and figure out what to do."

Lacking any sort of formal medical training, there was little David could do and he knew it. Warm, he decided, he could at least keep Charlie warm. Grasping the metal tab on his parka zipper, he pulled downward, but it refused to budge.

"A little help here, God," he begged, yanking on the zipper as hard as he dared but it still wouldn't move. "Just a little help here if you don't mind."

"Ellen," Charlie gurgled, "she needs—"

"Don't worry, I'll make sure she's fine," David said, raising his arms to slide the parka over his head. "Now you just be still and don't—"

That wasn't what Charlie was trying to tell him, but David wouldn't know that until much later. As Charlie's blood pressure crashed, it crossed a metabolic threshold and induced a *grand mal* seizure. Kneeling with the parka pulled halfway over his head, David was knocked flat on his back by Charlie's convulsing body. Recovering quickly, he rolled over and got to his knees. Tugging the parka back down, he tried to catch hold of Charlie's thrashing body but couldn't.

"Charlie, stop it, don't!" he screamed, weeping now. "Someone help us, please help us!"

Charlie's body went limp and he lay still. Desperate, David tried to think of something, anything, to help his friend.

"We're out of coffee," Charlie said and then he was gone.

CHAPTER 70

CLUTCHING THE RIGHT side of his throat with one hand and lashing out with the other, Gilbert struggled to wake from a terrible dream. Katie was sitting up in bed next to him, crying as if her heart would break.

"Was matter?" he asked, one foot still in the Land of Nod and in the firm grip of the nightmare. "You right?"

"It's, it's Charlie, he's dead, ah, ah, ah, a monster cut his throat and he bled to death," Katie replied, sobbing so hard that she was hiccupping. "And, and Ellen is going to die too unless someone helps her."

"Yeah, I 'member now," he said, grief ringing in his voice. "I think we better get to Frechette pretty quick or something awful is going to happen to Ellen."

"No offense, sweetie, but I'll drive because we gotta move it double quick," Katie said, blowing her nose and drying her eyes with a handful of tissues from the box on the night stand. "Now where'd I put my keys? I thought I put them right here on the dresser when we came in last night. C'mon, c'mon, dammit, where are, there they are!"

"You're right and I'm not offended," Gilbert told her. "Just don't get mad if I sleep most of the way because I really don't want to watch."

CHAPTER 71

QUIET FOOTSTEPS SOUNDED along the rear wall of the cabin, paused, and then faded away back toward the forest. Past caring, Ellen sat on the sofa staring at the weak light creeping in through the kitchen window. Dawn was here and she had survived the night, which amazed her.

Concentrating, she tried to remember what was ailing her. In, inc, damn it, yes, there it was, increasing neurological deficits, meaning that her central nervous system was deteriorating. By this evening at the latest, Ellen knew she would be dead or very close to it, a prospect which filled her with a strange kind of peace.

Thirsty, Ellen thought about getting a drink of water but knew that she was too weak to walk to the kitchen. Instead, she shifted her position on the couch, holding Charlie's shotgun across her lap and clutching the spay bottle of salt-water in her claw of a left hand. A minute later she fell into a light doze.

"Grandpa," she murmured in her sleep, certain that he had died in the early hours of the morning.

Around three a.m., her prisoner had begun shrieking, "Redbird dead, Redbird dead!" Agitated, the creature had started smashing against the floorboards until Ellen was certain that this time it was going to break through. Suddenly though it had howled and retreated, sounding fearful and confused. In the long hours since it hadn't resumed its assault on the floorboards. But it was still down there because she could hear it moving around and muttering.

"Oh Sweetums, wakey wakey!" the familiar voice roared from down below, jarring Ellen awake. "I've got something special for you and I can hardly wait to give it to you, bitch!"

"That's nice, Marcus," she mumbled, resting the fingers of her right hand on the shotgun's trigger guard, "because I have something for you too. Whenever you feel like it, come on up and get it."

CHAPTER 72

FORMERLY, THE WENDIGO had overwhelmed the throne's every dimension. Sitting on it now with his feet dangling several feet above the floor, he looked like Junior stealing a sit on daddy's La-Z-Boy. At ten feet tall and weighing over a ton, he was still a monster beyond nightmare, but nothing compared to the beast Charlie had battled for so many decades.

Cradling his chin in his hand, the Dark One sat thinking. Well, Redbird was finally dead. Which wasn't any great achievement on Mancun's part, Redbird had been as good as dead ever since he was bitten all those months ago.

The preliminary bouts were over, that was for sure. Nothing left now but the twelve round main card event, the title fight to end all title fights. It wasn't right that a creature of his vast importance and power had to do his own dirty work, but he was fresh out of troops thanks to Redbird and The Eldest. If that's what it took to gain possession of the staff, well, that was just the way it was going to be.

The humans had never been about much and they still weren't. Without Redbird's aid and counsel they would be helpless. Their lives were nothing more than lit candles soon to be extinguished. No doubt about it.

A clicking noise intruded on the monster's consciousness. Looking around, he located the source of the annoyance and glared, but the noise persisted. Angry, The Wendigo slammed his right hand down on top of his left, silencing the clatter created by the involuntary trembling of his talons against the arms of the throne.

CHAPTER 73

LAYING CHARLIE'S BODY under the transmission, David crawled out from under the Toyota. Working quickly, he started piling branches and brush around the SUV.

Finished building the brush barricade, David trotted back to where Charlie had fallen. Uncertain how to proceed, he stood there for a long moment looking puzzled. Maybe he should just leave it laying there on the ground and try to defeat The Wendigo without it. Somehow though he didn't think that was a very good idea.

"Well, ladies and gentlemen, boys and girls, children of all ages, and members of our studio audience, I guess this is the moment we have all been waiting for," he said aloud, bending down and picking up the staff.

Nothing happened and David snorted in disgust. Then the world vanished as he was engulfed in a shroud of blue fire. Opening his mouth, David tried to scream and found that he couldn't make a sound. Terrified, he tried to fling the staff away and discovered that he was bound to it as a fly is to flypaper. Then the fear passed and the rapture set in.

Once upon a wild undergraduate party years before, David had eaten a tab of nearly pure LSD-25, but that was nothing compared to this. He could hear the nearby trees respiring and could see the process of photosynthesis occurring at a molecular level.

A large male blue jay sat squawking atop a birch tree a hundred yards away. Focusing his vision, David was able to see every detail of the bird's bright plumage. Digging a little deeper, he was able to eavesdrop on the jay's simple, chaotic thoughts. Peeling back yet another layer, he was able to look at himself through the bird's eyes. The blue jay took flight and then he was the bird, wind sweeping over and under his wings, supporting him. Unbelievable.

In that instant, David knew he would never willingly surrender possession of the staff. The only exception would be if he fathered a son to succeed him as staff wielder. And since that blessed event was unlikely to happen, he would hold the staff against any and all whom who would claim dominion over it until the end of his life. Against all, no matter whom or what they were, no matter the cost.

Wrapped in the magic, David might have remained lost in reverie for hours had Rachel not interrupted. Raising his eyes, he scanned the surrounding landscape but couldn't see her. Puzzled, he started peering back even further between the trees before realizing that he had sensed, not heard, her.

Holding the staff at waist level, David slowly rotated his body until he fixed a bearing on Rachel. She was sitting at the base of a gentle slope, he saw, crying hard. Hoping that she wasn't too far away, he started jogging down the bearing. A hundred and fifty yards later he found her at the base of a small hill, still sitting, still crying.

"What's the matter, honey?" he asked, trying to catch his breath. "Where's your Mom?"

Hugging his shins, Rachel just shook her head and remained silent. Needing an answer, David reached down and tilted her face up so he could make eye contact with her.

"Who did that to your eye?" he asked, certain that he already knew the answer and hating it. "Did Mommy hit you in the eye?"

"Yes she did!" Rachel sobbed. "She said she wanted to go play dollies with Jillie and to leave her alone! When I tried to stop her, she pushed me down! I, I got up and tried to stop her and she hit me in my eye and pushed me down again! She, she said she didn't love me and didn't want to be my mommy anymore and then she ran away!"

"That wasn't your Mommy doing that, it was the boogie man making her do it," David said, struggling to keep the anger out of his voice. "I guess we better find her before anything else happens so we can help her and she can tell you that she's sorry. Do you remember which way she went when she ran away?"

"She went over that way," Rachel sniffed, pointing off to the left. "Between the big tree and the little one that looks like a bunny."

"You sure about that?" he asked, boosting her up on his shoulders. "Let's go take a look."

"I'm sure! See, there's her hat and her feet left marks and that's where she pushed me down. We gotta hurry, Mr. David, or the boogie man will get her for sure!"

"Okay, okay, keep your ears on. Now you hold on tight 'cause we're gonna go real fast."

Gripping Rachel's ankles with one hand, David leveled the staff with the other and willed something to happen. Slowly at first, then with increasing speed, they began moving even though his feet remained still. It wasn't running or any other sort of bipedal locomotion, and it wasn't flying, but rather an odd sort of hybrid that fell somewhere in between the two. Whatever it was, it was effortlessly covering hundreds of yards and David loved it.

The terrain began sloping upward and the trees and underbrush began thinning out. Even though the sun was still high in the sky the light was beginning to fail. Exerting his will, David slowed and then stopped. Reaching up, he lowered Rachel from his shoulders but kept her hand in his. Taking a deep breath, he stepped around the last tree and out onto a bare granite slope.

Twenty-five feet away, Gina was cowering between The Wendigo's feet. Deep in her mind, the monster was striding through the burning ruins of the garden The Eldest had given her. Becoming aware of Rachel and David, the beast swung his head around and stared at them.

"You should have run, humans," The Wendigo said, pinning Gina to the rock with a massive clawed foot. "Give me the staff and I will grant you a quick and merciful death. Cross me and I will flay your souls."

To David's eye, The Wendigo's form appeared mutable, in flux. Following a hunch, he envisioned the Mona Lisa and the monster assumed that form and pose. In rapid succession, he churned up consecutive mental images of an anaconda snake, a giraffe, and a koala bear. Each time, the monster morphed its form to match David's thought as soon as it jelled in his mind.

For the last permutation, David deliberately left his mind blank. After a second's hesitation, the beast mutated into a mottled, green reptilian creature no more than four feet tall. This, David realized, was the monster's true form.

Feeling the sudden decrease in weight on her back, Gina rolled to her left, sending The Wendigo crashing down on the stone. Getting up on her hands and knees, she scrambled over to Rachel and David. Wrapping both arms around Rachel, she collapsed at David's feet, babbling incoherently.

"We're not 'fraid of you!" Rachel yelled, fighting to escape David's grip so that she could wrap both arms around her mother. "You leave my Mommy 'lone!"

"I will rip you apart!" The Wendigo raged, talons ringing on the stone as he got up and started growing larger, much larger, with every syllable he spoke. "How dare you knock me down!"

"We dare, honest we do," David said, praying that this last premonition in a day chock full of them was also correct. "Tell you what, since you want it so bad, got get it!"

Cocking his arm back, he hurled the staff, not at The Wendigo, but at a small rock outcropping a few feet to the monster's right. As the staff left his hands, self-doubt swept through him, but by then it was too late to do anything about it. Blue flames exploded out of the staff's butt and a noise like a firing rocket engine sounded. Kicking his feet out from under him, David dropped down on top of Rachel and Gina, pinning them to the stone and protecting them.

Smashing into the outcropping, the staff buried half its length into the rock before the blue flames winked out. Silent now, it jutted from the stone as if waiting for someone to claim it. Unable to believe his good fortune, The Wendigo stood staring at the staff in disbelief.

"There it is!" David shouted, terrified that somehow everything would come undone at the last second, even though he had no idea what was supposed to happen. "Go get it, it's yours!"

"Weep not for your deaths, humans," the monster said, taking hold of the staff with both hands. "Your species, your world, is finished. Me and mine shall see to that, and over mine I shall rule as a god with the power you have so foolishly given me."

The staff began emitting a basso thrumming noise as the surface of the rock outcropping became molten and started spinning. Sensing the trap, The Wendigo released the staff and started scrambling backwards but it was too late. Increasing in size and speed, the vortex started drawing in loose leaves and debris from the rock face. Suddenly The Wendigo was sucked in up to his hips.

Fighting to keep Rachel and Gina anchored to the smooth stone; David raised his head and looked past the monster into the heart of the maelstrom. A pair of burning red suns hung low over a desert world of ocher sand and towering rock spires. Hordes of large insects scuttled across the stony ground and strange winged creatures resembling stingrays soared high overhead. The suction increased as the vortex roared ever louder and despite David's best efforts, they started sliding across the smooth stone toward the portal.

"Help me, human, help me!" The Wendigo shrieked, upper body flailing as he was sucked into the vortex.

"Help me and I'll give you anything you could ever desire! A-n-n-n-y-y-y-t-t-thing!"

"Anything?" David screamed back, barely able to make himself heard over the roar of the maelstrom. "Then give me your death, prick, in the name of my wife Jennifer and our daughter Allison and the life we should have had together!"

The Wendigo screamed again and then he was gone, consumed by the vortex and hopefully sent on to whatever lay at its other end. The maelstrom quickly decelerated and then vanished. The only sounds were the soft patter of leaves and debris falling out of the air onto the stone and Gina's incoherent babbling. Getting to his feet, David cautiously looked around, unable to believe that it was finally all over.

"Stay right here, honey," he said, addressing only Rachel. "Don't let Mommy wander off, okay?"

Walking the few steps over to the rock outcropping, David stood looking at the staff, wondering how he was going to free it from the stone. Taking hold of the staff with both hands, he pulled hard and nearly went over on his back when it slid smoothly out of the rock. A soft, dissonant chiming sounded as the granite congealed around a large iridescent crystal.

Stepping forward, he stared into the star-shaped sapphire. Although he wasn't certain, David thought he saw red eyes glaring out at him from far, far away. Good enough, or at least he hoped it was. Spreading his feet to shoulder width, he gripped the staff's carved headpiece with both hands.

"It is done!" he announced, tapping the staff three times against the stone, although he had no idea why he was speaking or acting in such a manner.

Rachel and Gina screamed and David's breath hissed out as the world suddenly went black. A second later, a thin crescent moon rose and strange star constellations started shining. Night, long delayed, had returned to First Land.

CHAPTER 74

"GILLIE, ARE YOU going to be all right?" Katie asked, rubbing his back. "Just breathe deep and you'll feel better in a little while."

Bending over, Gilbert vomited into the toilet bowl for the third time in less than a minute. Having never killed anything before, he was finding the experience less than salubrious. In fact, he thought it was the grossest thing he'd ever seen, never mind done.

When they had arrived a few minutes earlier, Katie had used her key to open the door after her knock went unanswered. Shotgun in hand, Gilbert had insisted on entering the dimly lit cabin first and had seen something monstrous erupt up through the living room floor. While Ellen had screamed in terror, he had emptied the shotgun's six-shot magazine into the thing. Most of the anatomical real estate north of the thing's shoulders had been blown into fine clouds of rank-smelling grey dust that flew all over the room.

Except that it really wasn't a thing. In the millisecond before he had started firing, Gilbert had recognized the creature as Marcus Taylor. Except that Taylor was supposed to be dead, *finis,* taking the old dirt nap, whatever, take your pick. Big of an asshole as Taylor had been, and he'd been a major one, he'd been a *human* asshole, or was the last time Gilbert had seen him.

Standing behind and to one side of Gilbert as the monster rose through the floorboards, Katie had a different impression of the chain of events. The creature had resembled Taylor, but she thought that it also had some female traits. Gifted with sharp eyes and acute perception, she was almost certain that the monster had self-destructed in the instant before Gilbert had started shooting. Not that it mattered in the least to Katie, she was proud of her husband's courage regardless of how the monster had died.

"Here, Honey, I got you a glass of water," Katie told him, wrapping his hand around the glass. "Swish and spit until it's gone and then I'll get you some more just to drink."

Swishing and spitting, Gilbert slowly emptied the glass. Taking a seat on the porcelain throne, he slowly drank the glass of ice water that Katie handed him. Feeling better wasn't in his vocabulary at the moment, but he'd live, although it would be a while before he felt like eating again.

"Gillie, I know you don't feel well," Katie said, taking his hands and pulling him to his feet, "but Ellen's really sick and needs to get into bed and I need your help to get her there."

"Ungh, shouldn't we take her to the hospital? Or better yet, we should call an ambulance, she looks awful."

"Gillie, we can't. Before she passed out, Ellen said she didn't want to go to the hospital because she's out on bail. If the police find about her injuries and come sniffing around here and get a look at this place, they'll put her back in jail for sure."

Although he had his doubts, Gilbert nodded his head and followed his wife out into the living room, mindful of the large hole in the center of the floor. Waving Katie out of the way, he knelt and picked Ellen up off the couch, hoping that he was doing the right thing by keeping her away from proper medical care. Carrying her back to Charlie's bedroom, he laid her down on the bed. Looking down at her drooping eye and mouth, he almost changed his mind and called an ambulance anyway.

"That was great, honey, but you didn't have to lift her all by yourself," Katie said, sitting down on the bed next to Ellen. "Now help me get her undressed so I can get her cleaned up."

"Huh?" Gilbert croaked, sounding like he was being strangled while someone simultaneously pulled hard on his short and curlies.

"Oh Gillie, come on, Ellen needs us!" Katie snapped. "Just pretend it's your grandmother or something."

When help wasn't forthcoming, Katie glared up at her husband. Coughing once, she then started giggling. Soon after she was down on the floor, laughing helplessly.

"Oh, oh God, Gillie, the look on your face!" she gasped, tears running down her face. "Wa, wa, what was it, the grandmother thing?"

Sobriety set in after a minute or so and Katie accepted Gilbert's hand and let him help her up off the floor. Leading him over to Ellen, she stood on her tiptoes and kissed him.

"Just don't get me started again," she said, biting down on her lower lip when she felt her funny bone getting tickled. "Let's just be clinical about this and get it done."

Looking away as much as possible, a beet-red Gilbert helped Katie get Ellen undressed. Soon enough, although it felt like hours to him, Ellen was laying covered under the sheets and blankets. After watching her for a minute, they walked out to the living room and sat down on the couch.

"Now that wasn't so bad, was it?" Katie said, snuggling up to her husband. "She didn't remind you of your grandmother did she?"

"No, not hardly," he replied, smiling through his embarrassment. "It was the high point of my life to date, no doubt about it."

"Well, you ain't seen nothin' yet," she told him, leaning forward and picking up a pad of paper and a pen off the coffee table. "As soon as I get done writing this list, one of us is going to have to go into Frechette and go shopping. The other is going to have to stay here and bathe Ellen and—"

"I'll go!" Gilbert declared. "Praise God and testify, I'll go!"

"Thought so," she said, trying hard not to giggle and failing. "Just give me a minute and I'll have this list done."

Walking out the door a few minutes later, Gilbert had the resigned look of a man with the attitude of, "In for a penny, in for a six-engine freight train's worth of long tons."

CHAPTER 75

THE SOULS THE Wendigo had enslaved for so long flowed forward, touched the staff, and were freed in strobing flashes of blue light. Their touch as they passed was warm on David's skin and their speech rang joyous in his ears. Soon, there was only four revenants left standing in the weak moonlight.

A young tow-headed spectre was trying to speak to Gina while the shade of her husband Eric looked worriedly on. Easing down on the rock, David gathered Rachel into his lap and leaned forward to speak to the spirits.

"Jillian and Eric, I know you're worried about Gina," he said, reaching out and taking the revenants' hands in his, "but it's time for you to move on now."

"She's real sick," Jillian told him. "Will you help her? Please?"

"I'll do everything I can for her," David replied, gently pulling her toward the staff. "Now it's time for you to move on and be happy again."

Smiling, Jillian's shade hugged Gina one last time. Stepping forward, she touched the staff and vanished in a flicker of blue fire. Eric Tolliver knelt and hugged his wife and daughter one last time. Smiling but weeping, he reached out, touched the staff, and was gone.

Sobbing inconsolably, Gina reached out for Rachel, who was also crying. Picking the child up, David settled her in Gina's lap and got to his feet.

"Rachel, you stay here with your Mom," he said. "If she starts acting strange or anything, you come get me, I'll be right over there. We've got one more thing to do and then we're going home."

"'Kay, Mr. David," Rachel mumbled, crying with her face buried in the breast of her mother's parka.

Walking a few yards away, David stopped and watched the glowing revenants of his wife and daughter approach. Opening his arms, he wrapped them in a gentle embrace. They were mostly insubstantial, not much more than the current of air spun up by a small fan on a warm summer's day. Yet somehow the essence of what they were, their souls and all they contained, was here with him.

"I, I, I have missed you both so much," he said, barely able to speak. "I, I searched and searched, but I couldn't find you."

"I know, David, I know," Jennifer told him. "We're almost out of time, so we better say our goodbyes."

"I, Jen, no, wait," he begged. "Since you've been gone, I haven't really been alive. Just let me take Rachel and Gina home and then I'll come back and we can go on together, you, me, and Allie. Please!"

"No, David, I'm sorry, but no," Jennifer said, kissing him. "It's not your time yet. You have much to do and far to go and you need to start rebuilding your life. We'll always love you and miss you and we'll be waiting for you when your time finally comes. Goodbye for now, David."

"'Bye, Daddy," Allison echoed, standing on her tiptoes so she could kiss him goodbye. "Love you."

Taking Allison's right hand, Jennifer Garrison reached out and touched the staff with her free hand. Cobalt fire flashed and arced and then they were gone. Time passed while David stood grieving with his forehead resting on the staff's carved headpiece. An insistent tugging on the bottom of his parka finally captured his attention and he looked down.

"'Scuse me, Mr. David," Rachel said, worried that she was bothering an adult. "Mommy's having a bad dream and I can't wake her up and it's real dark and I'm scared."

"Well, we can't have that going on now, can we? Let's go see if we can wake her up and then we can get going."

"Grampa Charlie's dead, isn't he?" she asked, taking David by surprise. "The bad man with the funny hair killed him, didn't he?"

"Ungh, yes, honey, he did. With everything that's been going on I kind of forgot to tell you. You're not mad at me, are you?"

"No, sometimes grownups forget to tell little kids things they need to know," Rachel commented, an observation that made him wince in embarrassment. "Mr. David, did you kill the bad man that killed Grampa Charlie?"

"Sort of, I guess," he said, uncomfortable about discussing such a terrible subject with a child. "I helped, kind of, is the best way to put it."

"Good, I'm glad!" she spat, almost screaming. "He scared Mommy and me and killed Grampa Charlie and I'm glad he's dead and I hope it hurt a real lot! I'm glad!"

"Okay, take it easy now," he said, startled by her bitter hatred, especially since it closely mirrored his own feelings. "Just calm down and don't cry. Grampa Charlie wouldn't want you to be sad, now would he?"

"No, sir, he wouldn't," she sniffed, bringing her tears under control. "Are we going home now? I don't like this place, it's scary."

"We're going home as soon as we say goodbye to Grampa Charlie," he said, taking her hand and steering her toward Gina. "Let's go wake your mom up and then we can get started."

Lying in a fetal curl on the cold granite, Gina twitched and muttered in the grip of an uneasy sleep. Kneeling down, David shook her shoulder until her eyes opened. Or as Rachel thought of it, her body woke up, but her mind remained asleep. Sitting up, Gina looked around and started holding an animated conversation with Jillian.

"C'mon, Gina," David said, helping her up, "time to go."

Looking into his eyes, Gina never missed a beat and kept on talking to Jillian, then to someone named Anita, and then to her mother and father. Bending down, David hoisted Rachel onto his shoulders. Taking hold of Gina's hand, he commanded the staff to take them back to Charlie's body, but nothing happened.

"Dammit, do your stuff!" he muttered, concentrating so hard that beads of sweat popped out on his forehead.

Giving up after a minute or so, David raised his head and opened his eyes. A narrow glowing blue line had appeared in the center of the trail leading back to Charlie's body.

"Shank's mare it is then," he sighed and started following the glowing ribbon down the path.

Two and a half hours later they arrived back at the blow-down clearing created by the Seismic Sonic Hammer. Lowering Rachel to the ground, David arched his spine and stretched his aching back muscles. As long as he held the staff, he possessed enough energy to continue on. But if he set it down, as he had during a couple of short breaks on the march back to the clearing, he became so weary that he could barely stand.

A commotion started shaking the brush a few yards away and David tensed up, then started laughing. A second later Susie charged out of the underbrush barking, indignant at having been left behind. Overjoyed, she ran circles around everyone for a few minutes and then settled into Rachel's lap.

Walking over to the wrecked Toyota, David climbed into the driver's seat. There wasn't much chance of finding what he was looking for, but he had to at least try. Twenty minutes, later his fingers skidded across a piece of plastic hanging down from the springs under the front passenger seat. His groping fingers found the piece of plastic again and he pulled it free. When he held the rectangle of laminated plastic up to the weak moonlight, Jennifer Garrison's beautiful face was looking out at him. Smiling, he zipped the driver's license into the inner breast pocket of his parka.

Looking over his shoulder, David saw a glimmer of red and white against the left side of the lift-gate. Climbing out of the passenger compartment, he walked around to the back of the SUV and stuck his head into the hole the lift-gate window had once occupied. Looking around, he located the splash of color in the darkness. Reaching down, he brushed the leaves and debris away. Taking hold of it with both hands in case it was damaged, he lifted his daughter Allison's rag doll out of the truck. Examining the doll and finding it undamaged, he placed it in the roomy map pocket inside his parka for safe keeping.

Two-for-two and against long odds, but that was easy compared to what came next. There was no way around it, David knew that. It had to be this way; it was the right thing, the only thing that he could do. But just because it was the right thing to do didn't mean that he wasn't dreading doing it.

Working quickly, David stacked the broken tree branches and brush surrounding the Toyota into a four foot tall rectangular pile in the center of the clearing. Allowing himself a short pause for one deep breath, he crawled under the truck and pulled Charlie's body out. Picking his body up, David carried it over and laid it on the makeshift bier. Only then did he dare to look down.

In death, Charlie looked serene. All evidence of the disease which had ravaged his final days was gone and his face was free from care. Sad but pleased that his friend was finally at peace, David stood leaning on the staff, thinking. A scuffling noise startled him and he turned away from the bier. Rachel and Susie were standing a couple of feet away, solemnly looking at him.

"Hi, Rachel," he said, kneeling down and gathering the child in his arms. "I guess you woke up from your nap. Did you come to say goodbye to Grampa Charlie? Do you remember what we talked about on the way back here?"

"I 'member about the Minnesota Vikings on the Discovery Channel," she replied, making David smile. "I'm all done saying bye to Grampa Charlie because it makes me sad. Mr. David, do you think Grampa Charlie went to Heaven?"

David had never believed himself good at speaking to children and although deeply spiritual, he had struggled with religious concepts his entire life. Rachel's question was an honest one, an earnest one, and it deserved the best answer that he could give. The revenants had gone somewhere, and he guessed Heaven was as good a name for it as anything.

"Yes, Rachel, he did," David said, reaching down inside his parka. "Before I forget, I have something here for you. This dolly used to belong to my little girl, Allison. The dolly's name is Amy and now she doesn't have anybody to love her. Would you like her for yours? I'm sure Allison would like you to have her to love and take care of."

"A dolly? For me?" Rachel exclaimed, reaching out for the doll with both hands. "Thank you! I'll take real good care of her for Allison, I promise!"

"I know you will, honey. Let's park you over here with your mom while I go do that Minnesota Vikings thing."

Leaving Rachel with her sleeping mother, David started walking toward the wrecked SUV. When he was about fifteen yards away, he stopped, lowered the staff to hip level, and let fly. Whatever Ma Toyota had put into the 4-Runner was no match for the power The Great Mother had put into the staff. In less than five seconds there was nothing left of the truck but a few burning scraps of rubber from each of the tires. Still not satisfied, David swept a stream of blue fire across the ground until he was certain that nothing belonging to his wife or daughter would remain in this awful place.

Done with the easier thing, David turned to the dreaded and the difficult. Stopping a few feet away from the bier, he stood searching for something appropriate to say. At first he found his mental vapor-lock amusing, but in short order it became annoying, and was well on its way to being a world-class pain-in-the-ass when he decided to speak from the heart and have done with it.

"Lord, Mother, we give into your loving arms our faithful friend and comrade, Charles Lantot Redbird," he began, hands trembling on the staff. "Charlie, we, we all miss you and love you and wish that you were still here with us. Goodbye for now until we meet again."

By his own admission, David was about as musical as a pair of galvanized trash can lids being smashed together. Now though, guided by the staff, he began singing. In part a dirge, in part a celebratory hymn, it was a song for Charlie Redbird, of his long life and brave struggle against the terrible evil that finally took his life. In two minutes it was finished, leaving David feeling bemused but well-pleased by the song's beauty and sentiments.

A glimmer of light and movement at the center of the bier caught his eye. Charlie's revenant was standing there holding hands with the ghost of a stunning dark-haired woman. At that moment, David thought that Mary Redbird was the most beautiful woman he had ever seen. They smiled and waved goodbye as he scythed blue fire over them and sent them onwards.

Turning away, David walked over to where Rachel and Gina were sitting. Looking up at him with a vacant smile, Gina babbled mindlessly on about a long ago slumber party with Jillian.

"Well how 'bout it, Sweetie, you ready to go home?" he said, kneeling down so that Rachel could climb on his shoulders.

"Yes sir, I am, and I hope we get there soon because I'm really hungry and I wanna watch cartoons. Will you hold Amy for me 'cause I'm scared I'll lose her?"

Smiling, David took the doll from her and put it in the map pocket inside his parka. Reaching out, he took Gina's hand, thankful that at least so far she was amenable to being led along. One last quick look around satisfied him that they hadn't forgotten anything, including Susie.

"Home, James," he ordered, tapping the staff three times against the ground and hoping for something a little more helpful than a glowing navigation beacon, "and don't spare the horses!"

As soon as the staff struck the ground for the third time, David knew that something had gone badly wrong. Bright pinwheels exploded in his vision and pulses thundered in his head as he fell forward into a spreading pool of darkness. Rachel screamed as she fell and was echoed by Gina and Susie. David heard nothing, already unconscious in a deep, exhausted sleep even as he slammed down face first on the ground.

CHAPTER 76

"GILLIE, I'M NOT trying to be a pest or anything," Katie said, rubbing her eyes as she stared out the front passenger-side window, "but would you please slow down, you're driving too fast again."

"Now this is a genuine Kodak moment if ever there was one," Gilbert replied, tapping the brake pedal.

Late on the evening of their arrival, Katie had a premonition, a dream. A man, a woman, and a child, faces indistinct, were standing in the dark in the middle of a two-lane paved road, freezing, near death. For the past two nights Katie and Gilbert had prowled the spider web of roads surrounding the lake from dusk to dawn but found nothing. On this, the third night, it was a balmy twelve degrees Fahrenheit outside driving on a strong north wind and snowing intermittently. Three hours now remained until dawn. They weren't giving up yet, but spirits and hope were running low.

"We better find them soon," Katie sighed, resting her forehead against the window then hastily wiping away the obscuring breath mist, "because if we don't, they're all gonna die."

"We'll find them tonight," Ellen said from the back seat, pulling a heavy blanket closer about her. "I honestly believe that. We must!"

Except for an occasional uncontrollable facial tic and a lingering migraine, Ellen's neurological injuries had healed during the past seventy-two hours. Her physical injuries though were another story. Those she would continue to be well-stocked up on for the next couple of weeks and beyond.

As Katie and Gilbert had prepared to leave the cabin just before sunset, Ellen had insisted on dressing and accompanying them. An epic clash of wills had ensued between her and Katie.

"I will," said Ellen.

"Oh no you won't," said Katie.

"I will," said Ellen, and then she had.

Somewhere in the middle, Gilbert had invented a pretext to go outside so he could laugh undetected. Katie was the love of his life, but she could be a tad, well, more than a tad, on the stubborn side at times. Ellen though was qualified to teach doctoral level classes on the subject.

Smiling at the memory, Gilbert looked down at the speedometer, frowned, and tapped the brake pedal again. When he raised his eyes, three people, two adults and a child, were standing in the road twenty-five feet ahead. Framed by the headlights, they stood frozen, watching the oncoming vehicle with stark terror on their faces.

"TOO LATE!" Gilbert's mind screamed in panic even as he stood on the brakes and cut the steering wheel hard left.

Blue fire flashed as Katie and Ellen screamed a warning and suddenly the road ahead was clear. The Subaru braked to a halt and Gilbert scrambled out, praying that he hadn't run anyone over. A gaunt scarecrow of a man was standing about twenty feet away on the other side of the road. A woman and a little girl were peeking out from behind his back.

"He-l-l-," the scarecrow rasped before a deep, rattling cough stole his voice for the next few seconds. "We've been lost for days and we need to get to a hospital. Help us, please!"

One of the car doors opened and Gilbert turned his head to look. Still wrapped in the blanket, Ellen was limping across the road toward the three ragged figures.

"Rachel honey, come here!" she called, kneeling and opening the blanket. "You must be freezing."

After a second's hesitation, Rachel darted out from behind David and rushed over to her.

"Hi, Miss Ellen," she said, snuggling into the warm circle of her arms. "I'm cold and hungry and I wanna go home."

"I'll bet you do," Ellen replied, kissing her. "We'll get you warmed up and then we'll get you something to eat."

Walking up to Gilbert, Katie wrapped both arms around his neck and leaned into his chest. Looking down at her, he saw the tears and felt his gut tighten.

"We don't know for sure yet," he argued, hoping that she was wrong, but already certain that she wasn't. "We haven't even had a chance to talk to them about it."

"Don't need to, I know already and so do you."

"Let's try and be optimistic until we know for sure," Gilbert told her. "In the meantime, let's get everybody in the car; it's not getting any warmer out here."

Nodding, Katie broke the embrace but kept hold of his hand as they approached Gina and David.

"Ungh, you must be Ms. Tolliver and Mr. Garrison," Gilbert said, sounding oddly formal. "We've never met, but I'm Gilbert Mason and this is my wife, Katie. Why don't you two get in the car and get warm and we'll get you to the hospital in Frechette."

"Yes, that's us," David rasped, his tortured breathing audible to Katie and Gilbert standing three feet away. "Thank you so much for helping us."

"I'm in the third grade," Gina announced. "What grade are you in? Do you like to play dollies? I do!"

"Gina's delusional," David explained, voice thick with despair, "but she's not violent or anything, just lost."

"Ungh, well, okay," Gilbert said, shrugging his shoulders in embarrassment although he didn't know why. "I guess we better get going before we all freeze to death."

Climbing into the back seat, David saw Ellen examining Rachel's black eye under the glow of the dome light.

"Her mother did that," he said, already weary of making explanations and knowing that he hadn't even really gotten started yet. "She's schizophrenic, but she's usually not violent."

"I can see that!" Ellen snapped, gathering Rachel in her arms in the far corner of the back seat. "I'm sure she's a perfect goddamn angel!"

Too tired and too ill to argue, especially with someone he had disliked on first sight, David closed his eyes but fought off sleep. A second later he leaned forward and tapped Katie on the shoulder.

"Excuse me," he said, hating to ask but knowing that it was critically important that he do so, "but do you have a cell phone I can use to make a long distance call? I can pay you for the call as soon as we get to an ATM."

"Yes, I do, Gillie makes me keep one in my purse," Katie replied, rooting around in her bag and then handing him the phone. "And you don't have to worry about paying me for the call."

Three times David tried to dial the number he wanted but each time his shaking forefinger refused to enter the digits in the correct order. Seeing his growing frustration, Katie could finally bear it no longer.

"If you'll tell me the number," she told him, holding out her hand, "I'll be happy to dial it for you."

Handing her the phone, David dictated the number and watched her fingers dance across the keypad. Finished dialing, she handed the phone back to him and he pressed it against his ear. Six rings sounded and he was losing hope when someone finally picked up on the other end.

"Terry Thomas speaking," a man's voice boomed out, making David smile, "and it is now 3:48 in the morning and this goddamn well better be important!"

"Terry, this is David," he croaked, excitement bringing on a bad coughing spell, "and I—"

"Who the fuck is this?" Thomas demanded. "David Garrison is my best friend and law partner. I know his voice like I know my own and you aren't him, asshole!"

"Terry, don't hang up, please don't!" David begged, near panic now. "We met and attended law school together at the University of Minnesota, took every class together for three years. We used to drink at the Hair of the Dog Saloon when we were students. Your favorite fly is a Grey Ghost. You collect over and under shotguns and antique fly-fishing reels. When we were roommates in that little apartment down on Miller I cooked and you cleaned because—"

"David, what the hell is going on and where have you been?" Terry asked, convinced now of his caller's identity. "You sound terrible; I didn't even recognize your voice."

"I got lost in the woods and just got out and now I've got pneumonia or bronchitis or some damn thing," David told him, relief easing the coughing spasm. "I've got Rachel and Gina Tolliver with me along with Ellen Talltrees and a couple of new friends. We're all on our way to the hospital in Frechette and I think we need some legal help."

"You aren't kidding you do," Terry said, the sound of a pen writing on paper now clearly audible to David. "Law enforcement has been tearing the country apart for days searching for that little girl. You tell everyone with you that as of now they are represented by the law firm of Thomas and Garrison and they are under no circumstances to speak to the police or anyone else about what has happened. Don't even discuss the case among yourselves. Clear?"

"Yeah, clear, I remember the drill, I think," David replied, remembering to ask one last question. "Are you driving up or—"

"No, I ain't got time for asphalt," Terry interrupted, his favorite euphemism for being in too much of a hurry to drive somewhere. "I'll charter a plane and be with you just as soon as I can. In the meantime, keep those lips zipped!"

"I, I, thank you, Terry, I know I haven't been much use to you these last few years and—"

"Bullshit, long as you've got a pulse, your name's gonna be on the door," Terry assured him, the sound of a pen scratching now replaced by the soft riffing of pages being turned. "Now I gotta go because I have to find a way to charter an airplane at four o'clock in the goddamn morning. Love you, Buddy, and I'll see you real soon."

Handing the phone back to Katie, David sat with his head bowed and his hands covering his face, fooling no one but maintaining at least a vestige of self-dignity. Raising his head after a minute, he wiped his eyes and reviewed Terry's instructions.

"I want you all to listen to me, please," he began. "I can only say this once because my throat is so sore I can hardly speak. Law enforcement has been searching for Rachel because she is a minor child kidnapped from state custody. When we get to the hospital, the staff will have a description and probably a picture or a drawing of her. As soon as they realize who she is, and it won't take them long, they will call the police. When the police question you, and believe me they will question you, you are to tell them that you are represented by the law firm of Thomas and Garrison and that you have nothing to say until you have consulted with your attorney, Mr. Thomas. No matter what they threaten you with, and they will probably threaten you with obstruction of justice charges or some such, your one and only answer is that you have nothing to say until you have consulted with your attorney, Mr. Thomas.

"Do not, I repeat do not, discuss what has happened even among yourselves because someone will hear you, even if it is around a corner or on the other side of a door, and tell the police. Save your questions and explanations for Terry, your attorney, when he gets here later this morning.

"Speaking as a person with a degree in law, I can assure you that refusing to answer police questions without an attorney being present is a right guaranteed you by the United States Constitution and is perfectly legal, although the police will try and make you believe otherwise. I'm not trying to be anal or anything, but could each of you indicate that you understood what I just said so that I can save my voice for what lays ahead."

Ellen, Katie, and Gilbert all stated that they understood what he had just said, although they sounded none too confident about it. Chiming in at the end, Rachel got a laugh from the adults by reciting David's spiel near perfectly. Satisfied, David laid his head back and closed his eyes. Intending only to rest, he instead fell fast asleep. All too soon the speed bumps and the sodium arc lights in the hospital parking lot woke him.

"Katie and Gilbert," Ellen said, "would you please take Rachel and her mother to the Emergency Room. I need to talk to David alone for a few minutes and then we'll be in."

Walking around the car, Katie opened the door and helped Rachel get out. Reaching across Gina, David opened the other rear door. Reaching down, Gilbert took Gina's arm and helped her out of the car while she babbled on about Barbie dolls. Sitting silently in the back seat, Ellen and David watched them start across the parking lot toward the brightly lit Emergency Room.

"I didn't mean to act as if I blamed you for Rachel's black eye," Ellen said, surprising David who was expecting nothing less than a full frontal assault. "And I wanted to thank you for getting me a lawyer and posting my bail. I'd never been in jail before and I don't think I would have lasted long in there."

"That's all right, I glad I could help," David told her, wondering yet again why this woman unsettled him so much. "Rachel's a wonderful little girl. When I first saw her eye, I would've strangled Gina if I could've gotten hold of her. But it wasn't her fault, she's not mentally competent enough to be responsible for anything, at least not right now."

"David, the main thing I wanted to talk to you about is my grandfather. I see that you're carrying his stick. I know much of what he did and I can make some educated guesses about a lot of other things he was involved in. Would you please tell me what's happened to him or where he is?"

One minute, then two passed while David sat thinking and Ellen waited.

"I didn't know your grandfather very long, but I liked and respected him a great deal," David began. "He, he died fighting the evil that he spent his life opposing. I'm so terribly sorry, if I could have brought him home safe to you I would've, but it was beyond me, beyond anyone. You were the last thing he spoke off and he told me to make sure you were all right and I told him that I would. That's all I want to say about it right now because, because it's still very painful for me to talk about."

Even though he was on intimate terms with pain and loss, David had never heard or seen anything like the paroxysm of grief that gripped Ellen Talltrees. For long minutes she wept inconsolably, so hard that her breathing became irregular and her face flushed dark scarlet. Growing concerned, David had just opened the car door intending to summon medical assistance from the hospital when she started calming down.

A few minutes later, David helped her out of the car. Walking slowly, the two coughed and limped their way across the parking lot. They had just stepped up onto the sidewalk in front of the Emergency Room when a Town of Frechette police cruiser raced into the parking lot with roof lights flashing and siren howling.

"Here they come," Ellen said, moving a step closer to David until their shoulders touched, "just like you said they would."

"Sometimes," David observed, barely keeping his cough in check, "being right isn't all it's cracked up to be."

Book V

And They All Lived Happily Ever After (Sort of)

CHAPTER 77

AFTER THEIR RETURN from First Land, as both Terry and David had predicted, the law had descended upon them like the proverbial ton of bricks. But with Charlie gone and everyone else either refusing to talk or not knowing anything worth talking about, the state found itself with a dearth of hard evidence. It took a while, three days shy of eighteen months after Ellen and David had watched the police cruiser charge into the hospital's parking lot, but finally the State's case collapsed from the weight of its own insufficiency.

Collapsed that is except for Rachel and Gina Tolliver. Armed with photos of Rachel's black eye taken that night at the hospital and Gina's obvious mental incompetency, the state proved her an unfit mother and Rachel was placed in foster care. Slightly harder, but still pretty much a legal slam dunk, the State proved that Gina met the legal definition of insanity and she was involuntarily committed to a lock-down psychiatric facility for the indefinite future.

Even though he was cured of his passion for Gina even before he left First Land, David did his very best for her. Given the facts though there was little he or any other attorney could have done for her. Still, it was a bitter pill for him to swallow.

Using a computerized legal database, David had hired a pair of psychiatric consultants to each write a report listing the twelve leading experts on schizophrenia. The experts' domicile, nationality, ethnicity, or any other modifiers were all matters of supreme indifference. All that mattered were that they be the world's leading expert on the illness; nothing else was relevant.

Receiving the consultants' reports within three days of each other, David had carefully compared the two. Noting the nine names the two reports listed in common, he had discarded the other fifteen names and called it good. Of the nine psychiatrists he had selected, seven had agreed to consult on Gina's case. He had mailed copies of Gina's medical and psychiatric records to these seven physicians along with hours of video-taped interviews and observations of her and a cashier's check for twice their requested fee. The same information had been mailed to the two declining physicians along with a blank check and a polite request to reconsider their refusals. Miraculously, they had both found time in their busy schedules to consult on Gina's case.

Even for a person of means, and David was a very wealthy man, the process was expensive and had put a healthy dent in his finances. Some ills though defy a cure no matter the amount of resources expended upon them and Gina's was one of them. Of the nine consulting psychiatrists, eight had believed that Gina would never be able to live outside of an institutional setting again.

The ninth had stated there was a remote, and she repeatedly stressed the word both in her phone conversations and in her final written report to David, that Gina might be able to live outside of an institution sometime in the indefinite future, but certainly no time soon.

Gina was lost to everyone, including herself. In the unanimous opinion of the nine consulting psychiatrists, she was trapped somewhere between her seventh and ninth year of life by the trauma of Jillian and her husband's disappearances and by the heartless vise of schizophrenia. If there was any solace for David in the situation, because comfort was too generous a word, it was that she seemed oblivious of her plight.

Regardless of David's concern about Gina or about anything else, the staff had its own agenda. Only occasionally at first, then with increasing frequency until he couldn't even get a good night's sleep, the staff let its demands be known. Finally one early September afternoon, David decided that enough was enough. Slamming down the novel he was trying to read despite the staff's non-stop nagging, he grabbed it and marched out to the barn.

As David's knowledge of the staff had deepened, he had become aware of how it and Charlie had maneuvered him, Gina, and Rachel into making the trip to First Land. At first he was disappointed in Charlie, then angry, and then for a few awful weeks he had hated him with a black passion. But as his knowledge of the staff deepened even further and finally became complete, the truth became bleakly apparent.

As Charlie had tactfully tried to tell him, he was a servant, not the master, and the staff would always serve its own ends regardless of the consequences for its wielder.

Whatever mistakes the wielder made, and the potential for doing harm with such a powerful supernatural artifact was enormous as Charlie had tragically learned when his flash of temper condemned his fellow villagers to the purgatory of First Land, the staff enabled and magnified those errors into human tragedies.

Awful as these truths were, they helped David both pity and understand Charlie and the difficult life he had led and the terrible choices he had been forced to make. With understanding came forgiveness and David was able to love his friend again.

Even though David now fully understood the nature of his servitude, that didn't mean that he was going to surrender his freedom without a fight. Starting up a wood chipper, he shoved the staff into the feeder hopper and in short order was the proud owner of an expensive pile of scrap metal. Siccing a chain saw on it yielded the same results. Never one to give up easily, he next tried burning it in a galvanized trash can with five gallons of gasoline, but that only further burnished the staff's lustrous finish. Recognizing a losing proposition when he saw one, David pulled the staff out of the trash can after the gasoline burned off, not surprised to find that it was ice-cold in his hand.

"All right, you win," he said, rapping it against the ground for emphasis. "I'll call when we get back in the house and set it up. But I'm telling you, this is a bad idea and it's never going to work. First though, you have to leave me alone and let me get a good night's sleep or else no go."

The staff remained silent but suddenly flushed warm in his hand and David knew they had a deal. After making a quick phone call, he climbed the stairs to his bedroom and started filling a large duffel bag with clothes. It was never going to work in a million years, he was near certain of that, but he did have some legitimate business at the same place so he could kill two birds with one stone.

Forty-eight hours later he rang the doorbell, still certain that it would never work. It had been years since he'd done anything like this and he was jumpier than a dozen long-tailed cats in a small showroom stuffed full of occupied rocking chairs. Thirty seconds passed and still no one answered the ring. Congratulating himself on a lucky escape, David had just turned to walk away when the front door swung open.

"Hi, Rachel, I thought I'd come by and see how you're doing," he said, forcing himself to smile. "I see you're still taking real good care of Amy."

"Hi, Mr. David," she replied, shifting the rag doll to her other arm so that she could unlock and open the storm door. "Amy's my favorite dolly and I take real good care of her. Come in and I'll tell Mom you're here."

By the time David walked into the foyer, Rachel had already disappeared, so he stood and waited. One minute, then two passed as he grew nervous to the point he laughed out loud about it. Footsteps and voices sounded in the near distance and he swallowed a lump in his throat that felt like it was the size of a basketball.

"Hello, David," Ellen said in a tone he usually associated with other stellar life events such as getting a flu shot or stubbing a toe. "What beautiful roses, what's the occasion?"

"They're for you and Rachel just because," he replied, smiling on the outside, but wondering on the inside why this beautiful woman nettled him so. "And I brought you some chocolate chip cookies from the All American Pastry Shop. I apologize for coming on such short notice, but I didn't think you'd mind this one time."

"That's all right, you're forgiven," she said in a tone that let him know it wasn't and he wasn't. "Let's go back to the kitchen and brew some coffee to go with those cookies and Rachel can have a glass of milk."

Following Rachel and Ellen through the townhouse, David tried to think of a diplomatic way to breach the business end of his visit. Sitting around the kitchen table waiting for the coffee to brew, Rachel solved the problem by raising the subject herself.

"Mr. David," She asked, getting up and standing next to his chair, "is my mommy ever gonna get better and come home from the hospital? It makes me mad because nobody will tell 'cause I'm little."

"Honey, I'd like to talk to Ellen about it first," David said, earning himself a furious look from Rachel, "then will talk about it, okay?"

"David, it's all right," Ellen told him, pulling Rachel up onto her lap. "I'm right here and Rachel really wants to know, she deserves to know."

Nodding his head, David sat for a long minute collecting his thoughts.

"Rachel honey," he began, wishing desperately that someone, anyone, other than him was giving her this awful news, "the doctors don't think your mom is ever going to get better and come home from the hospital. I'm real sorry, but that's what they say and I think they're right. Remember, your mother loves you very much and it's not her fault that she's sick and she would be here if she could. Most important though she wouldn't want you to be sad just because she's sick and can't get better."

"Thank you Mr. David, that's what I thought, but nobody would tell me 'cause I'm little," Rachel said, hugging her doll with both arms. "Mom Ellen, may I be 'scused? I'm sad and I wanna go sit in my room with Amy."

"Yes, Rachel, of course you may be excused," Ellen replied, lifting the child off her lap. "I'll come up in a few minutes and we can talk if you like."

"'Kay," Rachel mumbled, running out of the kitchen and heading for the stairs.

"Don't blame yourself, David," Ellen said, surprising him with the warmth in her voice. "She desperately wanted to know, it's been bothering her a lot. If I didn't hear from you by the end of the week I was going to call you Monday and ask."

"I don't blame myself, it's not mine or anybody else's fault, including Gina's," he replied, looking out the kitchen window in the vain hope that she wouldn't notice how upset he was. "It's selfish, but I would have given anything not to have to be the one to tell her. But I'm her mother's legal guardian and I know both of them so it had to be me."

They sat together in silence until the coffee was finished brewing. Rising, Ellen poured them both a cup and sat back down.

"David," she asked, catching him by surprise, "is there something else you wanted to talk about. I have a feeling there is."

There was, and relieved at having the initiative taken from him again, David spoke his piece. It didn't take him long and it took less time for Ellen to turn him down. She wasn't dating right now, she had explained, and besides which, she didn't think they were at all compatible. Then she had uttered those dreaded words which are the bane of hopeful males everywhere by saying they would always be "special friends," whatever that meant. Taking her refusal with good grace, he finished his coffee and escaped as soon as good manners allowed after promising to call in a few days.

Outside in the car, David tried to decide which had made him more miserable, talking to Rachel or Ellen's refusal. After mulling it over for a few seconds, he decided that it was a fifty-fifty split. Even though he'd dreaded telling her, Rachel's reaction to the news of her mother's indefinite psychiatric confinement was about what he'd expected. Looking back through the all-knowing lens of hindsight though he still couldn't believe that he'd asked Ellen out even when he was certain that she'd say no. And since she irked him any-damn-way, why was her refusal bothering him so much?

"That's what I get," he said, glaring over at the staff as he started the engine, "for listening to a haunted walking stick."

The next week was taken up with what David thought of as doing errands and catching up with old friends. The uncharitably disposed would have called it moping, but if ever a man was entitled to a good mope, it was David Garrison. Finding that nothing brought him peace, he visited a long neglected favorite spot during the mid-morning of his eighth day in the Cities.

Even for gifted law students, and David had been one, there are bad days. After a rough half-hour's grilling in a Contracts class near the end of his second semester, he'd gone for a ride and discovered a wildlife sanctuary near the edge of the Cities. The river formed a large inlet here that was home to many species of waterfowl and other birds. The sanctuary was usually deserted during the week and it had become one of his favorite places during his student years.

Taking a seat on a bench next to the water's edge, he was pleased to see that nothing had changed during his long absence. Although he didn't know it, Katie and Gilbert had gotten married in the apple orchard atop the hill that started a few yards behind him. Charlie could have told him that this was a magical place and that people had been coming here in search of peace for many centuries now.

A familiar honking reached David's ear and he turned his head to look. A flock of Canadian geese were taking flight from a nearby field. Smiling, he sat watching, waiting for that special moment when each goose's feet left the ground and it transformed from a clumsy, waddling bird and into a creature of sublime grace and power. Forming a vee behind their leader, the geese turned downwind and started honking their way south down the flyway.

Enough, David decided, this year he would follow them south. It was what he was going to do just before the final madness started and now he meant to go. Allison and Jennifer were gone, Rachel and Gina were safe, and there was no reason at all why he couldn't take an extended vacation. Big Cedar Key first, he thought, then on to Jamaica for a while, and after that Carnival in Rio and—

"Hi, Mr. David," Rachel said, startling him so badly that he leaped to his feet and almost dropped the staff. "Did you come to feed the ducks too?"

For a moment, David was certain that he could hear Charlie's soft laughter from somewhere just behind him.

"Hi, Rachel, you scared me. I usually don't feed the ducks; I just come and look at them."

"Hello, David," Ellen said in that arch-tone he'd come to know and love so well. "What are you doing here?"

"Oh, I've been coming here off and on ever since I was a law student," David told her, wondering how he could possibly run into the one person he least wanted to see in the middle of one of the most secluded parks in the Cities metro area. "It's pretty here and I like to watch the birds and think."

"What were you thinking about?" she asked, smiling for the first time and taking the frost out of her voice. "C'mon, inquiring minds want to know."

"Well, I just thought myself into a long vacation," he said, wondering why his thoughts or anything else about him would matter to her. "Some time away will do me good. It's been years since I took a real vacation and it's high time I went."

"You goin' 'way, Mr. David?" Rachel demanded, crying harder with every word she spoke. "Don't you like us no more?"

"Honey, it's just for a little while," he said, surprised by her tears. "I'll be back by spring at the latest. And of course I still like you; I like you a whole lot."

"Don't care 'bout no springs!" Rachel yelled, crying so hard that she could hardly speak. "You no like us no more!"

"I, ungh, oh boy," was all the reply that David could manage.

"David, can we talk about this, your vacation I mean," Ellen said, both surprised and a little frightened to discover that she cared greatly where he was going and what his plans were. "After I get Rachel calmed down and we get done feeding the ducks, there's a place not too far from here that has real good hot chocolate. That is, if you don't mind waiting or have other plans."

"I'd like that very much," he told her, taken aback by this latest turn of events.

Hot chocolate and pastries turned into an afternoon spent at the Children's Science Museum and then dinner at a Chuck E. Cheese store. Driving back to his hotel after dropping off Rachel and Ellen, David still had every intention of being southbound within seventy-two hours. Fond as he was of Rachel, he had no intention of altering his plans just because they upset her. Ellen had gotten her wish and in all truth they were now special friends and David was fine with that. On the way back to the hotel he even stopped at a Borders store and bought a new road atlas so he could start planning the drive down to the Florida Keys.

The next day David picked up Rachel and Ellen around ten and they spent a couple of hours shopping. After lunch they took in a new Disney film that got rave reviews from Rachel and so-so ones from the adults. A couple of hours spent playing video games in a mall arcade led to an early dinner at an upscale family restaurant and then David drove them home. Throughout the day he was still resolved to be heading south the next morning and had told Rachel and Ellen so.

That resolve remained firm until they arrived at Ellen's front door. Asking Rachel to go inside and close the door, Ellen turned and kissed a very surprised David. At that moment his resolve fled and he couldn't have cared less about going south or anywhere else for that matter.

"We'll have to wait until Rachel is asleep," she said, taking him by the hand and leading him inside. "She's had a couple of real busy days so she'll go to bed pretty soon. Once she's asleep she usually doesn't wake up unless she has a nightmare."

Not knowing what to say, David settled for nodding, smiling, and letting himself be led through the townhouse. Shortly after Rachel went to bed and an hour later so did Ellen and David.

In the morning, David was sitting at the kitchen table mulling it all over while Ellen cooked breakfast. Walking into the kitchen, Rachel did a double-take and invited herself up onto his lap.

"Mr. David," she worriedly asked, "are you still going 'way today?"

"You better not be!" Ellen interjected from over by the stove, smiling and shaking a spatula at him.

"No, honey, I'm not," David replied, absolutely certain about what he was saying. "I'm staying right here with you and Ellen."

Rachel cheered and Ellen applauded.

Picking up a salt shaker, David held it to his lip like a microphone and intoned in his best sportscaster voice, "And the crowd goes wild!"

"Mr. David, are you Mom Ellen's boyfriend?" Rachel asked with a guilty look on her face. "I'm not bein' nosy or nothin' 'cause Mom Ellen says that's not nice, but sometimes people—"

"Don't tell little kids everything they need to know," he finished for her, laughing. "Yes, Rachel, I am your Mom Ellen's very serious boyfriend."

"Rachel, stop pestering David and come over here and eat your breakfast," Ellen said, putting a plate on the table and pulling out a chair.

Twelve days later though David did go south, but he took Rachel and Ellen with him along with Katie and

Gilbert and Terry Thomas and his family. Twenty-four hours after they landed in Las Vegas, Ellen and he were married in a quiet civil ceremony.

After David kissed the bride, a flicker of motion at the back of the chapel caught his attention. The revenants of Mary and Charlie Redbird were standing there, waving and smiling. Not caring who saw, David raised his hand and waved back.

“Day, David, do you see them?” Ellen whispered, squeezing his hand so hard that it hurt. “Look, it’s, it’s—”

“I know, love,” he said. “I told you they’d come. You just have to think of them and they’ll be there for you.”

Smiling, Ellen took David’s arm and they started down the aisle toward the exit. By the time they reached the back of the chapel Mary and Charlie were gone, but both Ellen and David were sure of what they’d seen. After the reception the others flew back to the Cities while Rachel, Ellen, and David flew on to Hawaii for a two-week honeymoon.

Once they got home David broached another difficult subject with Rachel. After a week’s worth of long private conversations with Ellen, she decided that she wanted to be adopted. Three months after they started, the final papers were signed and Rachel Tolliver became Rachel Garrison. David had a family again and he didn’t think it was possible to be any happier than he was that day.

Twenty-four hours later a vicious thunderstorm lashed the Frechette area for hours and strange lights appeared in the sky. In the morning Rachel told her parents that someone had left a pair of picnic baskets outside on the deck. Walking outside with her, David saw a pair of wicker baskets, one large and one small, sitting on the far edge of the deck. As they approached, the larger basket began shaking. Sending Rachel back inside the house, he knelt and raised the lid a little on the larger basket.

A black and white form exploded out of the basket, knocking him flat on his back and scaring the hell out of him. Wiggling from head to tail, Susie licked his face, overjoyed to be home at last. Wrapping his arms around her, David sat up, unable to believe that she was back.

Somehow during the long dark nightmare that the road home from First World became, Susie had wandered off and gotten lost. Already seriously ill with what would later be diagnosed as pneumonia, David had chosen to push on rather than search for her, a decision that had probably saved all of their lives. It had been the right choice, the only choice, and David had known it, but that didn't mean that he had felt good about it. He'd taken his dogs to a distant and alien place and neither of them had made it back. Now, somehow, Susie had found her way home.

A heavy bond enveloped addressed to David was attached to the top of the basket. Opening the envelope, he pulled out a single piece of stationary and read the short message penned on it, and then read it again.

"Dear Counselor Davy,

"I found yews mutt wanderin' loose in a very bad neighborhood so I picked her up for yews and brought her home. Susie is a very nice dog and has caused me to reevaluate my previously unfavorable opinion of canines. Don't ever feed her hard-boiled eggs and pickles though because it makes her fart somethin' awful. I did and it took me two weeks to get the stench out of the house and out of her.

"Your Sincerest Friend,

"The Eldest"

Laughing, David refolded the letter and put it back in the envelope, deciding then and there that it was going into a safe deposit box with his other keepsake papers. The basket moved again and a familiar noise sounded from inside that he couldn't quite identify. Rotating the basket a few degrees, he saw that it was divided into another compartment with another envelope on top addressed to Rachel. Reaching out to open the envelope and the basket, he thought better of it and instead called his daughter out of the house.

Walking out of the house with Ellen, Rachel first sat down on the deck and had a joyous reunion with Susie. After girl and dog had calmed down a little, David led her over to the basket.

"Go ahead and open the basket, Rachel," he said, placing her hand on the hinged lid. "There's a present in there for you."

Lifting the lid a couple of inches, Rachel peeked inside and yelled in delight. Opening the lid the rest of the way, David tilted the basket up on its side. Six ducklings whose color could only be described as fluorescent tie-dyed waddled out and gathered at Rachel's feet.

"Look, Daddy, pretty duckies," she said, picking one up in each hand. "The nice man in the spaceship must have given them to me. Can I keep them?"

"Yes, of course you can," he replied, shaking his head in wonder at the ducklings' odd coloration. "But out in the barn, not in the house, okay? There's an envelope here addressed to you. Would you like me to open it and read you what's inside and then you can read it for yourself?"

Rachel nodded her head, so David unsealed the envelope and pulled out the card inside. On the cover there was a color drawing of The Eldest's ship parked on top of a strange looking cheeseburger which made them both smile.

"Dear Rachel," David read aloud, "Congratulations on yews new name and everything that goes with it. I remembered yews like duckies so I picked these out special just for you. I hope yews like the colors, I made them special just for yews. Maybe sometime you can come visit and we can cook hamburgers again. Love, Uncle E.."

"Can we go visit him sometime, Daddy?" Rachel asked, holding out her hand for the card so that she could read it for herself. "He's really nice."

"Yes, honey, he is," David hedged, picking up the smaller basket and balancing it on the top of the handrail. "Well, Mrs. Garrison, this one is addressed to both of us, so why don't you open it."

Smiling, Ellen opened the basket and gasped in shock. Nestled inside was a pair of ornate solid gold toasting goblets and a magnum of *Dom Perignon* champagne, vintage 1955. Picking up one of the goblets, David turned it over and examined the proof mark on its base. Unable to believe what he was seeing, he looked again, and then again. Moving deliberately, he put the goblet back in its nest, took the basket off the railing, and set it back down on the deck a good three feet away from the edge.

"David, what's the matter?" Ellen asked, certain that the goblets were valuable, but not why they were having such an effect on her husband. "What does that little f on the bottom of the goblet stand for?"

"It stands for Faberge, court goldsmiths to the Czars of Russia before the Communist Revolution in 1917," he replied, still in shock. "Those goblets are priceless and irreplaceable. The wine probably is too, but I'm not as certain about that."

"That's some friend you and Rachel have," she said, trying to be diplomatic. "But he does seem, ungh, a little eccentric maybe."

"He's a great friend," David told her, smiling at the memory. "But he very definitely marches to the beat of his own symphony orchestra."

Opening the envelope attached to the basket, Ellen unfolded the piece of stationary inside and held it up so they both could read it.

"Dear Ellen and David", the letter read, *"Congratulations on yews recent nuptials. I always knew yews two kids would come to yews senses, but I have to admit yews had me worried there for a minute.*

"Forgive me for not attending yews wedding, but Las Vegas is a little too close to Rosywell and that Area 51 place. Last time I got over that ways, yews wouldn't believe what happened. Maybe yews can come visit sometime and I'll tells yews all about it.

"I hope yews like the wine goblets, the bums that had 'em didn't appreciate 'em at all. 'Dem commies would run a rose over with a steam roller and call it progress. Be careful who you show dem to, now that the old bums are finally gone, the new bums will probably want 'em back.

"I hope yews likes the wine, bubbly is the only thing French I got any use for and I picked that bottle out especially just for yews. Remember now though, yews is supposed to share the bottle. Since Ellen is in a family way, yews will have to wait until after yews blessed event so yews can imbibe together.

"Well, I have to get going, the world(s) is/are a big place(s) yews knows.

"With Best Wishes Always on Yews New Conjugal Estate,
"The Eldest"

"But I'm not pregnant!" Ellen declared, near tears. "The doctors said it would be impossible after the miscarriage. I, I'm a little late, but that's nothing unusual. I'd love to have a baby and it's mean of him to say I'm pregnant."

"Humor me, please?" David said. "Go out and get a home pregnancy test just to be sure. Please?"

"If you want me to I will," she replied, "but I already know what it will say. I think this Eldest, whoever he is, is a heartless asshole!"

Turning away, Ellen stomped off across the deck. A minute later David heard her car roaring down the drive as she headed toward the drug store in Frechette.

"Don't worry, Honey, Mom's just a little upset right now, that's all," he told Rachel. "She'll be all right in a little while. Let's round up your ducklings and put them back in the basket and take them to the barn. There's an old chicken coop out there that will do them just fine with a little fixing."

An hour's worth of work and a few feet of wire and some staples fixed the chicken coop. Tipping the basket on its side, Rachel and David stood watching the ducklings explore their new home. Outside the coop, Susie perked up her ears as Ellen entered the barn. Even from twenty feet away, David could tell that she was still upset.

"Rachel, I didn't mean to be a grouch earlier," she said, swinging the coop door open. "I put some milk and cookies out for you on the kitchen table. Could you please excuse us for a few minutes, I need to talk to your dad about grown-up stuff for a little bit and then we'll come find you."

Smiling but still looking worried, Rachel started toward the house with Susie trailing along behind her.

"Ellen, what's the matter," David asked, walking over and putting his arms around her. "You're still upset."

"It's that damn test," she said, crying now. "It came out positive. I want a baby so bad, but the doctors said I could never get pregnant again after, after... So it can't be, it just can't!"

"Wouldn't be the first time in human history that a doctor's been wrong about something," David told her, trying to keep the elation out of his voice. "We'll run over to the hospital tomorrow and find out for sure."

"I want it so bad," Ellen wept, "but it can't be, it just can't."

But it was, as the blood test performed at the hospital the next day confirmed. The pregnancy went well but was complicated by Ellen's pre-existing injuries. The delivery, by caesarean section, took place in the Cities because of the superiority of the obstetrical care there. The afternoon of the surgery, David paced the waiting room, so frightened that he could hardly think.

"Hey there, hoss," a familiar voice boomed out. "I heard you might need a little company."

Turning, he saw Terry Thomas crossing the room.

"How did you know?" he asked, puzzled but very glad to see his friend. "They only decided to do the surgery a half-hour ago."

"Ah, Grasshopper," Terry answered, leading him over to a bank of chairs, "many are the wiles of woman. As soon as Ellen knew she called Katie, who called the office and had me paged."

David might have been led to a chair but he didn't stay there long. Soon he was up pacing around the waiting room again.

"David, you are the best friend I have ever had and I love you like a brother," Terry announced. "But if you don't come over here and sit down, I am going to nail your goddamn feet to the floor."

Smiling in embarrassment, David mumbled something inaudible and sat down next to his friend. Popping open his attaché case, Terry pulled out a lengthy appellate brief that he had written. David didn't feel like reading a legal brief or anything else just now. And although Terry normally valued his partner's opinion, he didn't trust it at all right at the moment. But both men knew it was as good a way as any to pass the time so they went through the motions. An hour and a half later Ellen's doctor stuck his head into the room and called David out into the hall.

"Congratulations, Mr. Garrison," he said, rubbing at a red spot on the bridge of his nose where his glasses must have rested, "you have a beautiful baby son, seven pounds, ten ounces worth. Your wife is doing just fine; she'll probably sleep until well after midnight. You can look in on her if you like, but please don't try to wake her. The surgery went well but was complicated by her previous injuries. But as I told you earlier, she'll be fine.

"If you follow the signs in the hallway, they'll take you to the nursery and the nurse there will introduce you to your new son. Now if you'll excuse me, I've got a date with a hot shower, a cold beer, and the inside of my eyelids."

"Thank you, Doctor," David said over his shoulder, already trotting down the hallway toward the nursery. "Thank you so much!"

"Call me, David," Terry called.

Without looking back, David raised his hand and waved goodbye, concentrating only on picking them up and putting them down. Arriving at the nursery, he spent an anxious few minutes waiting for the nurse to bring his son out. Finally, after what seemed like forever, she walked into the room and deposited the small bundle into his arms.

"Not too long now," she told him, "he just got here and he needs his rest. And remember to keep your mask on; we don't want him catching anything."

Delirious, David just nodded his head and rocked his son.

"Hey there, boy," he crooned to the sleeping baby, "how you doin'? I'm so glad you're finally here, I can hardly believe it."

In that moment, David was as happy as he'd ever been. Happiness though is ephemeral, mere smoke on a summer's breeze, and it never lasts long.

CHAPTER 78

CHARLES TERRENCE GARRISON sped toward the edge of the deck and the toddler-sized gap in the hand railing, giggling happily at the success of his latest escape attempt. He was a beautiful child with a sunny disposition, golden skin, and a full head of jet black hair. When he was two feet away from the edge of the deck, his older sister showed up just in time to head him off at the pass. Unperturbed, he just kept on laughing. After all, there was always next time.

"Bubby," Rachel lectured, picking him up and kissing him, "you know you're not supposed to be out here by yourself, you could get hurt. Now let's go inside 'cause were leaving in a few minutes.

The trouble, Rachel knew, had started with the arrival of the men-in-black at mid-morning yesterday. They had talked to Dad in his study and since then everything had been crazy, wrong. After the m-i-b had left, he and Mom had an argument so terrible that she had run upstairs and hid in her room to cry. And now she and Mom and Little Charlie had to go away for a while. In common with many children who know they are adopted, Rachel's greatest fear was something happening to her parents. Right now, she was so frightened that she would have started crying again except that it would have set Charlie off.

Ellen called and Rachel started walking toward the front of the house. Turning the corner of the wrap around deck, she saw her parents standing with their arms wrapped around each other, which eased her mind a little. They both looked somber and worried, but at least they weren't arguing any more. Releasing Ellen, David knelt and gathered Rachel and Charlie in his arms.

"C'mon now, Honey, don't cry," he said, kissing her and Charlie. "Everything's going to be fine, you wait and see. Help Mom with Charlie and I'll see you down in Scottsdale in a few days."

"P-p-promise?" Rachel asked, wanting those magic words of childhood from her father.

"I promise," David told her, giving her one last hug and a kiss. "Now you go on, you don't want to keep everyone waiting."

Standing up, David turned Rachel around and gave her a gentle push to get her started. Meeting her at the edge of the deck, Gilbert took Charlie from her and they walked down the steps together. The loose flannel shirt Gilbert was wearing didn't wholly conceal the magnum revolver he was wearing in a shoulder holster on his left side. There was also a cut-down semi-automatic shotgun riding in a pair of quick release clips next to the driver's seat in his new Dodge Caravan. Having once seen the elephant, Gilbert was taking no chances on a return engagement.

Seeing them coming, Katie got out of the van and helped Gilbert strap Charlie in his car seat. Muffled by the intervening sheet metal and safety glass, Susie barked from inside her traveling cage in the van's rearmost compartment.

Wrapping both arms around his wife, David buried his face in her hair and breathed in her scent. He'd known a lot of bad moments in his life, but few worse than this.

"I'll be all right," he finally told her, hoping that he sounded more confident than he felt. "I'll fly down to Scottsdale in a few days and we'll all drive home together."

"Ho, ho, hope so," Ellen said, the tears coming at the self-doubt she heard so clearly in his voice. "Guh, guh, God, I hope so!"

Bending down, David kissed her until he had to surface for air. Keeping an arm around her, David walked her down the deck steps and seated her in the back of the van. Walking around the vehicle, he saw Gilbert standing by the driver's door.

"I'll take good care of them, David," Gilbert said, sticking out his hand. "We'll call and leave messages on the answering machine just like we discussed and we'll see you down in Scottsdale in a few days."

"I know you will, Gilbert," David told him, shaking hands with him. "Thank you for everything and I'll see you all in a few days."

Stepping back, David watched Gilbert climb behind the wheel and start the engine. Raising his hand, he waved until they turned at the foot of the long driveway and were lost from sight. Taking a seat on the steps, David sat for long minutes with his face buried in his hands.

The men-in-black, as Rachel thought of them, had actually been FBI agents. The decapitated head of a missing woman had been found in a national forest a few miles away, they informed David, with a priceless 119 carat star sapphire stuffed in her mouth. On a rock outcropping a couple of yards away an inscription reading, "tell day-vid Gair-ri-son i am coming," had been scrawled in the victim's blood. In light of his first wife and daughter's disappearances, the agents had wanted to know, did he have any knowledge about the crime or why a message had been left for him using the murdered woman's blood? No, David had told them, he had no knowledge of the crime, no idea why the gruesome message had been left for him, no further comment, and excuse me agents, but good day.

Showing them out, David had closed the door and started running through the house, terrified that something might have already happened to his family. Finding them safe in the kitchen, he had taken Ellen aside and told her to pack for an extended visit to their condo in Scottsdale while he remained behind. Hurt, Ellen had refused and David had gotten angry and the worst argument of their marriage had erupted. Becoming desperate at her intransigence, David had finally come clean about the realization of his worst fear. Ellen had listened, believed, and finally agreed to leave for the children's sake, but she was still deeply hurt by what she considered his duplicity.

As soon as Ellen had agreed to leave, David had called Gilbert. Without even asking why, which raised him even further in David's esteem, he had agreed to drive Ellen and the children to Scottsdale.

The next call that David made was to an executive protection firm run by an old family friend. After a brief discussion, he had hired six of their best agents, all with extensive military or law enforcement experience and carrying more firepower than some small countries. Traveling in two cars, they had taken up point and trailing positions on Gilbert's van as soon as it left the driveway. Until he called them off at some time in the indefinite future, the agents, or more accurately bodyguards, would protect Ellen and the children twenty-four hours a day no matter where they went or what they did. Having already lost one family to the monster, David was taking no chances on losing another.

Not giving voice to your worst fears, David had tried and finally convinced Ellen through the depths of her hurt, was not being dishonest, it was being optimistic. From the first moment he had taken possession of the staff, he had feared this day would come, but he hadn't known for certain that it would until yesterday.

Without a male member of Clan Redbird being present at the end as there was at the beginning, the circle hadn't fully closed. A great victory had been won and a few years of precious peace gained, but the war still remained unresolved. Now the monster was afoot and ravenous in the land again.

Getting to his feet, David shouldered his backpack and stood leaning on the staff, looking at his home. Turning away, he strode off into the forest.

The End

A CLOSING NOTE FROM THE AUTHOR

Thank you for reading my book and I hope that you enjoyed it. Your interest and support are vital to mine, and every other aspiring author's, chances for professional success.

Although it is unlikely that we will ever meet, I would like to ask one small favor. I am absolutely shameless about damn near everything, but I am terrible at self-promotion. So if you liked this book, and I sincerely hope that you did, PLEASE TELL SOMEONE ABOUT IT. Write about it, blog about it, send a smoke signal or a fax or an email, it doesn't matter as long as you communicate that you liked it. If worse comes to worst I wouldn't be offended if you left a copy in the bathroom of your choice, although it would probably be better if it was one of those multiple stall facilities that sees a lot of traffic a day.

If you didn't like the book, I humbly apologize. Please feel free to recommend it to someone you really don't like who may have better literary taste than you do.

Seriously though, thank you again for reading my book. I hope that you enjoyed reading it as much as I did writing it and I hope to entertain you again in the near future.

Earle D. Spencer
August 15, 2011

EARLE SPENCER currently lives in the northeastern United States but has travelled extensively and lived many places. Although trained as a chef, he also holds degrees in Political Science and Law. Besides cooking, he has also worked as a deckhand on commercial fishing vessels, as a college instructor, and many other things as necessary. His favorite hobbies are reading, fishing, cooking, museums, and travel to anywhere with salt water, beaches, and palm trees. A Song for Charlie Redbird is his first (and hopefully not his last!) novel length work.

www.ingramcontent.com/pod-product-compliance
Lightning Source LLC
Chambersburg PA
CBHW072007020726
47501CB00006B/1713
9780615638942